TOUCH
& GO

LISA GARDNER

TOUCH & GO

A NOVEL

Doubleday Large Print
Home Library Edition

DUTTON

dryunt
5/30/13

Large print ed
MYS

This Large Print Edition, prepared especially
for Doubleday Large Print Home Library,
contains the complete, unabridged text of the
original Publisher's Edition.

DUTTON
Published by Penguin Group (USA) Inc.
375 Hudson Street, New York,
New York 10014, U.S.A.

Penguin Books Ltd, Registered Offices: 80 Strand,
London WC2R 0RL, England

Published by Dutton, a member of
Penguin Group (USA) Inc.

ISBN 978-1-62090-898-3

REGISTERED TRADEMARK—MARCA
REGISTRADA

Printed in the United States of America

PUBLISHER'S NOTE
This book is a work of fiction. Names, characters, places, and incidents either are the product of the author's imagination or are used fictitiously, and any resemblance to actual persons, living or dead, business establishments, events, or locales is entirely coincidental.

This Large Print Book carries the Seal of Approval of N.A.V.H.

TOUCH & GO

Chapter 1

HERE IS SOMETHING I LEARNED when I was eleven years old: Pain has a flavor. The question is, what does it taste like to you?

TONIGHT, MY PAIN TASTED LIKE ORANGES. I sat across from my husband in a corner booth at the restaurant Scampo in Beacon Hill. Discreet waiters appeared to silently refill our glasses of champagne. Two for him. Three for me. Homemade breads covered the white linen tablecloth, as well as fresh selections from the mozzarella bar. Next would be tidy bowls of hand-cut noodles, topped with sweet peas, crispy pancetta, and a light cream sauce. Justin's favorite dish. He'd discovered it on a business trip to Italy twenty years ago and had been requesting it at fine Italian restaurants ever since.

I lifted my champagne glass. Sipped. Set it down.

Across from me, Justin smiled, lines crinkling the corners of his eyes. His light brown hair, worn short, was graying at the temples, but it worked for him. He had that rugged outdoors look that never went out of fashion. Women checked him out when we entered bars. Men did, too, curious about the new arrival, an obvious alpha male who paired scuffed work boots with two-hundred-dollar Brooks Brothers shirts and made both look the better for it.

"Gonna eat?" my husband asked.

"I'm saving myself for the pasta."

He smiled again, and I thought of white sandy beaches, the salty tang of ocean air. I remembered the feel of the soft cotton sheets tangled around my bare legs as we spent the second morning of our honeymoon still sequestered in our private bungalow. Justin hand-fed me fresh peeled oranges while I delicately licked the sticky juice from his calloused fingers.

I took another sip of champagne, holding it inside my mouth this time, and concentrating on the feel of liquid bubbles.

I wondered if she had been prettier than me. More exciting. Better in bed. Or maybe, in the way these things worked, none of that mattered. Didn't factor into the equation. Men cheated because men cheated. If a husband could, he would.

Meaning that, in its own way, the past six months of my marriage hadn't been anything personal.

I took another sip, still drinking champagne, still tasting oranges.

Justin polished off the selection of appetizers, took a restrained sip of his own champagne, then absently rearranged his silverware.

Justin had inherited his father's twenty-five-million-dollar construction business at the age of twenty-seven. Some sons would've been content to let a successful business continue as is. Not Justin. By the time I met him when he was thirty-four, he'd already doubled revenue to the fifty-million mark, with a goal of achieving seventy-five million in the next two years. And not by sitting in some office. Justin prided himself on being a master of most trades. Plumbing, electrical, drywall, concrete. He was boots on the ground, spending time with his men, mingling with the subcontractors, first one on the site, last one to leave.

In the beginning, that's one of the things I'd loved most about him. A man's man. Comfortable in a wood-paneled boardroom but also played a mean game of pickup hoops and thought nothing of taking his favorite .357 to light up the firing range.

When we were first dating, he'd take me with him to his gun club. I'd stand, tucked into the solid embrace of his larger, stronger body, while he showed me how to position my hands on the grip of a relatively petite .22, how to sight down the barrel, home in on the bull's-eye. The first few times, I missed the target completely, the sound of the gunshot startling me, causing me to flinch even with ear protection. I'd fire into the ground or, if I was very lucky, hit the lowest edge of the paper target.

Time and time again, Justin would patiently correct me, his voice a low rumble against the back of my neck as he leaned over and helped me level out my aim.

Sometimes we never made it home. We'd end up naked in the closet of the rifle range, or in the backseat of his SUV, still in the parking lot. He'd dig his fingers into my hips, urging me faster and harder, and I'd obey, out of my mind with gunpowder and lust and pure mind-blowing power.

Salt. Gunpowder. Oranges.

Justin excused himself to use the bathroom.

When he left, I rearranged the pasta on my plate so it would appear as if I'd eaten. Then, I opened my purse and, under the cover of the table, doled out four white pills. I popped them as a single handful, chased down with half a glass of water.

Then I picked up my glass of champagne and steeled myself for the evening's main event.

JUSTIN DROVE US THE FIVE MINUTES HOME. He'd purchased the Boston town house pretty much the same day we'd confirmed that I was pregnant. From doctor's office to real estate office. He brought me to see it after reaching a verbal agreement, the big-game hunter showing off his trophy. I probably should've been offended by his high-handedness. Instead, I'd walked through four and a half stories of gorgeous hardwood floors, soaring nine-foot ceilings and intricate hand-carved moldings, and felt my jaw drop.

So this is what five million dollars bought you. Bright, sunlit rooms, a charming rooftop patio, not to mention an entire neighborhood of beautifully restored redbrick buildings, nestled shoulder to shoulder like long-lost friends.

The townhome was on tree-lined Marlborough Street, just blocks away from tony Newbury Street, not to mention walking distance to the Public Gardens. The kind of neighborhood where the poor people drove Saabs, the nannies spoke with French accents and the private school had an application process that started the baby's first week of conception.

Justin gave me carte blanche. Furniture, art, draperies, carpets. Antiques, no antiques, interior decorator, no interior decorator. He didn't care. Do whatever I had to do, spend whatever I had to spend, just make this our home.

So I did. Like that scene out of *Pretty Woman*, except it involved slathering painters and decorators and antiques dealers, all plying their wares while I sat my pregnant bulk on various divans and with an elegant wave of my hand ordered a bit of this, a dash of that. Frankly, I had fun with it. Finally, a real-world application for my fine-art skills. I could not only fashion jewelry out of silver-infused clay, I could renovate a Boston brownstone.

We were giddy those days. Justin was working a major hydroelectric project. He'd helicopter in and out, literally, and I'd show off the latest progress on our home, while he rubbed my lower back and brushed back my hair to nuzzle the side of my neck.

Then, Ashlyn. And joy, joy, joy. Happy, happy, happy. Justin beamed, snapped photos, showed off his precious baby girl to anyone who made eye contact. His crew filed into our Boston town house, muddy boots left in the gleaming foyer so a bunch of former Navy SEALs and ex-marines could make googly eyes at our sleeping daughter in her pink-coated nursery. They swapped tips on diaper changing and proper swaddling, then set out to teach a newborn how to burp the ABCs.

Justin informed them their sons would never date his daughter. They accepted the news good-naturedly, then made googly eyes at me instead. I told them they could have whatever they wanted, as long as they'd change diapers at 2:00 A.M. This led to so many suggestive comments, Justin escorted his crew back out of the house.

But he was happy and I was happy and life was good.

That's love, right? You laugh, you cry, you share midnight feedings and eventually, months later you have really tender sex where you realize things are slightly different, but still, fundamentally great. Justin showered me in jewelry and I took up the requisite yoga while learning hideously expensive places to buy baby clothes. Sure, my husband was gone a lot, but I was never the kind of woman who was afraid of being alone. I had my daughter and soon Dina, who helped out so I could return to playing in my jewelry studio, where I fashioned and created and nurtured and glowed.

Now, Justin slowed the Range Rover,

starting the futile search for curbside parking. Our town house included a lower-level garage, a luxury nearly worth the property taxes, but of course Justin saved the space for me, leaving him to play the highly competitive game of street parking in downtown Boston.

He passed by our town house once and my gaze automatically went up to the third-story window, Ashlyn's room. It was dark, which surprised me as she was supposed to be staying in for the evening. Maybe she simply hadn't bothered with the overhead light, sitting before the glow of her laptop instead. Fifteen-year-olds could spend hours like that, I'd been learning. Earbuds implanted, eyes glazed over, lips sealed tightly shut.

Justin found a space. A quick reverse, a short pull forward and he'd neatly tucked the Range Rover into place. He came around the front to get my door and I let him.

Last few seconds now. My hands were clenched white-knuckle on my lap. I tried to force myself to breathe. In. Out. Simple as that. One step at a time, one moment after another.

Would he start by kissing me on the lips? Perhaps the spot he'd once discovered behind my ear? Or maybe we'd both simply strip, climb into bed, get it over with. Lights off, eyes squeezed shut. Maybe, he'd be thinking about her the whole time. Maybe, it shouldn't matter. He was with me. I'd won. Kept my husband, the father of my child.

Door opened. My husband of eighteen years loomed before me. He held out his hand. And I followed him, out of the car, down the sidewalk, neither of us speaking a word.

JUSTIN PAUSED AT THE FRONT DOOR. He'd been on the verge of punching the code into the keypad, when he stopped, frowned, then shot a quick glance at me.

"She disarmed the system," he muttered. "Left the door unsecured again."

I glanced at the door's keypad and saw what he meant. Justin had installed the system himself; not a mechanically controlled bolt lock, but an electronically controlled one. Punch in the right code, the system disarmed the locks, the door opened. No code, no entry.

The system had seemed to be an elegant solution to a teenage daughter who more often than not forgot her key. But for the system to work, it had to be armed, which was proving to be Ashlyn's next challenge.

Justin tried the knob, and sure enough, the door opened soundlessly into the darkened foyer.

My turn to frown. "She could've at least left on a light."

My stiletto heels clipped loudly as I crossed the foyer to flip on the overhead chandelier. No longer holding on to Justin's arm, I didn't walk as steadily. I wondered if he noticed. I wondered if he cared.

I made it to the wall panel. Flipped the first light switch. Nothing. I tried again, flipping up and down several times now. Nothing.

"Justin . . . ," I started in puzzlement.

Just as I heard him say: "Libby . . ."

A funny popping sound, like a small-caliber gun exploding. Whizzing. Justin's body suddenly arching. I watched, open mouthed, as he stood nearly on his tiptoes, back bowing, while a guttural sound of pain wrenched through his clenched teeth.

I smelled burning flesh.

Then I saw the man.

Big. Bigger than my six-two, two-hundred-pound husband who worked in the construction field. The massive black-clad figure loomed at the edge of the foyer, hand clutching a strange-looking pistol with a square-shaped barrel. Green confetti, I noted, almost hazily. Little pieces of bright green confetti, raining down on my hardwood foyer as my husband danced macabre and the faceless man took another step forward.

His finger released on the trigger of the gun, and Justin stopped arching, sagging instead. My husband's breath came out ragged, right before the big man hit the trigger again. Four, five, six times he made Justin's entire body convulse while I stood there, open mouthed, arm outstretched as if that would stop the room from swaying.

I heard my husband say something, but I couldn't understand it at first. Then it came to me. With a low, labored breath, Justin was ordering me to run.

I made it one step. Long enough to glance pleadingly at the darkened staircase. To pray my daughter was tucked safely inside her third-story bedroom, rocking out to her iPod, oblivious to the scene below.

Then the huge man twisted toward me. With a flick of his wrist, a square cartridge was ejected from the front end of what I now realized was a Taser, then he leapt forward and planted the end of the barrel against the side of my leg. He pulled the trigger.

The contact point on my thigh immediately fired to painful, excruciating life. More burning flesh. Screaming. Probably my own.

I was aware of two things: my own acute pain and the whites of my attacker's eyes. Mask, I realized faintly. Black ski mask that obliterated his mouth, his nose, his face. Until he was no longer a man, but a faceless monster with white, white eyes, stepping straight out of my nightmares into my own home.

Then Justin lurched awkwardly forward, windmilling his arms as he rained feeble blows on the larger man's back. The black-masked figure turned slightly and with some kind of karate chop caught Justin in the throat.

My husband made a terrible gurgling sound and went down.

My left leg gave out. I went down as well. Then rolled over and vomited champagne.

My last thought, through the pain and the burning and the panic and the fear . . . don't let him find Ashlyn. Don't let him find Ashlyn.

Except then I heard her. High-pitched. Terrified. "Daddy. Mommy. *Daddy!*"

In my last second of consciousness, I managed to turn my head. I saw two more black forms, one on each side of my daughter's twisting body, as they dragged her down the stairs.

Briefly, our gazes met.

I love you, I tried to say.

But the words wouldn't come out.

The black-masked figure raised his Taser again. Calmly inserted a fresh cartridge. Took aim. Fired.

My fifteen-year-old daughter started to scream.

PAIN HAS A FLAVOR.

The question is, what does it taste like to you?

Chapter 2

THE TWEETING OF HER CELL PHONE woke her up. This surprised her for two reasons. One, because, in theory, she no longer had a job where phones rang in the small hours of the morning. Two, because it meant she must've fallen asleep, something else that, in theory, she hadn't done for months.

Tessa Leoni lay on the left side of her bed as her phone began a louder, tumbling cascade of chimes. Her hand was outstretched, she realized. Not reaching toward her phone, but toward the empty half of the bed. As if even two years after his death, she still reached for the husband who once slept there.

Her phone chirped louder, more obnoxiously. She forced herself to roll toward the nightstand, noting that actual sleep turned out to be more disorienting than chronic insomnia.

She answered her phone just as the last chime was fading. She registered her boss's voice, a third surprise as he was rarely the one who initiated contact. Then the last of her fogginess faded and years of training took over. She nodded, asked the questions she needed to ask, then had the phone down and clothes on.

A final moment's hesitation. Firearm or no firearm? Not a requirement anymore, unlike the days when she'd been a Massachusetts state police trooper, but still sometimes practical in her new line of work. She contemplated the brief amount of information her boss had relayed—the situation, the timeline, the number of known unknowns—and made her decision. Gun safe, back of her closet. She rolled the combo with practiced fingers in the dark, withdrawing her Glock and slipping it into her shoulder harness.

Saturday morning, 6:28 A.M., she was ready to go.

She picked up her cell phone, slipped it into her jacket pocket, then crossed the hall to alert her live-in housekeeper/nanny/longtime friend.

Mrs. Ennis was already awake. As with many older women, she had a nearly preternatural ability to know when she'd be needed and generally operated one step ahead. Now she was sitting upright, bedside lamp snapped on, notepad in her hands for last-minute instructions. She slept in an ankle-length red-and-green-plaid flannel nightgown Sophie had given her last year for Christmas. All she needed was a small white cap, and Mrs. Ennis would look just like the grandmother in "Little Red Riding Hood."

"I've been called in," Tessa said, an obvious statement.

"What should I tell her?" Mrs. Ennis asked. "Her" meant Sophie, Tessa's eight-year-old daughter. Having lost the only father she'd ever known to violence two years ago, Sophie wasn't keen on letting her mother out of her sight. It was for Sophie's sake, as much as her own, that Tessa had resigned from being a state trooper after Brian's death. Her daughter had needed more stability, to know at least one parent would be coming home at night. Tessa's new job in corporate investigations generally allowed for nine-to-five hours. Of course, this morning's call . . .

Tessa hesitated. "From what I can tell, the situation is urgent," she admitted. "Meaning it might be a day or two before I return. Depends on what kind of juggling I have to do to gain traction."

Mrs. Ennis nodded, didn't speak.

"Tell Sophie she can text me," Tessa said at last. "I don't know if I'll always be able to answer my phone, but she can touch base by text and I'll answer."

Tessa nodded as she said the words, satisfied with that answer. Sophie needed to be able to reach her mother. Whether with the touch of her hand, or the push of a button, Sophie simply needed to know, at all times, that her mother was there.

Because once, Tessa hadn't been, and even two years later, those kinds of wounds left a mark.

"She has gymnastics this morning," Mrs. Ennis said. "Perhaps she can invite a friend over afterward. That'll keep her busy."

"Thank you. I'll try to call before dinner, definitely before bedtime."

"Don't worry about us." Mrs. Ennis sounded brisk now. She'd been caring for Sophie since she was a newborn, including the long years Tessa had spent patrolling on graveyard shift. There was nothing involving the household or Sophie that Mrs. Ennis couldn't handle, and she knew it.

"Go on now," Mrs. Ennis said, waving her hand dismissively toward the door. "We'll be fine."

"Thank you." Tessa meant it.

"Take care of yourself."

"Always." She meant that, too.

Tessa eased down the darkened hallway. Her footsteps moved slower than she would've liked, pausing before her daughter's room. Going in, waking her sleeping child would be an act of selfishness. So she contented herself with standing in the open doorway, peering across the dusky room until she could make out the tumble of her daughter's dark brown hair across her light green pillow.

Two night lights burned, as Sophie was no longer comfortable with the dark. Tucked between her hands was her favorite doll, a Raggedy Ann–like toy named Gertrude with brown yarn hair and dark button eyes. After Brian's death, Gertrude wore a Band-Aid on her chest. Because her heart hurt, Sophie would say, and Tessa would nod in understanding.

Sophie wasn't the only one with scars from two years ago. Each time Tessa walked out the door now, whether heading to work, going for a run or popping down to the grocery story, she felt the separation from her child as a physical ache, a tearing of herself in half so that she couldn't be whole until she returned home again. And sometimes she still dreamed of snow and blood, of reaching for her husband's falling form. But just as often, she dreamed of herself still holding the gun, still pulling the trigger.

Tessa made it down the hallway. She paused in the kitchen long enough to scrawl a simple note and place it on her daughter's chair. She wrote: *Love you. Be home soon . . .*

Then she took a deep breath and walked out the door.

*   *   *

Tessa hadn't been one of those kids who grew up dreaming of being a cop. Her father was the neighborhood mechanic, a blue-collar guy much more interested in his daily Jack Daniel's than his only daughter. Her mother had existed as a shadowy figure who rarely left the back bedroom. She'd died young, leaving Tessa to mourn the idea of her more than the actual person.

Left to her own devices, Tessa had made the kinds of decisions that had left her alone, pregnant and destitute. And just like that, she'd grown up. Failing herself had never seemed such a big deal, but there was no way she was going to fail her child. First order of business, identify a career path suitable for a single mom equipped with little more than a GED. That had led her to the police academy, where she'd spent six long months learning to shoot, fight and strategize. She'd surprised herself by proving to have a knack for all three.

Even more so, she'd loved it. The job, the uniform, the camaraderie. Four years, she'd patrolled the highways of Massachusetts, collaring drunks, defusing fights and handling domestic disputes. Four whole years, she'd had a purpose and felt as if she was genuinely making a difference. She'd been happy.

She trusted in her training now, as she turned into downtown Boston, searching for a parking space while simultaneously beginning her analysis of the crime scene. The Denbes lived in Back Bay, one of the wealthiest neighborhoods in Boston, as would befit the head of a hundred-million-dollar company. The area featured elegant rows of stately townhomes, nestled close enough together that someone should have heard something, but expensive enough that the walls were no doubt filled with some insulation specially designed to give the rich the feeling of being on their own deserted island even amid the sea of downtown urban living.

No ME vehicle and no mobile command center, she noted, which made sense, given the call had come in as a simple B and E. On the other hand, she counted over six patrol cars, plus several unmarked detectives' vehicles. Lot of manpower for a break-in. Not to mention the presence of multiple detectives . . . Clearly the police were moving along from their initial assessment of the situation.

Tessa pulled around Marlborough Street to the back alley where lucky Back Bay residents had reserved parking, and even luckier ones, private garages. She found an empty space and grabbed it. Totally illegal, of course, but given that she now spotted additional detectives' vehicles, she wasn't the first investigator to take advantage. She grabbed her placard identifying her vehicle as Special Investigations and stuck it on the dash of her Lexus. She'd probably get ticketed out of spite, but it was what it was.

Tessa climbed out of her car, wrapped herself in her long chocolate-brown wool coat, then found herself hesitating again.

Her first instinct was to shed her Glock. Stick it in the glove compartment. Wearing it into this scene, in front of Boston detectives, would only invite comment.

But then that pissed her off. Cop 101: Never let them see you sweat.

Chin up, shoulders back, Tessa slipped her legally registered firearm into her holster, and got to it.

Sun was up now, casting the row of

redbricked and cream-painted town houses in a golden glow. Once back on Marlborough Street, she followed the redbrick sidewalk down to the Denbes' residence, admiring all the front stoops still harboring dried cornstalks and various harvest decorations in honor of Thanksgiving. Most of the townhomes boasted small curbside gardens defined by ornate black wrought-iron fencing. This time of year, the plantings were reduced to miniature boxwoods, larger leafy green shrubs and, in some cases, dead mums. At least the temperature today wasn't so bad, the sun promising some heat. But day by day, the sun would fall lower in the sky, the days growing shorter, the wind gaining bite as December dawned nearly painful with its early morning chill.

A young uniformed officer stood alone in front of the Denbe residence. He was juggling from foot to foot, maybe to keep himself warm, maybe to keep himself awake. This close, standing on the sidewalk before the striking cream-washed, black-trimmed town house, there was no sign of immediate tragedy. No crime-scene tape had been strewn across the front steps, no ME's gurney stood waiting on the narrow front walk. Relatively speaking, the scene was quiet, which already made Tessa wonder what Boston police didn't want people to know.

According to Tessa's boss, the Denbe family's housekeeper had placed the first call to police shortly after 5:30 A.M. She'd reported the residence appeared to have been broken into, at which point a Boston district detective had been deployed to the scene. What he'd found inside implied an incident a bit more urgent than a routine burglary, and had led to many more phone calls, including one from Justin Denbe's company to Tessa's boss.

Messy, Tessa had thought during her boss's initial call. Now, staring at the gaping black walnut front door of the house, she amended that to complicated. Very complicated.

She squared off against the young officer, flashing her investigator's shield. Predictably, he shook his head.

"Private party," he informed her. "Boston uniforms only."

"But I got a special invitation," Tessa countered. "Direct from the family's company, Denbe Construction. A firm that specializes in hundred-million-dollar building projects, handed directly to them by state senators and high-ranking Washington insiders. You know, the kind of people working stiffs like you and me can't afford to piss off."

Officer glared at her. "Which Washington insiders?"

"The kind of power brokers who've granted Justin Denbe a standing invitation to the presidential inauguration of his choice. Those kinds of insiders." Actually, that might be stretching things a bit, but she felt it got her point across.

The officer shifted his weight from his left foot to his right. Not completely buying the story of political connections, but given the residence's location in wealthy Back Bay, not completely willing to discount it, either.

"Look," Tessa pressed. "This family, this neighborhood. Hell, we're all out of our league. Which is why Denbe's company employed my company. Private firm to protect private interests. I'm not saying it's right, or that you have to like it, but we both know in these circles, that's how the world works."

She was winning, she could tell she was winning. Which of course was the moment Boston Detective Sergeant D. D. Warren appeared.

The hard-edged blonde walked out the front door, peeled off two latex gloves, took in Tessa's presence and openly smirked.

"Heard you became a rent-a-cop," the homicide detective stated. Her short blond curls bounced in the morning sun as she descended the front steps. An investigator known for her fashion sense, D.D. wore dark-washed jeans, a light blue button-up shirt, and a caramel-colored leather jacket. Her matching boots had three-inch high heels and she still didn't miss a beat.

"Heard you became a mom."

"Married, too." The detective flashed a blue sparkling band. She drew to a halt next to the uniformed officer, who was looking from side to side as if in search of a quick exit.

D.D. and Tessa had last seen each other in a hospital room two years ago. D.D. and her state partner, Bobby Dodge, had been interrogating Tessa regarding her husband's shooting, her fellow trooper's murder and two other deaths. Tessa hadn't liked D.D.'s questions. D.D. hadn't liked Tessa's answers. Apparently, time had not changed either of their opinions.

Now D.D. jerked her chin toward the distinct bulge beneath Tessa's open coat. "They seriously allow you to carry a gun?"

"That's what happens when a court clears a person of all charges. Innocent in the eyes of the law and all that."

D.D. rolled her eyes. She hadn't bought that story two years ago, either. "Why are you here?" the city cop asked crisply.

"To take your case."

"Can't."

Tessa didn't say anything, silence being the best show of strength.

"Seriously," D.D. continued. "Can't take my case, 'cause it's not my case."

"What?" Tessa couldn't help herself; the news was unexpected given D.D's status as Boston's reigning supercop.

D.D. jerked her head toward the front door of the brownstone. "Lead detective is Neil Cap. He's inside if you want to take up matters with him."

Tessa had to search her memory banks. "Wait a minute. The red-headed kid? The one who spent all his time at the ME's office? That Neil?"

"I raised him right," D.D. said modestly. "And for the record, he's five years older than you, and doesn't take well to being called a kid. Definitely, you're gonna need better manners than that if you want to muscle in on his case."

"I don't need manners. I have permission from the owners to enter."

D.D.'s turn to appear surprised. Her bright blue eyes narrowed shrewdly. "The family? You've spoken to them? Because we'd really like to speak to them. Right away, in fact."

"Not the family. Turns out, like a lot of rich guys, Justin Denbe didn't purchase his own home. His company did."

Detective Warren had always been a smart woman. "Shit," the detective exhaled.

"As of six this morning," Tessa filled in, "Denbe Construction retained Northledge Investigations to handle all matters related to this property. I'm authorized to enter the home, assess the scene and conduct an independent analysis of the incident. Now, we can all stand around waiting for the fax to reach your offices, or you can let me get to work. As I was explaining to this fine officer here, the Denbe family is just a little bit connected. Meaning you might as well let me enter and put my head on the chopping block. It'll save you the time and effort later of finding someone else to blame."

D.D. didn't speak, just shook her head. The detective studied the brick walk for a second, maybe composing herself, but more likely coming up with the next line of attack.

"What'd you serve in the end, Tessa?" D.D. quizzed. "Four, five years as a patrol officer?"

"Four."

The veteran detective looked up. Her expression wasn't mocking, but frank. "Not enough experience for this kind of case," she stated bluntly. "You've never processed evidence, let alone dissected a five-story crime scene, let alone taken on responsibility for this kind of situation. We're not talking speed-trapping motor vehicles or administering breathalyzer tests to drunks. We're talking an entire family, gone, including a teenage girl."

Tessa kept her face impassive. "I know."

"How's Sophie?" the Boston detective asked abruptly.

"She's doing well, thank you."

"My son's name is Jack."

"How old?"

"Eleven months."

Tessa had to smile. "Love him more than you ever thought you could love someone? Till you wake up the next day and realize you love him even more?"

D.D. didn't look away. "Yes."

"Told you so."

"I remember, Tessa. And you know what? I still think you were wrong. There are lines that shouldn't be crossed. As a cop, you knew that better than anyone, and you still shot a person in cold blood. Whether out of love, or out of hate, murder is never right."

"Allegedly," Tessa replied coolly. "Allegedly shot a person in cold blood."

D.D. did not look amused. She continued, voice slightly softer, "But . . . you got your daughter back. And there are days now, just like you said there would be, when I look at my son, and . . . I don't know. If he was in danger, if I feared for his life . . . Well, let's just say I still don't agree with what you did, but maybe I understand your actions better."

Tessa remained impassive. As apologies went, this was as close as D. D. Warren was ever going to get. Which already made Tessa suspicious of what the Boston detective would do next.

Sure enough: "Look, obviously, I can't stop you from entering the house and conducting your *independent* analysis, given that the *owner* of the house has granted you permission," D.D. said. "But respect our efforts, okay? Neil's a solid detective, backed by a seasoned squad. Better yet, we have a head start on evidence processing, and if what we think happened, happened, the fate of this family depends on us getting our acts together. Pronto."

Tessa waited a heartbeat. "It's not like you to use your nice voice."

"And it's not like you to be stupid."

"True."

"Got a deal?"

The sun was all the way up now. Warming the brick sidewalk, illuminating the cream-painted town house, reaching fingers for the yawning solid walnut door. Such a beautiful street, Tessa thought, for such a terrible crime. But then, she knew better than most that no one ever knew what really went on behind closed doors, even in a supposedly happy family, even among the wealthy Boston elite.

She took the first step forward. "I won't touch your evidence."

"I already said that—"

"I just want the computers."

"Why the computers?"

"I'll let you know when I find them. Now let's get moving. As you said, clock's ticking. Congratulations on your new family, D.D."

The detective fell in step behind her. "Yeah, well, congratulations on your new job. Tell me the truth: Are you raking in the dough?"

"Yep."

"Bet the hours are brutal."

"I'm home for dinner every night."

"But you still miss us, don't you?"

"Oh, only most of the time."

Chapter 3

THE WHITE CARGO VAN HEADED NORTH, sticking to major roads, Storrow Drive to 93 to 95 and beyond. It was nearly 1:00 A.M. and the highways offered the best bet for making time.

Nothing to worry about. Just a plain white van driving approximately eight miles above the speed limit through Massachusetts. The driver spotted two state police cruisers, lightly tapping the brakes the way any self-conscious motorist would, before resuming normal cruising speed. Nothing to look at here.

At 3:00 A.M., the van made its first stop, at an old roadside diner, shuttered up years ago. Located in a middle stretch of no-where, the diner had a sprawling dirt park-ing lot and looked like the kind of place a trucker might pull over to catch a few z's, or water the bushes. Most importantly, it was the kind of place that no one really noticed, because nothing that interesting ever happened this far out here.

The youngest member of the crew, a kid they called Radar, was sent around back to do his thing. He flung open the rear doors and inspected their packages. The girl and woman remained unmoving. The man, on the other hand, was starting to stir. He opened one glassy eye, peered at Radar groggily, then pitched forward, as if to attack this smaller, younger target. Obviously still under the effects of the sedative, the man fell forward about six inches, face-planted on the rubber mat, and went limp again. Radar shrugged, checked the man's pulse, then casually opened his kit, withdrew an already prepared syringe and plunged it into the man's upper arm. That would hold him for a bit.

Radar checked wrist and ankle restraints on all three, as well as the duct tape over their mouths.

So far, so good. He gathered up his kit, went to close the double doors, then paused. He wasn't sure what made him do it. Maybe because he really was good at his job, possessing an unerring sixth sense that had earned him his nickname during the first field deployment, so many countries, years, units ago. But for whatever reason, he set down his kit and though Z barked from the driver's seat for him to hurry it along, he reinspected each of their charges.

Cell phones, car keys, wallets, pocketknives, iPods, iPads, anything and everything that a person might consider useful had been left behind, neatly stacked in a pile on the center kitchen island of the Boston brownstone. Radar had thought that was a lot of precaution given their civilian targets, but Z had been explicit in his instructions. The man, they were told, had some skills. Nothing like their skills, of course, but he could "handle himself." Underestimating was for idiots, so they didn't underestimate.

And yet . . . Radar started with the girl. She moaned lightly as he patted down her torso, and he flushed, feeling like a pervert for running his hands up and down a kid, especially a young, pretty girl. Package, package, package, he reminded himself, compartmentalization being everything in his line of work. Next, the woman. Still made him feel self-conscious, dirty on the inside, but he comforted himself with the notion that it was better for him to be handling the women than Mick. As if reading his thoughts, Mick twisted around in the backseat, until he could stare at Radar with his unsettling bright blue gaze. Mick's eyes were still swollen and bloodshot, and he was definitely still pissed off about it.

"What the fuck?" Mick barked now. "Are you securing them, or feeling 'em up?"

"Something's wrong," Radar muttered.

"What's wrong?" Z, the big man, instantly alert from the driver's seat. He was already opening his door, climbing out.

"Don't know," Radar muttered again, hands moving, poking, prodding. "That's what I'm trying to figure out."

Mick shut his trap. Radar knew the blond didn't always like him, but they'd been together long enough for Mick to know better than to argue with one of Radar's hunches. If Radar knew something, he knew something. The question was what.

Z was already around the back. He moved fast for a big guy, and given that he was still dressed entirely in black, he made for an unsettling presence in the moonless night.

"What?" he demanded.

And just like that, reinspecting the husband, Radar figured it out. Roughly six hours into their mission, they had made their first mistake, and it was a costly one. He stood there, still debating options when, suddenly, Z was on the move.

Before Radar could blink, a knife appeared in the big guy's hands. He stepped forward, and Radar leapt out of the way, instinctively averting his gaze.

One stab, three cuts. No more, no less and Z was done. He inspected his work, grunted in satisfaction and walked away, leaving Radar, as the lowest man on the totem pole, to handle disposal.

Alone now, breathing unsteadily, Radar got to it. Happy he'd had the foresight to pick an abandoned diner. Happier still for the cover of night, which allowed even him to not really see what he had to do.

Then, disposal completed, he picked up his kit from the cargo van floor. Compartmentalization, he reminded himself. Key trick of the trade. He closed the rear doors, refusing to take a second glance.

Thirty seconds later, he was back in the van, settled uneasily next to Mick.

They resumed their way in the pitch-black night. White cargo van, headed due north.

Chapter 4

TESSA ENTERED THE DENBES' TOWNHOME with a mixture of trepidation and curiosity. Nervousness over inspecting a crime scene that may or may not involve a child. Curiosity over touring the inside of a multimillion-dollar Boston brownstone. Restored town houses in this area of the city were the stuff of legend, and upon first glance, the Denbe residence didn't disappoint. Tessa took in a sweeping expanse of meticulously polished hardwood floors, soaring nine-foot ceilings, original four-inch-thick dentil crown moldings and enough hand-carved woodwork to keep a crew of carpenters busy for an entire year.

Like most Boston townhomes, the home's footprint was narrow but deep. A yawning two-story foyer complete with a massive blown-glass chandelier—Venetian, she was guessing—set the stage for a gracefully sweeping staircase straight ahead and a great room with a beautifully restored historic fireplace to the left. Off the great room, stretching toward the back of the home, she spotted the beginning of what she guessed would be a state-of-the-art kitchen, complete with granite, Sub-Zeros and custom cabinetry.

Not a fussy house, Tessa decided. Nor an ultramodern one. Warm neutrals punctuated by unexpected splashes of color. Some contemporary art, mixed with obviously antique furniture. A home meant to impress, but not overwhelm, where one could entertain business cronies as well as the local kids with equal success.

Which made the scene in the foyer all the more disturbing.

Vomit. A large, watery pool, five feet inside the front door, near the far right wall.

Confetti. Bright green, a million little pieces, each of which would bear a serial number of the Taser used to fire the cartridge. Bitch to clean up, Tessa knew from personal experience, having spent time at the academy both shooting Tasers and being shot by them, and she still had the burn marks on her hip and ankle to prove it.

Yellow evidence placards were currently placed around the scene, identifying confetti and vomit, as well as a few traces of black scuff marks, probably from the bottom of someone's shoe. Tessa bent down to examine first the confetti, then the scuff marks more closely. Confetti was probably useless to them. On the one hand, the whole purpose of the serial-number-stamped bits was to be able to trace an incident back to the Taser in question, just as a slug could be traced through its rifling marks to a specific gun. In Massachusetts, however, Tasers were illegal for civilian use. Meaning whoever had fired this weapon had most likely purchased it on the black market and forged the paperwork accordingly.

The scuff marks interested her more. Not enough tread pattern to guess about make and model of shoe. She would guess, however, either a black-soled tennis shoe or work boot. Justin Denbe's? His attacker's? Already she was forming her list of questions, as well as a growing sense of dread.

For just one moment, Tessa couldn't help herself. She was standing in her own kitchen, fresh off patrol, duty belt snug around her waist, trooper's hat pushed low on her brow, reaching for her Sig Sauer, slowly removing it from its holster, dangling it in the space between herself and her husband . . . *Who do you love?*

"House has a state-of-the-art security system," D.D. announced crisply. "According to the housekeeper, it was not activated when she arrived at five thirty this morning. She doesn't use the front door, but enters via the rear garage into the lower level. Given that Justin Denbe is extremely security conscious, standard operating procedure involves punching in a key code to raise the outside garage door, then a second code to unlock the inner door leading from the garage into the basement. The garage door was lowered and secured; the inner door, however, was open. Then, she came upstairs and spotted the kitchen island."

D.D. hugged the front wall as she headed left into the main area of the house, by-passing the pool of vomit, the pile of Taser confetti. Tessa followed in D.D.'s footsteps, careful to limit their own evidence trail as they headed toward the kitchen.

Her own home that morning had been a modest three-hundred-thousand-dollar single-family dwelling in the middle of a working-class area of Boston. And yet, what had happened in her modest kitchen, versus what had happened in the great foyer here . . .

Violence, the great equalizer. Cared nothing for money, class, occupation. One day, it simply found you.

The kitchen was vast, stretching back forever to the rear of the home. It was also meticulously clean, and surprisingly empty. Tessa shot a quick glance at D.D. Outside, there had been at least half a dozen detec-tives' vehicles. But inside the house, Tessa had so far seen D.D., D.D., and only D.D.

Then, Tessa corrected herself. On the first *floor* of the home, she'd encountered a single detective. Meaning—she raised her gaze automatically to the ceiling above her—if the foyer was bad, upstairs, she guessed, had to be worse to have demanded the attention of at least five more Boston detectives.

"Look." D.D. pointed straight ahead.

Big center island. At least eight feet long, covered in an expanse of green-gold granite with darker gray veins that flowed like water. Currently, the high-polished surface was marred by a single jumbled collection of items, all piled directly in the middle.

Tessa approached slowly, reaching into her coat pocket for a pair of latex gloves.

Purse, she identified. Rich brown leather, looked Italian. Smart phone. iPod. Man's wallet. Another smart phone, two key fobs, one for a Range Rover, another bearing the logo of Mercedes-Benz. Two iPads. A red Swiss Army pocketknife, tightly folded. Finally, cotton-candy-pink lip gloss, a wad of cash and two sticks of bent gum, still in silver foil.

Purse most likely belonged to the wife. Wallet, pocketknife, at least one of the phones would be the husband's, while the two sets of keys translated to his car, her car. The rest she would guess belonged to

Ashlyn. Electronics, smart phone, lip gloss, cash, gum. Pretty much everything required by the modern teenager on the go.

Tessa was looking at the contents of an entire family's pockets/purses, single-mindedly extricated and piled like offerings on an altar in the middle of the kitchen island.

She glanced again at D.D., found the detective studying her.

"The two cell phones?" Tessa asked.

"Three. Third's in the purse, belongs to Libby. We contacted the carrier, who's in the process of faxing the past forty-eight hours of calls, texts and messages. Preliminary synopsis: no outgoing calls from any member of the family after ten P.M. last night. Ashlyn, the teenager, has a series of texts from various friends trying to contact her with growing degrees of urgency, but nothing the other way around. Last text message Ashlyn sent was at approximately nine forty-eight P.M. Last text message she received was shortly after midnight, the fourth from her BFF, Lindsay Edmiston, demanding her immediate reply."

"Perpetrator catches the family by surprise," Tessa said, testing out the scenario in her mind. "Hence no aborted calls or texts for help. Attacker uses a Taser to subdue them, hence the confetti in the foyer. Then he restrains them and divests them of their personal possessions."

"Some robbery," D.D. stated, voice challenging.

"Not a robbery," Tessa immediately concurred. "You're right. The smart phones, purse, wallet. Those would be the first items taken, not left behind."

Tessa wondered if the family had been conscious during this phase. Most likely. Tasering was intensely painful, but only briefly incapacitating. The moment the shooter squeezed the trigger, an electric current screamed through the victim's body, firing each nerve ending to intense, excruciating life. The second the trigger was released, however, the current ceased and the pain passed, leaving the subject shaken, but standing.

Most police officers preferred Tasering to pepper spray for just that reason. Pepper spray reduced the subject to a giant, blubbering, mucousy mess, which the officer then had to awkwardly heave into the back of the squad car. Tasering, on the other hand, generally involved two to three quick bursts of searing electrical charge, at which point most perpetrators tucked themselves obediently inside the squad car, anything not to be Tasered again.

So most likely the family was conscious. Restrained, subdued, while the perpetrator ransacked their pockets, rifled through their personal possessions, then placed everything neatly on the kitchen island. The parents, at the very least, must have realized the full implications.

That this was no robbery.

That by definition, therefore, the attack was something more personal. Something worse.

"Since you're doing a nice job of looking, not touching," D.D. said, "I'll let you in on a little secret."

Tessa waited. D.D. pointed to the pile.

"Beneath all those electronics, we found the family's jewelry. Engagement ring, wedding bands, diamond studs, gold hoops, two necklaces, a Rolex. My highly conservative estimate: at least a hundred grand in easy-to-pawn items."

"Shit." Tessa couldn't help herself.

"Yep. Some robbery."

"All right. Talk to me about the security system."

"Electronically operated. Denbe's firm has built a number of prisons, and he incorporated a system into his own home similar to what they use for jail cells. Doors all have multiple steel bolts, which are controlled by a master panel. Punch in one code, the system automatically locks down all means of entry and exit. Punch in a second code, the system automatically disarms, unlocking all egresses. I guess there's other codes, specifying unlocking just inner door A or outer door B, but given this system probably costs more than my entire house, I'm hardly an expert. Of course, the windows and doors are also hardwired to the security system, which would automatically contact the security company while blasting an alarm if someone tried to manually break down a door."

"And the system was disarmed when the housekeeper showed up at five thirty?"

"Correct. Which is highly unusual. Justin Denbe required the house to be locked at all times, whether anyone was home or not."

"City life one-oh-one," Tessa commented dryly. She went with the logical assumption. "Who knows the codes?"

"Family, housekeeper and the security company."

"How often are the codes changed?"

"Once a month."

"Can it be manually overridden? Wires cut, that sort of thing?"

"According to the security company, any tampering with the wires would activate the alarm. And there's redundancy . . . two sets of wires, both fiber optics and cable. Hell, I didn't understand it all, but Justin Denbe knows his shit, and applied it to his personal living situation. The security company can be contacted by first responders for emergency override—say, in the case of fire—but reported no such requests. Whoever gained access, they did it right."

Tessa turned to look at the detective. "You said the housekeeper enters through the garage. How about the family?"

"When on foot, they use the front door, just as we did. When Libby is driving, she enters from the lower-level garage where she keeps her car. But according to the housekeeper, Justin and Libby had dinner plans for the evening. And in a his-and-her situation, he always drove."

"But he doesn't park in the garage?"

"Nope, single bay, which gallantly, I suppose, he gave to her. They also have a reserved parking space around back, but the housekeeper uses it. Guess he's gone so much, he mostly keeps his car in the Denbe parking garage and limo's it from there. Then, on the few days a week he's back home, he takes his chances street side, like the rest of us schmucks." D.D. rolled her eyes.

"And the girl, Ashlyn? Where was she?"

"Parents' night out. She was staying in."

Tessa processed this. "So the teenager is already home. Parents return. Enter through the front door ... Attacker is already inside. Ambushes Justin and Libby in the foyer."

"Attacker or attackers?"

"Attackers. One person can't subdue an entire family with a Taser alone. And Justin worked in the field, yes? Hands-on, my boss said. Big guy, fit."

"Big guy," D.D. agreed. "Very fit."

"So attackers. At least one or two in the entryway. Element of surprise for the parents. Which just leaves the girl."

"If you were the kidnappers, who would you tend to first? Parents or child?"

"Child," Tessa said immediately. "Moment you control the child, you control the parents."

"Yep. Which is where our guys almost made their first mistake. Girl's room is on the third floor. Come on, follow me."

Chapter 5

MY FATHER DIED THE SAME WEEKEND as my eleventh birthday. To this day, when I think of him, I taste Duncan Hines yellow cake, topped with sugary buttercream frosting and rainbow sprinkles. I smell the melting wax of my twin number-one birthday candles, shoved side by side into the top of my lopsided round cake. I hear music, "Happy Birthday," to be exact. A song I've never sung to my own family and never will.

Motorcycle accident, it turned out. My father wasn't wearing a helmet.

Darwinism, my mother would mutter, but her blue eyes were always drawn, her expression deeply saddened. My first experience that you can both hate a man and miss him terribly.

Losing a parent isn't a great financial proposition. Up until that point, my father's job as an electrician and my mother's part-time work at the corner dry cleaners had kept us solidly blue collar. Cute little apartment in a working-class area of Boston. A single used POS car for my mom, the weekend motorcycle for my dad. We bought our clothes from J.C. Penney, or if my mother was feeling frisky, T.J. Maxx. I never worried about food on the table, or the roof over my head. My friends in the neighborhood were also working class, and if I didn't have much, well, at least I had as much as they did.

Unfortunately, the working-class lifestyle generally leaves households with just enough income to meet monthly obligations, while not quite enough to fund such luxuries as savings accounts or, better yet, life insurance.

After my father died, my mother and I lost seventy percent of our family's income. Social Security kicked in some survivor's benefits, but not enough to bridge that gap. My mom went from part-time work to full-time hours. When that wasn't enough, she started a cleaning service on the side. I'd go with her, two nights a week, plus every weekend, perfecting my own vacuuming, dusting and washing skills as we scoured our way toward one more meal on the table.

Good-bye, cute little apartment. Hello, one-bedroom subsidized living unit in a vast, soulless building where gunfire was a nightly occurrence and the cockroaches outnumbered the human occupants a thousand to one. On Friday nights, my mother would light the gas stove and I'd stand by with the can of Raid. We'd take out two to three dozen roaches at a time, then watch *Seinfeld* on a tiny black-and-white TV to celebrate.

Good times in the new world order.

I was lucky. My mom fought the good fight. Never gave in to hopelessness, at least not in front of me, though subsidized housing units have thin walls and many nights I woke up to the sound of her sobbing. Grief. Exhaustion. Stress. By rights, she was entitled to all three, and in the morning, I never spoke of it. Just got up,

and continued on with the business of surviving.

I discovered art in high school. Had a
great teacher, Mrs. Scribner, who wore
bright-colored peasant skirts and stacks of
silver and gold bracelets, as if a gypsy had
gotten lost in inner-city Boston. Students
made fun of her. But the second you entered her classroom, you couldn't help but
be transported. She covered the bone-
white walls in Monet's water lilies, Van
Gogh's sunflowers, Pollock's splattered
drips and Dali's melting clocks. Color, flowers, shapes, patterns. The dingy halls and
battered lockers and leaking drop ceilings
of an underfunded public high school faded
away. Her class became our refuge, and
guided by her enthusiasm, we tried to find
beauty in an existence that for most of us
was harsh and, for many of us, tragically
short.

When I told my mom I wanted to study
art in college, I thought she was going to
spit nails. Fine art, what kind of degree
was fine art? For the love of God, at least
study something practical like accounting,
where one day I could get a real job, and
earn enough money to get both of us out

of this hellhole. Or, if I absolutely had to be creative, what about a marketing degree? But at least study something useful that would one day qualify me for doing more than asking, "Do you want fries with that?"

Mrs. Scribner brought her around. Not by arguing that I had talent worth pursuing, or dreams worth chasing, but by mentioning there were a number of scholarships available for inner-city youths. At that stage of the game, free money was the key to my mother's heart. So I studied and painted and sculpted, exploring various artistic media, until one day I read about silver-infused clay and realized I could combine sculpting with jewelry design, the best of both worlds. My mother even liked it, because jewelry was tangible, something you could sell, maybe to some of her cleaning clients if it came down to it.

I got into college just in time for my mom to be diagnosed with lung cancer. Darwinism, she would mutter, while gazing longingly at her pack of cigarettes. She had options, but none that she pursued very hard. Honestly, I think she still missed my father. I think, nine years later, she just wanted to see him again.

I buried her my sophomore year. And just like that, I was twenty years old and alone in the world, armed with a college scholarship and the desperate need to create, to find some beauty in a world that was just so grim.

I did okay. My parents raised me right. By the time I met Justin, he marveled over both my innate resilience and inner vulnerability. I worked hard but accepted his helping hand. I never questioned his desire to work hundred-hour weeks, as long as he never questioned my need to be alone in an art studio, armed with precious-metal-infused clay. I never expected to be saved, you know, didn't go looking for Prince Charming or think that once I met him, now I'd get to live happily ever after and never want for anything ever again.

And yet . . . I fell hard. Completely, passionately in love. And if this strong, handsome, incredibly hardworking guy wanted to give me the world, well, who was I to argue?

We had balance, I told myself. We had love, mutual respect and a whole lot of lust. Which was shortly followed by the Boston brownstone, the cars, the clothes, not to mention an entire lifestyle beyond my wildest dreams.

Then we had Ashlyn.

And if I'd once fallen hard for my husband, I fell even harder for my child. It was as if my entire life had been building to this one moment, my finest work, my greatest accomplishment, this tiny bundle of precious life.

That first night, her sleeping form bundled against my chest, I solemnly stroked her pudgy cheek, and shamelessly promised her the world. She would never want for anything—food, clothes, safety, security. She would not live forever haunted by the taste of birthday cake or the smell of melting wax. She would not fall asleep to pops of gunfire or wake up to the sound of her mother crying.

For her the skies would be bright, the horizon unlimited, the stars always within reach. Her parents would live forever. Her every need would be met.

This, and more, I promised her, my darling girl.

Back in the days when my husband and I were still in love and I was convinced that, together, we could handle anything.

Chapter 6

THE BASE OF THE STAIRCASE CURVED, but once on the second floor, it surrendered to the more traditional switchback approach. D.D. didn't stop on the second floor, but continued climbing to the third.

Tessa still didn't see any more detectives, and only a smattering of yellow evidence placards, most of which seemed to be identifying black scuff marks. From the attackers, she was more and more willing to bet. A good housekeeper would've cleaned up the marks before now, while a good wife would've demanded the offending boots be left by the front door.

"There's an elevator," D.D. said.

"Seriously?"

"Yep. Shoots all the way from the basement garage to the fourth-story rooftop patio. The beautifully wood-paneled double door you see off each hallway—the elevator door is tucked behind it. Panel slides to the right, you hit the button and voilà. I bet the wife uses it every time she returns home from yoga."

Tessa didn't say anything. Apparently, running a hundred-million-dollar construction firm had its perks.

"Also, in the basement," D.D. continued, "a wine cellar, built-in gun safe and an au pair suite. Wine cellar and gun safe are both locked and appear undisturbed. The au pair suite wasn't locked, but equally undisturbed."

"Do they have a nanny?"

"Not anymore. Probably when Ashlyn was young, though. Now they just employ the housekeeper, Dina Johnson, and she doesn't live on the property."

"Big house for three people," Tessa observed. "What are we looking at, about two thousand square feet per family member? How do they even find each other?"

D.D. shrugged. "A lot of families seem to prefer it that way."

"Sophie still crawls into my bed half the time," Tessa heard herself say.

"Really? I only wish Jack would sleep. Apparently, he's on a five-year plan."

"Don't worry. Preschool will take the fight out of him. Toddlers chase other toddlers around all day, and next thing you know, they're asleep by seven."

"Great. Just two more years to go."

"Assuming you're only going to have one child."

"Hah, I was doing good to reproduce at forty. As far as I'm concerned, the baby factory is out of business. You're the youngster; you have a second, and I'll borrow."

They arrived on the third floor, the staircase dumping them into a wide hallway liberally sprinkled with doorways. Tessa immediately spotted half a dozen evidence placards, plus one lanky, carrot-topped detective leaning against the wall, surveying the scene.

"Neil," D.D. called out. "Brought you a guest."

Neil looked up, blinked his eyes. Tessa still thought the redhead looked approximately sixteen, but then he narrowed his gaze, and she saw crow's-feet crinkle the corner of his blue eyes.

"What?"

She stepped forward, offering a hand. "Tessa Leoni. Northledge Investigations. The owner of the property, Denbe Construction, hired me to conduct an independent assessment of the situation."

"The owner? Denbe Construction . . . Wait. Tessa Leoni? *The* Tessa Leoni?"

It had been only two years, and given the media attention at the time . . . Tessa waited patiently.

Neil swung his attention to D.D. "You let her in? Without asking me? If I'd done that when you were in charge, you would've skinned me alive with a rusty razor, then gotten out a shaker of salt."

"I made her promise not to touch anything," D.D. said mildly.

"I only want the computers," Tessa interjected. "And I won't even take them. Just need to check something first. You can watch. But"—she shot a glance at D.D. just for sport—"your turn to promise not to touch."

Neil scowled at both of them. "This is a time-sensitive investigation!"

"Yes."

"Not to mention a highly complex crime scene!"

"How many perpetrators do you think?" Tessa asked him.

"At least two. Taser guy. Boot guy. Wait. I don't have to share any information with you."

"True, but Denbe Construction would appreciate your cooperation, which in turn will help you later, when no doubt you're going to need information from them."

Neil scowled again, then pursed his lips, considering. Tessa wasn't touching anything, and they would need help from Justin's construction firm, with requests to view corporate financials and personnel files being on the top of any good detective's next-steps list.

"I think there were three to four guys," Neil said, more considerate now. "But I can't pinpoint exactly why. That's what I'm doing now. Staring at the walls and willing them to talk."

Tessa understood. Police work often felt exactly like that. And sometimes, the walls did talk, at least forensically speaking.

Now she gestured to a collection of evidence placards, which seemed to mark a trail of water drops. "What spilled?"

"Urine." Neil pointed toward a doorway at the end of the hall. "Girl's bathroom. Looks like they surprised her in there. Must've made a noise, I don't know. But she was peeing, as there's also urine in the toilet, but no toilet paper."

"Sure it wasn't a guy?" D.D. asked.

"Well, not being a total idiot, I thought we'd test it to be sure," Neil drawled, obviously still cranky with his mentor. "But most logical scenario: Ashlyn Denbe was peeing. They made a noise. Scared her. Startled her. Something. Either way, she didn't take the time to flush, but grabbed hair spray and launched a counterattack."

"Really?" Tessa was intrigued. "Can I see?"

"Look, don't touch."

Tessa took that to be a yes. She walked down the hall, D.D. behind her now. She passed a double door that appeared to lead to the master suite, then a single door that led to a study, currently occupied by an older detective who was already sitting at the computer she wanted. Next up, on the left, came an obviously female room, bright pink walls covered in rock star posters, while the plush-carpeted floor was covered in clothes. Three detectives stood in there, probably how many it took to determine which items were evidence and which items were everyday teenage mess.

She arrived at the bathroom. Keeping with the theme from the rest of the house, it was a luxurious, double-sinked affair, featuring miles of earthy Italian tile, a walk-in glass shower and a bunch of brushed-nickel fixtures Tessa had once seen in a TV commercial. If memory served, the shower fixture alone cost about as much as a small automobile.

If Tessa was impressed, apparently, Ashlyn Denbe could've cared less. Rather than revel in her gold-veined granite countertop, she'd buried it beneath piles of cosmetic must-haves. Hair scrunchies, brushes, lotions, sprays, makeup kits, acne solutions. You name it, Ashlyn Denbe had it piled across her long, double-sinked countertop. Countertop finally gave way to the toilet, the back of which was equally cluttered.

Now Tessa stared at the toilet, stared at the countertop, then turned and stared at the open door.

"Lights on or off?" she asked Neil.

"Technically?"

"Okay," she dragged out, unsure what *technically* could mean.

"Technically," he repeated briskly, "it appears the intruders tripped the circuit breakers in the master electrical panel, meaning that the entire downstairs was lights-off. We found a light switch flipped to the on position in the foyer, however, which I'm assuming is from when the parents first entered the home. You know, walk in, turn on a light."

Tessa digested that. Made sense. First, that one of the Denbes would try to turn on a light. Second, that if the intruders were smart enough to override a state-of-the-art security system and come armed with Tasers, of course they'd killed the lights. "And up here?"

"Circuit was still working. Maybe they realized the girl was on this level and to suddenly plunge her into darkness might spook her. She'd call her father or something."

"Got it. So, on this level then, hallway light on or off?"

"On."

"Bathroom light?"

"Off."

"Female point of view?" Tessa offered. "Ashlyn hadn't closed the door. She was alone, her parents out, right? Ashlyn was all tucked in for the night. Probably not asleep, given we're thinking ten P.M. on a Friday night. But wearing comfy clothes, all holed up in her bedroom. Then she had to pee. Pads in here, sits to do her thing. The kidnapper appeared. That's what scared the crap out of her. She's sitting here, peeing in the dark, then looks up, and there's a guy standing in the doorway."

"That would do it," D.D. muttered.

"She grabbed the hair spray from the edge of the counter," Tessa continued. "See this one empty spot? Bet it sat right there. Ashlyn grabbed it, jumped up and started spraying. Kidnapper, grown man, probably not expecting resistance from a kid, takes it in the face. He stumbles back, and she starts to run."

Neil studied her, nodding thoughtfully. "She ran for the master bedroom," he murmured.

Tessa felt a little catch in her throat, couldn't quite stop the sigh. Fifteen years old, scared out of her mind, the kid had run automatically for her parents. Forgetting in the moment that they weren't home, couldn't help her, couldn't, in fact, do a damn thing to save her.

She followed Neil out of the bathroom, down the hall into the master suite. If the girl's room had looked like a refugee camp, the master suite, in soothing shades of rich beige and chocolate brown, was a calm oasis. Huge king-size bed bearing some kind of leather-studded headboard. Dramatic floor-to-ceiling drapes, a chaise longue situated perfectly in front of a master fireplace, framed with yet more Italian marble.

The massive desk in the left corner held the first signs of fight or flight. The overstuffed executive chair had been toppled, wheels now pointing sideways. A heavy gold desk lamp had fallen to the floor. She could see where a drawer had been pulled out, quickly rifled.

"Letter opener," Neil said. "Girl was a quick thinker, I'll give her that. She grabbed the brass letter opener and went back at him."

"Blood?"

"Not that we've found, but it was enough to get her by him again. Next, she headed for her room."

Back into the hallway they went, a somber trio. No urine drops leading to the girl's room, which explained how Neil had known that Ashlyn had run for the master bedroom first. By now, clothing back in place, bladder recovered, the girl was shifting gears from initial panic to fledgling strategy.

Tessa stopped in the hall, considering. "Why her bedroom? Why not go for the stairs?"

"When we find her, I'll ask her," Neil said. "For the moment, my best guess is she went for her phone."

Tessa nodded. "Of course, lifeline for any teenager. First instinct is parents. Second instinct is phone a friend. When in doubt, text."

The girl's bedroom was a disaster. Upon closer inspection, Tessa could see that clothes hadn't just been dropped on the floor, but flung around the room. Books, another table lamp, an alarm clock.

The intruder must've been close, maybe right on her heels, chasing her into the room and apparently around the bed as she threw various items behind her, hoping to trip him up, as she scrambled to grab her cell.

On the far side of the rumpled bed, Tessa spotted the dull brass letter opener, with a crystal handle. Chic-looking, she thought. Something bought to look classy on a desk, not necessarily to tear out an attacker's jugular.

"She made it all the way here," Tessa murmured. Then took in the rest of the story. A broken lamp, a cracked laptop computer, a shattered snow globe. "Jesus, she must've put up a helluva fight."

"Don't think she won," Neil commented.

"And I don't like to think about what it might have cost her," D.D. added more quietly.

The blade of the letter opener was clean. Ashlyn had armed herself but not managed to retaliate.

"I think it took two of them," Neil said. "Kidnapper one had to yell for kidnapper two for backup. I think kidnapper two had the black-soled shoes, because there's no scuff marks in the bathroom or the master bedroom. Just the staircase. Meaning kidnapper two made the scuff marks as he ran up the stairs into the bedroom as reinforcement."

Tessa nodded. Scuff marks were imperfect evidence, but on face value, that theory made sense.

"Now, while my esteemed colleague"—Neil shot a glance at D.D., who was beaming proudly at her top pupil—"was letting private investigators into the house, I was calling Scampo, which is where the housekeeper said the Denbes went for dinner. We'll pull security video footage, but a parking valet at the Liberty Hotel remembers fetching Justin Denbe's vehicle around ten P.M. The Denbes are apparently regulars, not to mention Justin tips well, so they're well-known by the staff. Given the five-minute drive time, that puts the Denbes entering the house anytime around ten fifteen, give or take."

"One of the first unanswered texts on Ashlyn's phone is ten thirteen P.M.," D.D. filled in.

"Yep," Neil agreed. "I'm thinking the kidnappers were in the house by then. At the very least, two of them were chasing Ashlyn around upstairs. Meaning at least one more had to be stationed by the front door, waiting for the happy couple. They walk in, he Tasers Justin Denbe, going after the most logical threat first. Get the husband down, the wife shouldn't be much of a problem."

"He threw up?" Tessa asked with a frown.

"No, the wife threw up."

"And you can tell . . . ?"

"Again, according to the waiter at Scampo, the husband ate. The wife, on the other hand, mostly drank. Wasn't so steady on her feet by the time they left. The pool of vomit, if you noticed—"

"Liquid. Which would be consistent with a woman who drank her dinner, instead of eating it," Tessa filled in.

"And there you have it," Neil summarized. "Husband got Tasered, wife got ill, and teenage girl fought like a hellion, requiring not one, but two kidnappers to drag her out of her bedroom."

"So at least three guys."

"I wouldn't take on Justin Denbe with only a single man in the foyer," D.D. said.

"Okay, four guys," Tessa granted. "So, why do you think the entire family was taken?"

Both Neil and D.D. stared at her, didn't say a word.

"Denbe Construction hasn't received any ransom demands, nor contact by the kidnappers of any kind," she supplied.

D.D. arched a brow, then looked down, expression more subdued. Still, she and Neil didn't say a word.

Tessa knew what they were thinking. Maybe she didn't have their years working homicide, but she did have eight weeks of intensive criminology training, courtesy of Northledge Investigations. Given their elite clientele, training had included two days on kidnapping 101, covering situations both foreign and domestic. First rule of ransom cases: Kidnappers will seek to establish immediate contact. Their motivation had nothing to do with a family's peace of mind, or expediting law enforcement's handling of the situation. More relevantly, abduction cases involved complicated logistics. First, the taking of the subjects. Next, the transporting and hiding of said subjects. Third, the ongoing care and feeding of subjects while waiting for demands to be met.

Basically, the longer the subjects were held, the more involved the logistics became. Meaning higher risk of discovery, exposure or the subject's untimely death, screwing up proof of life and the ability to demand a major payoff. Given that this situation involved the abduction of an entire family, logistics would be significantly complicated. Two adults and one teenager to be handled, transported, managed.

If this was a kidnapping for ransom situation, the kidnappers should be champing at the bit to make contact. Perhaps through a written note, neatly placed in front of the altar of the Denbes' personal possessions. Or, a call easily placed to Denbe Construction's main line. Or another call dialed straight into the home, to be picked up by the good detectives who were no doubt already working the scene.

Except—Tessa glanced at her watch—it was now nearly 11:12 A.M. Meaning most likely, the Denbe family had been kidnapped over twelve hours ago.

And they had yet to hear a thing.

"I think," Tessa said quietly, "I should take a look at the family computer now."

Chapter 7

THE THREE MEN IN THE WHITE CARGO VAN SLEPT. The big man reclined the front seat, the second big man reclined the passenger's seat, and the little guy sprawled in the back, his black duffel bag serving as a makeshift pillow. Not the most comfortable positions in the world, but they had each slept in worse. In ditches in faraway lands, lying straight as corpses, arms crossed over their chests while the hot desert sun beat against their closed eyelids. Under dense green leaves, curled up with their heads upon their knees as sheets of rain poured down from soaring jungle canopies and beat incessantly against the brims of their hats. In the vast cargo hold of military planes, seated ramrod straight, shoulder harnesses digging into their necks as turbulence bobbed their exhausted heads up and down, up and down, up and down, and still, no one cracked an eye.

They were men who'd been trained to sleep when they were told and to wake when they were told. Mission first. Personal comfort second.

Which made this brief respite an unexpected treat. Z had made the call. They'd been up for the past thirty-six hours, between preparation, travel time, then deployment. By definition, those hours had been long with significant events requiring the cover of night.

Now, having successfully concluded the initial phase of operations, they were 80 percent of the way back to target, making good time, feeling comfortable with themselves, their progress, their objectives. Daylight was not an issue. At this point, they had traveled so far north, they were closer to the border of Canada than to Massachusetts. They had passed through mountains so tall and forests so wild that they had a greater chance of being spotted by a bear than a human being. Given that this far north, the bears were already holed up for the winter, they basically had minimal risk of encountering any life-forms at all.

Z had debated making one of the others, Mick or, more likely, Radar, keep watch over their charges. But, freshly drugged, they had yet to stir. Which was just as well. Missions inevitably came with parameters and one of their first parameters was to minimize physical harm to the woman and the girl, especially during transport.

Once at their destination, they would receive fresh instructions regarding the next phase of operations.

At which point their charges might or might not become fair game.

Whatever. It was not their place to reason why.

They took a job. They executed it at the highest standards of performance. Then, at least in this case, they would be paid such a fucking shitload of money, Radar personally planned on never working again. White sandy beaches, sweet rum drinks and large-breasted women. That was his near future. Hell, maybe he'd even marry one of the large-breasted women. Have a couple of babies and settle into paradise. Fish all day, have sex with his beautiful wife all night. Sounded like a plan to him.

So when the van had first pulled over, tucking into an old campground, where it was quickly obscured by walls of dense evergreens, Radar had administered a fresh round of sedatives. For the sake of napping, fishing and large-breasted women everywhere, he'd given an extra-large dose.

Radar had started packing up his gear, mentally skipping ahead to three hours' sleep, when his internal sensor had once again begun to ping. The woman. Something about the woman.

He'd studied her closer. Noticed that her face had lost some color, was covered in a faint sheen of sweat. Her eyes were not open. In fact, her eyelids appeared squeezed shut, twitching even, as her breathing accelerated rapidly.

She didn't look so good. Maybe from the sedative, though it was mild enough. He took her pulse, listened to her heart, then checked her temperature. Nothing.

She just looked . . . wrong. Car sick? Flu? Shock?

Maybe she was dreaming, he'd decided. Judging by her heart rate, not a nice kind of dream.

And not his problem.

Radar packed up his bag, climbed into the back and within minutes was out cold.

Three men in a white cargo van, asleep.

Then the first man opened his eyes, sat up in his seat, started the engine and turned back onto the winding mountain road.

Eleven o'clock Saturday morning, one white cargo van headed due north.

Chapter 8

IN THE PAST SIX MONTHS, ever since That Day, I'd taken to avoiding sleep. There was a phase, maybe around the second or third month, where I was nearly phobic about evenings. If I just stayed awake, kept my eyes open, my body moving, somehow, I could keep tomorrow at bay. Because I didn't want it to be tomorrow. Tomorrow was too scary a proposition. An unnamed deadline where I'd have to make major life decisions about my marriage, my family, my future. And maybe, tomorrow was just too sad. Tomorrow was loneliness and tenement housing units and Friday-night cockroach raids and every lesson I had learned in childhood and wanted so badly to leave behind.

So for a while I didn't sleep. I roamed the house. Ran my hand across the granite countertops in the kitchen, remembered the day Justin went with me to the quarry, where we gazed at slab after slab of natural stone. At the exact same moment, we'd both pointed to this one, then laughed like two schoolkids, giddy to discover we shared the same favorite color or pet or sports team.

From the kitchen, I'd journey down to the wine cellar, housing bottles I'd meticulously researched and stocked to impress Justin, his business associates, even his crew. You'd be amazed how many drywallers, plumbers and other general contractors know their wines. With success, everyone cultivates tastes, until even the most rugged dirt hauler can appreciate a well-balanced Oregon Pinot Noir or a more robust Spanish red.

Justin was sleeping in the basement apartment at that point. The au pair's suite, people called it, except we'd never had a nanny, preferring to raise our daughter ourselves. The door was at the opposite end of the hall from the wine cellar. During my nightly roamings, I would stand in front of it, sheltered by the deep dark of a windowless basement. I would place my hand upon the warm wood and wonder if he was on the other side, actually asleep. Maybe he'd gone back to her. Or maybe, a thought so painful it bordered on nearly intoxicating, he'd brought her here.

I didn't open the door. Never knocked, never tried to peer beneath it. I would just stand there, thinking that at one time in our marriage that would've been enough. My mere presence would've spoken to him, beckoned him like a magnetic force, until he would've thrown open the door, grabbed me into his arms and kissed me hungrily.

This is what eighteen years of marriage does to a couple. Minimizes the polar fields, mutes the laws of attraction. Until night after night, I could stand in a darkened hallway just eight feet from my husband, and he never felt a thing.

Inevitably, I would return upstairs, arriving outside my daughter's bedroom. Again, no knocking, no entering, no disturbing of a private space where I wasn't wanted anymore. Instead, I would sit on the floor in the hallway, lean my head against the wall and picture the white-painted shelving unit positioned on the other side. Then, by heart, I would systematically catalog each item that had been placed there. Her ballerina music box from the first time we took her to see *The Nutcracker*. A jumbled pile of her most beloved childhood paperbacks, *Where the Red Fern Grows, Little House on the Prairie, A Wrinkle in Time*, placed haphazardly on top of her more neatly organized hardcovers such as the Harry Potter series and the Twilight saga.

She'd gone through a horse-crazy phase, which would explain the herd of Breyer horses now relegated to the back corner of the lower shelf. Like her mother, she had an eye for beauty and an urge to create, hence the random collections of polished seashells and artfully strung sea glass she still added to each time we visited our second home on the Cape.

The top of her dresser held two vintage china dolls, one brought back by Justin from Paris, another she and I had found together at an antiques store. Both had been expensive, and once, both had been treasured. Now, their sightless blue eyes, glossy ringlet hair and frothy lace dresses served as makeshift jewelry stands for piles of beaded bracelets and long snarls of nearly forgotten gold necklaces. More piles of silk-wrapped hair bands and decorative hair clips adorned their feet.

Sometimes, when I entered the chaos of my daughter's room, I wanted to toss a match. Scorched-earth policy and all that. Other times, I wanted to take a photo, draw a map, to somehow immortalize this complex web of toddler dreams, young girl obsessions and teenage desires.

In the dark of the night, however, I simply sat and named each treasured item over and over again. It became my rosary. A way to try to convince myself the past eighteen years had had some value, some worth. That I had given love and that I had been loved. That it hadn't all been a lie.

As for the rest of the days, months, weeks currently unfolding ahead of me . . . I tried to tell myself I had not become the clichéd middle-aged woman, abandoned by her cheating husband, alienated by her teenage daughter, until she now existed as a mere shadow in her own life, with no identity or purpose of her own.

I was strong. Independent. An artist, for God's sake.

Then I would get up and wander out to the rooftop patio. Where I would stand in the faint ambience of city lights, my arms wrapped tightly around my body for warmth, taking step after step closer to the edge . . .

I never managed to stay awake an entire night.

Five thirty A.M. was probably the longest I made it. Then, I'd find myself curled up once more on top of the king-size bed in the master suite. And I'd watch the dawn break, tomorrow forcing itself upon me after all. Until I closed my eyes and succumbed to a future that happened whether I wanted it to or not.

It was during the second month of forced sleep deprivation that I opened my medicine cabinet and found myself staring at a bottle of painkillers. Justin's prescription, from when he hurt his back the prior year. He hadn't liked the Vicodin. Couldn't afford to feel that fuzzy at work. Besides, as he put it bluntly, the constipation was a bitch.

It turns out, walking all night will not keep the future at bay.

But the right narcotic can dull the edges, steal the brightness from the sun itself. Until you don't have to care if your husband is sleeping in the basement beneath you, or your teenage daughter has locked herself in a time capsule down the hall, or that this house is too large and this bed too big and your entire life just too lonely.

Painkiller, the prescription promised.

And for a while, at least, it worked.

Chapter 9

WALKING INTO THE THIRD-STORY STUDY, Tessa immediately recognized the detective sitting at the computer as the final member of D.D.'s three-man squad. An older guy, heavyset, four kids was her memory. Phil, that was it. He'd been at her house, too, that day. Then again, most of the Boston police and Massachusetts state cops had been.

Apparently, he remembered her, too, because the moment he spotted her, his features fell into the perfectly schooled expression of a seasoned detective, seething on the inside.

She figured two could play at that game.

"My turn," she announced crisply, heading toward the computer.

He didn't address her, turning his attention to Neil and D.D. instead.

"It's okay," Neil, the lead officer, proclaimed. "The owner of the house, *Denbe Construction*, hired her to assess the situation."

Tessa could tell Phil got the nuances of that statement loud and clear, because a vein throbbed in his forehead. If Denbe Construction owned the house, then in theory, Denbe Construction owned the contents of the house, including the computer, which this fine Boston detective had been searching without permission.

"File a missing person's report?" Phil asked Tessa, voice curt.

"Based on what I've seen here, I'm sure that will be the company's next move."

Another investigative quandary. For the police to become involved in a missing person's case, a third party must first file a report. Even then, the standard threshold was that the family hadn't been seen for at least twenty-four hours.

Meaning at this stage of the game, without a report filed, without twenty-four hours

having passed, D.D.'s squad was stuck responding to a call, but not yet handling a
case.

"Any contact . . . ?" Phil again, voice less
certain, more searching.

"From the family, no."

"Kidnappers?"

"No."

A fresh tic of the vein in his forehead.
Like Neil and D.D., Phil understood lack of
contact was not a good thing. Ransom
situations generally involved keeping the
victims alive. Whereas in an abduction
case with no financial demands . . .

"Anything good on the computer?" Tessa
gestured to Phil, who was still seated at
the keyboard.

"Been looking at the Internet browser.
Family liked Facebook, Fox News and
Home and Garden. Already guessing the
iPads will be more personal. Not enough
activity here for a family of three. I'm assuming they each do their own thing on
their individual devices."

Fair assumption, Tessa thought. She
gestured to the keyboard. "May I?"

Grudgingly, he stepped aside. Tessa
reached into her inside coat pocket and

withdrew a small notebook. She had written the name and manufacturer on it. Now she started scanning computer icons until she found the desired program.

"Justin Denbe has a new toy," she explained as she double-clicked the icon. "His crew gave it to him in the fall, partly as a joke, but he loves it. Apparently, these job sites—prisons, hospitals, hydroelectrical plants—are quite large. And Justin, as the hands-on owner, inevitably holds the answer to every question. Meaning his guys spend a fair amount of time searching for him. Sites are also often in rural areas with shitty cell-phone coverage, making it hard to snag him by phone when they can't locate him physically. So"—she paused a second, scrolling through the directions that had just popped up on screen—"his guys bought him a coat."

"A coat?" D.D. asked with a frown.

Neil, however, was already ahead of her. "A GPS jacket. They got him one of those fancy outdoors never-get-lost-in-the-woods kind of jackets."

"Bingo. Not cheap, either, like nearly a thousand bucks. So apparently it's a really nice outdoors jacket, and Justin loves it.

Wears it everywhere. Including, hopefully, out to dinner last night."

"Scampo is a nice restaurant," D.D. commented.

"Navy blue fabric with tan leather trim. He could wear it to Scampo. Hell, from what I'm told, this is a guy who wore his work boots everywhere. Why not a nice outdoors jacket?"

They fell silent, watching Tessa work the keyboard. "The jacket's GPS device is built into the back liner," she explained. "There's a slot for removal, as the battery is good for only fifteen hours, then has to be recharged."

"Do you have to activate it?" D.D. asked. "Or is it just always on?"

"This particular device must be activated. From what I'm reading here, that can happen two ways: The wearer manually activates it at the beginning of his hike or, say, day on the job site. Or it can be activated remotely using this software, which can also be installed on a cell phone. Kind of wild," Tessa muttered to herself, fingers flying over the keyboard. "Turns any smart phone into a digital search dog. Find Justin Denbe."

A map had just opened up on the computer screen. She eyed it carefully. Saw nothing.

"Is it activated?" D.D. again, voice impatient as she moved to stand behind Tessa, peering intently at the screen.

"In all of the US, we have nothing. So I'm guessing Justin hasn't turned it on."

Neil looked at her. "Then you do it. Ping it."

"Thought you'd never ask."

She moved the mouse to a green button in the lower right-hand corner of the menu. "Activate," it read. Like a bomb. Or a hand grenade. Or the key to saving a missing family's life.

She clicked the icon. The colored map of the US shifted, zooming in, focusing left until it was no longer the entire US map on the computer screen but just the eastern seaboard. There, due north of them, a red dot suddenly pulsed to life.

"I'll be damned."

In front of her, she heard a small beep. She glanced up, to see Phil setting a timer on his watch. "Fifteen hours," he said. "Battery life, remember?"

"Yep."

"Zoom in, zoom in, zoom in." D.D. hit Tessa on the shoulder to hurry her along. Since Tessa was sitting closer than D.D., and could already make the distinction the Boston crew hadn't been able to see yet, she did just that.

The East Coast became New England. Massachusetts expanded in front of their eyes. Then, New Hampshire. Until right there, definitely over the border, definitely crossing state lines into central New Hampshire, the GPS device in Justin Denbe's fancy outdoor jacket blinked back at them.

Tessa pushed back from the computer, turning around till she met D.D.'s eyes. "Assuming Justin Denbe has been abducted wearing that coat, he's no longer in the Commonwealth of Massachusetts . . ."

"I was right at the start," D.D. grumbled.

"Not your case," Tessa agreed.

Neil put it more succinctly. "Damn feds."

THE BOSTON DETECTIVES did not pack up their toys and go home.

Jurisdiction was a legal distinction. Basically, federal laws carried stiffer penalties than state laws, meaning the US Attorney's Office packed a bigger punch than the Suffolk County DA when prosecuting suspected kidnappers.

Given that it was in everyone's best interest for accused criminals to face the largest legal hammer possible, the Suffolk County DA would call the US Attorney's Office, District of Massachusetts, and inform them of a crime that most likely crossed state lines. The US Attorney would then contact their investigative body of choice, the FBI. At which point, FBI agents from the Boston field office would promptly deploy to the Denbe residence, arriving in ten minutes if they chose to drive, or twenty if they chose to walk.

The local field agents wouldn't expect the Boston detectives to simply disappear. Instead, the federal agents would politely but firmly redirect all evidence collected— the urine samples, the vomit, Taser confetti, scuff markings—from the Boston PD lab to the federal crime lab. Next, they would form a multi-jurisdictional task force, where conveniently enough, they would serve as the brains of the operation, while the Boston cops became the brawn.

Neil grumbled, D.D. and Phil sighed philosophically. Tessa remained indifferent.

Her job was to locate the Denbe family. She would work with whichever playmates she was given, though she was already guessing the Boston cops were better at sharing their sandbox than the feds. And given D.D.'s notoriously cranky temperament, that was saying something.

Tessa pushed back from the computer. She made one last pass of the upstairs crime scene, while D.D. checked in with the efforts of the uniformed officers, Phil returned to working local contacts and Neil made a last series of calls. While they were distracted, it was possible that Tessa also reentered the kitchen, powered up all three family cell phones and jotted down the contacts that appeared in their various favorites lists. She could go through official channels, of course, but this was more expedient.

Then, the Boston squad reappeared and, gathered around the pile of family possessions, began the summarization process. To give the rookie lead detective credit, Neil's investigative efforts thus far had been quick but thorough:

Initial police canvassing of the neighborhood had yielded no sightings of any member of the Denbe family. Calls to relatives, friends and known associates hadn't produced any member of the Denbe family. Same with all outreach to local businesses, area hospitals and nearby establishments.

Justin Denbe's vehicle had been located four blocks down, empty. Libby Denbe's Mercedes was still tucked in the garage, empty. All cash, credit cards and ATM cards appeared to be sitting on the family's kitchen counter. According to the local bank, no financial activity had occurred on any of the family accounts since 4:00 P.M. on Friday, when two hundred and fifty dollars had been withdrawn from an ATM in Copley Square (video from the bank pending). Likewise, no member of the family had placed an outgoing call or text on a mobile phone since 10:00 P.M. on Friday (faxes from cellular provider pending).

At this time, all three members of the Denbe family appeared to have been missing for the past fourteen hours. The investigator's only lead: Justin Denbe's outdoor jacket, which was now broadcasting a GPS signal from the wilds of New Hampshire.

In an aggressive move that surprised Tessa, Neil Cap got out his phone, pulled up a New Hampshire map and translated the missing jacket's GPS coordinates to a local law enforcement agency.

Then, without waiting for the FBI's official blessing, Neil made what would probably be his last call as Boston's lead investigator: He contacted the New Hampshire sheriff's department and asked them to track down the signal on the coat. A quick and efficient move to glean the most amount of information in the shortest amount of time. The FBI would hate him immediately for stealing their thunder.

Tessa took that as her cue to exit stage right.

Best she could tell, she'd seen what there was to see. Boston had control of the crime scene where the family used to be. Some local cops, too far north for her to assist, would handle the investigation of the next location where the family might be. Which left her with one central question: Who would've wanted to abduct and/ or harm the Denbe family to begin with?

She decided it was time to learn more about her new client, Denbe Construction.

Chapter 10

WYATT FOSTER WAS A COP who wanted to be a carpenter. Or maybe a carpenter who wanted to be a cop. He'd never completely figured it out, which was just as well. In this day and age of constant budget crises, the going rate for protecting and serving the good citizens of North Country New Hampshire made two jobs a necessity for himself as well as most of his fellow officers. Some guys picked up refereeing. Other guys bartended on weekends. Then there was him.

This fine Saturday morning, sun shining, air brisk with late-fall chill, he was staring at a collection of old pine boards, reclaimed from his neighbor's hundred-year-old barn, and trying to put together a design for a rustic bookshelf. Or maybe a kitchen table, the kind with bench seats. Or a wine cabinet. People paid good money for wine cabinets. Hell, he wouldn't mind a wine cabinet.

He'd just made up his mind, reaching for the first board, when his pager went off.

Early forties, buzz-cut hair that used to be a dark brown but these days held a fair amount of silver, Wyatt had served the county sheriff's department for the past twenty years. First as a deputy, then as a detective, now as a sergeant in charge of the detectives unit. Best part of being a sergeant was the hours. Monday through Friday, 8:00 A.M. to 4:00 P.M. 'Bout as regular as one could get in a profession not known for its regularity.

Of course, like any county officer, he served on call a couple of nights a week. And, yeah, things happened, even in the wilds of New Hampshire, perhaps especially in the wilds of New Hampshire. Drugs, alcohol, domestic violence, some interesting embezzlement cases as an employee sought new ways to fund his or her drug and alcohol issues. Lately, the murder rate had been spiking uncomfortably. Death by hatchet. A disgruntled employee who'd brought his high-powered bow to his former job site at a sand and gravel company. A number of vehicular manslaughter cases, including an eighty-year-old woman who swore she ran over her eighty-five-year-old husband by accident. All three times. Turned out he'd been cheating on her with their seventy-year-old neighbor. Hussy, the wife had declared, which came out more like *fuffy,* because before "accidentally" running over her husband three times, she hadn't bothered putting in her teeth.

Certainly, the job was never boring, which Wyatt appreciated. A quiet man by nature, he liked a good puzzle, followed by a just resolution. And, as crazy as it sounded, he liked people. Interviewing them, investigating them, arresting them, people never failed to fascinate. He looked forward to his work, just as he looked forward to coming home from work. Build a case, craft a wine cabinet. Each project was compelling in its own way, and each, on a good day, yielded tangible results.

Now Wyatt checked his pager, sighed a little and hoofed it back inside his cabin to grab his cell. Missing Boston family. Fancy jacket with a built-in GPS emitting a signal forty miles to the south. He knew the area. Long on trees, short on people.

Wyatt asked a few questions, then started in on his next list.

No more wine cabinet. Instead, he prepared to assemble some manpower and go snipe hunting in the woods.

ON WYATT'S FIRST DAY AS A COUNTY OFFICER, the sheriff had given him the lay of the land: Basically, there were two New Hampshires. There was the New Hampshire south of Concord, and there was the New Hampshire north of Concord. The New Hampshire south of Concord served as a Boston suburb. The neighborhoods featured either 1950s ranch houses for the working class, or 1990s McMansions for the wealthy Boston executives. That New Hampshire, being a small geographic area with a dense, tumbling-over-each-other population, was entitled to a police force where multiple officers worked every shift, with backup never being more than a couple of minutes away, and each department boasting its very own collection of modern forensic tools to better facilitate criminal investigation.

Then, there was the New Hampshire north of Concord. Where the remaining one-third of the state's population sprawled helter-skelter over the remaining two-thirds of the state's terrain. Where entire towns were too small to justify their own police force, and even the towns that did generally deployed one officer at a time, patrolling vast expanses of rural roads, woodland forests and lake borders all alone. Backup could be an easy thirty to sixty minutes away. And heaven help you if you had a complex investigation involving real forensic tools; chances were you would have to borrow them from another department, maybe even two or three other departments, in order to get the job done.

New Hampshire south of Concord had city cops. Whereas New Hampshire north of Concord had basically the Wild, Wild West. City cops traveled in packs and could go an entire career without ever drawing their weapons on the job. Wild West cops handled entire shoot-outs alone, and drew down at least a couple of times a year. Hell, Wyatt had been on the job for all of four hours when he'd pulled his sidearm for the first time. Called to a scene of a domestic disturbance. Getting out of his patrol car just in time to be charged by a knife-wielding drugged-out lunatic. Wyatt had kicked the guy in the stomach first, so shocked by the sudden attack he actually forgot for a second that he was a cop and had a whole duty belt complete with Taser and pepper spray, and, oh yeah, a Sig Sauer P229 .357 semiauto.

Sky-High Guy popped back up, which was the problem with drugged-out lunatics—they just didn't feel the pain. This time Wyatt had his act together enough to produce his weapon. At which point, Sky-High Guy, staring down the barrel of a loaded gun, sobered up record quick and dropped his steak knives.

By the time backup finally arrived—a mere thirty minutes later—Wyatt had the first druggie secured in the backseat of his car, plus a second who'd tried to bolt from the rear of the property. He'd also taken a witness statement from the owner of the residence, the druggies' mother, who now swore she never wanted to see either of her sons again as they were good-for-nothing pieces of shit that owed her at least twenty bucks, or a dime bag, whichever they could get their hands on first.

Definitely, never a dull moment in the wilds of New Hampshire.

BEING A SHERIFF'S DEPUTY involved more than practicing the art of the quick draw, of course. County officers were empowered to write their own search warrants and even arrest warrants, a logistical necessity as the nearest courthouse could be fifty hard miles away, meaning by the time a detective spent two hours driving there and back, the suspect had either split town or covered his tracks. New deputies were generally enthralled by this unparalleled example of police power. Then, inevitably, the full implications would come crashing down—by virtue of writing up legal documents, they each needed to become mini lawyers. Because, sure, they could write up any old damn thing they wanted, and search the property, or arrest the suspect, at which time a judge would review the warrant and if it wasn't absolutely, positively to the letter of the law, throw the whole thing out, leaving the county detective with no one to blame but him- or herself.

Wyatt read law magazines in between woodworking publications.

The final distinction of the sheriff's departments was that they had jurisdiction over the entire state. Even the New Hampshire state police had to ask for permission to patrol various town and county roads. Not the sheriffs, though. Wyatt could drive anywhere in the state, policing his heart out while displaying his superior knowledge of legalese. Of course, most of his part of the state was populated by bears and moose who could care less, but a man liked to feel good about these things. His powers were considerable, his grasp of law enviable and his domain vast.

It helped him fall asleep late at night. Assuming his pager didn't go off.

Now Wyatt headed for the county sheriff's department. Normally, he'd work out of his cruiser, especially in a matter that warranted some urgency. But his cruiser's GPS could only take him as far as the nearest road. Given the working theory of an abduction scenario, odds were their target would involve more rugged terrain, possibly the deep woods. Hence, he wanted the handheld GPS tracker, two of his fellow detectives and at least a couple of uniformed officers.

Inside, the three guys and one gal were already suited up and ready to go.

He briefed them on the situation, a Boston family, missing since 10:00 P.M. last night, signs of foul play discovered in the home, biggest lead currently being the GPS locator in the husband's jacket, which had approximately thirteen hours of battery life remaining.

Wyatt entered the GPS coordinates first on his main computer, and they all gathered round the monitor to see. Good detectives appreciated the stalking power of the Internet as much as any serial killer, and with a few clicks of the mouse, Wyatt was able to bring up satellite images of their target coordinates. He zoomed in on snapshots of a rural road, then a large dirt parking lot surrounding a much smaller, dilapidated building, bordered heavily by deep woods. The exact coordinates appeared to be a spot just beyond the cleared parking lot in the woods.

"I'm thinking that's the old Stanley's diner," Wyatt said.

Gina, one of their new deputies, nodded vigorously. "Yes, sir. Drove by it just a couple of days ago. Boarded up tight."

"Not a bad place to hide hostages," Jeff commented. The forty-five-year-old father of two was one of the county's best detectives, with a knack for financial crimes. "Near a road for easy access, but also isolated. Sure as hell aren't that many other people or residences around."

"Shouldn't the GPS signal be emitting from the building, then?" Gina countered. Wyatt liked the fact she argued. Tough part for any new officer, but particularly a new female officer, was speaking up. Clearly, Gina could hold her own.

"Range is give or take a hundred feet," Jeff said. "So it could be from the building."

Gina nodded, hooking her thumbs in her duty belt as she accepted his answer.

"So here's the deal," Wyatt spoke up. "We have three possibilities. We're going to find a jacket. We're going to find a jacket and some or all three members of the missing family, possibly alive or dead. Or, we're going to find a jacket, a missing family and their kidnappers. Possibly up to four definitely living kidnappers. Which, if you include three family members, totals seven people at one site, with five of us to approach, control, contain. Let's talk strategy."

He looked at Kevin, the second detective, who had yet to speak. Kevin had taken some courses on workplace violence and hostage negotiations. They called him the Brain, not just because he was thin and bookish looking, but because he really did like to study. New legal rulings, new forensic techniques, new criminology reports, just ask Kevin. He also knew all the hockey stats for any given player on any given team in any given year. And, no, he could not get a date most Friday nights.

"Code one," he suggested now. "Approach quiet, get the lay of the land. If the kidnappers are around, we don't want to spook them."

"So five patrol cars convening in one parking lot isn't gonna work?" Wyatt asked with a droll smile.

"We can take two vehicles," Jeff said. "Double up occupants."

"Only gonna buy us so much," Gina pointed out. "Even two cars, turning at the same time into a deserted parking lot . . ."

"One car could pull in, the other should drive past, heading south," Kevin amended. "Once out of sight, that car can pull over and the officers hike back up. That gives us one car appearing to stop randomly— maybe a driver needing to check a map, stretch his legs, that sort of thing. Better yet, Gina should be in the car that pulls over. So it looks more like a couple pulling over than cops descending on a scene. Just till we know more."

Made sense to Wyatt. One by one, they agreed.

"Vests?" he double-checked.

They were a good crew. They were prepared. Better yet, they were excited to get out there and do some good.

Wyatt grabbed the handheld GPS tracker. They booted it up, plugged in the coordinates.

And just like that they were ready to go.

WYATT HAD BEEN MARRIED ONCE. Stacey Kupeski. Beautiful girl. Great laugh. That's what originally caught his attention. Literally, across the room in a crowded bar, he'd heard that laugh and just known he had to hear it more. They'd dated six months, then tied the knot. She owned a high-end boutique that specialized in fancy Western belts and glittery tops and lots of other bling women seemed to think they needed for big nights out. Being retail, Stacey worked holidays and weekends, which seemed a good fit for his job, given that criminal activity inevitably spiked during every major holiday, not to mention most lazy Sunday afternoons.

Except, that became the problem. She was working and he was working, their paths crossing basically on Monday night, when she'd want to go "do something" and he mostly wanted to varnish a piece of wood just so he could watch it dry. They made a go of it for eighteen months. Then she started going out and "doing something" with the husband of one of her best customers. That wife went crazy, trashed Stacey's store, while the husband got a restraining order, and Wyatt got out of his marriage. Turned out, he only liked drama on the job, not in his personal life.

Besides, he found he wasn't really that upset with Stacey, which struck him as not a good thing. If your wife was sleeping with some other guy, you should probably care. At least he and Stacey were still friends to this day. Mostly, because Wyatt still didn't much care.

His only regret: He would've liked kids. Not with Stacey. Oh no, that would've been a disaster. But in an abstract gain-two-point-two-kids-but-not-an-ex-wife sort of way, he would've loved children. Boy, girl, didn't really matter. Someone to build tree houses and toss a ball and just be with. Maybe a little version of himself he could teach a few things to before it inevitably grew into a teenage version of himself and passionately declared, You just don't understand me! But even that would be good. A rite of passage. The way the world was meant to go round.

Not going to happen at his age, he figured, so he borrowed his friends' kids, helping them build clocks and jewelry boxes and once, even a pirate's chest. Good Saturday afternoon activities. Made the little ones proud to have made something with their own hands, and made him feel like he had something worth sharing other than investigative skills 101.

These days, his mom was trying to get him to adopt a dog. Maybe an older rescue animal. He had a good mojo for that kind of thing, she kept telling him, which seemed to imply that his current lifestyle was one step away from a monk's.

Sometime soon, he'd go on a date. But first, he wanted to build that wine cabinet. And today, rescue a missing Boston family.

They'd reached the old diner. He and Gina had volunteered to be the turn-in vehicle. Not the biggest undercover operation in the world, given that even an unmarked police car screamed cop and they were both in uniform. Their hats were off for now, making them appear civilian at least from the shoulders up, as Wyatt casually slowed the car, put on the blinker.

No sign of any vehicles in front of the diner. As Gina had said, the old building was boarded up. He drove to the left side, away from the blinking GPS target, as he didn't want to get too close too fast. Mostly, he wanted to peek behind the building.

Still no sign of any vehicles. Or an open door. Or cracked window.

He looped an easy circle, as if just turning around and now preparing to head back on the road.

Gina had the handheld tracker on her lap. She was looking down at it. "Due north, fifty feet," she murmured.

Wyatt looked due north. He spotted trees, lined by dense vegetation. He also spotted twin tire tracks, fresh, more deeply rutted, approaching the edge of the woods. A second set of tracks, slightly parallel to the first, showed where the vehicle had backed up, then headed back to the road.

"Shit," he muttered.

Gina glanced at him.

"Vehicle was here. Looks like it pulled up to the woods, then left again." He didn't say the rest. As if to dump something. Perhaps just a jacket, but, more likely, a body wearing said jacket.

Gina reached around for her hat. Wordlessly, she shoved it down on her head, while he got on the radio and relayed their status to their backup car. He heard back from Kevin; ETA on foot in five minutes.

Close enough, Wyatt figured. Action here was over and done. Not even a matter of what he could see, the tracks and all, but what he could feel. The property was abandoned. Plain and simple.

He and Gina got out together, taking a moment to pause with their doors open for cover, just in case. When nothing moved, no shots were fired, no suspects magically bolted from a boarded-up building, they continued on.

Wyatt had out a digital camera. Gina still worked the handheld.

"Watch the ground," he instructed her. "Avoid tread marks, footprints, any other signs of disturbance. Feds are gonna work this later, and I'll be damned if they chew our asses."

She nodded in agreement.

She was keeping a cool face, expression neutral, but he could see a slight tremor in her hand as she held the GPS tracker in front of her. Not fear, he'd guess, though maybe. But either way, adrenaline. He had it crashing through his bloodstream as well, heart rate slightly accelerated as he faced a known unknown. Something and/or someone loomed before them.

They approached together, him in the lead, Gina two steps back, tucked slightly behind him because presenting one target was bad enough; two targets would be just plain stupid.

Wind blew, rippling the low bushes, swaying the trees. Broad daylight, sun shining. A bird, here and there. The sound of a car, rushing by at forty-five miles per hour on the rural road, passing them by.

"Fifteen feet," Gina murmured.

He placed his right hand on his holstered weapon, as prepared as one could be.

"Ten feet."

And then, Wyatt didn't need her anymore. He saw it, plain as day. A darker lump tangled in a sea of sparse green. Not a body, thank heavens, but a large swath of fabric, wadded up, tossed in a twiggy bush.

His hand came down. He approached more briskly, brow already furrowing. Gina had seen the blue material as well. She lowered the handheld tracker and got on the radio to let the others know.

Then they both came to a halt, regarding the lump of fabric, thrown waist high in the bush.

"Doesn't look like much," Gina said. "Not even a whole coat."

Wyatt pulled on gloves, then gingerly untangled the lightweight material, holding the long strip up in front of them. Nice fabric, he thought. Some of that high-tech stuff meant to keep you warm and dry and still look good in pictures at the summit. Cost some dough, he'd bet, as befitting some rich Bostonian.

He felt around with his gloves, until he came across a flat, thin shape in the lower part of the strip, the GPS device. He fingered the edges, where the material was jagged and frayed.

"Kidnappers figured it out," he said after another minute, glancing around the scene. Kevin, Jeff and the other deputy had arrived, walking the length of the dirt parking lot to meet them. "Maybe Justin Denbe confessed, or the kidnappers discovered it upon closer inspection, but they figured out the jacket contained a GPS device, so they cut it out, looks like with a serrated blade, and tossed it."

"Why cut it out?" Gina asked with a frown. "Why not just toss the whole coat?"

Wyatt had to think about it. Then it came to him. "Denbe's tied up. Hands most likely bound. Meaning, to get the coat off him, they'd first have to remove his restraints. He's a big guy, I was told. Strong. Probably, the kidnappers didn't want to risk it. Easier, quicker, to remove the device itself and toss it aside."

He couldn't help himself. He flipped the fabric back over, inspecting for droplets of blood. Hunting knife. No good reason, maybe because he was a New Hampshirite, but he pictured a hunting blade. Plunging into the blue material, ripping down. Fast, that would be the way to do it. Two tears down, one across. Slash, slash, slash.

But not a trace of blood on the surviving strip. Fast and controlled. Disciplined.

The kidnappers had discovered their mistake, but they hadn't panicked. They'd simply taken evasive action. Fast, disciplined and smart.

It gave him a bad feeling. He turned his attention to the tread marks. Not wide, such as the kind on some of the souped-up SUVs guys drove around here, or the deeper grooves of the snow tires many would soon be sticking on their trucks to prepare for winter, but average Joe tracks. Like car tires, except given they suspected three to four kidnappers plus a family of three . . . cargo van. Had to be to hold a party of seven.

So a van, under the cover of night, pulling in, ripping apart a jacket, tossing the strip with the GPS device into the bushes. But why did it pull in? Because they already knew about the GPS device? Seemed unlikely to him that Justin Denbe would volunteer that kind of information. The jacket was his family's best shot at being rescued. So maybe it had nothing to do with the coat; that came later. The kidnappers were simply taking a comfort break. Someone had to pee. Or the kidnappers needed to sleep. Or just get their bearings, check a GPS system or a map. Not much going on in this area any time of day, let alone in the small hours of the morning. Good place to pull over, maybe better secure the family, pat down pockets. Interrogate. Hand off.

That intrigued him. He glanced up at Kevin.

"I see one set of tracks. You?"

His detective walked around, took his time with it. "One set of tracks," he agreed.

"Footprints?"

More studying. The others were fanning out, searching the bushes. Maybe the jacket wasn't the only thing that had been tossed. And while the jacket had been discarded at the edge of the woods, in plain sight, that didn't mean there weren't other discoveries to be made deeper in. "Maybe some footprints," Kevin finally called back, crouched down. "Ground's disturbed over here, between the tracks. As if a person or persons had been milling about."

"I'm thinking cargo van, to hold seven," Wyatt supplied.

"Makes sense. Pulls in, parks by the edge of the woods, at least one guy gets out, comes around to the back. Fiddles around. Can't make out individual sole patterns, though. Dirt's too firm."

"Guy or guys came around to the back." Wyatt picked up the thought. "Opened the doors. Most likely, to check on their hostages, tied up and tossed on the floor."

Kevin shrugged. Couldn't be known or unknown at this time.

"Discovered the GPS device in the jacket," Wyatt continued, "ripped up the coat, tossed the device in the woods. Then they continued on their way."

Kevin straightened. "Continued north," he added, pointing to the way the tire tracks exited the parking lot.

"Looks about right." Wyatt reconsidered the strip of fabric, moved on to the next logical question. "Why toss the GPS device? Even discarded, it's still traceable. Why not smash the device, render it inoperable?"

"Didn't know how?" Kevin suggested. "Or, they didn't care if the police traced them to this point. This area"—he waved his hands at the desolated building, deep woods—"isn't relevant to their final destination."

"Lets us know they're in New Hampshire," Wyatt said mildly.

"*Were* in New Hampshire," Kevin corrected. "Driving north, hell, they could be in Canada by now. Or have turned off toward Maine or Vermont, all easy routes from here."

Wyatt shrugged, unconvinced. The kidnappers should've smashed the device. That's what he would've done. Not rocket science. Just take a hammer or a rock and be done with it. Otherwise, jacket became the first bread crumb, and why leave behind a trail if you could help it? Not to mention this particular bread crumb proved the crime had crossed state lines and brought the feds into the game. Again, an unnecessary risk that could've easily been avoided given thirty seconds and a large rock. The discovery of the jacket seemed to imply that the kidnappers were shortsighted, but Wyatt wasn't convinced a stupid crew could've abducted a family of three from downtown Boston with such precision and speed.

Meaning maybe it meant the opposite? Not that their suspects were dumb, but their suspects were so experienced, they didn't believe having their activities traced this far hurt their efforts. They were executing according to plan, and the police discovery of a GPS device three hours north from the abduction site didn't matter to them one way or another.

That thought, the coldness behind it combined with the kind of precision it took to effortlessly slice up a thousand-dollar jacket without any collateral damage, unsettled him.

Kevin straightened from his study of the ground. "So based on the GPS device, the missing family was here. Question is, where are they now?"

They both looked north, toward the fading tire tracks.

This time of year in northern New Hampshire, there were hundreds of shuttered campsites, boarded-up homesteads and deeply isolated mountain cabins. And the farther north you went, the better the opportunities for never being seen by another living soul.

The kidnappers didn't need to care about one strip of material discovered in an isolated spot in central New Hampshire. Because from here on out, trying to find even three missing people in a state this rural, this wild, this mountainous . . .

Wyatt's powers were considerable, his grasp of law enviable and his domain vast.

He turned toward his assembled task force; two detectives plus two deputies. Not much, but enough to get the party started.

"All right," he informed them crisply. "Kevin, contact the media and release a description of the family. Kidnappers need fuel, need food, so in particular, follow up with truck stops, gas stations, roadside diners, all the quick in-and-out sort of joints.

Jeff, you work on the vehicle, issue a BOLO for any suspicious cargo vans, and while you're at it, request video footage from the Portsmouth tolls. Rest of you, time to bang the drums, rally the troops. We have only about three hours of daylight left. Let's get it done."

"At least we can assume the family is still alive," Gina provided hopefully. "Since the kidnappers dumped only the GPS tracker and not any bodies."

"We can assume," Wyatt murmured. "For now."

Chapter 11

"WAKE HER UP."

"I'm trying!"

"What's the problem? Did you administer too much sedative?"

"No—"

"Then wake her up!"

"I . . . shit!"

Pain. Instantaneous. Absolute. One second, I was floating in an abyss. The next, my stomach cramped violently and I bolted upright. Going to vomit. Trying to roll onto my side, but flopping awkwardly. My hands, my arms, my shoulders burning . . . couldn't move, didn't understand. My stomach heaved more insistently. Car, I was in the back of a vehicle, going to throw up in the back of a vehicle. Instinctively, I angled my head toward fresh air, rolling toward the open cargo doors where I could just make out the rear bumper, black tennis shoes and asphalt drive.

Then . . . Tape. My mouth. Taped shut. Oh God, oh God, oh God. I was going to puke, then suffocate on my own vomit. Panicking now, flailing wildly as my stomach rolled again and I clenched my jaw, trying to will the bile down. Not going to make it. Throat gagging . . . An unbelievable pressure building in my chest.

A man's hand darted forward, grabbed the edge of the duct tape and ripped it, *ripped* it from my mouth.

I screamed short, then vomited long, a watery stream of old champagne and yellow bile that spewed past the bumper onto the black tennis shoes and gray asphalt. A man's voice, swearing again. The tennis shoes, dancing back.

"Why is she sick?"

"I don't know, man. Crap. Look at my shoes. These are brand-new!"

"Is it from the sedative?"

"No. Shouldn't be. Hell, it could be any-thing. Shock. Motion sickness. Exhaust fumes. I mean, she's been Tasered, drugged and stuffed in the back of a van for the past fourteen hours. An upset stom-ach isn't out of the question."

The voices fell silent for a moment. I opened my mouth, thought I would vomit again, but my stomach was empty. I dry heaved instead. Then the last of my strength left me, and I collapsed onto my side, finally registering the rub-bery mat beneath me and the blue sky above me.

Except not all sky. Barbed wire. I made out rolls of razor wire spanning the horizon.

"Walk," a voice said.

A man appeared, looming over me. Mas-sive shoulders. Perfectly shaved head sporting a cobra tattoo, inked in shades of green. The coils twined around his neck and skull, the snake's fanged mouth bared around his left eye. I stared at that tattoo, and for a shuddering instant, I swore the tattooed scales moved.

Then it came back to me. The hulking form at the edge of my foyer. The Taser. My husband's terrible convulsing. My leg's fiery pain. And my daughter, screaming. Calling out our names.

I sat up. The world spun, but I didn't care. I had to find my daughter. Ashlyn, Ashlyn, where was Ashlyn?

My wrists were bound at my waist. Too late, I figured out my ankles were restrained as well, as I flopped out of the back of the van and landed hard enough to knock the wind from my chest and send my stomach spasming again. This time, I rocked onto my side until the worst of the dry heaving passed.

"She's sick. She get car sick?" Tattooed man. Had to be. A menacing voice to go with a menacing face.

The tearing sound of tape being ripped from flesh. A short, hiccuping cry. Then my daughter's voice, thin, reedy, uncertain. "Not . . . usually. Mommy?"

The man was moving. I could hear his steel-toed boots ringing out against the asphalt. My head hurt. My stomach, my back, my hip. I wanted to close my eyes. I wanted to curl up in a ball and squeeze my eyes shut, as if that would make it all go away. I would will myself back to sleep, except this time, when I woke up, I would be in my own bed, with my husband snoring softly beside me and my daughter tucked safely down the hall.

I opened my eyes. For my daughter's sake, I worked myself around until, for the first time, I could make out our surroundings.

We were outside, under some kind of covered drive. A large white van was parked a few feet away, back doors still open. Behind it more fence. Tall, maybe twenty feet, topped by razor wire, and buffered by even more rolls of razor wire.

My eyes widened. I searched out my daughter, found her standing next to the smallest of three men. Her shoulders were rounded, her chin tucked defensively against her chest, while her long wheat-brown hair hung down in a curtain, as if to protect her. Her feet were bare and she wore her favorite comfy clothes, fuzzy ice-cream-cone-patterned pajama bottoms with a long-sleeved waffle-knit top. My first thought was that her feet had to be freezing. Then I noticed a dark stain streaking across the shoulder of her pale blue shirt. Blood? Was that blood? My daughter hurt, bleeding . . .

And Justin? What about Justin? I glanced wildly around the space, then spotted his booted feet, bound with zip ties and poking out the back of the van.

The tattooed guy, who wore a black commando outfit, turned to the younger kid next to my daughter.

"Watch her," he said, and pointed at me, as if I were somehow going to magically make my escape now that I was tied up on the ground instead of being restrained in the back of the transport vehicle.

The man crossed to the rear of the van, where he was joined by a second guy, also garbed in black and almost as big and frightening looking, except his buzz-cut hair had been dyed into a checkerboard pattern of black and blond. Between the two of them, they heaved Justin's bound body out of the van and placed him on his feet. Immediately, Justin started struggling.

Cobra-tattooed guy reached up and ripped off Justin's duct tape.

My husband didn't scream. He roared, hopping forward and trying to head butt his nearest opponent.

In response, the tattooed guy stepped back, unholstered his Taser and pulled the trigger. Justin dropped like a rock, blue jacket flapping, whole body convulsing. He no longer roared, but ground out gibberish through clenched teeth.

I glanced away, unable to see my husband in so much pain.

Across from me, Ashlyn was crying.

The tattooed guy pulled the trigger a few more times. When he seemed to feel Justin had had enough, he nodded once, and the second man jerked Justin back onto his feet, wires still dangling from his body.

"Here is the deal," the tattooed guy boomed, and at the sound of his voice, Ashlyn started crying harder, her hands bound at her waist, her teeth digging into her lower lip.

I closed my eyes, not wanting to see my daughter's tears any more than my husband's pain. I pictured colors, flowers, melting clocks.

I smelled oranges, and tasted yellow birthday cake.

"You can call me Z. I am your new boss. You will speak when I say you can speak. You will eat when I say you can eat. You will live as long as I say you can live. What is my name?"

Silence. Belatedly, I opened my eyes, found the man staring at me. "What is my name!" he boomed at me.

"Z." My voice came out weak. I licked my lips, wondered if I should try again, but he was already moving away.

This time, I tried to catch my daughter's attention, tried to will her to look at me, as if by holding each other's gazes, this would be easier to take.

"This is Mick." The tattooed guy pointed to the checkerboard-hair man. "And this is Radar." He pointed at the smaller, younger guy standing next to my daughter. The one not in black commando garb, but instead jeans and vomit-covered black tennis shoes. He bobbed his head slightly, as if pleased to make our acquaintance. Then he flushed self-consciously.

"And this"—Z turned half around, gesturing grandly—"will be your new home." The man beamed, appearing particularly pleased with himself. I forced my aching body to turn again, take in the building I was only half aware of. Except this time, it became clear to me it wasn't just a building, but a sprawling complex. An institution. Four stories tall with narrow slits for windows, surrounded by fencing topped with rolls of razor wire.

What kind of building had such tiny windows? What kind of landscaping involved so much razor wire? Then it came to me. A prison.

These men had dragged us from our home and brought us to a prison. Except . . . the place seemed eerily quiet, still. Not a populated facility, but empty. Abandoned, maybe.

"I will pay you money," Justin spoke up clearly. "Any amount you want. Double, triple whatever you've been offered."

For his response, Z pulled the Taser trigger. Once more my husband's body arched. Once more his lips peeled back from his teeth, forming a macabre grin that went on and on.

He didn't make any noise this time. He just took the pain.

Z finally released the trigger. Justin's body sagged, would've collapsed, except the other guy held him up.

"You will speak when I say you can speak," Z repeated. He stared at Justin's heaving form. "When will you speak?"

My husband raised his head. His eyes were bright with rage. I could see a muscle clenched in his jaw. Such a competitive man. One of the things I had admired about him in the beginning. Down but never out. Battered but not broken. Now I silently willed him to give up. Keep his mouth shut. Not say another word . . .

"Daddy," Ashlyn pleaded softly.

Justin's look changed. From fury to panic and in the next instant, I understood, as Z wheeled about, headed for our daughter.

"No." I gasped the word out loud, trying to roll forward, do something. I could hear Justin growling, knew he had to be struggling, desperately trying to break free.

Too late, my daughter realized her mistake. She watched Z's rapid approach, her sobs reaching hysterical pitch as she raised her bound arms in front of her face . . .

The kid stepped forward. Straight into Z's path.

"Hey," the kid said, "isn't that a patrol car?"

He pointed his finger, and just like that, everyone was on the move.

"Inside, now," Z snapped. "You get the women. You get Denbe."

Checkerboard Hair was already slicing through Justin's leg restraints, with a single stroke of a huge knife, then dragging my husband's stumbling form toward the front doors.

Radar fumbled for a moment with my daughter's restraints, then made it to my side long enough to free my ankles and help me stagger to my feet. I tried to shoot him a grateful look, to let him know I knew what he'd done for Ashlyn, but he wouldn't make eye contact. Instead, with one hand on my daughter's elbow and another on mine, he hustled us both toward the doors.

Behind us, I could hear the engine as the van started up. Hiding it, I supposed. The van would be tucked somewhere outside, we would be tucked somewhere inside, and then no one would be the wiser.

Doors, closing behind us. First one set, then another.

The kid and the second commando dragged us deeper inside a vast, empty space. If this was a prison, then this must be the receiving area. I could make out stark white cinder-block walls, a dingy yellow linoleum floor, some kind of command post straight ahead with thick windows all around it.

The room was dimly lit, only a fraction of the overhead lights in use. I had a feeling that was to our advantage, that when every light was flipped on, the starkness would be nearly blinding, miles of bone-white walls to bounce the light and hurt the eyes.

I tried to sneak a glance at my daughter again. She stood on the other side of Radar, her head still bowed, hair down, shoulders trembling. Z was not around, but I still didn't dare to speak. I noticed for the first time she wasn't wearing her usual gold hoops in her ears, or the small diamond pendant Justin had given her on her thirteenth birthday.

Belatedly, I glanced down only to discover my engagement diamond and wedding band were also missing. Damn thieves, I thought irrationally, considering everything else they'd done. Robbing us of our own jewelry while we were heavily sedated.

I stole a glance at my husband's wrist, confirming that his Rolex was also gone. Then my gaze drifted up, and I found my husband's eyes. He was watching both me and Ashlyn, his features etched with sorrow.

If I could've, I would've reached out my hand then.

For the first time in six months, I would've touched my husband and meant it.

Instead, the three of us just stood there, not speaking, waiting to see what terrible thing would happen next.

Z REAPPEARED SHORTLY, his footsteps ringing down the hall as he approached from a different direction. His minions hadn't spoken in his absence, and I had a feeling that's the way things worked. Z called the shots, the other two did the shooting.

The kid, in his jeans and tennis shoes, didn't bother me. He had a tendency to duck his head and hunch his shoulders self-consciously, almost as if embarrassed to be there.

The other one, with the checkerboard hair, worried me. His eyes were too bright, some shade of neon blue I associated with drug addicts or lunatics. He held Justin's arm in a white-knuckled grip, his face openly daring Justin to do something about it. The bully, looking forward to the fight.

I noticed the kid, with one hand upon each of our elbows, kept Ashlyn and me a good distance from his partner. And I noticed Justin made no attempt to close that gap.

When Z appeared, both the kid and the checkerboard commando stood a little straighter, ready for the next set of instructions. I wanted to brace myself, call upon some kind of internal reserve. I had nothing.

My stomach hurt. My head pounded.

I needed my purse.

For the love of God, I needed my pills.

"Would you like a tour?" Z's voice sounded taunting. Because he had not said we could speak, none of us answered.

"It's a twelve-hundred-bed medium-security facility," Z continued crisply. "State-of-the-art, completed just last year and, conveniently for us, currently mothballed."

I glanced up. My confusion must've showed on my face, for he expanded: "Welcome to your tax dollars at work, where one hand builds the prison, but a different hand funds the opening and operating of said facility. Basically, capital expenditures fall under appropriations bills, whereas operational costs fall under the government's annual budget. Except the state's budget has been facing the usual shortfalls, so this prison has never been opened. It simply sits here, a very expensive shell wasting away in the mountains of New Hampshire. It's perfect for us."

He turned on his heel, walking down the hallway toward the direction he'd come, and his commandos dragged us into place behind him.

"Did you know," he continued over his shoulder, "that eighty percent of prison escapes occur when an inmate is already out of his cell, maybe tending to his prison job, or in the infirmary? That's because no one, absolutely *no one* can escape from a modern jail cell. Walls are five-thousand-pounds-per-square-inch concrete poured twelve inches thick. The windows feature one-inch-thick bars formed from saw-resistant steel and positioned every five inches in front of fifteen-minute ballistic-rated glass. That means"—he gave me a glance—"you can fire a small-caliber pistol at point-blank range and the glass might spiderweb, but still won't break.

"Doors are twelve-gauge steel with a solid one-inch-thick dead bolt. All locks are triggered electronically, meaning there is no way to manually override the dead bolt system. Not to mention there are at least seven locks between you and the outside world. First lock is on your cell door. Get by that, you're in a locked dayroom. Which leads to a double-locked sally port, where the system only allows one locked door to be opened at one time. After that is a locked corridor leading to a main wing entrance where there is yet another sally port. Two more doors, two more locks.

"Should you finally exit the prison, you must now confront the perimeter fencing. The fences are completely electrified and built in two layers, each sixteen feet high and separated by a twenty-eight-foot-wide no-man's-land filled with seven rolls of razor wire. Even if you somehow disabled the electric fencing, and/or survived scaling the first sixteen-foot fence, you must still drop down into the no-man's-land and navigate seven rolls of razor wire in order to make your way over the second sixteen-foot-high fence. After which, you will find yourself plopped in the middle of six hundred acres of some of the most rugged wilderness the North Country has to offer. Nighttime temperatures are currently forecast to be below freezing. Oh, and this area is known for bears and bobcats."

Z stopped walking. Abruptly, we all drew to a halt.

He stared at my husband. "Did I miss anything?"

Justin didn't speak. I looked at him in confusion. He and Z seemed to be involved in some kind of staring contest.

"Not that there's any need to leave the prison," Z said now, still staring at Justin. "As part of the building contract, this facility was fully stocked. Bunk beds, rec tables, state-of-the-art medical equipment, state-of-the-art dental. Two cafeterias, including a separate, self-enclosed cooking space for the preparation of nut-, dairy- and gluten-free items. Can't have any of the inmates dying of food allergies, yes? The complex also runs on 'duel fuel,' both natural gas and oil, with fifty thousand gallons of oil on site. Plus its own water tower, sewer system and utility plant. A fully independent operation. With redundancy. I believe that's what you call it? So utilities can't be disrupted, water cut, sewer stopped. We could hole up here for years without anyone being the wiser."

Z still stared. Justin still didn't speak.

On the other side of Radar, my daughter shuddered.

"I served eight years as a soldier," Z said abruptly. "Still never had it as good as the convicts who will one day occupy these cells."

My husband spoke up: "I just build—"

"I didn't say speak."

"Then stop talking to me."

"I'll hurt you again."

"Then do it. Just tell me what the fuck you want and stop terrorizing my family!"

Ashlyn and I both recoiled, tucking ourselves ironically against the kid, who stood as still as stone.

Z didn't move. He continued to watch my husband, as if evaluating something. The look on his face was not harsh, but clinical. Sizing up his opponent. He would hurt my husband in the end. He would hurt all of us, I realized. He just wanted to do it properly.

"Please," I heard myself whisper. "We have money . . ."

"Not what this is about."

Justin snorted. "Money is what it's always about." He swung his gaze to Z's cohorts, the kid, the checkerboard man with the neon-blue eyes. "Sure you two couldn't use some extra cash? I got a company worth a hundred mil. Whatever he's paying you, I can do better."

"Just let our daughter go," I added quietly.

The kid didn't move. Checkerboard man actually smiled, but it wasn't a nice expression.

Ashlyn shuddered again.

"Girl stays," Z stated. "You stay." He looked at me. "You stay." He looked at Justin. "And I don't have to tell you why or for how long. Because I know you, Justin. I know exactly how your mind works. You're a born problem solver. Even now, you're not panicking; you're simply waiting for the situation to reveal itself. Because in your experience, information is power. It enables you to dissect, control, resolve.

"Which will make breaking you all the more interesting. Now then, the fun is just beginning."

Z moved his hand, pushed open the door behind him to reveal a supply closet neatly stacked with piles of orange material.

"Your new wardrobe," he announced. "Get dressed. From here on out, you're our prisoners. And this is your new home."

Chapter 12

LAW ENFORCEMENT OFFICERS such as Boston detectives and FBI agents generally went straight to the source. Would descend upon a company, badging the receptionist and proceeding to milk every last drop of information from the rank and file.

Since Tessa was no longer a cop, she went about things the private investigator's way: She identified the name of Justin Denbe's right-hand man, tracked him down on his personal cell and arranged to meet him twenty minutes later at a coffee shop several miles and at least two neighborhoods away from Denbe Construction's downtown Boston headquarters.

She went with the right-hand man, figuring he'd know the most about Justin's personal and professional life. She lured him off campus because anyone was more apt to talk without known friends or associates looking over his shoulder.

Chris Lopez, construction manager, was already waiting for her at the Starbucks. She recognized him immediately because even from thirty feet away, his clothes and demeanor screamed construction. Well-worn jeans, red plaid shirt with rolled-up sleeves layered over a plain white T, scuffed work boots complete with a layer of grime ringing the heavy soles. He wore his black hair short and she could see rings from a dark blue tattoo just creeping out above the collar of his shirt.

Former military. The buzz-cut hair, muscled forearms, stocky build, lounging in the hard wooden chair, denim-clad legs sprawled forward.

Currently, he was appraising her as openly as she appraised him. Which didn't surprise her, either. Uniform was forever attracted to uniform. If she pegged him as former military, she bet he'd already pegged her as former law enforcement, some sort of internal radar system pinging both of them onto high alert.

She took her time crossing the room. Bright, sunny Saturday afternoon, the Starbucks was still jammed, people loading up on mid-afternoon lattes and muffins. She doubted she'd pulled Lopez from work when she'd dialed his cell. Given the military and construction personnel's reputation for working hard and playing harder, she'd bet she'd pulled him out of bed, or someone else's bed, where he'd been sleeping off Friday night.

She went with someone else's bed. Hence the work clothes, including work boots; all he'd had to drag on when summoned to a last-minute meeting.

He didn't look away as she approached. If anything, he met her gaze head-on, a smile playing around the corners of his mouth. Ballsy, she thought, for a guy most likely still wearing another woman's perfume upon his skin.

And maybe, slightly flattering. Women like her didn't garner a lot of glances across a crowded room. She had a tendency to hold herself too rigidly, always on guard against some unknown threat, but also walled off from polite chitchat. Then, after the events of two years ago . . . There were mornings she didn't even recognize her face in the mirror. Her blue eyes were too flat. Her face too grim.

People moved away from her on crowded subways. She told herself it was good to be tough, but there were days she still found it depressing.

Her husband had been killed, and she lived now as an island. If not for Sophie's unconditional love, she would exist in total isolation. It made her value her daughter more, while also worrying that having an eight-year-old as her main source of companionship was not healthy for either of them. Sophie's job was to grow up and leave her.

And Tessa's job was to let her.

She'd arrived at the table for two. She removed her long coat, too warm for a sun-baked coffee shop, and given she'd left her gun in her vehicle's locked glove compartment, unnecessary. She draped her coat over the back of the chair, moving unhurriedly, then, at long last, took a seat.

Neither of them spoke, and now Chris Lopez's smile grew.

"So," Tessa said at last. "What was her name?"

His smile vanished. "What?"

"The woman. Last night. Or not the kind of thing where names are necessary?"

He scowled.

She held out her hand. "Tessa Leoni. I'm here in regards to the Denbe family."

"You're the former cop," Lopez said, voice a tad sulky. He shook her hand but no longer appeared so amused. "The state trooper. You shot and killed your own husband."

"Allegedly," she corrected. The story of her life.

"What do you miss most? The uniform, the gun or the really uncool car?"

"The easy parking. Now, tell me what you do for Denbe Construction."

They'd covered the basics by phone beforehand. Justin Denbe and his family were missing—Lopez had already been aware of the situation, no doubt called by either Denbe Construction or the Boston cops, probably both, during the initial search phase. Lopez reported last seeing Justin at a 3:00 P.M. meeting on Friday afternoon in the corporate office. Hadn't spoken or met with him since. As for the family, the house, Lopez hadn't seen them or visited Justin's Boston town house in months. Too busy on a job down south.

Tessa wasn't having this conversation because she thought Chris Lopez could lead her to the Denbe family. She was interviewing Chris Lopez as part of the next step of the missing persons' process—developing a victimology report. Who was Justin Denbe? And who were the winners and the losers when a man like him vanished into thin air?

"You know construction?" Lopez asked her now.

She shook her head, taking out her phone and holding it up for inspection. When he grudgingly nodded permission, she tapped the recording app and set the phone on the table between them.

"Denbe Construction is a major player. We bid on projects that cost at least tens of millions and often hundreds of millions. Think prison construction, senior care facilities, military barracks, et cetera. Big money, significant timeline, make-it-or-break-it kind of risk."

Tessa decided to start with the basics. She got out her notebook, turned it horizontally and presented it to Lopez. Here was a trick she'd never learned at the police academy, but had come up day one in corporate security school.

"Org chart," she asked. "Major players."

Lopez rolled his eyes but took the paper, her offered pen and drew the first box on the top of the page. Justin Denbe, CEO. Made sense to her. Beneath Denbe came three boxes. CFO Ruth Chan; COC Chris Lopez; and COO Anita Bennett. Tessa recognized Bennett's name, as she'd been the one to contact Tessa's boss bright and early this morning. Now, beneath the chief of operations's name, Lopez drew two more, smaller boxes: MIS Tom Wilkins and Office Admin Letitia Lee.

"COC stands for chief of construction," Lopez explained, tapping the box bearing his name. "Anita Bennett and I act almost as cochiefs of operations. She handles business affairs, while I manage the building gigs. So admin reports to her, while the tradesmen report to me."

Lopez didn't draw any more boxes. He pushed the org chart back and Tessa frowned.

"That's a pretty small corporate structure for a hundred-million-dollar company," she observed.

He shrugged. "First rule of construction: It's all about the subs. Especially these major projects, no way you can provide all the boots on the ground, not to mention it'd be too expensive to maintain that kind of overhead in down cycles. We partner. Think of Denbe as being the head of a centipede. We develop the RFP—"

"RFP?"

"Request for proposal. How these big jobs start, especially if they're government funded. The agency involved—"

"Agency involved?"

Lopez sighed. He leaned forward, placing his forearms on the tiny table while explaining: "Say we're bidding on a hundred-million-dollar project to build new barracks for the navy. Obviously, that RFP is generated through military channels. Then there are hospitals, which can come through private or state channels. Or prisons, which might come through the Bureau of Prisons, depending on whether we're talking a county, state or federal facility."

"But it sounds like you mostly do government work?"

"True. There are firms out there who specialize in major hotel projects, conference centers, casinos, that sort of thing. The hospitality industry. In comparison, we're the opposite end of the spectrum— the institutional industry." Lopez chuckled, pleased at his own irony.

"Why?"

"Government game is connections, and Justin has connections. That's one of his strengths. The man knows how to work a room, and when you're competing against a dozen other firms for an RFP worth hundreds of millions of dollars, personally knowing the senator on the appropriations committee, or having had the head of the Bureau of Prisons over to your house for dinner, isn't a bad thing. Some firms even employ lobbyists. We attend some key conferences, get to know the major players and Justin will take it from there."

"So you get to know the key people who are issuing RFPs for these major projects. In New England?"

"We build nationally."

"Okay, national building projects. But these projects are for hundreds of millions of dollars, and must take, what, years to complete?"

"Just the on-site build will tie up a couple of years," Lopez clarified. "But take a major prison project we just completed. Took us ten years, start to finish. Our client's the government, right? And governments don't move fast."

"I get it. So, on the one hand, you're landing projects in the hundreds of millions, but on the other hand, it's taking you up to ten years to complete them. Big money, big risk, like you said. But Denbe's a second-generation firm, right? Started by Justin's father. Meaning you guys have longevity on your side."

"We are not the new kids at the party," Lopez agreed, "but nor are we resting on our laurels. When Justin took over after his father's death, he became obsessed with growing the firm. Way he saw it, the industry was at a major turning point, where the big were gonna get bigger, but the small, smaller. He didn't want to get smaller. Of course, the challenge in construction is how to grow a company without growing your overhead. We're a boom-and-bust industry, right? We increase our staff, double our costs during the boom, and suddenly, we can't survive the bust. Hence, Justin's centipede model: Denbe Construction provides the leader for each segment of the build process—the best project manager, the expert tradesmen, et cetera, for guidance and troubleshooting. Basically, we provide the generals, our subs provide the troops. Meaning Denbe can staff lean, while still being a leader in the industry."

"So does that make you the expert on the experts?" Tessa asked Lopez. "After all, if your guys are the best of the best, and you're the overseer of the best of the best . . ."

Lopez rolled his eyes. "I don't know if I'd say I'm that smart, or just that stubborn. Look, I can draw you all the pretty pictures you want, but basically large-scale construction means large-scale headaches. First, I gotta hand-hold dozens of subs to put together one coherent RFP. Except putting together a building proposal is a lot like a political campaign. All the subs put on their best faces and make their brightest promises, hoping you'll pick them for your winning team. But maybe, when the HVAC subcontractor was campaigning that hard, he forgot to read the fine print on the spec sheet. Or he mistook the number seventy for, say, the number seven, so he underbid the project by quite a lot. Most subs will try to weasel out of such mistakes. My job, three years later when we've actually started building, is not to let him. On a good day, that can mean forcing a sub to eat an error worth tens of thousands of dollars—no big deal when the sub's total contract is for fifty million. On a bad day, however, when the error runs into the tens of millions, meaning the sub is now losing money on a project I'm not letting him quit—a quote is a legally binding contract—that can mean threat of lawsuits or even death. Hey, it happens."

Tessa was impressed. "So you're the company bad cop. Does that make Justin the good cop?"

"Pretty close. Justin is strategic. When

a sub sends us twenty sets of boots on the ground, but the overall timeline of the project clearly demands forty, he sorts it out. When the electrical plan manages to violate four basic codes, he'll get on the phone and hash it out. When an RFP gets tied up in a committee, he does some schmoozing and pulls it out. Justin's not just smart, he's *useful* smart. He not only gets things done, but makes you happy to have done it. Guys like me, we respect that."

"Guys like you?"

Lopez shrugged. "Army ranger."

"Lot of former military on the payroll?"

"You could say that." He held out his hand for her notepad. When she handed it over, he drew a line down from his name on the org chart and added four horizontal boxes beneath. Design Manager; Structural Engineer; Superintendent of Security; Quality Engineer.

"This is the core build team," he explained. "Design manager oversees the architects. That's Dave, only one of us whose misspent youth wasn't funded by Uncle Sam. Now, the structural engineer, Jenkins, is former air force. Everything is funneled through him, including layers and layers of plans. You think I like details? Jenkins dreams in blueprints. He's also an antisocial son of a bitch, probably has some kind of Asperger's, but the man is scary smart and not too bad with a forty-five, so we forgive him his other sins. Let's see, that brings us to Paulie, the superintendent of security. Now, security systems have two components, electronics and hard line. Paulie handles both and is the craziest mother you'll ever meet. Former Navy SEAL, and how Justin ever gets him through security clearance, I'll never know. Especially after that last incident, involving two bars, the entire town's PD, and Paulie's new court-mandated anger-management classes. But Paulie's not really too bad, just as long as you keep him off the sauce. That's my job, and Justin's. Which brings us to our quality engineer, Bacon. His real name is Barry, but call him that and he's liable to hurt you. Bacon is ex-marine, Force Recon. He wears a spoon around his neck. Claims he used it once to kill a guy. We don't argue much with Bacon." Lopez looked her in the eye, his voice dead serious. "This team, we're the ones who work with Justin the most. We work close, we work well. And I can tell you, to a man, we have his back."

"Interesting circle of friends."

Lopez just shrugged. "These aren't projects for the faint at heart. It's a tough job, moving around the country to follow the work. It's a rough job, spending the first year living in a trailer, pissing in a pot. Us military types—we're used to it. We don't expect indoor plumbing. We can fix three squares with a hot pot. Not to mention, for most of us, these paychecks are a nice step-up. Justin's good to us. Pays well, respects us. Construction's a shitty industry these days. Firms are folding all around. But Justin's kept doors open, jobs secure, paychecks coming. Even a muscle head like me is smart enough to appreciate that."

"Justin is a good boss," Tessa stated.

"Yeah. And we're terrible employees, a bunch of disrespectful, drunken, wiseass personal fuckups. So that's saying something."

"You mentioned Justin had to get the crazy former SEAL through security clearance. Does everyone on your crew have to pass background checks to work these sites?"

"Basic CORI Criminal Offender Record Information check," Lopez supplied. "Looks for outstanding warrants. Frankly, if a building is new and unoccupied, they often waive even that. The trades, we're not the noblest bunch. Even the government understands that if you set the security standards too high, there'll be no one left to work the site."

"Rough-and-tumble crew, to go with the rough-and-tumble management team?"

"The kind of guys who know how to show a girl a good time," Lopez assured her. He had his smile back.

Tessa switched gears: "If the employees at Denbe Construction love Justin so much, who would hate him?"

"Every rival that lost a job to him. And every sub we awarded a contract to, who then lost his shirt on his legally binding bid he completely fucked up. Priced out seven items instead of seventy, remember? Couple of times, we've had angry subs show up on site, packing heat. 'Course, we're not the kind of guys you want to draw down on. And I include Justin in that category. He shoots with us at least once a week, and he gets his slug through the center of the dime just as often as the rest of us."

Tessa blinked her eyes. "You are a crazy crew."

"Hell, it's a crazy business. Got a fresh piece of paper? I'm gonna need the whole thing if you want a proper enemies list."

TESSA WRAPPED WITH LOPEZ an hour later. It took that long to establish the long list of rivals and subs who held grudges against Justin personally, or Denbe Construction generally. The list was further complicated by the complex dynamics of an industry in which firms bought and sold subs and rivals, let alone folded under one name just to reemerge a month later under a new moniker. Lopez highlighted two firms, ASP Inc. and Pimm Brothers, who were long-time Denbe nemeses. The Pimm Brothers were two sons from another family-operated business. When they struck out on their own, they'd assumed Justin would switch his relationship from their father's company to theirs. When he hadn't, they'd never forgiven him.

More soap operas here, Tessa thought, than in most Mafia enterprises.

Which brought her to the next topic of conversation. Justin Denbe's personal life.

Lopez, so insightful on the intricacies of the construction industry, immediately turned stupid when it came to the subject of Justin's marriage.

Best she could get from him was that he respected Mrs. Denbe and had a soft spot for Ashlyn. Apparently, most of the core build team had known Justin's daughter since she was a toddler. From the time she was three, Justin had often brought her on site and let her run around with power tools. Justin liked to boast she'd take over the firm one day. Why not? Lopez had offered with a shrug. Girl seemed capable enough.

All in all, Lopez couldn't think of a single reason the family would willingly disappear. The firm's finances were a bit thin, but in their industry, that was typical enough. And, no, Justin hadn't seemed particularly stressed or angry or irrational. Hell, they were working hand in hand on a major RFP to repair an aging nuclear power plant, and Justin had seemed his usual nose-to-the-grindstone self. And, yeah, Lopez had heard talk of a date night on Friday. Justin had seemed in a good mood, looking forward to it. Scampo, right? Swanky place, just right for impressing the missus.

As for who might abduct the entire family . . .

Lopez had grown noticeably agitated. Sitting up straighter, hand thrumming against the top of his leg. From what Tessa could tell, it didn't seem to be Justin's kidnapping that bothered Lopez so much, but the abduction of Justin's wife and child. Someone possibly harming women definitely pushed Lopez's buttons.

Tessa gave him credit for that.

"I'll do some poking around," Lopez volunteered at last. "I mean, I can't think of anyone inside Denbe who'd hold a grudge against the family, but . . . I'll monitor the mood of my fellow inmates. If I hear anything, I'll give you a call. We can talk about it over dinner."

"I don't date on the job," she informed him.

"Why? You're not a cop anymore. Who makes those rules?"

"Basic professionalism. And I can make any rule I want."

"Hard-ass," he said.

"Well, I did allegedly shoot my own husband."

Lopez laughed. Apparently, a suspected murderess only attracted him more.

Very interesting people in construction, Tessa decided.

She wrapped up with Lopez just as her phone rang.

She exited the coffee shop before picking it up, assuming it was Sophie and already feeling guilty she hadn't taken the time to call. But it wasn't home. Instead, it was D. D. Warren.

"The eagle has landed," the detective said by way of greeting. Tessa interpreted that as code for arrival of the FBI.

"Trimming your wings?"

"With a rusty razor," D.D. replied dryly. "But, turns out Neil gets the last laugh—the New Hampshire cops, some sheriff's department, has picked up the ball and is now running with it."

"The GPS beacon?" Tessa asked hopefully.

"They found only the device. Looks to them like the kidnappers must've discovered the GPS capabilities of the jacket, so they pulled over at some abandoned diner, cut out that piece of the coat and dumped it in the woods. Tire tracks show the vehicle resuming a northern route."

Tessa frowned, tried to picture a map of New Hampshire in her head. "They were already three hours north of Boston. How much more north is there?"

"Two hours to Canada. But also twenty minutes from the Maine border, so possibly they veered east at some point, which would really place them in the middle of nowhere. Basically we're looking at hundreds of square miles of wild mountains, abandoned campsites and boarded-up summer homes. But other than that . . ."

"Crap," Tessa said, chewing her bottom lip. "Any word?"

"No. FBI brought with them a Behavioral Analysis Unit agent whose specialty is missing persons. According to her, if this is a ransom case, we should hear by end of day or things aren't looking good."

"It's not kidnapping for ransom. It's something . . . more personal."

"The FBI expert has a theory about that, too," D.D. supplied.

"Which is?"

"In cases of retribution, people have a tendency to think in terms of an eye for an eye. They want to dish out as much harm as they feel they sustained. Under this theory, a suspect who felt his person or reputation was damaged by Justin would seek revenge against *only* Justin."

"Except," Tessa said slowly, "it wasn't just Justin who was attacked. They also abducted his wife and daughter."

"Meaning if this *isn't* a kidnapping-for-ransom case, then whoever orchestrated the kidnapping feels Justin Denbe harmed his entire family, maybe cost him his own wife and child."

"That doesn't sound like business anymore," Tessa agreed. "That definitely sounds personal."

"Food for thought," D.D. agreed. There was a pause. "So, given that the feds are now here and working their magic . . ."

"Last insider's call regarding this case you're going to get to make for a bit?" Tessa guessed. Which begged the question of why her one-time nemesis had been so considerate as to use that call on her.

As if reading her mind, D.D. said, "Speaking for the entire Boston squad, we don't really care who saves the Denbes. We just want to hear that they've been located safe and sound. But if the family happens to be rescued by a local investigator versus, say, the very irritating feds who just commandeered our crime scene . . . well, all the better in our petty little world."

Having said her piece, D.D. disconnected. Tessa stood in the parking lot another moment, considering the detective's update. What if money had nothing to do with the Denbes' kidnapping? What if, as the FBI expert suggested, it wasn't a professionally motivated crime, but a personally motivated crime?

Not a matter of ransom, but retribution.

Tessa checked her watch, skimming through the list of favorite contacts she'd gleaned from the Denbes' phones. Justin's right-hand man had claimed to know very little about his boss's personal life. But what about a member from Libby Denbe's inner circle? Sister, best friend, close confidant?

Tessa Leoni, former state trooper, current investigator extraordinaire, selected her next target.

Chapter 13

How do you know when you've fallen out of love?

There are entire songs, poems and greeting cards dedicated to the notion of falling in love. The power of the first glance across a crowded room. That moment right before the first kiss, when you're still wondering will he or won't he, while angling up your head in centuries-old invite.

The first giddy days, weeks, when you are consumed by thoughts of him. His touch, his taste, his feel. You invest in better lingerie, take more time with your hair, pick out a new form-fitting sweater because you can imagine his hands following the same lines as the soft knit and you want, more than anything, to invite those hands anywhere.

When the phone rings, you snatch it up in hopes of hearing his voice. When your lunch break arrives, you hastily calculate if you can make it to his office and back before the hour's up. Wearing a trench coat and nothing else.

Planned dinners out become hastily scrambled eggs eaten out of bowls in the middle of his king-size bed, because your new sweater worked its magic and neither of you made it back out the door. And now he lounges around in his boxers and you lounge around in his button-up oxford and you think to yourself, admiring the hard expanse of his bare chest, the rippling muscles of his upper arms, my God, how did I get so lucky?

Then, his eyes darken, he reaches for you and you don't think of anything else again.

I knew when I fell in love with Justin. Felt it like the proverbial lightning bolt.

And I thought, That Day, confronting him with the evidence, watching his face pale, then set, that I would feel my love for him die an equally thunderous death. Certainly, I caught my breath. Felt my stomach churn with growing nausea.

As he looked me in the eye and quietly said, "Yes, I've been sleeping with her . . ."

I yelled at him. Threw whatever was closest at hand. Raged and screamed with growing levels of hysteria. Ashlyn came racing down the hall to our room, but Justin turned and, in the sharpest voice I'd ever heard, ordered her back to her room *right now.* She literally spun around on one toe and went running for the sanctuary of her iPod.

He told me to calm down. I remember that.

I believe that's when I went after him with the bedside lamp. He caught it, grabbed it with those strong arms I used to love and twisted me around until I was caught in his embrace, my back to his front, my arms locked by my sides where I could no longer hurt him. He held me. And he whispered, softly against the top of my head, that he was sorry. So sorry. So really, really sorry. I felt drops of moisture against my hair. My husband, moved to tears.

The fight left me.

I sagged against him.

He held me up. Supported me in his embrace, and for a while, we stood together, both of us breathing hard, our tears comingling. I cried for the loss of my marriage. For the trust I'd had in this man, and for the terrible, terrible feeling of not just betrayal, but failure. That I had loved my husband with my entire being, and it still hadn't been enough.

And Justin? Those drops of moisture against the top of my head? Tears of shame? Pain at having caused me pain? Or simply regret at finally being caught?

I hated him then. With every fiber of my being.

But I don't think I fell out of love with him. I only wished that I could.

Afterward, I kicked him out of the house. He didn't argue, just quietly packed his bag. I told him not to come back. I told him he was a terrible man and he'd hurt me too much, and what kind of man ripped apart his own family, and what kind of father abandoned his own daughter? And then, for a while, I said things that didn't even make sense but simply poured out, a raging flow of hurt and spite. He took it. Stood in front of me, holding his black duffel bag, and let me hate him.

Finally, I emptied myself of all words. We stared at each other across the silent space of our bedroom.

"I was an idiot," he said.

I made a noise. It wasn't kind.

"This is my fault, my mistake."

Another noise.

"Can I call you?" he tried again. "In a few days, after you've caught your breath. Can we just . . . talk?"

I regarded him with pure, stony rage.

"You're right, Libby," he said quietly. "What kind of man hurts his wife and tears apart his family? I don't want to be that man. I never wanted to be like . . ."

He hesitated, and I knew what he meant to say. He didn't want to be like his own dad.

I don't know why that should've made a difference. Justin's father had been a hard, misogynistic 1950s man who'd idolized his only son while driving his wife to drink with his nearly legendary unfaithfulness. So the apple hadn't fallen far from the tree. That's all Justin's unfinished statement should've meant to me.

Except . . . it made me remember other things, too. All those quiet moments of true confession during our dating years. The kinds of conversations that occur in the afterglow, sprawled naked on a bed, Justin stroking my bare arm, talking about the man he'd both worshipped and abhorred. Loved as a father, while being quietly appalled by the way he'd behaved as a husband.

Justin had wanted his father's business sense, but he'd vowed even then to be a better husband, a better man.

Just as I looked back at my own parents and swore never to smoke and to always wear helmets.

That's the problem, you see. It's so much easier to fall in love, and so much more complicated to fall out of it. Because I couldn't just see this moment. I had eighteen years of memories of this man, including our younger days, and the hopes and dreams we'd both nurtured. When we'd magically assumed we could do better than our own parents, because we hadn't walked in their shoes yet. We didn't realize just how complicated and lonely even a good marriage can get.

"I don't want to lose you," my husband had said That Day. "I'm willing to try harder. I want to do better. Libby . . . I love you."

I made him leave. But I did let him call. And later, he settled into the basement bedroom, as we officially moved into the "working on it" phase of our marriage. Which meant he traveled just as much but brought me flowers more often. And I fixed his favorite meals, while withdrawing deeper and deeper inside myself. Both of us waiting for our marriage to magically feel normal again.

Time heals all wounds, right? Or if not, what the hell, six months later, you can always try date night.

I told myself I stayed in the marriage for Ashlyn. I told myself you just don't walk away from eighteen years together.

But the truth?

I still loved him. My husband had cheated on me. My husband had lied to me. He'd sent texts to another woman using the kind of endearments I thought were once reserved only for me. He'd slept with her.

Then, based on what I could piece together, returned home and, on several occasions, made love to me.

And yet, my heart still skipped a beat
when he walked into the room. The sound
of his laugh filled an ache in my chest. The
feel of his long, strong fingers retained the
power to make me shiver.

And I hated him for that. For hurting me
and then being decent about it. I didn't
want him kind or gentle or remorseful.
I wanted him to be the bad guy. Then I
could've just left him. Changed the locks
on the doors and never looked back. But
dammit, he kept trying. He ended the relationship as I asked. He moved out of our
bedroom into the basement as I asked.
He suggested marriage counseling, though
in the end, I was the one who proved re-
sistant. But he kept at it, dozens of tiny little
gestures, trying to reassure me of his love,
and that he was sorry and he really did
want me back. Except, instead of making
me feel better, all of his outreaches simply
made me feel worse.

I wondered, did he spoon with her afterward? Feed her oranges? Watch her lounge
around in nothing but his favorite dress

shirt? Did he whisper to her the kind of innermost dreams he once used to share with me?

I couldn't let her go. She had entered our marriage, some pretty young thing, and I didn't know how to get her back out again. So I'd pop open the orange prescription bottle, shaking out two, then four, then six chalky white pills. Trying to halt the endless stream of painful imagery running through my head.

But even I understood it wasn't the memory of That Day I was trying to dull with the pills. Not even the pain of betrayal that I needed to go away.

It was my love for my husband I was desperately trying to let go.

Because if I could love him less, then maybe I could forgive him more.

And it had amazed even me, how many pills it was taking to get the job done.

ASHLYN HAD TO GO TO THE BATHROOM. She whispered her need in my ear as we were ushered into a single cell, her trembling body pressed to my side. I nodded once, half listening to her and half hearing the *clang* of the steel door slamming shut behind us.

We were together, a pathetic party of three, now garbed in identical prison orange jumpsuits. The smallest size was still too large for Ashlyn, rolled up at the ankles and still swimming on her slight frame. The jumpsuits all had short sleeves, which I thought would be cold, except the cell was hot, the whole wing almost oppressive with its stale, overheated air.

Z had informed us the thermostat was set at a fixed seventy-six degrees. Winter, spring, summer, fall. Didn't matter in a prison. Likewise, the overhead lights were on 24/7. Morning, noon or night, also irrelevant for life behind bars.

Our dingy white cinder-block cell was narrow and deep, with a set of cream-painted steel bunks on either side, topped by what appeared to be a few inches of foam covered in a vinyl I could only describe as Smurf blue. The end of the cell featured a tall, narrow window bisected by a single steel bar. The door, comprised mostly of twelve-gauge steel, also boasted a thin viewing window, probably for a guard to check on the inmates. The window in the far wall overlooked bare, brown earth. The window in the door overlooked the cell block's cavernous dayroom, where prisoners could commune at hard metal tables, or tend to hygiene in exposed showers. In the middle of the space sat a lone command post, most likely where one corrections officer supervised an entire two-story wing of stacked cells.

I checked for Z, Radar or the one called Mick. Best I could tell, all three had disappeared. The dayroom was empty. We were finally alone, shuttered up with a mere seven locked doors between us and freedom.

I relayed Ashlyn's need to Justin. He nodded once, jaw clenched, eyes hard with equal parts rage and helplessness. When he turned to our daughter, however, his face softened and he sounded almost normal.

"So, here's the first part of prison life." He spoke briskly, as if describing a strange, new adventure. "One toilet, one sink for all of us to share—"

"Daddy—"

"Think of it as summer camp—"

"I can't—"

"Ashlyn, stop. I need you to hold strong. We're going to get through this."

Her lower lip trembled. She was on the verge of tears.

I wanted to reach out to my daughter, but I didn't. Because what would be the point? Don't cry, darling, we'll all be okay?

We'd been abducted by madmen out of our own home. We were clad in thin orange jumpsuits with slippers on our feet, shoved into a white eight-by-ten cell where there was barely enough room to stand and the only places to sit were prison bunks topped by the world's thinnest vinyl mattresses. Things were not all right. Things were wrong, very, very wrong, and probably going to get worse.

Justin moved to stand at the far window, his back to the toilet, his broad shoulders covering the exposed window. I moved to block the window in the doorway, my back also to my daughter, who'd begun demanding privacy at age eight, and by age fifteen, found anything involving the human body totally mortifying if not completely shameful.

The quiet was unbearable. The rustle of Ashlyn awkwardly struggling with her oversize jumpsuit ricocheting around the hard-edged space.

I started humming. Thought of Justin's tone, as if this were nothing but a camping adventure, and found myself singing: *I like to eat, eat, eat apples and bananas.* Which led Justin to adding, raspy and off-key, *I loke to ote, ote, ote opples and bononos.*

I filled in with the *I* verse, Justin handled the letter *A*, then we combined for *E* and *U*. We had just wrapped up, when I heard, right behind me, Ashlyn break down into total, body-heaving sobs. I turned, caught my daughter as she collapsed and held her against me. Justin moved away from the window, wrapping his larger arms around us, and we stood together, nobody speaking a word.

First family hug we'd shared in months.

I wanted to cry with my daughter, but I didn't.

EVENTUALLY, I tucked Ashlyn into bed on one of the lower prison bunks. No blanket to cover her. No words to comfort her. I sat on the edge of the squeaky blue vinyl and stroked her hair.

Justin paced. He roamed the tiny cell like a caged beast, running his fingers around the dull edges of the bunk beds, top and bottom. Then inspected the far window, the door, the strangely built stainless steel contraption with a lower half that formed the toilet, while the top half jutted out sideways to serve as the sink.

I turned to give him privacy as he used the facilities. The advantage of years spent sharing a master bath; I didn't have to sing. When he was done, I peed as well, then rinsed out my mouth with a dribble of water from the sink. I still tasted bile and rust. What I would give for a toothbrush and toothpaste, but apparently, our captors weren't concerned about such amenities.

When I finished, Justin moved from the far window and sat on the lower bunk across from Ashlyn, his back to the door. He indicated for me to do the same, so I returned to my seat next to Ashlyn, this time turning away from the door and staring at the narrow window.

"No bugs," Justin said, as if this were great news. I stared at him blankly. He continued, "That means they can see us—there are video cameras everywhere—but not hear us. So as long as we keep our backs to the electronic eyes, we can speak privately."

The subtleties of this were lost on me, but I nodded, encouraged if he was encouraged.

"This is a state facility. Means our cell door is operated electronically, from the control room. Bad news is that this means there's no chance of a manual override, or for us to escape by stealing someone's keys. But it also means they have to split up each time they want to retrieve us. While one or two may come to our cell door, the third has to remain in the control room to work the touch screen."

I turned my head just enough to stare at my husband. "How do you know all this?"

He turned to regard me curiously. "Libby, the project we wrapped last year in northern New Hampshire? The prison? I built this."

I blinked my eyes, honestly startled. I knew Justin's firm had constructed a number of prisons over the years. New Hampshire, West Virginia, Georgia. But somehow, it hadn't occurred to me . . .

"Then you know this facility. The whole facility. You can get us out!"

Justin didn't speak right away. Instead, his expression turned sober. "I do know this facility, honey. Including all the reasons we probably aren't going to get out. Z was telling the truth. This prison's state-of-the-art, with all of the state and all of the art designed to keep people wearing these jumpsuits trapped in these cells."

My shoulders slumped. I leaned against the metal pillar supporting the top bunk. My hands were shaking. I could watch them tremble on my lap, almost like two separate entities, pale, dehydrated, claw-like fingers that belonged to anyone but me.

"Ashlyn," I whispered, a single word that said enough.

Justin's jaw hardened. His face took on a fierce expression I knew so well. And because we'd been married eighteen years, years where I'd seen the look in his eyes when he'd held our baby daughter for the first time, watched him patiently balance her tiny hands in his when she was learning how to walk, still caught him standing in her doorway late at night just to check on her, I knew how much pain was behind that rage.

"They'll demand money," he said roughly. "I don't give a fuck what Z says to terrorize us. This is about money. Sooner or later, they'll issue a ransom demand. Denbe will pay it. And we'll go home. All of us."

"Why bring us here?" I asked. "If this is just about money, why bring us this far north, lock us up . . ."

"Where better to hide an entire family? This place is deserted for now. State's too busy cutting costs to fund the operating budget of a whole new prison. It's also re- mote, with nothing around for fifteen, twenty miles. Local PD probably does an occa- sional perimeter check, such as what hap- pened when we were first dropped off, then moves along."

"They'll see the lights on," I spoke up hopefully. "Investigate further."

Justin shook his head. "The whole prop- erty is wired with motion sensors. Every time a cop approaches, this place lights up like the Fourth of July. Nothing unusual there."

"There's three of them," I whispered. "A whole . . . commando team. They have Tasers, weapons, obviously spent some time planning this. If this is about money, they're going to want a lot of it. And tomor- row's Sunday, so even if the company is willing to pay . . ."

Justin thinned his lips. "We're probably looking at least a couple of days' internment," he granted.

I brushed our daughter's hair. Ashlyn still slept soundly, exhaustion and shock having caught up with her. "How long have we been gone?" I asked now. "Fourteen, sixteen hours? They haven't even offered food or water."

"Sink has water. As for food, we can make it a couple of days."

I watched my hands tremble again. Felt my stomach churn, my headache build. Things I should probably tell him. But I didn't. Because while we had eighteen years together, we also had the past six months. And that had changed things.

"I don't want her alone with them," I said, turning the matter back to Ashlyn.

Justin shrugged away my concern. "They've put us together in a single cell. Nicer of them than I would've thought, actually."

He was right. Three separate cells would've been worse. Each of us trapped in a separate cage, helpless to assist the others. In that scenario, if they'd come for Ashlyn . . . What would Justin do? What would I do? Stand by powerlessly while they led our daughter away . . .

"Whatever happens," I reiterated, my own thoughts starting to run away with me. "I don't want Ashlyn alone with them. Especially that one with the checkerboard hair . . . Mick? Did you see his eyes? Something's not right there."

"Not going to happen."

"Really? Because we're so in control of the situation? In case you haven't noticed, they're the predators, and we're the prey. And what kind of prey ever gets to choose its own fate?"

I wish I hadn't spoken the words the second I said them. My voice was too high, verging on hysterical. I fisted my hands on my lap, bit into my lower lip as if that would keep the panic at bay.

"Libby." Justin's voice was serious. I looked up, found him studying me. He didn't speak right away. Instead, he regarded me with a fierceness I hadn't seen in years, but still remembered well.

"I know things are challenging for us right now. I know I've hurt you. If I could go back in time . . ." He paused, squared his shoulders, soldiered on. "I want you to know, Libby, somehow, someway, I'll keep you and Ashlyn safe. Nothing and no one is going to harm my family. You can trust me on this."

And I believed him. Because my husband was that kind of guy. The modern caveman, I'd often called him. He would lay down his life for his daughter, just not remember her favorite foods. And he would slay dragons for me, just not, apparently, remain faithful.

Ironically enough, his alpha male tendencies were one of the things that had first attracted him to me.

Justin held out his hand. His palm was large, ridged with callouses. His nails were short, his skin rough. I'd spent so much of my life admiring those hands. It made it easy for me to place my fingers upon his and make my one request.

"Keep our daughter safe, Justin. That's all I want. Keep Ashlyn safe."

His fingers closed around mine. He leaned forward. I could see his eyes, somber and resolute, and then, his head angled down, and my head angled up . . .

Clanging, from the steel door. So loud both of us startled, jerked back, then turned around.

The crazy blue-eyed one stood in front of the window, leering at us. Clearly, he'd been watching for a bit. Clearly, he'd liked what he saw.

I couldn't help myself; I recoiled, reaching for my daughter, as if holding her arm would somehow keep her safe.

"Get up," Mick barked from the other side of the door. "Think this is some kind of vacay? Come on. Time to work."

Chapter 14

WYATT DIDN'T CALL THE FEDS. If they wanted to join the party, they knew where to find him. In the meantime, he and his deputies went to work.

Maps. He liked maps. Sure, you could look this stuff up on a computer in this day and age, but there was something satisfying about unfolding a massive, color-coded scale map of mountainous New Hampshire. The dozens of blue blobs of lakes. The endless squiggly lines of hundreds of winding rural roads.

New Hampshire was a funny state. Long, skinny at the top, with a wider base.

Nestled like a puzzle piece into the opposing shape of Vermont, as if the two were long-lost friends. New Hampshire wasn't a very big state as the crow flies. A dedicated driver could make it from the southernmost border with Massachusetts to the northernmost border with Canada in three and a half, four hours tops. Horizontal routes, however, were another matter entirely, thanks to the White Mountains. They jutted up like jagged teeth and bit their way through the middle of the state, forcing east-west roads to zigzag, stair step and generally give way before their greater might. As the locals liked to say when contemplating drives across the state, *"Why, you just can't get there from here . . ."*

Given those dynamics, Wyatt was betting their suspects had continued due north. Mostly, because that's what drivers did in New Hampshire. You went up, or you went down, but it was too painful to move side to side.

For kicks, he'd sent one deputy, Gina, to drive due north from the diner. Told her to perform basic recon. Note rural turnouts or deserted campgrounds where a driver might pull over to refresh. Stop in at any isolated gas stations or unpopulated grocery stores where a bunch of kidnappers might feel it was safe enough to grab food, water, refuel. Start asking questions, passing along the description of the missing family and getting the locals watching.

She could also mark major turnoff points, or larger towns where they could involve local PDs, but Wyatt was guessing their suspects would do their best to drive through such areas. An entire family was hard to conceal. Why even risk heavily populated areas for stopping, when the North Country had so many safer havens to offer?

Frankly, he respected the kidnappers. When heading for the wilds of New Hampshire, they had picked wisely.

He bent back over the map, tracing Route 16 up the eastern edge of the state, as the feds swept through the door.

He knew it was them without looking up. For one thing, he spotted one pair of low-slung black heels and one pair of glossy brown men's dress shoes. Only lawyers wore those kinds of shoes in this neck of the woods, and lawyers rarely visited the sheriff's office on a Saturday afternoon.

The female spoke first. "Wyatt," she said, and inside, he immediately groaned.

He knew that voice. Crap.

Wyatt straightened. Took his finger off the map. Prepared to give the devil her due.

Nicole Adams, aka Nicky. Except last time he'd used that nickname, she'd been waking up in his bed. He had a feeling he didn't get to use that nickname anymore. Or, for that matter, remain an intact male in her withering presence.

"Special Agent Adams," he replied. Seemed the safest answer.

She smiled. It didn't meet her cool blue eyes.

She wore a dark pencil skirt, matching jacket, high-collared silvery silk blouse. Being one of those tall blondes with up-swept hair, the ice-princess look really worked for her. She also carried a thick black leather computer case, which she now dropped to the floor with a heavy *thud*.

"Sergeant Wyatt Foster, Special Agent Edward Hawkes." She introduced him to her partner.

Wyatt nodded, shook hands. Special Agent Hawkes also carried a heavy bag.

Apparently, they were planning to stay for a bit.

"We understand you found the missing man's jacket," Nicole continued.

"Got it wrapped up special in an evidence bag, just for you."

"So you knew we were coming?"

"Made sense."

"But you didn't call with an update."

"Update implies progress. Not so sure we got progress. Mostly"—he tapped the map—"we got a helluva lot of real estate and no real leads."

The feds seemed to accept that. They crossed to the table where Wyatt had spread out the map, leaned closer.

"Catch us up," Nicole ordered briskly. "What are you looking at?"

Wyatt swallowed another sigh and got down to business. This was why he should've listened to his gut before getting involved with a fellow member of law enforcement. Except at the time, in the Concord courthouse, about to testify at a trial, he'd spotted this beautiful blonde across the hall and lost common sense. Couldn't say it was her laugh that got him, because it still wasn't clear to him that Nicole Adams ever giggled. But he'd gotten it into his head that he needed to meet her, which had led to drinks, which had led to a hotel room. Then, probably to the surprise of them both, they had an on-again-off-again thing that went on a couple months.

Except one day he started to realize he liked the off more than the on. Nothing against her. But she was clearly federal agent to the core: upwardly mobile, urban powered, tightly disciplined. And, as he tried to point out to her when breaking up, he was none of those highly admirable things.

In hindsight, he should've waited another week. At which point, she probably would've dumped him. Then, this moment would've made him laugh, instead of shiver from deep freeze.

He pointed to a spot on the map, midway up the state, closer to Maine, which would be relevant in a moment. "Jacket was recovered here. Abandoned roadside diner, no other businesses or residents around for miles."

"Witnesses?" Hawkes spoke up.

"No one around to witness. Welcome to the North Country. Now, tire marks show the vehicle resuming a northward course. Which brings us to"—he drew a large circle around the northern tip of the state—"hundreds of square miles of absolute nowhere. In other words, the perfect place for a bunch of kidnappers to hide."

Nicole was frowning at his map. "You're assuming they maintained a northern route."

"Yes, ma'am." Wyatt explained his logic, the mountains muddling up east-west routes and all. Based on the jacket's disposal site, the kidnappers had taken 95 into New Hampshire, veering left onto Route 16, which followed the eastern border of the state. Call him crazy, but it seemed to him if you were a bunch of kidnappers with a family of three stashed in the back of your van, you'd go with the most direct route possible. Which would place them squarely in northern New Hampshire, an area remote enough to easily hide hostages that was also conveniently located just three to four hours from Boston, making for easy access come time for ransom drop or hostage exchange.

Special Agent Nicole Adams seemed to accept his logic.

"Large search area," she commented, her own finger starting to trace the various shaded regions on the map.

"Yeah, and being a rural sheriff's department, we're not exactly rolling in manpower, so I called in some backup."

"Backup?" Hawkes spoke up. He had an accent. Maine maybe? Wyatt was still trying to peg him.

"US Forest Service, as well as Fish and Game. You know Marty Finch, the forest service investigator?"

Both agents nodded. While Finch worked out of Vermont, the federal agent's territory also included New Hampshire and Maine. Given that US Forest Service lands were becoming a haven for drug operations, Wyatt had worked with Finch on a number of cases. He figured the same should be true for FBI agents out of Concord.

"I gave him a ring," Wyatt continued now. "Gotta figure the largest chunk of real estate we're facing is the seven hundred and fifty thousand acres of the White Mountain National Forest—Finch's jurisdiction. At my request, he's mobilizing the forest rangers, sending them to search parking lots at the various trailheads and camp-grounds for a possible transport vehicle—I'm thinking a van based on the tire marks and need to hold at least seven. The rangers will also check out hiking huts, various rest stops. If you want to keep a low profile, hiding out in the various state parks or national wilderness areas would do it."

"Do the rangers have enough experience to know what they're looking for?" Nicole asked crisply.

Wyatt rolled his eyes. "Please. In New Hampshire, we all attend the same training academy. Sheriff, state, local, Fish and Game, we all go in, we all come out. Meaning that clearly, we're all brilliant."

Nicole raised a brow but didn't say anything. It went without saying that her precious FBI Academy remained a step above. Wyatt didn't feel like pressing the point.

"What about the tolls?" Nicole spoke up. "Have you requested video footage? If your assumption about the kidnappers taking Interstate ninety-five to sixteen is correct, then they've passed through four major tollbooths."

Wyatt shrugged. "Have a detective making the request. Can tell you now, given all the privacy concerns, actually obtaining that footage will be a royal pain in the ass."

"Not like you to back down from a fight."

"Consider it more like a strategic use of resources. I have two detectives and four deputies. There's only so many investigative avenues we can effectively pursue. And given the urgency of the situation, I want to deploy my people smart. In my book, that means searching all local, state and federal recreation areas and campgrounds. Now, your turn to share."

Nicole didn't volunteer right away, so Hawkes did the honors.

"Boston PD ran a preliminary trace of the Taser confetti, identified a dealer out of Chicago. The serial number ties back to a batch of fifty he sold to another dealer for a gun show in New Jersey. That dealer says all fifty were sold at the show. If the individual buyers didn't register their Tasers, that's not his problem."

"What kind of gun show?"

"Open to the public, with attendance from the survivalist and ex-military crowd."

"We think the kidnappers are professionals," Nicole stated curtly.

That got Wyatt's attention. "How so?"

"They accessed a house armed with a top-of-the-line security system, and managed to overcome two grown adults and one teenager without ever alerting the neighbors. Furthermore, Justin Denbe is experienced in firearms and by all accounts, a man capable of defending himself and his family. As it is, there's evidence the teenager put up a decent fight. The suspects, however, were still able to overpower her and ambush her parents without ever spilling a drop of blood. It takes discipline to pull off that kind of controlled operation. Not to mention training and resources."

"Ransom?" Wyatt asked with a frown.

"Not yet."

"But you assume demands are coming?"

"As of this time, we have no other theories on motive."

Wyatt got that. Especially if the situation involved professionals, who by definition were interested in payment. "Family has the ability to pay?"

"The family firm, Denbe Construction, is running the show. And, yes, the officers of the company have been in touch with local law enforcement and are willing to release whatever funds are necessary."

"Except significant funds can't be released before Monday."

"True."

"Meaning if these guys planned ahead, by definition they knew they'd have to hide a family of three for at least several days."

"In our minds, further evidence that the suspects are professionals. This isn't a rush operation. They obviously put thought and planning into the abduction scenario. Odds are, they put equal thought into the best place to secure their hostages for the long haul. When they feel ready, we'll hear from them. But not before, I think. Even now, they are establishing a hierarchy of control, one where they give the orders, and we do exactly as they command."

Wyatt didn't like the sound of that. He returned to his map, considering the logistics behind such an operation. "They're here," he said, tapping the White Mountain National Forest. "It's logistically perfect. Far enough away from Boston to keep out of sight, but not so far away they can't return to accept payment. Rural, but not too rural. Wild, but not too wild. This is our haystack. Now, we just gotta find the needle."

"All right. You work the haystack. We're heading to Boston to conduct initial interviews. Justin Denbe owns a second-generation mega-construction firm. By all accounts, he made big money but also big enemies. We'll prepare the list."

Wyatt got the message clearly enough—the feds were running the investigation, though he was welcome to play in the woods. He simply decided to ignore it.

"Great," he declared. "One of my detectives and I will meet you in Boston to assist with the interviews. Give us thirty minutes or so, and we'll be on our way."

Nicole rewarded him with an icy look.

He smiled back, already reaching for his hat. "And here I thought you'd never ask."

Chapter 15

IN TESSA'S EXPERIENCE, if you wanted to know what was really going on in a woman's life, you had to track down her prime confidant. And in at least 80 percent of the cases, that included the woman's hairdresser. A single check of Libby Denbe's favorites list from her phone had revealed the Farias & Rocha salon in Beacon Hill. Tessa had showed up in person, flashing her credentials. Which had earned her an introduction with James Farias, one of the single most beautiful-looking men she'd ever encountered. Frosted blond hair, strong jaw covered in artful stubble, piercing blue eyes and the kind of sculpted shoulders and arms rarely seen outside Hollywood.

Unfortunately for her, she had a feeling she was packing the wrong equipment to garner James's attention. Yet another reason Sophie would remain an only child.

Also, James had taken one look at her and exclaimed that the real crime she should be investigating was the one that had been committed against her hair. Didn't she realize that shade of brown—her real color, sadly—was too dull, totally washing out her complexion? Not to mention pulling her long hair back into a single hair clip was much too severe for her face. She needed softness, she needed warmth, she needed an immediate hair intervention. That was it, she must return for his next available appointment. Which turned out to be in six months.

Tessa dutifully made the appointment. In return, Farias agreed to answer her questions regarding Libby Denbe.

"The husband did it," he declared now, leading her to a back room marked Experts Only. She took that to be a euphemism for Employees Only. "Trust me, honey. Justin will appear out of nowhere, sweet little Ashlyn will be found. But Libby will never be seen again. Don't you read the papers? That's always how these things work. Mango-pomegranate tea?"

"Um, no, thank you."

"Wouldn't hurt, you know. Rich in anti-oxidants for the investigator on the go."

It seemed important to him, so she finally agreed. Maybe having been denied access to her under-tended hair, the man needed to at least provide vitamins and minerals.

"Did Libby love her husband?" Tessa asked, taking a seat at a black lacquer table while Farias fished out two bags from a beautifully decorated container.

"He wasn't worth it," James declared.

"How so?"

"Wasn't even home most of the time. His job, his crew, his buildings. *Puuullleeeze.* Everyone was allowed to need him except Libby. She just had to maintain the perfect home, raise the perfect child and greet him each Friday night with a smile. I told her at the beginning she gave too much. And trust me, honey, men don't appreciate what women give willingly. A thousand years of evolution later, it's still about the chase." James paused in the act of reaching for a row of mugs. "You know how many Libbys I see in a salon like this? Beautiful, talented women, each and every one. And they do everything their rich, self-centered hubbies ask of them, right up to the moment the rich, self-centered hubbies kick them to the curb in favor of the younger, fresher model. It's like driving by an auto accident. No matter how many of them you see, you still think it'll only happen to someone else."

"Justin had a younger, fresher model?"

"Yep. Went on for months before Libby found out. She was blindsided by the discovery. Simply blindsided. File for divorce first, I advised her. Hire the power lawyer and go after him, big legal guns blazing. But no. They had a daughter, they had a marriage, they had a life. I'm telling you now, he didn't stop seeing the bimbo just because his wife found out. I mean, maybe he told her he did, but a leopard never changes his spots."

"Who was it?" Tessa asked, frowning.

James returned to the table with two mugs of fragrant tea. He set them down, then jabbed her in the forehead with his index finger. "Stop it. Didn't your mother ever tell you your face will freeze like that? You don't need to be developing any frown lines. Your face is stern enough as it is."

"Well, I am an investigator."

"That may gain you a suspect, honey, but it'll never help you find your man."

"So true. So did Libby know the bimbo?"

"Travel agent. His. Justin's on the road all the time. Guess his firm uses a travel agency with offices in the same building to handle all their arrangements. Pretty soon, it became a *full-service* relationship."

"Did Libby know the woman?"

"Please, *girl* is more like it." James took a seat, leaning close. "Libby went in one afternoon. Wasn't going to talk to her, wasn't going to approach. Just wanted to size up the competition, you know. According to her, she walked through the doors of the agency, took one look and walked right back out. Said the girl couldn't have been a day over twenty-one. Just some starry-eyed kid who no doubt hung on every word Justin ever said before catching up with her friends at a concert."

"Name?"

"Kate. Christy. Katie. Something like that. Libby couldn't take her seriously. If anything, she seemed to feel bad for her, just some young girl getting involved with a married man. In her mind, Justin had taken advantage."

"Generous of her," Tessa remarked.

"Oh, she's that kind of woman. Not a catty bone in her body, which is more than I can say for most of the felines around here."

"How long have you known Libby?"

"Oh, honey, I never give out that information. Next thing I know, you'll guess my age."

"Okay. A longtime client?"

"Certainly. Woman needed help in the beginning, too. She grew up in the projects. A regular Little Orphan Annie with a hard-knock life. I understand no one thinks of Back Bay as being the mean streets of Boston, but trust me, love, they're tough in their own way."

"Didn't exactly fit in?"

"Her husband's in construction. Wears work boots. Seriously?"

"Yeah, but a hundred-million-dollar company . . ."

"And once word got out, trust me, attitudes softened. Plus, Libby herself is a fabulous artist."

"Jewelry?"

"Exactly. The ladies who lunch liked that. Maybe Libby's upbringing wasn't Back Bay, but her fine-arts education was a step in the right direction. Not to mention her home is gorgeous. Have you seen it? I've been over several times, and with the exception of that chandelier in the foyer, there isn't a single thing I would change."

"Did Libby like the ladies who lunch?" Tessa asked. "Have a circle of close friends?"

For the first time, Farias hesitated. He covered the pause by taking a sip of his tea. "Libby . . . Libby is a kind soul. I've never heard her say a bad word about anyone. She doesn't hold to social circles the way some do—she would have these dinner parties from time to time that would include, say, myself and her neighbors, but also Justin's construction crew." James shivered. "Delicious bunch of men, positively divine, each and every one of them, even if they did make me fear for my life."

"Libby got along? Liked everyone, was liked by everyone?"

"Libby is genuine." James stopped, repeated the word, seemed pleased with the description. "Not much of that going around here these days. And up until a few months ago, I would've also said she was happy. Justin's job didn't bother her, his absence didn't bother her. She loved her daughter, had her jewelry. She went out when Justin was away. I know she'd talk about going to the movies with some ladies, various lunch dates, but . . ." He paused again, hands wrapping around his mug. "Libby was a bit of an island. I don't know any other way of saying it. Neighbors, organizations, the local pecking order, I never got the impression she cared about any of that or for any of them. Her world was Justin and Ashlyn. As long as they were happy, she was happy. And that worked for them."

"Until Justin took up a side project. She must have been devastated."

"Oh, Libby doesn't do devastated. She does withdrawn. Last few times I saw her . . ." James sighed heavily. "Trust me, honey, there's no haircut in the world that can compensate for a shattered heart. She claimed she and Justin were trying to work things out. She claimed she hadn't given up. But let me tell you, that's not what her hair and skin were saying about things. Woman was a wreck. And that's no way to win your cheating husband back."

"Rumor is, Friday night was date night."

James merely sniffed. "Really, like going back in time is any way to move forward. A couple like that . . . you have trust issues, you have insecurity, you have a family business that routinely destroys any hope of true family time. What kind of dinner date can fix all that?"

"Well, when you put it that way," Tessa murmured. Her tea had finally cooled to the point where she could take a sip. It was fruity; she liked it.

"What do you think?" Farias asked.

"I can already feel the antioxidants rushing in," she assured him.

"Hmm, I'd recommend at least two to three cups a day. And no more frowning. Otherwise, in another year or two, it's Botox for sure."

"Good to know. So, tell me about Ashlyn."

"Beautiful girl," he provided immediately. "Definitely her mother's daughter."

"Did you do her hair?"

"Absolutely. Very fine, very silky. Yours is coarse. It doesn't sound appealing, but trust me, coarse hair is easier to work with. Your hair, I can fix." He gazed at her pointedly. "Ashlyn's hair we worked to keep as smooth and well-maintained as possible."

"What's she like? Quiet, outgoing, athletic, artistic, what?"

"Quiet. Artistic. Gorgeous smile. Like Mona Lisa. You had to work to get it, and even then, the expression was so fleeting you wondered if you didn't just imagine it. Sweet child. She'd done some school plays, had an interest in her mother's jewelry, that kind of thing. She liked to ask me questions about cutting hair, running a salon. Always polite, but curious. I think hair and fashion interested her, but her own style was more . . . eclectic. Not an in-your-face rebellious child, or a spoiled girl, but then, she was only fifteen. Give her time."

"Did she know there was trouble in paradise?"

James paused, seemed to consider the issue. "How much they told her, I don't know. But Ashlyn's sensitive. There was no way she could be living in that household with her mother looking the way Libby looked and still believe her parents were doing fine."

"Was Libby protective of her?"

"Ab-so-lute-ly! Libby grew up without a father. Yet another reason to keep her fickle, rutting husband around. Heaven forbid her own child should suffer the same."

"Heard Justin was grooming Ashlyn for the family business."

"Oh yes. Gave the girl pink power tools for her fifteenth birthday. What teenager wouldn't be impressed?"

Tessa contemplated James's tight-lipped expression. The man's words had radiated sarcasm, his face clear disapproval. "Ashlyn didn't like the tools? Or Libby didn't approve?"

"Oh, I don't know. Probably neither one. Just sounded silly to me. I mean, couldn't the man be a little more subtle? Just because he doesn't have a son is no reason to stick a penis on his daughter."

It occurred to Tessa that her witness might have his own daddy issues. For example, a father who'd wanted other things for his son's life than hair care brilliance.

"Did you cut Justin's hair?"

"No. Barber shop. Definitely. Or maybe, he and his crew sit around and buzz each other with clippers, right after picking each other over for nits. That's possible as well."

"When was the last time you saw Libby or Ashlyn?"

"Three weeks ago. They came in together. Ladies day."

"How'd they seem?"

"Usual. Libby was pale, still looked to me like she wasn't sleeping well at night. I advised more fish oil in her diet; her hair seemed very brittle. But she kept a brave face on, shared some laughs with her daughter. To most people, I'm sure they looked like they were having a very nice time. You had to know them better to read the signs."

"Such as?"

"The circles under Libby's eyes. And Ashlyn was glued to her iPod. She kept putting in her earbuds, Libby kept pulling them back out. Talk, she would say. Share. That's what this day is supposed to be about. I'd never seen Ashlyn quite like that, so . . . purposefully withdrawn from a situation."

"Libby disclose anything more about her marriage?"

"No, but of course, she had her daughter sitting right there. They had some shopping bags, though, including Victoria's Secret. Nothing says wife of a cheating husband quite like new lingerie." Abruptly, Farias reached across the table, fingering her hair where it was gathered at the nape of her neck. "You know, I could at least tend to the ends."

"Sorry." She set down her mug. "Calendar's a little full today, finding a missing family and all. But I'll come back." She made a move to stand.

Farias regarded her steadily. "No, you won't."

"Yes, I will. May twentieth, two thirty. I have the little reminder card and everything."

"No, you won't. You'll work too hard, micromanage your child, obsess over your career. Then one day, you'll wonder why you are not the beautiful, proud woman you remembered yourself to be." His voice softened. "A good haircut is not about the hair, darling. It's about the woman beneath. Shortchange her now, and you can't really blame others for doing so later."

Tessa had to smile. Because she would've thrown away the reminder card and blown off the appointment. Not immediately, but within a week or two or three, when, yes, Sophie needed her for something, or a new assignment was heating up . . .

She started to understand why Libby came here, and brought her own daughter. In his own way, James Farias ran a side business in nurturing lost souls.

"I'll return," she promised.

Farias merely *hmmph*ed.

"Find my Libby," he said abruptly. "Whatever happened, wherever they've gone . . . She's a good person. And there aren't nearly enough of them left these days."

"The dinner parties," Tessa asked. "Who else were among the attendants?"

James sighed, then wrote up a list.

Tessa took it with her. Four P.M. Nearly sundown this late in November. Temperature definitely dropping. As she walked down the street toward her car, she hunched her shoulders reflexively against the chill.

She thought about the Denbes. Couldn't help but wonder where they were, how they were faring, as day transitioned to another bitterly cold night. Did they have food, shelter, adequate clothes and blankets for warmth? She supposed it depended on how much incentive their captors had to keep them safe and sound.

Personal or professional, that's what this case would boil down to in the end.

Had the Denbes' abduction been motivated by vengeance? Maybe a business rival who'd felt personally slighted when Denbe Construction had been awarded a significant building contract? Or perhaps related to Justin's affair. The jilted ex-lover, having lost her man to his family, striking back? Or, the most sinister and interesting theory, that Justin had staged the abduction of his whole family as an elaborate ruse to disguise the murder of his estranged wife. Because given the threat divorce would pose to his personal wealth, not to mention the family business, Justin would clearly be the prime suspect if anything happened to Libby. Unless, of course, the whole family was attacked, and he and his daughter miraculously happened to be the sole survivors . . .

Except, why now? Six months later, when the Denbes seemed to have survived the immediate aftermath of Justin's betrayal? Libby was definitely trying to save her marriage, according to her hair stylist. Maybe not succeeding yet, given her fragile emotional state, but still trying.

Tessa shook her head. For the Denbes' sake, she hoped this was a professionally motivated crime. Because a team of kidnappers looking for a ransom payout had incentive to keep the Denbes as comfortable as possible. Whereas the people the Denbes thought they knew and held most dear . . .

Tessa couldn't help herself: She flashed back two years ago, to her kitchen, the look on her husband's face. The shock of the exploding Sig Sauer. The feel of the white, white snow against her frozen fingertips. Her daughter's empty bedroom.

It wasn't that strangers couldn't hurt you. It was simply that the people you loved could do it so much better.

Just ask Libby Denbe.

Chapter 16

THE CRAZY BLUE-EYED COMMANDO wanted Ashlyn to step out of the cell first.

"No," Justin said.

Ashlyn was awake, sitting up on the lower bunk. Her bleary gaze shot from her father to the steel door to her father again. I had my body positioned in front of her, as if by blocking her from view, I could keep the man from remembering she was there.

"Girl steps up," Mick repeated. "Girl presents wrists through the slot. I secure girl's hands, she exits cell. Those are the instructions."

"No," Justin said. His shoulders were

set, his hands fisted by his side. "I'll go first. Then my daughter. Then my wife."

Mick raised his black Taser till it was visible through the narrow strip of window.

"Girl steps up," he repeated, and this time there was a load of menace behind each word.

I gazed from my husband to the commando, still feeling confused, then I got it. The scenario Justin was trying to avoid: If Ashlyn exited the cell, Mick could simply slam the door shut behind her. Trapping us inside the cell. Leaving Ashlyn alone and vulnerable on the other side of it.

I stepped forward, standing beside Justin with our shoulders touching. I wanted to feel brave, resolute. My stomach was cramping. I could feel fresh beads of sweat across my forehead, and I dug my nails into my palms, calling upon the pain to ground me.

Mick lowered a metal plate, opening the slot in the middle of the cell door. His eyes were flat, his face expressionless as he lined up the Taser in the opening, aiming for Justin's torso.

"The girl—" Mick started harshly.

"Fuck you!" Justin bellowed back.

"I'll go."

Both men paused, blinked, looked at Ashlyn, who'd risen from the lower bunk.

"Stop it." She wasn't talking to Mick; she was talking to her father. "What are you gonna do, Dad? Protect me? Pretend everything's all right? Nothing bad's ever gonna happen to your precious little princess? Kind of late for that, don't you think?"

The bitterness in her voice caught me off guard. I looked down, embarrassed for my daughter, hurting for my husband, who I knew had to be shocked by such an outburst.

"Ashlyn . . ."

"Stop it. Just stop it. You should've left us, you know. Moved in with your new girlfriend, built a new life. We could've handled that. But, no, you have to hang around the house, pretending you still love us, pretending you still care. You made a mistake, but now you're sorry. If we'd just give you a second chance, boo hoo hoo. You're the one who's trying to have his cake and eat it, too."

Ashlyn pushed past her father, thrusting her hands through the open slot. Justin made no move to stop her, just stared at her back, openly stunned.

On the other side of the cell door, Mick laughed.

"Feisty one!" he declared, reaching for a zip tie.

"Fuck you," our daughter told him, and my eyes widened for a second time. I'd never heard Ashlyn use such language. And I definitely hadn't known . . . hadn't even begun to suspect that she'd resented the past few months so much.

Mick laughed again.

Our family needed to hold together. Instead, barely an hour into prison life, we were tearing apart.

The commando secured Ashlyn's wrists. There was a short buzzing sound, then the door swung open. Mick stood in the opening, Taser pointed at Justin's chest.

I should rush him, I thought. He was so focused on Justin, I could run forward, throw all hundred and ten pounds of my body at the commando's massive two-hundred-pound frame. If I hit him around the knees, he'd go down. Then Justin would charge forward and then . . .

Then there would be six more electronically controlled doors between us and freedom. We would've exchanged our cell for the prison dayroom. And we would've pissed off three armed men, one of them sporting a fang-baring cobra tattoo.

I shuddered. Another buzz. The heavy steel door closed and our daughter stood on the other side, next to the psycho commando. She didn't look scared. She just stared at her father as if she'd never hated him so much.

"I am such an asshole," Justin whispered.

I didn't argue. I stepped up and presented my wrists through the slot.

MICK LINED US UP IN FRONT OF HIM. Still no sign of the other two commandos, so it was up to him to shepherd three bound prisoners out of the dayroom into the corridors of the abandoned prison. He didn't seem nervous about his prospects. More like tense. He had the Taser held at his waist, pointing forward. The first time one of us flinched, he'd pull the trigger.

The moment we started walking, I knew I'd be the first one down. My legs shook uncontrollably, each step requiring more effort than the one before. It felt as if the atmosphere had taken on weight, until just getting my knee off the ground, my foot in the air, demanded a tremendous amount of energy. I was like a character in slow motion, barely churning my leg up, forward, down.

I stumbled, swaying right.

Mick didn't pull the trigger, but caught my arm, shoved me forward.

I noticed that Justin and Ashlyn were now several steps ahead, a gap opening up in our group. They didn't look back to check on me.

We arrived at the sally port. The first set of doors buzzed open, Big Brother always watching. Mick ushered us forward. When we were assembled inside the small portal, the first door rolled closed behind us; then, after a moment's pause, a second door rolled open ahead of us.

Justin was looking up and to the right. I followed his gaze until I spotted a small electronic eye protruding from the corner. I wondered whether we should wave, or whether that would be childish.

We exited the sally port into a towering white corridor. At least two stories tall, with huge steel girders forming intersecting Vs above us. Keeping with the prison theme of soullessness, the floor was poured gray cement, the walls painted stark white and the windows, high above us, dark eerie panes of glass. Periodically, cement staircases protruded from the right side of the wall, leading to second-floor doorways.

"We're behind the cell blocks," Justin murmured. He looked at Mick, his gaze still challenging. "This is the exit hallway in case of fire. Hey, *man.* Tell us where we're going. I'll lead us there."

"Walk," Mick ordered.

Justin and Ashlyn took the lead again. And I fell immediately behind once more, still trying to force my limbs to fight gravity. Arm swinging slowly forward. Knee raising slightly, trying to cycle ahead. The lights were bright. Bouncing off every hard white surface. While my head ached and my stomach cramped and I wanted to curl up in a ball in a cool dark place. I would cover my face with my hands. I would succumb, sinking down, down, down into a darkness without end.

"Move."

Mick's hand on my arm, shoving me forward. I stumbled, he tried to correct, I stumbled again.

Dimly, I was aware of Justin and Ashlyn, well ahead now. Justin had his arm around our daughter's shoulders. His head was low. He was speaking in her ear.

I was the distraction, I realized. Mick had to tend to me. And while he and I tussled with my weak, uncoordinated limbs, Justin could lead our daughter out of here. He knew where he was, behind the cell blocks, he'd said, with three locked doors already behind us . . .

I tripped, almost went down. Mick grabbed my upper arm, dragging me upright and twisting me around till we stood mere inches apart, chest to chest, face to face. I stared into his crazy blue eyes, framed by his even crazier blond-and-black checkerboard hair.

"Walk, goddammit! You move, you perform, you work, or I'll blow out your fucking brains myself."

I wished I had my husband's courage. I would've settled for my daughter's bitterness. Instead, I smiled up at the crazy commando, watching his eyes widen in surprise.

His left hand, bruising my arm. His right hand, with the Taser, dangling forgotten by his side.

"Shhh," I whispered at him.

"What the—"

"Shhh."

Then, faster than I knew I could move, definitely faster than he thought I could move, I grabbed the Taser with my bound hands, twisted it between us and pulled the trigger.

It's true what they say: The bigger they are, the harder they fall.

I would've liked to enjoy the moment more, except from up ahead, my daughter started to scream.

Z had materialized in the corridor. Big Brother always watching.

He had a Taser, too, except his was pointed at Justin, who was now on the ground, entire body jerking crazily. Ashlyn stood beside her father, her face clearly beseeching.

"Whatever you can do," Z stated clearly from the other end of the hallway, "I can do better."

At which point, he popped a cartridge out of the end of the Taser, turned deftly and dry fired into my daughter's exposed forearm.

Ashlyn no longer screamed. Now she more like shrieked.

Her skin, blistering. I knew, because I bore the same burn mark on my upper thigh.

I released my Taser. It dropped to the ground. I stepped away from Mick's convulsing form, putting space between myself and Z's fallen comrade.

Much more slowly, Z lifted the Taser from my daughter's pale skin. He stood, twenty feet away from me, holding up the Taser like a gunslinger, and I half expected him to purse his lips and blow the smoke from the end of the barrel.

Ashlyn was crying. She danced on her toes, bound hands dangling before her, as if that would help ease the pain. Justin had stopped twitching on the floor, but he didn't immediately rise to his feet. My husband had been hit how many times in the past twenty-four hours? How many unfried brain cells could he have left?

"The background report did not indicate you would be a problem," Z said, still looking at me. "Interesting."

I wanted to jut out my chin at him. Yell at him for harming my child, torturing my husband. But the heaviness was back, an internal lethargy that would sink me yet. I tried to plant my feet, found myself swaying instead.

"Ashlyn . . . ," I might have whispered.

Except, suddenly, with an ear-splitting roar, Mick leapt to his feet, fists clenched, face enraged. In exactly half a second, his gaze found me, locked on target, and he charged.

I collapsed, trampled like a dandelion before a rampaging bull. He was bellowing, Ashlyn was screaming, and I could hear another voice, maybe Z, calling out something, but mostly I was trying to curl up, to tuck my head into my bound arms as Mick grabbed my hair, lifted my head and shoulders half off the floor, then slammed me back down onto the concrete.

Cracking. Maybe a rib. More likely my skull.

More screaming. More yelling, and then a strange sizzle and burn until I realized that Mick was off me, once more on the floor, once more convulsing wildly, except this time it was his own guy who stood above him, Z and his creepy cobra-tattooed head, pulling the trigger.

"Get. Yourself. Fucking. Under. Control." Z released the trigger. Mick groaned audibly. "Do you hear me?"

"Y-y-yes."

"Yes what?"

"Yes, sir."

"I can't hear you."

"Yes, sir! Yes sir, yes sir, yes sir!"

"Fucking right. Up. Get your sorry ass to the control room. I'll take things from here."

Mick got up, staggered for a second, then marched down the corridor.

The moment he was halfway down the hall, Ashlyn rushed forward, dropping to her knees beside me.

"Mom, are you all right? Mom? Please?"

I felt her long hair against my cheek. Her own fingers, trying to push my lighter strands back so she could better see me.

"I just . . . need a minute."

Z didn't talk. He stood. After a few minutes, I was able to sit up, Ashlyn helping support me. Somewhere along the way, Justin had managed the same, his back propped against a wall, his legs splayed in front of him.

Our first attempt at rebellion. My ribs ached, my head ached, my leg burned. Ashlyn's forearm sported a square of blistered flesh. Justin had yet to make it to his feet. The Denbe family had tried to take on the evil commandos, and the evil commandos had won.

As if reading my mind, Z looked down at me. "If you ever try that again," he said firmly, "your daughter will pay the consequences. Whatever pain and damage you inflict, she will bear the cost twice over. Do you understand me?"

Slowly, aware of my pounding skull, I nodded.

"It's okay, Mom," Ashlyn said, and once again I was startled by the vehemence in her tone. "I don't care. I hate you," she spit out at Z, as if that should bother him. "I hate you, I hate you, I hate you!"

"Forget the money," Justin spoke up behind us. "I will see you fucking killed for this. One day, sooner or later, you're gonna take a bullet to the brain, and I'll be the son of a bitch who put it there."

Z merely snorted.

"Please," he said, indicating for us to rise. "Mick has already picked out your graves, and Radar would kill his own mother if the price was right. Around here, I'm the best friend you got. On your feet. You still got chores to do."

Chapter 17

TESSA CALLED ANITA BENNETT to arrange a meeting with the chief of operations at Denbe Construction. At this stage of the game, Tessa figured it was time to get a better sense of the core group of company officers who'd be called upon to handle the ransom demand, if/when it should occur.

As long as she was visiting Denbe's worldwide headquarters, Tessa also decided to make a quick detour to the travel agency, located in the main lobby of the steel-and-chrome high-rise office building. Kate, Christy, Katie, the hairdresser had thought.

Sure enough, front desk, facing the double-wide glass doors, sat a fresh-faced brunette whose brass desk plate identified her as Kathryn Chapman. A younger Katie Holmes, Tessa thought, which was scary, as Katie Holmes was young enough.

Tessa would estimate the girl's age at twenty, twenty-one. With perfect skin, warm brown eyes, and a positively beaming smile.

Tessa glanced at her watch. Fifteen minutes before she was due at Anita Bennett's twelfth-floor office. She approached.

"Can I help you?" Kathryn Chapman greeted her.

"I hope so. I'm here on behalf of Denbe Construction. I understand your firm handles their travel plans."

"Absolutely. Are you a new employee?"

"You could say that. My first assignment is to track down the big boss, Justin Denbe. Do you happen to know where he's traveling? Because he doesn't seem to be at home this weekend."

At the mention of Justin's name, the girl's smile didn't falter. Some of the luster left her, though. She turned to the monitor on her desk, tapped her keyboard. "Let me see. And your name?"

"Tessa Leoni."

"My name is Kate. Pleased to meet you, Tessa. When you have a moment, we have a basic travel worksheet for you to fill out. Covers your legal name, date of birth, frequent flier numbers, seating preferences, that sort of thing. Once we have all that info on file, we can better assist you with your travel arrangements."

"Good to know."

Kate turned back, frowning slightly. "I don't show Mr. Denbe traveling this weekend. Perhaps he's on a personal trip."

"You only assist with his business travel?"

"We're a corporate agency."

"Huh. And you assist everyone at Denbe? I mean, I should just call you, instead of, say, Expedia.com?"

"I don't know if Denbe has a specific policy, but, yes, we handle the majority of the travel arrangements. With no disrespect to Expedia, it's nice to have a number to call should something go wrong, and we're happy to be that number."

"Can I use you for personal travel, too, or only business?"

"Many of Denbe's employees use us for both."

"But not Justin? You think maybe he made his own plans this weekend?"

"I . . . I don't know."

"You always the one who helps him? Or maybe someone else?"

"There aren't assigned agents, if that's what you mean. We all take turns helping everyone."

The girl was withdrawing. Not deliberately rude, not yet. But her smile had dialed down a few notches. Inside her sharp navy blue blazer, her shoulders were starting to round, her body hunch.

Talking about Justin Denbe hurt her. And she was just a kid, not wise yet in all the ways to hide that kind of pain.

"Maybe he swept his wife away on some romantic getaway weekend," Tessa said. "Office rumor mill said Friday night was date night. Sweet, if you ask me, after all these years."

"Would you like the traveler's profile now?" Kathryn asked softly.

"Kathryn . . . Kate?"

"Yes?"

"Justin Denbe has gone missing. So have his wife and child."

The girl looked up sharply. "What?"

"I am with Denbe Construction. As corporate security. The family disappeared last night. We're trying to find them."

"I don't understand."

"How long have you known Mr. Denbe?"

"Just, you know, since I started here. Nine months."

"I'm told you and Justin were pretty close."

The girl blushed, looked down at her desk. "You were misinformed," she said quietly.

"Kate. Now is not the time. This isn't about reputations, or job security, or the state of Justin's marriage. This is about finding a family while they're still alive."

The girl didn't speak right away. She seemed to be conducting an in-depth examination of her dull gray keyboard. Then, "Can we step outside?"

"Sure."

Kate rose to standing, walking around her desk toward the double-glass doors. She was about Tessa's height of five-six, but with a lithe build that had all the right curves. Male clients probably flocked to Kathryn Chapman. It didn't surprise Tessa that Justin had been part of the pack, nor that he'd emerged victorious. The consummate alpha male.

Jerk, she thought, but it made her sad now. Because in many ways, Justin Denbe sounded like just the kind of strong, successful guy a woman like her hoped to find one day. And look where that had gotten his own wife.

Turned out, Kate was a smoker. They exited the back of the building, to the last refuge smokers had left: a five-foot patch of real estate next to the Dumpsters. The girl lit up; Tessa let the silence work its magic.

"I didn't mean to get involved with him," the girl said abruptly. "I'm not a home wrecker, you know. But, I mean, have you met him?"

Tessa shook her head.

"He's good-looking. Even for an older man, and, and . . . I guess I got a thing for older men. Daddy issues and all that, right?" Kate's lips twisted. She took another drag of her cigarette. "There was this snafu with his plane tickets, so Justin came down to work it out in person. I looked up, and . . . there he was. Tall, broad shoulders, wearing construction boots, for God's sake. When was the last time you saw a guy in an office building in downtown Boston wearing honest-to-God work boots? I just . . . I wanted him from first sight.

"But, I mean, I never woulda," the girl interjected hastily. "He was a client, and it was just business, and I saw his wedding band, not to mention part of the ticket snafu was he wanted to return on Thursday night so he could have a three-day weekend with his family. Then, he got to talking about his wife and daughter. He gushed, you know. Actually beamed with pride . . . It was so clear he loved them so much. I couldn't help thinking . . ." She sounded wistful. "I just thought, God, why can't I meet a guy like that?"

Tessa didn't say anything. Kate looked up at her.

"Are you married?" the girl asked.

"No."

"You ever go to the clubs? You know, go out drinking and dancing, hoping to meet a cute guy?"

"Can't say it's come up."

"Don't bother. The clubs, the bars . . . they're filled with assholes. Petty, self-centered drunks who won't remember your name in the morning. Trust me on this one."

"Okay."

"Justin . . . he was different from all that. A nice guy. When I spoke, he listened. He even looked into my eyes, you know, instead of staring at my chest the whole time."

"And yet . . . ?"

"Lunch," Kate whispered. "It started one day at lunch. I was heading out of the building, and there he was. And he just kind of said, want to do lunch? And I said yes. It sounded so innocent. But I knew. I just looked at him, and I knew. But I wanted him. I even told myself I deserved him. I needed him more than his wife and kid."

"Where'd you go?"

"The Four Seasons." She blushed. "He, ah, went right up to the front desk, got a room key, and up we went. Room service, he said. We'd order room service. But we never did."

"Sounds like a pro," Tessa stated dryly.

"No! I mean, he said . . . he said I was his first. He'd never cheated on his wife before, wasn't that kind of guy. But there was something about me . . ."

"You were special."

"Exactly."

Tessa stared at the girl, gaze hard. After another moment, Kate flushed again, looked away.

"Yeah, there were probably others," the girl said, tapping her cigarette. "Stupid thing is, I expect that kind of bullshit in the bar scene. You know they're feeding you lines, you got your guard up, your armor on. Then, I came to work, sat at my own desk . . . and, yeah, he totally reeled me in, hook, line and sinker. I believed every word he said. Because I wanted it to be special, something other than the slutty travel agent stealing away with the big boss guy for lunchtime quickies."

The girl's voice broke off bitterly. She gave up on her cigarette, her arms wrapped tightly around her waist, that whole armor thing, except it was too late.

"How long did it go on?"

"Not long. Maybe four, five months."

"Ended?"

"His wife found out. We'd started texting. I mean, he traveled a lot. Four, five days a week. Then his family . . . It wasn't easy to get together. I imagine his wife felt like she got the leftovers of his attention once his work commitment was done. But I was one rung even below that. I got the leftovers of the leftovers. The whole . . . affair . . . It wasn't what I thought it would be."

"He ever fly you out to meet him?"

"Maybe, um, a couple of times."

"Define couple."

"Five or six times. In the beginning."

"Definitely you were one rung above leftovers, then."

Kate flushed, looked away. "Only the first month. When everything was new."

"So the relationship starts to cool. You see him less. Text him more."

"He didn't like me texting. He worried about his wife. 'That's how they all get caught,' he'd say. But toward the end . . ." The girl looked up, her face suddenly set. "I wanted him to get caught! I wanted the whole thing exposed. Because I thought"— she swallowed hard, eyes welling—"I thought, stupid, stupid me, that he'd choose me. That his wife would find out, kick his sorry ass out the door, and he'd come running to me. To *me*!"

Tessa waited a beat, let the girl calm down. "But that's not how it played out."

"He dumped me. Called me up, said he'd made a terrible mistake, he loved his wife and it was over. Don't contact him again. And that was that. I waited. Thought maybe, after a few days, he'd call or text. Or even just show up downstairs. But nothing. His secretary took over his travel plans. That was it. I loved him, you know. I was stupid and naive and . . . and I loved him. I thought, maybe, he loved me, too."

"You ever visit his house?"

The girl shook her head.

"Ever meet his wife?"

"No. Just saw her once or twice, in the lobby. I thought she was beautiful. She had on this real artsy skirt and form-fitting turquoise top. She looked like she took care of herself, you know. People said she was nice. I didn't . . . I didn't ask too many questions."

"What did Justin say about her?"

"He didn't. Our time was our time. He wanted to keep it that way."

"And you never asked him questions? Like why he was having lunch with you, instead of her?"

The girl had the good grace to flush again. "He just said they'd been married for a long time. She was a good mother, he respected her—"

"Seriously?"

"But, um, you know, then he'd seen me. And there was something magical—"

"Ah, please." Tessa bit her lip, belatedly trying to call back her own interjection. Always better to let the subject talk.

But Kate was nodding right along. "I know. I look back at it now, and I was so unbelievably stupid. I knew, I think I always knew. But he was just so attractive, and he had this way . . . He made me feel special. As long as I didn't think about it too much, of course. But for those moments, when we were together . . ."

"He gave you gifts?"

"A bracelet. From Tiffany's. I keep thinking I'll give it back, but I haven't, um, seen him."

"Did his wife know? About the bracelet?"

"I don't know."

"She ever find you?"

Kate shook her head. "I wondered if she might try. If she'd call, or worse, come to the office. I tried to think of what I might say . . . I don't know, what do you say?"

"She came. She saw you. She thought you were very young. And given Justin's skills, you never stood a chance."

The girl wilted. Why not, Tessa figured. Imagining yourself as hated by the ex-wife was one thing; discovering you were actually pitied, instead . . .

"Are they really missing?" Kate asked.

"Yes."

"I don't know anything about that. I mean, I haven't even seen Justin for weeks and I never spoke to his wife. I guess I figured they were working things out. I mean, when Justin ended it with me, he *ended* it. Just like that. He loved his wife, and he wasn't coming back."

"And you let him go?" Tessa pressed. "No notes slipped under his windshield wiper, calls to his private line, visits to his job sites?"

"Oh, I called. Third time, he even answered. Told me very firmly . . . like, like *a father*, that I was not to bother him again. That his decision was made and his family came first, and he knew he'd been selfish, and now he needed to work on the irreparable harm he'd caused to his loving wife, blah, blah, blah."

The girl broke off suddenly, flushing as if she understood how callous she sounded. She added, heatedly, "He said if I was struggling this much with the end of our relationship, maybe it would be better if I sought a new place of employment. Well, I got that message loud and clear. He was threatening to get me fired! I haven't finished college yet. You know how many jobs I *can't* get out there? I need this one. Trust me, I got the message just fine. I let him go and that was it."

Tessa studied the young travel agent. She seemed sincere enough. And yet, the girl's recollections seemed to rely a lot on simply *knowing* things. She'd known Justin had wanted her. She'd known he was trying to get her fired. Made Tessa wonder just how much she should trust the *knowings* of a twenty-one-year-old girl. Especially one who was apparently learning many of life's lessons the hard way.

"One last question," Tessa said. "Justin never spoke of his family when you were together, but how about work? Any construction jobs he was worried about, either current or in the pipeline?"

Kate shook her head. "We didn't have much time together, remember? Let's just say we didn't waste it talking."

"You know you're better off without him."

"That's what I keep telling myself." The girl dropped her cigarette, ground it out with her foot. "If you don't mind, I should head back. Like I said, I need this job."

Tessa nodded, glanced at her watch. They'd been talking longer than she'd expected. Kate's absence would be noted, not to mention that Tessa was now five minutes late for her first Denbe Construction meeting.

She grabbed the handle of the office building's back door, about to reenter, when it came to her: the oldest trick in the book, the lie of omission.

She turned around, studied the young travel agent carefully. "Hey, Kate, you said you never met Justin's wife. But what about his daughter?"

Chapter 18

THE PRISON'S KITCHEN WAS HUGE, a commercial space filled with stacked ovens, bakery-quality mixers and endless miles of stainless steel counters. The kind of kitchen meant to serve hundreds of people in an overcrowded cafeteria. It was fully stocked with pots, pans, bakeware, mixing utensils, measuring cups, etc., though it appeared Z and his crew had replaced the knives with plastic utensils.

Our first test, the team leader informed us. If we wanted to eat, we would cook. Enough for all six of us. Z cut the zip ties binding our wrists, allowing the three of us to stand together, unrestrained, for the first time since this ordeal had begun. While the knives had been removed, the kitchen still held cast-iron skillets, graters, peelers, rolling pins. Plenty of options for violence, if we felt motivated enough.

Z stated this directly, standing loosely before us, his back to a rolling, stainless steel island. He had the Taser stuck in a leather holster around his waist. Other objects protruded in discreet black leather pouches attached to his belt. I had a feeling we didn't want to know what was in those other pouches.

I noticed that when Z spoke, his dark green snake tattoo seemed to undulate around his head, the scales moving sinuously beneath the too bright overhead lights. As if the cobra were advancing. As if the cobra would come for us next.

Mick would simply kill us. Z, on the other hand, would hurt us in ways that would make us wish we were dead.

Z finished his friendly reminder that should we choose to cause trouble, our punishment would be immediate and include but not be limited to a loss of food privileges for the remainder of our incarceration.

He said it just like that. The remainder of our incarceration. As if we were somehow serving hard time, maybe life without parole.

I felt like giggling, but I didn't.

The commandos had procured supplies. Not much in the way of fresh produce—again, because we were serving a life sentence?—but an impressive array of canned foods, bagged lentils, and dry goods. Enough to fill several long shelves in the twelve-foot-by-twelve-foot walk-in pantry. I tried not to think about how much food was present, how long this supply could conceivably last and what that might say about our kidnappers' plans, as I worked my way through the pantry, trying to assemble enough ingredients for a credible dinner.

For our first night of gourmet prison dining, I went with pasta with tomato sauce. We had plenty of cans of crushed tomatoes, olive oil, dried herbs, and garlic cloves. I added a jar of olives, a jar of pearl onions, then canned carrots and baby corn to the stack on the stainless steel island. Without fresh produce, we were reduced to a diet of processed vegetables, terrible in taste, nearly deadly in sodium content. Not much I could do about salt levels, but incorporating items such as carrots and corn into a marinara sauce would help supplement the nutritional content without totally sacrificing edibility. The olives and onions would assist with flavor, creating a sauce that might not win any awards in the North End but would be medal-worthy inside a state institution.

Z seemed intrigued that I would know such things. I didn't feel like telling him about my life with my mother in the projects. That not only could I cook out of cans, but I could clean a toilet with Coke and remove grout stains with bleach and baking soda.

Justin was put to work preparing two pounds of pasta. My husband could cook. Very well, in fact, if there was a grill involved and some choice-cut fillets. But for now, he tended spaghetti while Ashlyn and I assembled the sauce. My daughter went to work opening cans, then diced up mushy carrots and slippery onions with a plastic knife. I used a second plastic knife on the olives. At least with canned vegetables, a sharp-edged blade was hardly necessary.

For a while, none of us spoke. We worked, and working felt nice. To have a purpose again, a focus and direction. Ashlyn's stomach growled as the scent of boiling noodles filled the air. Twenty hours without food? I tried to do the math, but my brain wouldn't go there. So I chopped more, stirred together, played with herbs, started the simmering process. Cooking was something I'd been doing my entire life. Motions that could be performed on autopilot.

The problem started when Justin asked me for a spoon.

He wanted to test the cooked noodles. Could I pass him a spoon?

I stared at him, standing in front of a saucepan of stewed tomatoes, and for the life of me, I couldn't remember . . . a spoon, a spoon, a spoon?

"Libby," he said.

I stared at him, more and more curiously.

"Whoa, whoa, whoa. Burner's too hot." He reached in front of me, turned the dial down. That made sense to me. The dial controlled the fire, the fire controlled heat, and I didn't want my sauce to burn.

But then Justin ruined the moment, by asking me again for a spoon. I turned to him in near exasperation.

"I don't have a sfpoof," I heard myself say.

"A what?"

"A sfpoof."

That didn't sound right. I frowned. Ashlyn was staring at me. Z, too. My head hurt. I put a hand to my forehead, and realized I was now swaying on my feet.

Z approached me.

"Tell me your name," he ordered.

"Kathryn Chapman," I said tiredly.

My husband paled, though I wasn't sure why.

"Mom?"

Z touched me. I flinched, couldn't help myself. That cobra, those fangs, those gleaming scales . . .

My back hit the hot-burning, bubbling sauce.

"Libby!"

Justin jerked me to the side, away from the stove. Then Z placed his fingers around my eyeball and steadily pulled my eyelids open.

I think I whimpered. Someone did.

"How hard did that fucker hit you?" Z murmured. "Count to ten."

I stared at him blankly, trying to disappear into my husband, who stood beside me solidly now, arm around my shoulders for support. I wished I could turn in to him. When we were first dating, I'd loved to tuck my body into him, the feeling of his hard planes against my softer build. Two pieces of a puzzle that clicked into place. He had made me feel safe then, and I could use a feeling of safety right about now.

His fingertips curled around my shoulder. A subtle squeeze of reassurance, and I felt the weight of his earlier promise. He would keep Ashlyn and me safe. He had sworn it.

"One, two . . . ," Z prodded.

"Eight?" I whispered.

"Ah, crap." Z stepped back, looked at Justin. "I think your wife has a concussion."

"I think your psycho gave it to her. Can't you control your own men?"

"Apparently, no more than you can control your own family. No matter. Radar's a crack medic. He can handle her."

Z made a motion with his hand toward the camera in the ceiling. An electronic eye to go with the snake's eye, I thought, feeling my mind spiral further away. Justin led me to a stool, telling Ashlyn to please stir the sauce. Then, he left me, and I was once more all alone, watching the overhead lights bounce crazily off miles and miles of stainless steel, and I was going to be sick except what was the point? In the past twenty-four hours, I had thrown up way more than I'd taken in. I tried to explain that to my churning, twisting stomach, as I sat and watched my husband lift the heavy pot of pasta off the stove, carry it to the sink and dump it into a colander. Then Ashlyn, voice sounding stilted, said the sauce was done, except she was staring at me, not the sauce at all, and in her eyes I saw worry and anger and fear, and that made my head ache more. I didn't want my child worried and angry and afraid. I was supposed to take care of her. Wasn't I?

Justin and I against the world.

Justin clicked off the burner and Radar walked through the kitchen doors.

He looked me up and down, seemed to study my eyes, then nodded to himself.

"Can you walk?" he asked.

"Spfoof," I said.

"Excellent. I'll help get you there."

"We'll all go," Justin started.

"You will sit," Z instructed firmly. "Your daughter will sit. Eat. Last chance you're gonna get. Radar, tend to business."

The kid put his shoulder under my arm, helped me to standing. I only swayed once, then the world righted itself. Walking wasn't so hard. No need to think, just place one foot after the other.

Except my footsteps carried me away from my family. I felt like I should say something. Try to communicate some message of hope, reassurance. Or maybe even love. It shouldn't be too hard, should it? On this eve of our lives falling apart, shouldn't I be able to call out across the void, I love you, I'm sorry, I love you.

Forgive me.

I left my husband and daughter sitting at the stainless steel counter.

And as so often was the case these days, none of us said a word.

IF THE MOTHBALLED PRISON had an impressive commercial-grade kitchen, the infirmary was equally state-of-the-art. Radar led me straight into an exam room, complete with stainless steel sink and locked drawers filled with all sorts of interesting equipment. The bed appeared bolted to the floor. Maybe so you didn't float away.

Radar checked my pulse, my blood pressure, then shone a pinpoint light straight into my eyeballs. I bit my lower lip to keep from screaming in pain. Next, he started to inspect my skull with his fingers, working them through my unkempt, uncombed, dirty-blond hair. I felt self-conscious until his fingers landed on a spot behind my ear. This time, I did cry out, and he hastily withdrew his hands.

"Could be concussion," he muttered. "Could be contusion, could be straight-line fracture. Do you know what the Glasgow Coma score is?"

I didn't answer. He mostly seemed to be talking to himself.

"I'd put you at a ten, which is better than an eight, but still . . . You need a CT scan. Toys here aren't quite that fancy, but we can start with a basic X-ray."

New room. Definitely not walking so well

now. Sweating. I could feel my pulse starting to flutter. Pain, agitation, distress.

I wished . . . I wished Justin were here, his arm once more around my shoulders.

X-ray machine. I got to lie down on a table. Radar positioned a heavy mat over my chest, then a cover over my eyes, then a machine over my head.

"Close your eyes. Don't move."

He left. A buzzing, then a flash.

Radar was back.

"Digital system," he announced, as if that should mean something to me. "But gotta wait a bit."

"How did you . . . learn, all this?" I managed to wave my hand around the room.

He stared at me straight-faced. "In school, I applied myself real hard."

"Doctor? Is that what you studied?"

"Doctors are pansies. I'm a field medic. We have real skills."

"In the military? Army?"

Kid didn't say anything, just stared at me.

"What's your name?" he asked after another second.

I opened my mouth, but nothing came out, so I closed it again. "He tried to kill me," I heard myself say.

Radar rolled his eyes at me. "Pretty fucking stupid thing to do, Tase a guy twice your size. Take it from me, your survival skills could use some work."

"Bigger they are, the harder they fall," I murmured.

"Yep, and the faster they crush your skull."

"Are you friends?"

The kid shrugged, shifted uncomfortably. "We know each other. That's enough."

"There's something wrong with him."

Radar shrugged again. "Tell me something I don't know."

"He would've killed me. Then my husband. Then my daughter."

"Z stopped him."

"Is he the boss?"

"In any grouping of more than one, there is a boss."

"Can he control Mick?"

"Z?" Radar laughed. "Z can control the world. Question is, does he want to?"

"I think I'm going to vomit now."

"Now, see, you tell that to a real doctor,

they run away. I, on the other hand, already have a bag."

The kid held up a plastic grocery bag. I rolled slightly to the side, and threw up a small stream of water. Then I dry heaved, then I fell back, holding my aching stomach. Radar wasn't impressed. "You need to drink. Look at your skin." He pinched the back of my hand, then shook his head. "Already dehydrated. What do you think, you're on a pleasure cruise? First rule of thumb in an adverse situation: Tend to your own health. You need fluids. You need food."

"I need my purse." I whispered the words without thinking, already licking at my cracked lips.

"Can't," the kid said levelly. "No Vicodin as long as you have a head injury."

"How did you . . . ?"

"Some people limit themselves to going through life using all five senses. Then, there are guys like me. Prescription painkillers, right? Ritzy housewife from Back Bay, no way you're hitting the hard drugs yet—that would imply a real problem. But popping Percocet, oxycodone, pills prescribed by your own doctor, that not's so bad, right? Meaning you're going on twenty-four hours without a hit . . . Bet you're really tired right now. Just barely hanging on. Like the world is an ocean dragging you under. You know you need to pull it together, focus for the sake of your family, but of course you can't. You're suffering from depression, abdominal cramping, agitation, constipation and nausea. Oh yeah, and now a knock on the head. But other than that, sure, you got your shit together."

I didn't answer.

He spread his hands. "Might as well tell me everything. Just you and me here, and at the rate you're going, we're going to have a lot of quality time together. More you tell me, more I can maybe help. 'Cause you're kind of useless right now. FYI."

"Water," I said.

He crossed to the sink and poured a little in a plastic cup. I used the first sip to rinse my mouth, then spit in the puke pouch.

I thought Radar looked like his TV namesake—too young to sound so old. Too fresh-faced to appear so cynical. But then I thought of Z and I thought of Mick and I wondered how innocent he could really be while hanging with the likes of them.

"Ten," I said. "I try to limit myself to ten a day." Or fifteen.

"Oxycodone or Percocet?"

"Hydrocodone. It's for my neck." I said the words straight-faced. He didn't correct me.

"Dosage?"

"Ten milligrams."

"That's the opiate dosage. So you're taking at least another five hundred milligrams of acetaminophen per pill. Times ten . . . How long?"

"Couple months."

"Stomach bleeding?"

"It hurts."

"When you drink alcohol?"

"Hurts more."

Radar looked at me. "So you take another pill."

"If I could just . . . my purse."

Radar shook his head at me. "You live in that house. You got a husband, a pretty daughter. Seriously, what the hell are you escaping from? Maybe you need to spend more time in the slums. Or, hell, military barracks. That'll teach you a thing or two."

He got up. Left the room. Probably had to check the X-rays, or maybe I disgusted him that much. I didn't bother to correct him, to tell him I had once lived on the other side of the tracks, and, yes, I understood the advantages of my new and improved station in life.

Maybe I was a romantic, however. I'd never wanted the big house, the Back Bay address. I'd just wanted my husband.

Except that wasn't entirely the truth, either. From the moment I'd taken that first pill . . .

Once upon a time, I'd lost my father. And then, still too soon, I'd lost my mother. And I had borne it, I'd been strong. Until That Day, realizing I was going to lose my husband, hearing him whisper the truth about his affair with another woman, realizing that this family, too, was doomed to self-destruct . . .

It turned out, a giant well of emptiness had always existed inside me. A void so deep and black and ugly, I wasn't just empty, I was hollowed out by the losses in my life. Until there were days I didn't dare go outside because I worried the wind would blow me away.

The pills became my anchor. And sometimes, knowing something isn't right still doesn't change anything. You are who you are. You need what you need. You do what you do.

I wondered if Justin told himself the same when he was having sex with that girl. I wondered if afterward, he felt as guilty as I did, while still knowing he was going to do it again. And again. And again.

I had thought love would make us better people. I was mistaken.

Now I curled up in a ball, trying to ease the cramps in my stomach, while closing my eyes against the ache in my head.

Door opened. I didn't open my eyes, just waited for Radar to make his pronouncement. Would the patient live or die?

Instead, a hoarse voice whispered in my ear, "I'm gonna kill you, pretty white bitch. But first, I'm totally gonna fuck your daughter. You can hide down here as long as you want. I got time. I got patience. I got a whole prison, with three hundred and forty-two places where I can jump out and yell boo!"

I didn't move. Just lay there, as if I were sleeping. Mick departed. Radar reentered.

Informed me I had a concussion. Told me I needed to rest, drink more fluids and bone up on omega-3s, building blocks of the brain. He handed me two fish oil capsules, then said he would return me to my family, who would monitor me overnight.

I said nothing, just accepted the gel capsules, then the support of his arm, as we made our way slowly down the corridor. I could tell from the smell when we neared the kitchen.

What had Radar said? The first rule of thumb . . . tend to your health.

"Could I eat a little dinner?"

Radar eyed me dubiously.

"Maybe plain pasta. Something simple."

He shrugged, as if to say it would be my problem later.

I accepted that. A lot of things, it seemed, would be my problem later. But now I had to pull it together. Find some way to get myself to stop drowning and start swimming, to think of my husband and daughter and put their safety first.

Justin had sworn to protect Ashlyn and me. But I already doubted he could take on a professionally trained psycho like Mick all alone. We needed to come together, him, me and Ashlyn. Hate a little less. Love a little more.

Once upon a time, inside one of the most luxurious town houses in Boston, our family had fallen apart. Now, inside these harsh cinder-block prison walls, we needed to find ourselves again.

Because Mick didn't strike me as the kind of killer who made idle threats. And trapped inside this prison, it's not like we could get away. He was the predator. We were the prey. And there was no place left for any of us to run.

Chapter 19

PARTICIPATING IN A MULTI-JURISDICTIONAL IN-VESTIGATION was a lot like dancing. Unfor-tunately, Wyatt didn't care for dancing. Never had. Never would.

Currently, he had Kevin in the car, riding shotgun. When playing with the feds, it never hurt to have a smart guy around, and Kevin was as geeky as the North Country knew how to get.

They had instructions to rendezvous with Special Agents Adams and Hawkes at the Denbe Construction headquarters in downtown Boston. Though it was a Saturday, the FBI had already received permission to start interviews of various company officers and employees. Given that in a missing person's case, time was of the essence, no one was arguing.

Nicole mentioned a private investigator might be present as well, some corporate security expert retained by Denbe Construction to conduct an independent assessment of the situation.

Which is where things got complicated. Not competitive, necessarily, though sometimes that happened as well. But complicated. To say everyone wanted the Denbes recovered safe and sound oversimplified the matter. Denbe Construction wanted them found in the most efficient (i.e., least costly) manner possible. The FBI wanted them found in a way that would highlight not only the bureau as a whole, but advance Nicole's and her partner's careers individually. And Wyatt . . . Well, hell, he wasn't immune to a little glory. He was already blowing his budget on the search operations. He wouldn't mind coming out of this looking like a good guy. A sheriff's department had to fight for funding just like everyone else. A high-level success went a long way to keeping them operational another year.

In other words, a lot of cooks in the kitchen. Which could lead to some really great collaboration, or one massive fuckup.

Wyatt's job was never boring.

They took 93 into Boston. Sun was long gone, the city lights blazing with full Saturday night glory. In his younger days, Wyatt would head down to Boston to catch a concert, or maybe a Red Sox game. Now, following in the footsteps of most New Hampshirites over forty, he shunned the city entirely. The drive, the traffic, the parking, the crowds . . .

Yep, he'd gotten old and, mostly, he liked it.

Red arrows appeared on the navigation system, trying to illustrate which of the myriad of exits he was supposed to take, but mostly confusing the issue. Kevin did the honors. Being a hockey nerd, he still drove to Boston regularly for the Bruins games.

Between the two of them they managed to find the Denbe Construction building. Underground parking lot, which was useful. They got their ticket, parked the car, then shook out their limbs. They wore their uniforms: Tan pants with dark brown stripes. Dark brown shirt topped with a light brown tie, county patches and gold badge indicating rank. Duty belts, high-polished boots, tight-brimmed hats.

The feds would blend with the other suits in the room. Wyatt and Kevin, on the other hand, knew how to make an entrance.

The building lobby was composed of mostly glass, steel and dark-gray slate. The kind of architectural design that kept Wyatt forever happy to be a hick. He noticed one coffee shop and what appeared to be a travel agency. Otherwise, there was an information desk, currently empty, then a bank of elevators beside a huge directory of the building's occupants.

Kevin located Denbe Construction, twelfth floor. They hit the button and the elevator obediently carried them away.

Exiting the elevator, they encountered a narrow hallway and a great deal more glass: an entire wall of it, with the glass door so artfully fit into the broader panes Wyatt felt like a blind man using Braille to feel out the edges. Door was locked.

Behind it sat a cherrywood receptionist's desk, topped with bold metallic letters that spelled out Denbe Construction. Right place. If only they could enter.

Kevin finally found an intercom, hit the button.

Thirty seconds later, an older woman with short-cropped silver hair, dark gray pants and a long-sleeve white silk turtleneck appeared. She had the tight look of a woman under a great amount of stress but holding it together.

She took in their uniforms, then opened the door.

"Anita Bennett," she said briskly. "Chief of operations, Denbe Construction. And you are?"

Wyatt did the honors, could see her bright blue eyes immediately connect the dots.

"You found Justin's jacket and will now be assisting with the New Hampshire search," she stated, gesturing for them to enter.

Wyatt was tempted to quibble over the word *assist*, but resisted. "Nice to meet you, Mrs. Bennett—"

"Anita, please call me Anita. The others

are in the conference room. Coffee and refreshments are on the side table. Restrooms just down the hall. I have a few final details still to tend. This whole day . . . We're a bit rattled. Nothing like this has ever happened to us before."

Wyatt and Kevin nodded their sympathies. Anita led them to an impressively large conference room, with the requisite wall of windows overlooking downtown Boston. Wyatt guessed that in an industry where contracts ran to the tens of millions, image mattered, because nothing in this room was cheap. Massive birchwood table. Dozens of plush leather chairs. Huge graphic prints. Wyatt hadn't gotten to visit the crime scene at the Denbes' town house yet, but just looking at Justin Denbe's offices made him very curious about Justin Denbe's home.

Half of the leather chairs were taken. Sitting with their backs to the Boston view were the two feds, Nicole Adams and Ed Hawkes. Next to Nicole sat a stocky-looking guy, buzz-cut black hair, red plaid shirt rolled up to the forearms, tattoo creeping up his neck. Definitely one of Denbe's, same with the three guys beside him, also clad in worn flannel, heavy cargo pants and work boots. None of them were large, but each of them exuded the kind of inner swagger that came with years of winning bar brawls. Former military, Wyatt would bet his life on it. Which he already found interesting. Hadn't realized Denbe employed so many of the military types, guys who would have, say, hands-on experience with Tasers. Not to mention, these guys looked like top of the food chain— they probably had interesting connections to even more interesting military specimens.

He finished his inspection of the Denbe crew about the same time they finished their inspection of him. They didn't seem impressed, but then, the first guy, Mr. Buzz Cut, already appeared more captivated by Nicole. Good luck with that, Wyatt wanted to tell him, but didn't.

Across the table, currently sitting alone, he got his first surprise.

Female, heart-shaped face, flat blue eyes. Jolted him a second, because at first glance, the face seemed young, but then, those eyes . . . He met her gaze, and she returned it frankly.

Definitely another former something. Not in uniform now, but had been. The face niggled at him. A sense of déjà vu, as if he should know her.

"Tessa Leoni," she spoke up. "Northledge Investigations. I've been retained by Denbe Construction to handle an independent assessment of the situation."

Ah, the independent investigator.

He crossed over and pulled out a rolling leather chair next to her. Kevin took a seat beside Wyatt.

Wyatt did the honors, holding out his hand. "Wyatt Foster, sergeant, criminal investigations. This is Detective Kevin Santos. We had jacket duty."

"You launched the hotline," Tessa said.

He nodded modestly. "Don't tell anyone, but I like the public. More often than not, they have useful things to tell us. I mean, once you weed out the crazies. And given that we have few leads and very little information, I thought we could use some useful tips right about now."

"Have you received any?" Nicole Adams spoke up from across the table.

"Nah. But we only have the description of the family, and I doubt the kidnappers are parading three abductees through public spaces. More useful would be a description of the vehicle."

Nicole nodded briskly. "We have agents still canvassing the neighborhood. So far, however, we have more theories on the subject than solid leads."

Wyatt was about to ask about the theories, when Anita Bennett returned.

The hostess of the party, she carried a large stack of spiral-bound photocopies. Company financials, he realized quickly. She handed out the presentation on Denbe Construction, and they quickly got down to business.

First, introductions. From Denbe Construction, they had Anita Bennett, COO and now acting president given Justin's disappearance. (Wyatt made a mental note: first person to gain from the Denbes' loss— Anita Bennett.) Next up, the stocky lothario, Chris Lopez, chief of construction, who made a point of emphasizing his title while gazing deeply into Special Agent Nicole Adams's very cool, very unimpressed pale blue eyes. Next to him was a trio Wyatt immediately pegged as the three stooges: Jenkins, Paulie and a guy seriously called

Bacon. The core building team, Lopez explained. They worked with Justin, they knew Justin, they had his back. Whatever happened, these were the go-to guys for knocking heads and taking names.

Jenkins, who was former air force and current structural engineer, actually cracked his knuckles. And yet he was still more subtle than the Bacon character, who kept stroking a small, rough-hewn metal spoon he wore on a leather cord around his neck.

Wyatt translated "core building team" to mean "posse." Justin Denbe had a posse. Of apparently some of the most dangerous, crazily unbalanced former military types Wyatt had ever met. Meaning he and the other law enforcement types would have to manage information carefully, as guys like this would definitely go off on their own, violence being their best friend and primary coping mechanism.

Mental note two: Isolate posse, interview each one alone and do deep background checks. These guys knew things, knew people. Probably including the type of people who could abduct a family of three, no problem.

Missing in action was the fourth member of the build team, an architect who was currently on site in California. He'd be on a plane first thing in the morning, available for interviews by Sunday at five. Also, the chief financial officer, Ruth Chan, was on vacation in the Bahamas. They were still trying to get word to her of the "current situation," as Anita Bennett put it.

"Now then," Bennett declared, "we are here for you. I understand you must have questions, and of course we will do everything in our power to make ourselves available to you. As you can see, I have already made a copy of last quarter's financial statements. The head of HR is also on call, ready to line up whichever employee interviews you feel are most appropriate. Right here in this room, we are the ones who work with Justin most closely, and I think I can speak for all of us when I say assisting him is nothing short of a privilege and an honor. Of course our number one priority is his safety, as well as the safety of his family."

"And none of you have heard from Justin or any member of the Denbe family today?" Nicole spoke up briskly, assuming her role as lead agent.

It seemed like a stupid question, except Wyatt had been in investigations before where right at this moment, someone raised his or her hand and went, wait, dude, did I mention he called me thirty minutes ago? Today, however, was not one of those cases. Each person around the table shook their head.

"Has Mr. Denbe mentioned to anyone personal plans, a weekend away with his family?"

"Justin generally made his own travel plans. I took the liberty of checking his computer here at work, and there's nothing on his calendar," Bennett supplied.

"Has he expressed frustration with a current project, angst over the direction the company is going?"

A larger pause this time, then one by one, each person of the Denbe crew shook his or her head. Wyatt didn't get too excited yet. Group answers were always suspect. A starting point, sure, but what would be more interesting is what they got out of each person individually, when they didn't have to worry about their fellow employees overhearing.

"How are the financials?" Wyatt asked, earning a dirty look from Nicole for stealing her thunder. "Bottom line?"

"We are profitable." Bennett said this a bit stiffly, paused. "But cash-flow challenged."

Wyatt got that tingling feeling. As Anita Bennett explained it, Denbe's last major build had had some cost overruns and Denbe had gotten pinged pretty hard. They'd covered the project's net loss out of cash reserves, but that meant they'd entered their current build, some hospital down in Virginia, with no cushion and, of course, encountered their first cash-flow crisis right out of the gate.

Big picture good, Bennett went out of her way to emphasize. The hospital was still on track to generate five million in profit. Last quarter, however, looked dreadful, and, yes, things were tight. But Justin liked tight, she added quickly. For him, money management, which really meant finessing banks and suppliers and subs, was all part of the fun of a major build. If there was one thing he loved even more than negotiating terms, it was renegotiating terms. Definitely not the kind of guy to run from a fight.

Wyatt thought that was a very interesting story. He jotted down: Embezzlement? Money laundering? Because from what he could tell, with these kinds of dollars flying around, this industry had to be rife with such opportunities. Meaning if Justin was a numbers guy, maybe he'd started to figure it out, or was at least sniffing close enough to someone else's cash-skimming trail. Making his imminent departure necessary.

Bennett had one last piece of what she considered to be good news. Denbe Construction carried insurance on Justin. Boatloads of it. Ten million in life, but also a two-million-dollar kidnapping policy. Better yet, the kidnapping rider also covered members of his family. One million for his spouse. One million for each kid.

Nicole did the honors: "Are you saying this policy guarantees up to four million dollars in possible ransom money?"

"Yes." Bennett beamed.

"Have you notified the company?"

"Not yet. We haven't received any ransom demands."

"How long would it take for the insurance company to procure such funds?" Nicole asked.

Bennett appeared a little less excited. "I don't know. We've never used it."

Wyatt thought that was missing the point: "Excuse me, but how many people are aware of this policy? You know, that kidnapping the Denbe family is worth at least four mil? Because it sounds to me like the company doesn't have the cash to ransom Justin back, but this policy sure as hell does."

Silence in the room. The Denbe employees looked at one another, then glanced away. "Well, most of us, I believe," Bennett supplied warily.

"Justin liked to joke about it," Lopez, the construction manager, spoke up. "That we should remember he was worth money alive, not just dead. But, for the record, I didn't know about the family clause. I just knew Justin was insured. I mean, he's the owner, this is a pretty serious firm that handles mega–financial deals. Seems to me, if you know Denbe Construction at all, then you assume the owner, Justin Denbe, is loaded to the hilt, whether it's insurance money, his money, firm money. Either way, kidnapping a guy like Justin Denbe should equal easy money."

The other members of the posse nodded.

"Except, of course," Lopez continued, "nothing about Justin is easy. And we're the ones who know that, too. So don't go staring all flinty-eyed at us." He shook his finger at Nicole in particular. "We shot with Justin at least once a week. The guy could take care of himself. Not to mention, most of us were around for his wedding, plus we helped change Ashlyn's diapers. He's one of us, his family is our family. We're not the fucking problem here. You're gonna have to sniff somewhere else for that."

Lopez appeared to have said his piece. He sat back, crossed his arms over his chest. His guys nodded beside him.

Score one for the hood, Wyatt thought.

"I think we can all agree," Bennett interjected diplomatically, "that we are deeply concerned about Justin, Libby and Ashlyn. Please, you're handling this investigation. What can you tell us?"

"We do have some initial leads," Nicole supplied. "For starters, Taser confetti was recovered at the scene, which we can use to trace the weapon used in the attack."

"Won't help," the Bacon guy spoke up.

All eyes turned to him. "Illegal in Mass." He shrugged, apparently not a big talker. "Meaning Taser's probably not registered, meaning serial number on confetti won't tie back to a listed weapon."

Nicole thinned her lips, and Wyatt could tell by her expression that she'd already known that. Still, *knowing* you had no leads didn't necessarily mean *admitting* you had no leads.

"Neighbors didn't see or hear anything?" Wyatt asked.

"No. But sometimes a negative can be a positive."

Good line. Which was why Nicole had a real career with the FBI, while Wyatt was still a semi-carpenter.

"For example," she continued, "to transport a family of three, as well as multiple kidnappers in a single vehicle, would require at least a van or SUV. Presumably, for the kidnappers to remove three bound-and-gagged individuals from a home without arousing suspicion means such a vehicle would have to be parked in the immediate vicinity. Inside the Denbes' garage would be one option, but none of the neighbors saw the garage opening and closing that night, let alone Libby's vehicle being moved onto the street. How, then, did the kidnappers manage to illegally park a large vehicle right near the house without arousing suspicion?"

"Delivery van." Tessa Leoni spoke up for the first time. Her tone wasn't cool, just matter-of-fact. Wyatt's first guess: She had yet to hear anything at this table she didn't already know.

Nicole frowned slightly, clearly not thrilled to have had an outsider beat her to the punch. "That is our current theory, correct. We're assuming the vehicle was disguised as a caterer's van, which is the kind of thing few people would notice in such a neighborhood. The Denbes have rights to an aboveground parking space, located next to the garage entrance at the rear of the town house. It would've been easy enough to park a van there, and quickly remove the family members from the house under the cover of night."

"How'd they enter the house?" Wyatt asked, as he knew the least about the Boston scene.

"Overrode the security."

"No." One of the posse, Paulie, spoke up. "I installed that system myself. Can't be overridden."

Paulie rattled off about double this and reinforced that. Nicole let him talk, her expression more patient than surprised.

"Then it wasn't overridden," she stated calmly, when he was finished. "It was disarmed."

"You'd have to know the code," Paulie began.

"Exactly."

"Meaning . . ."

"Exactly."

Around the room, the various members of the management team all stared at one another, the message loud and clear.

An inside job. The Denbes had been abducted by people who knew them, their security code and, most likely, the ransom insurance policy. Definitely a friend had masterminded the kidnapping, not a foe. And most likely, given that it was a Denbe employee who'd installed their security system, and the Denbe management team that had approved Justin's insurance policy, it was someone sitting right at this table.

Tessa Leoni leaned forward, taking the initiative for the first time all meeting: "In the event of a divorce between Justin and Libby, what would happen to Denbe Construction?"

Absolute, immediate uproar from the Denbe contingency. Never, couldn't happen, how dare she . . .

Wyatt leaned back, crossed his arms over his chest and took it all in. No doubt about it, 9:00 P.M. Saturday night, they were finally getting down to business.

Yep, his job was never boring.

Chapter 20

DINNER DIDN'T MAKE IT. I threw up within the first few minutes of returning to the cell. Ashlyn held back my hair as I leaned over the stainless steel toilet. Afterward, I rinsed my mouth with water from the sink, then, given that there were no towels, patted my face dry with the sleeve of my orange jumpsuit.

"Are you okay?" Ashlyn whispered, my fifteen-year-old daughter who hadn't spoken to me in months, now the epitome of motherly concern.

"Just need to rest," I said. "I'll be better by morning."

She nodded, though morning seemed a strange concept, locked up in an over-bright prison cell. What time was it, any-way? I peered out the far window, the one overlooking the barren dirt outside. The sky was pitch-black. Meaning, this time of year, it could be anytime after 5:00 P.M. I felt the hour was probably around eight, maybe nine, but was mostly guessing.

The three of us stared at one another, stuck together in a tiny cell, unsure of what to do next. Justin was gazing at me with open concern. Then he caught me star-ing, and quickly smoothed his expression.

"We should compare notes, assess what we know," he said briskly. He moved away from the door, toward the left-hand bunk. He winced as he sat down.

I couldn't help myself: "How are you feel-ing?"

He waved a hand. "Fine, fine."

Watching him closer, I detected the tight set of his jaw, the fine lines creasing the corners of his eyes. He was in pain, defi-nitely. How many hits had he taken with the Taser? Six, eight, twelve? Enough to cause permanent damage? Maybe Z and his cohorts had fried my husband's spinal cord. God knows, Ashlyn and I were sporting decent-size burns from the Taser's contact points. Justin must have nearly a dozen of those, not to mention one extremely overstimulated central nervous system. Of course he hurt.

"The front door was locked." Ashlyn spoke up earnestly. I sat down next to her on the lower right-hand bunk. She took my hand, her face pleading with me. "Honest, Mom, I told Dad on the way to dinner. I never touched the system after you two left. I was in my room the whole time, playing games on my iPad and texting Lindsay."

I looked at Justin. He'd armed the system when we left. He always did, Mr. Safety and Security. If I thought back hard enough, I could even picture him doing it. His fingers moving quick and sure over the keypad.

"Did you hear anything?" I asked softly. My head still throbbed, but if Justin could will his pain away, I could do the same. He was right, after all. We needed to figure out what we were up against.

"No." Ashlyn flushed. "I was, um . . . going to the bathroom, and this guy, he just . . . appeared in the doorway. It was the larger one, Mick, I guess. And I, I got scared and I grabbed hair spray and went after him—"

"Good girl," Justin said.

She flashed a look at him. "I ran for your room. But you weren't there, of course, and I . . ."

Her voice drifted off. She didn't look at either of us, and I realized that, all of a sudden, my daughter was near tears. Because she'd needed us, run to our room, and we hadn't been there. Said a lot about our family these days.

I squeezed my daughter's hand in silent apology, but wasn't surprised when she pulled back, tucking once more into herself.

"The younger guy, Radar, showed up," she whispered. "And between him and Mick . . ." She glanced up at Justin. "I heard you downstairs, the front door opening. I wanted to scream or yell or something, but Mick put his hand over my mouth. I tried . . . but there wasn't anything . . ." She shrugged, shoulders rounding inside her oversize jumpsuit as she fell quiet.

"It's all right," Justin reassured her. "Nothing you could do. These guys, they're trained. Professionals. And they had a plan we never saw coming."

"What do they want?" Ashlyn asked plaintively.

"Money."

I glanced up sharply, a motion that made me wince.

"Think about it," he said, as if sensing my doubt. "They're carrying Tasers, not guns. So their goal is to control, but not harm. They've Tased us, drugged us, bound us. Again, all strategies devised to subdue, but not injure."

"Until the Mick guy beat the shit out of Mom," Ashlyn muttered.

"Young lady," Justin began, "I don't want to hear that kind of language—"

"She's right," I interjected, already feeling Ashlyn's growing hostility. "He beat the shit out of me."

Justin scowled at our joint rebellion. "Which their leader, Z, immediately halted by Tasing his own guy, then he sent you for medical treatment. Again, if their intent is to harm, why would Z care if you have a concussion? Why bother having one of his men tend to you, taking up time and resources? For that matter, why feed us?

Because he wants us subdued but un-harmed, all the better for demanding ran-som, where he'll have to deliver proof of life."

"Proof of life?" Ashlyn asked.

"As part of the ransom demand, Z will have to prove we're still alive and well. Hence he went after Mick when Mick at-tacked your mother. It's not enough to simply ask for money. Z has to prove he really has us, but also, we're undamaged enough to be worth wanting back; hence your mother can't be in a coma."

"Kidnapping," Ashlyn murmured. "Ran-som. Proof of life." She tested out each word, as if trying to determine how such phrases had come to apply in her life.

"The kitchen is well stocked," I said, my gaze flickering to Justin with unspoken meaning. Such as, there were enough dry goods in this prison to last weeks, let alone days.

"Ransom cases can take time," he said evasively. "Especially, given there's an in-surance company involved."

Ashlyn and I stared at him blankly. He explained that Denbe Construction carried not only a life insurance policy on him, but kidnapping as well. Corporate insurance 101, he claimed, especially in this day and age when executives traveled to places such as South America and the Middle East, only to disappear in the middle of the night. Except Justin never traveled to any of those places, I thought. But apparently, he still had kidnapping insurance, and by extension, Ashlyn and I did as well.

Ashlyn perked up. "How much are Mom and I worth?"

Justin hesitated. "One mil. Each."

"Cool!" Our daughter found this exciting. "And you?"

"Don't remember . . . couple mil maybe."

Ashlyn rolled her eyes at me. "Why are the men always worth more?"

"You don't want to provide too much incentive," Justin said, tone still deadly serious. "The point of insurance is to cover worst-case scenarios, while not making the insured—say, you or your mother or myself—appear so valuable that you become a target."

He looked at me, and once again, wordless communication passed. Such as, while individually our abduction would not earn enough money to significantly compensate a trio of commandos, our family as a whole was worth at least four million, possibly more, if the commandos planned on stretching above the policy limit. For example, perhaps Z figured that if the insurance would kick in four million, then the company, Denbe, ought to be good for at least another two, meaning they'd demand six million for our safe return. That would translate to two million dollars per commando. Incentive, all right.

Justin was still staring at me, and in his direct blue eyes, I saw the other piece of the puzzle, the real reason he sat so straight and grim: Whoever had come up with this scheme must know about the insurance, must know us. Factor in what Ashlyn had said, that the front door had been locked, the security system armed, and that meant they also had access to our security codes.

Someone we knew. Someone we trusted. Someone we most likely considered a friend had hired Z's team, researching our schedules, identifying this mothballed prison from Justin's work history and planning each step of this operation. Maybe that person got three million, and Z's team one apiece. Still plenty of incentive.

To betray a buddy and put his entire family at risk.

I shivered slightly. I hadn't felt so violated since . . . well, since finding another woman's sexually explicit texts on my husband's cell phone.

"They're professionals," I murmured.

He nodded slowly.

"Military backgrounds," I added. "I tried, in the infirmary, to ask Radar questions. He was careful with his replies, but he mentioned military barracks. Plus, the way they look, act . . ."

Justin wasn't speaking, but he appeared troubled. "A lot of former military in the trades," he said at last. An admission of sorts. Maybe the threat didn't come from his company specifically, but from the construction industry as a whole.

Ashlyn was studying us, picking up on the unspoken communiqués. "What?"

"Nothing," Justin said.

"Bullshit!"

"Young lady—"

"Stop it! *Stop it!*" She lurched to her feet, temper flaring. "I'm fifteen years old, Dad. I know all my swears. Shit, fuck, damn, bitch. And who are you to tell me how to talk? I've been on your job sites, I know how guys speak. What, it's good enough for you, but too real for me?"

"Pretty girls don't need to use ugly words—"

"Who says I want to be pretty? Maybe I like using ugly words. Maybe someone in this family should finally be honest about how they feel. Maybe Mom should start using the work *fuck*, instead of running around trying to be so perfect and accommodating. Maybe, if she said the word *fuck* once and a while, you wouldn't have found another woman to *fuck*. There's a thought."

Justin paled. I sat, frozen across from him, staring at my daughter as if she'd just grown two heads.

Then Justin reached up and slowly, but firmly, pinched our daughter's lips shut. "I do not want to hear that word from your mouth. Not now. Not ever. You might be fifteen, but I'm still your father and in this family, we have standards."

Ashlyn crumbled. From shock, from shame, I couldn't tell which. She collapsed on the bunk beside me, buried her face against me and wept. I stroked her long wheat-brown hair, wanting to ease the moment, but not knowing where to start.

"It's not fair," Ashlyn moaned. "You did everything to make him happy, and for what? Men are pigs. Men are pigs. *Men are pigs!*"

The way she said the words gave me a second jolt. A female didn't speak with that much vehemence in defense of another woman's feelings, but in defense of her own.

I closed my eyes, wondered what his name was, how long it had been going on and when we had all drifted so far from one another. Even nine months ago, I would've sworn we were a solid little family. Sure, Justin's job took its toll. . . . But I would've said that we loved each other, trusted each other, told each other everything.

A whole family can't fall apart just like that. Even with infidelity. There had to have been cracks, weaknesses in the foundation. But I hadn't seen them, or hadn't wanted to see them. Ashlyn was right about one thing: I did run around trying to be perfect and accommodating. I wanted my husband happy. I wanted my daughter happy. And I hadn't thought that was such a bad thing.

Justin still wasn't speaking. He watched me comfort our daughter and he didn't appear angry anymore as much as hollow.

"You shouldn't have told her so much," he said finally, to me.

"I didn't."

"I figured it out for myself," Ashlyn interjected. "I'm not an idiot, *Dad*."

She pressed her head harder against my shoulder, giving him her back. I continued to stroke her hair.

"We need to stop fighting," he tried again.

Ashlyn sobbed against me.

"We need . . ." His voice caught, he soldiered on. "We need to rest. It's been a long day. But if we just stay calm . . . They're going to ask for ransom. The company is going to pay it, and then we'll go home. Tomorrow is Sunday, so it'll probably take a few more days. But two, three days tops and this will all be over. We'll be back in our house. Everything will be okay."

Ashlyn remained with her head buried against me, so I returned Justin's look, nodding once so he knew that I had heard him. Then, because I just couldn't help it, I smiled at my husband sadly.

Poor Justin. Through sheer force of will he'd quadrupled his father's company, completed dozens of hundred-million-dollar projects and become one of the foremost names in construction. Of course he thought his word was law, that if he could think it, he could make it so.

But he was wrong about things. In a few days, this would not be all over. Kidnapping or no kidnapping, ransom or no ransom, it didn't matter.

Best I could tell, the total destruction of our family was just beginning.

Chapter 21

TEN P.M., the meeting in the conference room broke up. Not to go home. In an investigation with this much ground to cover, sleeping was a luxury reserved for people who didn't know the Denbes, had never worked with the Denbes and were not currently assigned the task of finding the Denbes.

In a missing person's case, the odds of finding the people alive diminished dramatically after the first forty-eight to seventy-two hours. Which was worrisome, because the Denbe family had now been gone for almost exactly twenty-four hours. And as of this moment, the police had no direct contact from the family, no eyewitness accounts of a kidnapping, nor any reported sightings of the family from the general public.

Tessa texted her daughter good night. She had not heard from Sophie all day, which either meant that Mrs. Ennis was doing a great job of keeping her occupied, or that Sophie was currently plotting her revenge. Tessa placed her odds at fifty-fifty, then told herself to let it go.

If Sophie was upset, that was a conversation for later.

Right now, the Denbe family needed her more.

Tessa joined the blond FBI agent, Nicole, and the burly sergeant, Wyatt Foster. They were interviewing Anita Bennett first, and not only was Bennett Tessa's paying client, but as COO, the person most in the know about possible corporate scandals.

Anita led them to her office. An expansive corner suite with light wood-paneled walls, a stunning Boston view and its own leather sofa. Definitely some money in the construction biz.

Tessa wondered how hard Anita had worked to get this office, a top woman in a predominantly male industry. She had a feeling that for all of the room's opulence, this was mostly the place where Anita worked, worked and worked some more.

She took a seat on the chocolate-colored sofa. The blond FBI agent positioned herself in a hardback chair directly in front of Anita's desk. The North Country detective didn't sit at all, but leaned casually against the wall. He seemed enamored by the fine wood paneling, running one hand along the grain.

Decent-size guy, Tessa thought. She'd place him mid-forties, aging well. Not a big talker, but he had a look about him. Deep thinker, she predicted. The kind who knew a lot more than he let on. Worked the good-old-boy routine, then emptied your wallet in poker.

She made a mental note never to gamble with him, but perhaps buy him a beer. A little collegial warm-up, and he probably had some insights worth hearing.

Special Agent Nicole Adams started with general background. When had Anita first started in Denbe Construction? Her subsequent rise within the corporation?

Anita smiled, clasped her hands and placed them on the desk. "Believe it or not, I've been with Denbe thirty-five years. I started fresh out of school. Which gives me the dubious distinction of being the company's longest-serving employee. Not counting Justin, I suppose, though he was just a teenager back then."

"So you worked for Justin's father?" Tessa spoke up.

"That's right. I was Dale's secretary. Business was much smaller then. Operated out of an old warehouse in Waltham. But construction is construction. One of those businesses where the more things change, the more they stay the same."

"You went from secretary to COO?" Special Agent Adams quizzed. "That's quite a career trajectory."

"Well, you know, thirty-five years later . . ." Anita's smile was more wistful now. The good old days. "Dale was a hard-ass. No doubt about that. Much of Justin's management style still comes from his father—be the first on site and the last to leave. Demand the most from your employees, but also treat them with respect. Dale was famous for free-beer Fridays. The guys would wrap up for the week, then hang out in the warehouse kicking back with six-packs. You can't do that sort of thing anymore, of course, the liability alone would kill us. But free-beer Fridays wasn't just about rewarding the crew; it was about bonding. Making the employees also feel like part of the family. Justin has continued that tradition in his own style. He and Libby are famous for dinner parties with the crew, Sunday afternoon cookouts. Speaking as a key member of Justin's management team, I've never felt that I work *for* him, as much as I work *with* him to continue the great tradition of this company."

"Great family," Special Agent Adams repeated evenly. "Great company. Great family company."

Anita beamed, nodding shortly.

Special Agent Adams leaned forward and stated coolly, "Please stop wasting our time."

The COO startled. Tessa felt her own eyes widen, while against the wall, she watched the sheriff's detective quickly suppress a grin.

"We are not shareholders. We are not with the Better Business Bureau, nor are we prospective clients. We are here to locate and assist Justin, Libby and Ashlyn Denbe. To be even more frank, we have roughly twenty-four hours to get that job done, or chances are, you won't see any of them alive again. Do you understand?"

Slowly, the COO nodded.

"Now, to do our job," Special Agent Adams explained briskly, "we require information. Better yet, we need unvarnished truths. To start with, you went from secretary to COO. How do you account for that level of success, especially as a woman succeeding in a predominantly male industry?"

Anita's lips thinned. She answered the question in the same brusque tone the FBI agent had used to ask it.

"By working twice as hard as everyone else, of course. Look, Justin's father was hardly an enlightened male. Dale liked to have a pretty receptionist, and thirty-five years ago, I fit that bill quite nicely. But I was also smart. It didn't take me long to see that Dale needed help with more than answering phones. He was terrible with paperwork, notorious for losing contracts and a train wreck at account management. I started with arranging his calendar, then took over organizing the entire office. While I was at it, I also started making phone calls, finding vendors who could supply us with cheaper office supplies, then better health insurance, then better workman's comp. Dale might have been a chauvinist pig, but even he recognized that he was saving tens of thousands of dollars a year. As I said *honestly* before, Dale was always one to treat his employees with respect. I proved my value, and he promoted me accordingly. By the time he died, I was already running the admin side of things. As Justin grew the company, so did the complexity of our operations. I moved into chief of operations accordingly."

"Tell us about Justin. When did he take over the company?"

"He was twenty-seven when Dale died—"

"How did his father die?"

"Heart attack. Dropped dead in the office. Dale was a work-hard, play-hard kind of guy, with the play-hard side of the equation including copious amounts of red meat and hard alcohol."

"Women?" Tessa spoke up from the couch.

The COO flicked her a glance. For a second, Tessa thought she'd refuse to answer, but then: "Given that Dale himself hardly kept it a secret," Anita said tightly, "yes, he maintained a pretty *active* social life outside his marriage."

"How'd Justin's mom take it?" Tessa asked curiously.

"Drank a lot. Martinis mostly. Then would come to the office and scream at Dale over the latest discovery. At which point, he'd promise her a new car, or a fur coat, or a trip to the Bahamas to patch things up."

"You seem to know a lot about the couple's marriage," Special Agent Adams observed.

Anita smiled again but was not amused. "Like I said, Dale hardly kept things a secret. I suppose also, it's the nature of a family-run business. The employees get to know the family, almost as well as the business."

"Is Justin like his father?" Tessa again.

"Yes and no. Dale groomed Justin. From the time the boy could walk, he was the designated heir to Denbe Construction. Other sixteen-year-olds went to the beach. The summer I started with Dale, he'd just shipped his son off to work eighty-hour weeks with a drywalling firm. Dale believed firmly in hands-on education. And learning the trades inside and out. The more you know, he'd say, the less they can rip you off."

"Justin didn't mind?" Special Agent Adams.

"Best any of us could tell, he loved it. So, yes, from that perspective, Justin is very much like his father. He's a hands-on boss. Extremely dedicated and hardworking, which in turn inspires the loyalty of that bunch of reprobates that pass as his crew."

Anita uttered the term *reprobates* with a touch of affection. So apparently, they had inspired her respect in return.

"So he maintained his father's work ethic." Wyatt finally spoke up, pushing away from the wall. "That's how he's like his father?"

"Yes."

"And the ways he isn't?"

Again, that faint hesitation. Tessa was noticing a trend: Denbe employees seemed very comfortable talking about the business, say, Chris Lopez explaining the business model, or Anita talking about the company's history. But those same insiders suddenly clammed up tight when it came to talking about their boss's personal life. Loyalty? Fear? Or an almost cult-like need to never violate the code of the inner sanctum?

"Justin's parents hardly had a happy marriage," Anita said at last. "Then, when Dale died and Mary learned that he'd left the entire company to Justin, well, she didn't take that very well. In fact, she's never spoken to Justin since."

"Dale disinherited his wife. Gave it all to his son?" Special Agent Adams, frowning.

"Yes, which she took personally. Except, rather than hate Dale, which would've made sense, she took out her rage on Justin. Moved to Arizona and cut him out of her life completely. She's never met Libby, let alone her granddaughter."

The office fell silent as the three investigators digested this.

"Meaning," Anita said after another moment, "that Libby and Ashlyn are the only family Justin has left. He . . . he valued them. Maybe even placed them on a pedestal. His daughter, Ashlyn . . . he worshipped her. Brought her to the office, taught her personally how to use power tools. In fact, last I heard, they were taking shooting lessons together. Daddy-daughter day on the firing range. Go figure.

"As for Libby, I've never heard him speak of her except in glowing terms. He took pride in how she arranged their home, her success with her jewelry, then the dinner parties she'd host on his behalf . . . I always felt that he genuinely loved her, was openly appreciative of how lucky he was to have her. But that's not to say he didn't make mistakes."

Anita's gaze was on Tessa now, no doubt recalling her earlier question about the company's future in the event of a divorce.

"He cheated on Libby." Tessa stated it as a fact, not a question.

"Yes."

"You knew?"

"Most of us heard about it eventually. Late spring, early summer? Justin started showing up late at work, looking haggard, not himself. Eventually, the story came out."

"What did he have to say?" Special Agent Adams.

"He didn't. I mean, certainly I never heard him . . . make excuses. He screwed up. He knew he screwed up. He was raised in that kind of marriage. He had a firsthand seat to just how damaging infidelity can be. Though, of course . . ."

"Yes?" Special Agent Adams pressed.

Anita sighed, gazing at the two female investigators as if they had the best shot at understanding: "In the immediate aftermath, he sent Libby a diamond necklace. A rather large and flamboyant diamond necklace. Just because you know better doesn't mean you can't be stupid."

"What did Libby do?" Tessa asked.

"Being a jewelry designer with a nice collection of tools, she apparently took the necklace apart, link by link, and left it in a pile on the front seat of his car. After that, I believe he got the message."

"Were they going to counseling?" Wyatt again.

"I don't know those kinds of details. But they were working on their marriage. Justin had moved back into the house. And certainly, all day Friday he kept talking about their upcoming dinner at Scampo. He sounded excited for it."

Tessa leaned forward. The COO's face seemed open enough, as if she'd joined their program of full disclosure. And yet . . .

"When did Justin first start cheating on his wife?"

Anita stiffened. "What do you mean?"

"Come on, a guy as good-looking as him. Had a job that kept him on the road. Plus, like you said, grew up with a father who apparently thought a hard day's work justified a hard night's play. Did Justin really believe in being more faithful to his wife, or was he just better at covering his tracks?"

"I don't get involved—"

"Sure you do. You're the chief of a family-owned business. In your own words, that involves dealing with the family, as much as the business. Six months ago, this family fell apart. Libby discovered Justin had been cheating on her with a travel agent downstairs. What else did she finally figure out?"

"Ashlyn," the COO said abruptly.

"What about Ashlyn?"

"She came to the office, three months ago. She confronted the girl Justin was rumored to be involved with. And she made quite a scene."

ANITA HAD JUST BEEN ENTERING THE BUILDING when she'd heard the commotion. Ashlyn Denbe, still clad in her private-school uniform of green-and-blue plaid, was screaming at one of the dark-haired young travel agents. Words such as *slut*, *whore*, *cunt*.

The travel agent was standing there, shell-shocked, when Anita had intervened. She'd dragged Ashlyn upstairs to the relative privacy of Anita's office—Justin had been out of town on business, thank goodness. Anita had barely gotten the door shut when Ashlyn had burst into tears.

She hated travel agents. She hated this building. She hated Denbe Construction. But most of all she hated her father. All these years, preaching honor and loyalty, then he'd gone and cheated on her mother. Now their family was a mess, and her mom was a mess and it was all his fault. She wished he were dead.

Anita sighed heavily. "Teenage girls," she murmured. "Thank God, I have three boys instead."

"What did you do?" asked Special Agent Adams.

"Informed her of the facts of life. What had happened had happened, and there was nothing she could do about it now. Then I told her to go home and stay there. No returning to this building, no yelling at travel agents. This was her parents' business, not hers."

"And how did she take that?"

"Glared at me mutinously." Anita rolled her eyes. "Teenage girls," she murmured again.

"Did she return?"

"Not that I heard of. It's possible. I also informed her that if I saw her again, I'd tell her mother. Libby didn't deserve that kind of added stress, and Ashlyn knew it. The girl is loyal to her mother. She's just . . . hurt. Fathers aren't supposed to be human, you know, especially not the ones who've raised their girls to be Daddy's little princesses."

"Sounds to me that family was still going through a rough patch." Special Agent Adams, clearly fishing.

The COO shrugged, not taking the bait.

Wyatt's question was more direct. "Talk to us about divorce. Date night doesn't do the trick, Libby decides to go ahead and hire a lawyer. What happens to the family firm?"

For a change, Anita seemed genuinely perplexed. "I . . . I don't know. Justin is the sole shareholder. He was wealthy when he first met Libby, so there may be a prenup. If not, I would assume she'd be entitled to fifty percent of their assets, which would include fifty percent of the business."

"Hefty price to pay for an *active* social life," Tessa said dryly.

"Do the crime, serve the time," Anita answered just as succinctly.

"You think Justin would be willing to part with half his firm?" Wyatt again, his tone patient but probing.

"I don't . . . I can't answer that."

Which Tessa personally took to mean no. Protect the boss, that seemed to be

Denbe Construction's standard operating procedure. Meaning if they weren't answering a question, there was something they didn't want you to hear.

"And if he dies?" Wyatt again, tone still even. "If Justin Denbe isn't found alive . . . ?"

"I would assume the company reverts to his surviving family. First Libby, then Ashlyn."

"And in the event they're dead, too?"

That guarded look again. "I would think there is some kind of provision in Justin's will. You should follow up with his lawyer, Austin Ferland. He'd know."

"What about the employees?" Special Agent Adams. "In the event that the entire Denbe family died, would there be an opportunity for, say, the core management team to purchase the company?"

Anita's gaze definitely sliding sideways . . .

"Ever try to buy in before?" Wyatt, piling on. "After all, hundred-mil company, you got thirty-five years of blood, sweat and tears tied up into it. Why should Justin have all the glory?"

"We would never try to take over—"

"Not saying take over. Just . . . buy in. Happens. Hardworking employees get to become profit-worthy shareholders. Ever approach Justin? Raise the question?"

"Once." She said the word grudgingly. "Cash flow was tight. Some of us, myself included, offered to invest into the company in exchange for an ownership stake."

"Define others?" Special Agent Adams, clearly intrigued by this line of questioning.

"Myself, Chris Lopez, Ruth Chan. It was a win-win proposition. Doesn't matter, though. Justin declined. He felt the company could weather the economic downturn, which it did."

"Except, you still didn't have an equity stake to benefit from its hundred-million-dollar success."

"Our bonuses were particularly large that year," Anita replied curtly.

But even Tessa could read between those lines. A bonus wasn't the same as ownership. Clearly, Justin Denbe didn't share his toys. Which already made Tessa wonder what he'd do in the event of a divorce. If he wasn't willing to share the company with his most trusted management team, would he really share it with his jilted ex-wife?

"Besides," Anita continued, "I wouldn't

include myself as a prospective buyer any-more. In the last few years, there's been a shift in the industry. We're a design-and-build firm, and unfortunately for us, the future of institutional construction seems to be companies that can design, build *and* operate. For example, a fully turnkey company that designs, builds, then runs the senior care facility on behalf of the state. Justin himself doesn't believe this mega model will last. He's convinced that, eventually, the operating costs of running these facilities will overextend the private firms just as much as it did the government agencies. Or, perhaps more prophetically, there will be some kind of scandal—an escape at a major prison, a death at a senior home—that will cause public backlash toward private handling of public institutions. But, in the meantime, given the number of jobs on which we've recently been outbid . . ." The COO thinned her lips, stopped talking.

"Tensions are high?" Special Agent Adams asked.

"We have the necessary cash reserves," Anita replied, which Tessa took to mean that tensions were very high, and in fact, the future of Justin's hundred-million-dollar firm wasn't so certain after all. Interesting. If memory served, just an hour ago, in the conference room, the COO had stated emphatically that Justin had no angst over the future of the company and all was well on the corporate front. Now, suddenly the future wasn't so bright, and here was a thought—Justin's disappearance/untimely demise might allow for a significant change in corporate direction, possibly even save a sinking ship. Seemed like the column for winners in the event of Justin Denbe's death was steadily racking up names.

"However," Anita said abruptly, as if she'd read Tessa's mind, "even if this firm ceased to exist, most people around here would survive just fine. There are old-timers"—she used the word dryly—"such as myself, who've logged enough of the good years, stuffing our mattresses. As for the younger guys, Chris and his crew, most of them could easily find a similar job at a rival firm with very little fuss. At the end of the day, this is all just . . . business." Anita waved her hand. "And what about a day's work is worth harming someone over?"

Good question, Tessa thought, and yet people got killed over money and business transactions all the time.

"Would you like to know the true paradox of the Denbe male?" Anita asked abruptly.

"By all means," Tessa assured her.

"They may not be faithful, but they are loyal. Dale loved Mary. Justin, from everything I've ever seen, loves his wife, too. He would never choose divorce. And he would certainly never do anything to harm his family. Especially not Ashlyn. Dear God . . . I mean, maybe if only Libby were missing, some of your questions would make more sense. But you can ask anyone, everyone . . . Justin Denbe would never harm a hair on his daughter's head. And if you understand that most of us here have watched Ashlyn grow up before our eyes . . . We'd never harm her, either. Whatever has happened . . . we're not the problem. Justin's not the problem."

"Then who is?" Tessa couldn't help herself.

"I don't know. The kind of person who is heartless enough to attack an entire family. I mean, why?"

"Question of the day," Tessa assured her. Personal or professional. Ransom or revenge?

"There is, maybe . . . one last thing."

They glanced at Anita expectantly. "Last time I saw Libby was several weeks ago. She came in to sign some forms. She seemed . . . off. Actually, I had a flashback to Mary Denbe and her four-martini lunches. Except, Libby didn't smell like alcohol."

"You think she was under the influence?" Special Agent Adams pressed.

"I would guess she was on something, you know, trying to dull her pain. I almost said something to Justin, but then I thought, they're already dealing with so much . . . We're pulling for them. Despite what you may think, each of us here, we're hoping the marriage works out. Once upon a time, they were such a great couple. We remember those days, even if they don't."

Anita seemed to finally run out of things to say. With no more revelations, they wrapped up the interview and exited the office. It was now after midnight. The other officers had already completed their interviews, the conference room deserted when they reentered it.

Just to be sure, Special Agent Adams walked the perimeter, peering through the frosted glass panes that overlooked the rest of the offices.

"The Boston detectives recovered a prescription bottle for hydrocodone in Libby Denbe's purse," she stated without preamble. "Filled two days ago, already one-third empty."

Wyatt picked up the thought trail first. "Libby was abusing painkillers."

"According to the pill count on the bottle, she'd taken twenty pills in just two days . . ."

"Can't just be one prescription, then," Wyatt mused. "Not if she's using at that level."

"Doctor shopping," Tessa supplied. "A woman of her socioeconomics. Most likely she's going from doctor to doctor, cataloging fictional pains."

Wyatt turned to Nicole. "You said the prescription bottle was in her purse?" he asked.

She nodded.

"Meaning it was left behind."

"Makes sense," the blonde replied. "Their personal possessions were all piled on the kitchen island."

Tessa got it, the point Wyatt was trying to make. "Detox," she murmured.

The New Hampshire detective glanced at her, nodding appraisingly. "And how. Wonder if her abductors expected that little development. That one of their abductees would"—he glanced at his watch—"right about now start suffering from extremely painful, extremely high-maintenance withdrawal symptoms."

Special Agent Adams turned at the end of the table. "She might even need medical care."

"Avenues to start pursuing," Wyatt said thoughtfully. "Assuming the kidnappers are willing to risk discovery by taking her to a local hospital. But, yeah, I'll put out a bulletin to keep an eye on emergency rooms for a woman matching Libby Denbe's description."

"You think they're still alive?" Tessa couldn't help herself. She glanced at the FBI agent, then the New Hampshire sheriff's detective. They both shrugged.

"Don't know," Special Agent Adams replied honestly, "though I certainly hope so."

"I still put the odds in our favor," Wyatt said. "If they wanted the family dead, no reason they couldn't have taken care of business up close and personal, then left behind three bodies. The use of Tasers suggests to me there's more at play here than simply eliminating the family."

Tessa nodded, if only because it was late, and given their lack of immediate progress, she needed something to believe in.

"Tell you something else," Wyatt continued. "This company, these people"—he grimaced—"what a bunch of liars."

He said it so flatly, Tessa almost burst out laughing. But she recovered herself quickly enough to ask, "What makes you say that?"

"They've all got Justin Denbe's back, except, you know, when they're trying to buy his company. And the business is doing great, except, of course, there's this whole new branch of mega-corporations that are stealing their jobs. Oh yeah, and they don't know anything about the family's secrets, except of course, when they *are* the family secret."

"Who's the family secret?" Special Agent Adams, looking confused.

"Anita Bennett. You didn't pick up on that?"

"Pick up on what?"

Wyatt gave them both a look. "The expression on her face every time she said Justin's father's name. Telling you now, she wasn't just one of Dale's employees. She was one of his conquests. That whole unfaithful but loyal speech? Because Dale was unfaithful with her but remained loyal to his wife. Meaning when he died, both of the women in his life got shafted."

"Mary left, Anita stayed behind," Tessa murmured. "Continuing to rise up the corporate ranks, but thirty-five years later, still just an employee, never an owner."

"Some people might get a little bitter about that," Wyatt observed.

Special Agent Adams smiled for the first time all night. It was a particularly scary look for her. "And some people might decide to finally take what they believe they so richly deserve."

Chapter 22

THEY TOOK JUSTIN AWAY.

Ashlyn had fallen asleep. I was drifting in and out, exhaustion dragging me under only for an achy, restless pain to prick me back to consciousness. My concussion, withdrawal, who knew. I dreamed of dark, turbulent seas, monsters and bared fangs and striking cobras. Then I would wake up, curled into a ball, shaking uncontrollably, head nearly shattering in agony.

I don't think Justin was sleeping. Each time my eyes opened, I would find him standing at the cell door, shoulders back, face tense, a caged beast still seeking a way out. Or maybe a sentry, standing guard.

Either way, it didn't save him.

The door blew open. That's how it felt. I had dozed off, then suddenly, *bam!*

The steel door, flying open, two intruders pouring in. They each bore mattresses, held as shields below their dark helmeted heads. Faceplates obscured their features, until they appeared as dark, armor-plated beetles coming to get us. One of my own crazy dreams coming to life.

They were shouting, wielding clubs. The largest went straight after Justin, knocking him to the floor and beating him with a stick. *Bam, bam, bam.* Then the second was on Ashlyn, who was asleep on the lower bunk. A rabid beetle pouncing on her with the mattress, smothering her down.

I heard muffled screams, then I toppled off the top bunk, rolling onto the back of the beetle from hell. I whacked instinctively at his shoulders, except everything I smacked was padded or plated. My fists were useless. My daughter screamed and I hit and none of it made a difference.

Justin shouting from the floor: "I'll go, I'll

go. Just leave them alone. Leave my family the fuck alone!"

That quickly, Ashlyn's attacker straightened, removing the mattress from her body, brushing me off his back. I fell hard, catching myself at the last second with my hands, because my head had already suffered enough.

Justin, already dragged to his feet, lurched to standing near the open cell door. Blood on the corner of his mouth, hands manacled before him.

His attacker grabbed his cuffed wrists and dragged him away.

Our attacker had his shield once again positioned against his body. He eased backward toward the open door. At the last moment, he flipped up his faceplate.

Mick smiled, blew us a kiss. Most fun he'd had in ages, you could see it on his face. Couldn't wait to do it again.

Then he stepped out, the steel door clanged shut and Ashlyn and I were alone.

WE DIDN'T CRY. By mutual consent, we curled up on the top bunk, out of immediate reach of smothering beetles. From this vantage point, I could see out the narrow window to a dark, dark sky. Still middle of the night, not even the next day, and yet it already felt like we'd been in this hellhole forever.

My daughter lay on her side, with her back to me. I put my arm around her waist, my face against the top of her hair.

When she was little, Ashlyn used to creep into our room. Never say a word. I'd simply open my eyes and find her standing next to my side of the bed, a pale little ghost. I would lift the covers and she'd crawl in next to me, our secret as Justin didn't approve of such things.

I never minded, though. Even then, I knew these moments wouldn't last forever. That the first five years of my daughter's life, for all of the exhausting sleeplessness, were one of the only times she would truly belong to me. First, she'd learn to crawl, then walk, then run away on her own.

So I liked to hold her close, smell the baby shampoo scent of her hair. Feel her like a hot little furnace, nuzzled up next to me.

My girl wasn't little anymore. At fifteen, she stood at nearly my height. And yet her rib cage still felt so slight. She was growing like a colt, all skinny arms and legs. Given Justin's size, she would probably top my head next year. It was one of those things, I guessed. She'd always be my little girl and yet, she never would be again.

My body started to shake, my stomach cramping. I willed the tremors away, but they didn't listen.

"Mom?" my daughter asked. Her voice was soft, subdued.

I brushed back her long wheat-brown hair, and for the first time in a long time, my own weakness shamed me. I never should've taken that first pill. I never should've let something as stupid and pathetic as my husband's affair become an excuse to fall apart. Maybe my marriage was done. But I still had motherhood. How had I forgotten about that?

"My concussion," I mumbled, a vague enough excuse.

My daughter wasn't fooled. She rolled over, staring at me. She had my eyes, everyone always said that. Not gold, not green. Somewhere in between. She was beautiful and smart, and growing up too fast. I touched her cheek, and for once, she didn't flinch.

"I'm sorry," I said. My brow was starting to sweat. I could feel the beads of moisture, except in my hazy state, they felt less like water, more like blood.

"You need your pills," she said.

"How did . . ." I wasn't sure I wanted to know.

"I've been going through your purse," my daughter stated matter-of-factly. "And your cell phone. Dad's, too. Both of you, you didn't just stop speaking to each other. You stopped speaking to me."

I didn't say anything, just searched her gaze, tried to find myself in my teenager's unflinching stare. "We love you. That will never change."

"I know."

"Sometimes, parents have to be people, too."

"I don't want people," she said. "I want my mom and dad."

She rolled back over. Then my time was up. One side effect of taking an opiate: severe constipation. Meaning once you go off that drug, your body has some catching up to do.

I made it to the toilet just in time.

The diarrhea was violent and smelly and

awful. I would've cried, except between the chronic vomiting, sweating and now this, my body didn't have any moisture left.

Ashlyn remained on the top bunk, did her best to give me privacy. Not that it really mattered anymore.

I was being broken down, I thought, clutching my cramping stomach. Devolving from human to animal. From a respectable wife and mother who once knew her place in the world, to a woman who might as well collapse in a gutter.

Then, the worst of the diarrhea was over. All that remained was shaking and sweating and aching and the deepest, darkest despair.

I made it off the toilet. Curled up on the floor.

And waited for the world to end.

LATER, Ashlyn told me that Radar came. He had a jug of water, a pile of towels and a bunch of pills. An antidiarrheal, some acetaminophen, an antihistamine. It took both Radar and Ashlyn to get the pills down my throat.

Then Radar was gone, and Ashlyn was left with the task of dampening towels and wiping my face. She couldn't figure out how to move me to the bunk, so she sat with me on the floor.

At one point, I remember opening my eyes, watching her watch me.

"You're going to be okay," she murmured. Then, "I don't feel sorry for you, Mom. It's the least you deserve."

Except later, I heard her crying, hushed, wracking sobs and I tried to touch her face, tried to tell her she was right and I was wrong, but I couldn't move my arms. I was underwater again, sinking down, down, down, watching my daughter drift away from me.

"I hate you," my daughter was saying. "I fucking hate both of you. You cannot leave me like this. You can't *leave me.*"

And I didn't blame her. In fact, I wanted to tell her I understood. I hated my father, too, because he hadn't wanted to wear a helmet. And I hated my mother, who even when we couldn't afford dinner, always had a fresh pack of cigarettes. Why were parents so weak, so fallible? Why couldn't my own parents have seen how much I loved them, needed them beside me?

They died, leaving behind the kind of

void that is never filled, a relentless ache that follows an abandoned child through-out her entire life. And I stood alone, a pil-lar of brittle strength until the day I met Justin. Wonderful, gorgeous, larger-than-life Justin. Who swept me off my feet and made me feel beautiful and loved and de-sired beyond all reason. And now we were living happily ever after, the king and queen of Camelot.

I think I might have started giggling. Maybe I laughed until I cried, because the next thing I knew, my daughter was once again in focus and this time Ashlyn's face was frightened, and she kept saying, "Please Mom, please Mom, please Mom," and that shamed me all over again.

I was supposed to take care of my daugh-ter, not the other way around. I was sup-posed to keep her safe.

Radar reappeared. He did not look at me. He did not speak to my daughter.

He had another handful of pills.

These ones got the job done. My aches and pains disappeared. The dark void whittled down, down, down. My panting, shivering and sweating stopped.

My body stilled.

I slept.

After a bit, my daughter curled up on the floor beside me. This time with her arm around my waist, her face pressed against my hair.

She slept, too.

For a moment.

THE CELL DOOR EXPLODED OPEN. The first armored beetle rushed in, screaming and yelling and wielding his mattress, jerking us once again from slumber to full alertness.

The beetle whacked us with his mattress. Yelled at us to get up, up, up.

On the floor, my daughter's arm tightened around my waist. I wrapped my fingers around her hand and held on tight.

Don't let her go don't let her go don't let her go. She is mine they cannot have her.

More screaming, more yelling, more whacking.

Mick, finally releasing his shield, grabbing Ashlyn's shoulders, trying to physically yank her up off the floor. Me, gripping tighter. Him, pulling, pulling, pulling, so relentlessly, freakishly strong.

Our hands parted, Ashlyn's fingers slipping through mine.

Mick lifted her away from me.

I staggered to my feet and kicked him in the balls.

More protective padding, but maybe not foolproof. Mick fell back, released Ashlyn, considered me instead. This time, I kicked his knee, then rained feeble, kitten-like blows at his kidney. I had virtually no strength, could barely stand, but I didn't pause. I just kicked and hit and hit and kicked, until he finally fumbled for his mattress shield and Ashlyn bolted away, up onto the top bunk, where she formed a crouch, as if preparing to launch at him.

Suddenly, a fresh set of hands, huge, ungodly strong, lifted me off the floor and held me in midair. Ashlyn's eyes went wide in her face.

Z stating quietly, his voice an inch from my ear: "Mick, you are a fucking waste of human DNA. Stop dicking around and get the job done."

Mick didn't reach for Ashlyn, but huffed out of the cell.

Z set me back down, his hands still holding me firmly in place. His next command was directed at my daughter: "You. Sit."

She sat.

Then Mick returned, except this time he wasn't alone. He shoved Justin before him, my husband stumbling toward the nearest bunk, grabbing for the metal frame to support himself.

Z released my shoulders, and as quickly as they'd come, both men disappeared.

Justin looked up, his formerly handsome face now beaten nearly beyond recognition.

"Libby," he whispered. "Libby. I was wrong. We have . . . to get . . . out of here."

Then, my husband collapsed into a bloody heap upon the floor.

Chapter 23

WYATT COULDN'T SLEEP. He didn't mind sleep. Had nothing against it. But tonight, after a long investigative day tackling a high-stakes case, his brain wouldn't shut up. He lay in the moderately priced hotel Kevin had found using the modern miracle of their vehicle's built-in navigation system, and his brain was running a mile a minute.

His current 2:00 A.M. musing: Why a whole family?

So far, most theories of the case had to do with financial gain. After all, Justin Denbe was a wealthy man, heading an even bigger dollar corporation. A guy like that gets Tasered and abducted from his elite Boston brownstone, money was the first thing that sprang to mind.

According to his company, he carried an insurance policy making him worth a cool two mil—hard to argue with that. And looking at the company itself—going through a difficult industry transition, maybe some infighting among the management team—you could see where a key player might perceive gain if Justin didn't show up for a bit. Hell, maybe a good old-fashioned kidnapping would sour Justin on the whole business. He'd step aside permanently, allowing either the old guard, or the new blood, to take over the reins and move the business triumphantly into the full glory of design, build, operate.

Whatever.

Wyatt wasn't into businesses. He was into people. Case like this, no matter where you started, would never end up being about P and Ls. It would be about people, what made them tick, and what made some of them tick differently.

Which brought him back to his first thought: Best they could tell, there were a couple of lucrative reasons for kidnapping Justin Denbe, but why his whole family?

Kidnapping three was tricky. For one thing, you immediately added coconspirators in crime, and if there was a coconspirator out there who could keep a secret, a prison official hadn't met him yet. Second, the logistics increased exponentially. Transportation—now you had multiple perpetrators *and* multiple victims. Hell, getting from point A to point B was no longer neat and discreet, but involved a regular party boat. Might as well rent a stretch limo and call it a day.

Then, lodging. Where do you put that many people? Granted, this is where northern New Hampshire made sense, especially this time of year. Some of the campgrounds involved decent-size seasonal lodges. They'd be a bitch to heat, and uncomfortable as hell, as they weren't meant for winter occupancy, but they'd definitely provide a private, inconspicuous way to house a bunch of hostages.

Of course, now you gotta feed a whole party as well. And sure, you can stock these lodges; that's what happened in the summer months. But it still involved *effort*. Trips to the grocery store, which as an experienced shopper himself, Wyatt knew were nearly impossible to get right the first time. You always forgot something on the list. Or, something unexpected came up—say a rich Boston wife suddenly going through opiate withdrawal and now requiring aspirin and Imodium and all sorts of TLC.

Work, work, work.

Risk, risk, risk.

If these guys were truly professionals, why expose themselves to the hazards of grabbing an entire family? Especially if the most financial gain could be made by simply kidnapping Justin himself?

Wyatt didn't like it.

Two A.M. to three A.M. to four A.M.

Why take the entire family? Why not just kidnap Justin Denbe?

And thirty hours later, where the hell was the ransom demand?

WYATT ROLLED OUT OF BED AT SIX. He showered, which made him feel moderately human, then shaved, which definitely made him feel better, and finally changed into a fresh uniform he kept packed in a duffel bag, because in his line of work, an initial call out had been known to involve several days away from home.

Too early to call the North Country yet. If his people had real news, either from the hotline or direct public contact or from the campground searches, they would've let him know, regardless of the hour. His cell phone had no messages, same with his voice mail, which led him to believe they were still in the all-pain, no-gain phase of their investigation. Fair enough.

HE HEADED DOWNSTAIRS to retrieve a fax from the Boston PD, and found Kevin already in the lobby, holding two large cups of Dunkin' Donuts coffee.

"Good man," Wyatt said, grabbing the thick bundle of papers, then accepting the offered coffee. He looked around. The lobby was deserted.

"They provide a continental breakfast," Kevin commented. "Can you believe it doesn't open till seven thirty on a Sunday?"

Wyatt grunted, took a sip. He liked Dunkin' Donuts regular. Nearly white with cream and heavy with sugar. Good stuff.

"Sleep?" Kevin asked.

"Who needs it? You?"

"I watched pay-per-view. But not porn. I know they make this big deal about *none* of the movie titles showing up on the hotel bill, but that just makes everyone look like they've been viewing porn."

"Good to know."

"You don't talk much in the morning."

"And you talk entirely too much."

The men headed for a small table in the common room. No one around, so they didn't have to worry about prying eyes or keen hearing.

"Game plan for the day?" Kevin asked.

"Stick around. Unless we get a development from up north, only real crime scene is here, not to mention all the players are in the city as well. Tricky, trying to profile an entire family. The number of interviews, background reports . . . We need more manpower. 'Course, we don't have it to give."

"FBI will start throwing more bodies at it, especially now that the family's beyond the twenty-four-hour mark," Kevin said. "Won't have a choice. It's been, what, a day and a half, and we have no leads, not even a ransom demand."

"FBI's gonna set up a command center. I'm guessing they'll bring in a mobile unit, park it in front of the Denbes' town house. They'll be thinking seriously about preparing for contact from the kidnappers, wiring the house, tapping the landlines, all that stuff. I bet they keep the Denbes' mobile phones as well. Just in case a call comes through them."

"Can you text a ransom demand?" Kevin mused. "Especially on the teenager's cell. There's something suitably ironic about that."

"Hell, if you can sext, why not ransom text? Textortion? Sounds good to me."

Kevin took a sip of his own coffee. "So what do you think of Tessa Leoni? You got to interview with her last night."

Wyatt shrugged. "She asked good questions. Can't get a vibe on her relationship with Denbe Construction, though. On the one hand, they're her client, on the other hand, it seemed to be her first time meeting any of them."

"First," Kevin confirmed. "Looked it up last night. Denbe has had Northledge on retainer for the past seven years, but it doesn't appear to be a major account.

Northledge probably provides routine background checks on prospective employees, that sort of thing, which is handled lower on the Northledge food chain than Tessa Leoni. Her boss saves her for more strategic situations."

"This would be a situation needing some strategy," Wyatt concurred, but he was frowning. "She seems kind of young to be the investigative big guns."

"Twenty-nine. Served four years as a Massachusetts state police trooper. Two years at Northledge."

"Twenty-nine? Shit, that's barely out of investigative diapers."

"She seems to be able to make it work," Kevin said. "Her last employee review was positively glowing."

"How can you know that? Seriously? From surfing the Internet in the middle of the night?"

"Oh, you'd be surprised."

Wyatt shook his head, finished up his coffee. "I want to head over to the Denbes' residence. So far, we're taking everyone else's word for what happened. Nothing personal, but I want to know for myself."

"We need contact," Kevin observed,

downing his own cup. "A ransom demand, something. That will get our wheels humming again."

"Nah, we don't need to wait for the kidnappers to find us. We need to use good old-fashioned investigative techniques in order for us to find them. Starting with answering my question of the day."

"Which is?"

"If this is just about money, why take the entire family?"

"Oh, I can answer that."

"Really? Dazzle me, Brainiac."

"Economies of scale. You heard the construction team's description of Justin Denbe. Big guy, handy with a gun, tough in body and spirit. Would you send one person to grab a man like that?"

Wyatt saw his point. "Guess not."

"Except, the moment you get more bodies involved, you're also slicing up the ransom pie. One guy grabbing Justin Denbe would earn two million. But three guys grabbing Justin Denbe only get six hundred sixty-six thousand six hundred and sixty-six dollars. Not nearly the same payday, given the amount of work. However, add in the wife at one mil and the daughter at another mil, and suddenly, the math becomes attractive again."

"Economies of scale. Except, the wife and child add risk, too. Three people to control, transport, house and feed. Seems like you're back to adding manpower and diluting payoff. Except . . ."

And suddenly Wyatt had it. The thought that had been with him since 2:00 A.M. Why you would take a family, and not just a man. Why a case was never about P and Ls, but always about what made people tick.

"Control," Wyatt stated, and the moment he said the word, he knew he was right. "Think about it. A guy with Justin Denbe's reputation—the kidnappers figure they'll need multiple men to grab him and even then, they're nervous. Which is an even better reason for taking the wife and daughter. Justin Denbe, on his own, might fight back. But now, with these guys holding his family . . . Whatever he tries, his wife and only child will pay the price." Wyatt paused, shook his head. "Man, these guys are good."

THEY FOUND THE DENBES' BROWNSTONE shortly after 8:00 A.M. Wyatt wasn't an ur-

ban guy, but their quaint, tree-lined ave-
nue, featuring row after row of meticulously
restored historical town houses, he could
get into. This was the face of Boston that
tourists paid good money to see. Not to
mention an architectural advertisement for
how the other half lived.

The neighborhood was quiet this early
on a Sunday morning. The street was completely lined with cars, of course. Porsche
Carreras, Volvo station wagons, Mercedes
sedans. If this is what the residents felt
comfortable parking on the street, Wyatt
could only wonder at what they had stashed
in private garages.

He didn't see any sign of a mobile command center outside the Denbes' home,
wasn't even sure where there was space
for such an immense vehicle to park. He
also couldn't make out the sign of major
police presence but figured Boston had
ordered roving patrols, that sort of thing. In
case the Denbes suddenly resurfaced. Or
even luckier for them, the kidnappers returned to the scene of the crime.

For now, the only sign that something
wicked had this way come was a relatively
discreet line of yellow crime-scene tape

across the top section of the front door. Probably to keep from over-alarming the neighbors. Or, even to maintain good relations within the community. After all, people who paid this kind of money for real estate probably didn't want any perceived disruptions to their homes' net worth.

Kevin circled the block four or five times. They finally parked in a public garage and hoofed it back. Nice morning for a walk. Chilly, as the air carried a late-fall bite. But the sun was out, the redbrick sidewalk warming and the town houses' various-colored facades glowing as they narrowed in on their target.

The Denbes' front door—dark-stained walnut, he thought—was closed. Wyatt started with the basics: He knocked.

And the door opened.

For a second, he stood there, slack-jawed. Watching the heavy wood swing open, thinking, My God, they're back! But then the walnut door completed its inward arc and he found himself staring at Tessa Leoni, in crisp black trousers and a white dress shirt. She could've been a Realtor, except for the rather large gun holstered at her hip.

"Figured you'd pay a visit," she stated without preamble. "A good investigator always has to see for himself."

She took a step back and allowed Wyatt and Kevin to enter the home.

WYATT FELL IN LOVE WITH THE STAIRCASE. He tried not to stare. Hell, it was all he could do not to run his hands over such richly grained hardwood. Mahogany, he was guessing. Freshly oiled, patina darkened. And, oh, the graceful curve of the lower landing, the hand-hewn craftsmanship of each individual spindle, the hours of meticulous, painstaking labor.

Except, then he turned away from the staircase toward the front sitting room to discover built-in shelves, a gorgeously restored fireplace mantel, the original crown dentil molding . . . He gave up. He stood in the middle of the foyer, strewn with crime-scene placards and dusted with fingerprint powder, and he beheld a carpenter's wonderland.

"Impressive, huh?" Tessa remained standing next to the door. He noticed she had a thing for personal space. And she wore her dark hair pulled back a tad too tight, as if she cared less for hairstyle and more for control.

"Holy shit," he observed politely.

She smiled, her shoulders coming down a fraction. "By all accounts, Libby Denbe was the hostess with the mostest. Had a degree in creative arts, something like that, which you can see in some of the color choices. At least, they seem very creative to me, given that my own house is mostly white, white and, well, white."

"Where do you live?"

"Just bought a little bungalow in Arlington. Small probably by New Hampshire standards, but works for me."

"You got a family?"

"A daughter." She eyed him thoughtfully, as if slightly surprised. "My husband died two years ago." Another expectant pause. Wyatt looked around the foyer. Kevin was already busy examining the evidence placards, his brow furrowed in concentration, which meant that Wyatt was on his own.

"Sorry to hear that," he drawled politely.

She smiled again, but it was ironic now. "It's because you're from New Hampshire," she murmured. "I forget, sometimes, that not everyone cares about Boston news. Would you like the nickel tour? The feebies have yet to leave their mobile command center, meaning for the moment, the place is ours."

Wyatt drew up short. "Mobile command center? Where?"

"The back alley that runs behind the townhomes. That's where everyone has garage access, parking spaces, the less glamorous stuff. That's how Back Bay works. You get these beautiful scenic streets, say, Marlborough, where you behold the front facade of each town house. Then you get a narrow back alley that runs behind it, featuring the much less glamorous rear of each building. Boston FBI pulled in last night. Big white mobile command center, very pretty on the outside, I'm betting lots of cool toys on the inside. Now, my turn: Is it just me, or do you have a history with the blond agent?"

"Nicole?" Wyatt fell in step beside Tessa and she led him away from the foyer toward what appeared to be the kitchen. "History is the operative word."

"She good?"

"I'd say so. Smart, resourceful, ambitious. If I were missing, I wouldn't mind her handling my case."

"Good to know."

Arriving in the state-of-the-art kitchen, first thing Wyatt spotted was the pile of personal possessions topping the granite island. The FBI had left the items intact, Tessa informed him, as they had some behavioral expert returning today to further study the scene. Not to mention, it wasn't necessary to remove the mobile phones to analyze them; the cellular provider had already faxed over transcripts of messages, texts and call histories.

There was something about the cache of personal possessions that bothered Wyatt. It was more than simply removing items that could be used to call for help or potentially aid in a victim's escape; it was dehumanizing. Divesting the fifteen-year-old of her metallic orange cell phone with her Swarovski crystal initials stickered on the back. Stripping off the wife's engagement ring and wedding band. Taking the husband's obviously well-used, well-loved, battered red Swiss Army knife.

It also invoked a sense of déjà vu. He had to think about it, circle the pile for a moment, consider multiple angles. Then, it came to him:

"Prison intake," he said.

Tessa glanced up from her own inspection.

"When you're first admitted into jail, they take all your personal possessions," he continued. "Jewelry, wallets, money, keys, phone, cash, everything. You place it in a pile, slide it over. That's what this looks like. Prison intake."

Tessa nodded thoughtfully. "So possibly one or more of our offenders has a history."

"Unfortunately, that doesn't limit the suspect pool much," Wyatt said dryly. "We were already thinking professionals, and many of them have logged time. You know, that way they can continue their education with even more experienced felons, while forming new alliances to assist with fresh criminal activities upon release."

"But never call you cynical."

Wyatt looked at her. "Versus your natural well of optimism?"

That smile again. Larger, more genuine. Made her look, for a second, like a woman still in her twenties. It occurred to him that Tessa Leoni's natural state seemed to be almost wary, as if on guard against some danger he hadn't identified yet. A story there. Definitely a story there.

"Pessimism is an occupational hazard," she granted. "So, one of our suspects has probably served time. Most likely, the FBI is already on it, but I'll mention it when they next emerge from their cocoon. Anything else?"

"For a crime we keep saying is financially motivated, there's a lot of financial motive right here. I mean, as long as you're grabbing a family for ransom, why leave behind the gold and diamonds? The kidnappers don't want a bonus for their efforts?"

"Disciplined," Tessa stated. "That's my theory. The kidnappers had a plan, and they stuck to it. Which scares me a little as Libby's diamond alone must be worth an easy hundred grand. If you think about it, when the other guys aren't looking, you could simply slide it in your pocket . . ."

Wyatt saw her point and it worried him a little, too. Essentially, they weren't just looking for a professional, well-disciplined predator. They were hunting a professional, well-disciplined team.

"I think they kidnapped the wife and daughter in order to better control Justin," he said abruptly. "Guy like him sounds like a natural-born fighter. With the lives of his wife and kid at stake, however . . ."

Tessa nodded shortly, that tight look back on her face. "Limits his options," she murmured. "Another argument that the abduction team did their homework and came prepared."

"But no ransom?"

"Nothing yet. Come on. I'll take you upstairs."

Upstairs turned out to be the third floor. A lot more evidence placards and signs of a struggle. Tessa walked him through the scene, the Boston cops' theories on the chain of events. It all sounded good to him. God knows, he'd never had the occasion to use urine drops to diagram a crime scene.

They completed their inspection, then Tessa once more headed downstairs. When they came to the second-floor landing, she was still walking, but he paused.

"What's here?"

"Family room, guest bedroom, library."

"I mean, in terms of the kidnapping."

She shook her head. "There isn't anything on this level."

"And the top level, above the third floor?"

"Nothing."

Wyatt frowned. "Meaning the activity was limited to the third floor, where the intruders got the girl, and the foyer, where they got the parents, then the kitchen, where they stacked the family goods after everyone had been subdued?"

Tessa nodded.

Wyatt looked at her. "Pretty precise, if you ask me. This is what, a six-thousand-square-foot town house? How many levels, how many rooms? And yet, to judge by the *lack* of evidence on certain levels, the kidnappers never wasted a step. In, out, done."

She stilled slightly, and he could see the implications sinking in. "We already figure it's an inside job—or at least, someone the Denbes knew gave out the security codes. But what you're suggesting . . ."

"They've been here before," Wyatt said bluntly. "Either as guests, or the same person who gave out the security codes also gave them a personal tour. Enough so they'd know exactly where to find Ashlyn's bedroom and precisely where to stand to grab the parents walking in."

"For that matter, they were briefed on

the family's habits," Tessa added. "Because if Libby had driven, she and Justin would've entered from the lower-level garage, but he drove, meaning they used the front door."

"Who would know such details?"

"The housekeeper, Dina Johnson. I would guess some close friends and acquaintances. Also Justin's management team, the crew we met last night. I'm told they were all frequent guests in the home, plus it makes sense Justin might have given them security access in case they needed to fetch something for him, that sort of thing."

"In other words, a decent-size pool of suspects," Wyatt said. "Who've already fed us a bunch of stories."

They'd arrived back in the main foyer. Kevin was no longer hunched over the floor, having probably worked his way to the kitchen.

"If this is about corporate gain," Tessa said, "why kidnap? How does abducting Justin and his family assist with taking over Denbe Construction?"

Wyatt considered the matter. "Missing its leader, the company goes into crisis mode, meaning the management team can assume emergency control of Denbe Construction."

"To what end? Justin is found, he takes it back over."

"Unless he's incapacitated. Hurt." Wyatt paused. "Killed."

Tessa nodded but wore a troubled frown. "It's possible. God knows, there have been enough cases involving murder-for-hire by disgruntled business partners. It's not always easy to understand what some people find worth killing over." A chiming sound came from her pocket. She pulled out her cell, glanced at the screen. "Excuse me, I have to take this."

Wyatt nodded, wandering to the family room, where he eyed the hand-carved mantel one last time, then pulled out the thick sheaf of papers from his bag, and set about reading.

Next thing he knew, Tessa Leoni was standing beside him, bouncing on the balls of her feet.

"Got it!"

"Got what?"

"The answer to my question. Wait, is that the evidence log?" She pointed to his stack of papers. "You got the FBI to share the evidence log?"

"Not the FBI. Boston cops. I found their jacket, remember, and now I'm horning in on the FBI who horned in on them. Figured the detective in charge, Neil Cap, might feel like doing me a favor."

Her eyes widened. "Well played."

"The mountains aren't all bears and moose," he assured her modestly. "Sometimes, we deal with foxes, too. Now, your answer to your question?"

"How did Libby discover her husband's affair?" she said immediately.

Wyatt blinked. Truthfully, he hadn't thought about it. "The daughter? She visited the building to check out the competition, according to Anita Bennett."

"Good guess, but according to Libby's hairdresser, Libby found out about the other woman six months ago, whereas Ashlyn showed up in the lobby only three months ago. So *how* did Libby find out? Something she saw? Or something someone said?"

Wyatt perked up. He could see where this was going now. "Interesting."

"This morning," Tessa continued, "I requested the transcript from Libby's phone.

And get this: She received a text in the beginning of June, telling her she needed to keep a better eye on her husband. Then, two days later, asking her if she knew what he was doing during lunch. Then, a third text, the day after that, telling her to check his phone messages. Now get this: The texts to Libby's phone come from a pre-paid cell, no caller ID available."

"Covering his tracks," Wyatt mused.

Tessa smiled again. And her blue eyes were definitely brighter, and her face animated, and call him crazy, but he found himself holding his breath.

"Funny that you should say *his* tracks, because my first thought was *her* tracks. And the only woman I could think of who'd be in the know is the other woman, Kathryn Chapman. So I asked one of the research analysts at Northledge to run a full background. And guess what? You were right. I think it was *his* tracks. According to my brilliant research analyst, Kathryn Chapman's uncle is none other than Justin's second in command, Chris Lopez."

Chapter 24

THE FIRST TIME I MET JUSTIN I was working at a friend's clothing boutique. I helped with customers on the weekend, while tending to my fledgling jewelry business on the side. In return, my friend paid me next to nothing but agreed to display some of my pieces.

I heard the jangle of the front door opening, looked up from a rack of scarves I was rearranging and Justin walked in.

I can tell you everything about those first fifteen minutes of our relationship. I remember his brown hair, longer then, darker, the way it fell to the side of his forehead almost boyishly. I remember the size of him, the sheer physical presence of his broad shoulders, the way he seemed to literally block the sun. He wore blue jeans, but not the designer kind. Real honest-to-God, broken-in, clinging-to-his-long-legs jeans, as well as an olive green L.L. Bean barn coat and scuffed-up work boots.

Then, his smile. Quick, instantaneous. He looked at me, he broke into a huge grin and he declared, "Thank heavens, I'm saved!"

And just like that, I was lost.

I wanted to run my fingers through that hair. I wanted to feel the hard wall of his chest. I wanted the scent of him in my nostrils. I wanted to hear the rumble of that deep voice in my ear, over and over again.

He had needed a present that day, for a female friend. I, of course, sold him one of my original necklaces.

With my phone number on the tag.

Which led to our first date, where I can tell you exactly how his face looked, a little more sheepish now, almost shy as he offered up a single yellow rose, then held out his hand to boost me into his old Range

Rover. Please excuse the mud, the scattering of pencil bits and, oh yeah, the rolls of building plans. He was in the construction business, he said, hazards of the trade.

I remember the look in his eyes the first time we made love, not that evening, though I would've. Not until date number four, and his blue eyes were so intent, so focused on my face, every sigh coming out of my mouth, every undulating move of my body, I felt as if he were trying to memorize me. This is Libby. This is what Libby likes.

Later, he confessed that he'd been nervous, and that made me laugh so hard he swore he'd never tell me a secret again.

Except he did. He told me he loved me before I ever confessed that I loved him. He told me I'd be his wife one day, before I knew it myself.

Then, that Thursday night, when he returned home from a particularly long and grueling business trip, and I greeted him with a bouquet of pink and blue balloons and the news I was pregnant, the total sea change of expressions across his face. From weary exhaustion to squinty-eyed confusion to slow-dawning joy. Followed by complete and utter adoration. He dropped his bag. He swooped me up, and the balloons broke free, escaping out the open door as we laughed, then cried, and I can taste to this day the salt on his cheeks.

The memories of a marriage. The faces of my husband. So many moments, when I saw him so clearly. So many moments, when I *know* he saw me.

Is that what you lose over time? Not so much a loss of affection, as a slow clouding of your own sight? We became less and less focal points for each other, and more like pieces of furniture to maneuver around in the course of everyday life. I know there were times in the past few months when I sat across from my husband, as high as a kite, and willed him to look at me. Then, when he continued to calmly shovel dinner into his mouth, I poured myself another glass of wine in order to fill the void.

It's hard to realize you're invisible in your own life. But maybe the blindness was mutual. Because if not for three texts sent to my cell phone, I never would've guessed Justin was having an affair. Meaning that somewhere along the lines, my own husband had also become unnoticed by me.

But I was seeing him now.

I traced the swelling of his right eye. The five lacerations on his cheek. The lower lip that still welled with a single drop of blood. The ugly evidence of more bruises around his neck and shoulders.

His brown hair, silvered now with age, felt damp, as if the pain of the beating had made him sweat. And he smelled rank and terrible, or maybe that was me.

The dehumanization process, meant to break us, to turn us into animals.

But I wasn't going to let it. I refused to let our kidnappers win.

I was looking at my husband. I was seeing him again, a good man who'd taken a beating to protect his wife and daughter. A brave man, who had to be in agonizing pain, but didn't utter a single complaint as Ashlyn and I slowly roused him to standing, then eased him into the lower bunk.

My husband.

I sent my daughter to bed. She'd had enough for one night and needed the rest. Then, though my hands still shook uncontrollably, and I had to pause on occasion to recover my breath, I slowly and gently washed the worst of the blood from Justin's face.

He sighed.

I kissed the corner of his mouth.

He sighed again. "I'm sorry."

"It's okay."

"I wish . . ."

"Shhhh. Rest now."

I got him to quiet down. Then I fell asleep, still sitting up on the edge of the bunk, holding my husband's hand.

THEY DIDN'T COME FOR US first thing in the morning. Maybe they decided they'd tortured us enough the night before. Or, more likely, they were catching up on their own rest.

Our narrow window lightened with daylight. I awoke with a crick in my neck from sitting with my back against a metal bunk post. I felt weak but less achy. More like a middle-aged woman, badly in need of water, food and a good night's sleep.

The pills, I figured. Whatever Radar had provided was masking the worst of my withdrawal, temporarily reducing my symptoms. I didn't know what that might be. Not

Vicodin, because that always provided a lovely glow, a softening of life's hard edges. I felt none of that. No melting wonderland, just fewer tremors, less nausea and despair.

I should ask Radar about the medication, but I wasn't sure I wanted to know. Right now, this moment, I was doing better. Given our current situation, I had a feeling that was as good as it was going to get.

I used the toilet while my family slept, then refilled the water jug from the sink, which, given the barely-there trickle, was an accomplishment. This must be what inmates did with their time in prison. Stood around waiting to get enough water out of the faucet to wet a finger, rinse their mouths, wash their faces.

I took tiny sips out of the jug, working on hydration while I peered out the window in the cell door, eyeing the cavernous, overlit expanse of the dayroom, wondering where our attackers might be lurking next.

To the far left end of the dayroom was a bank of showers. Broad, white-tiled stalls, six down, six up. On the left end of the stacked rows loomed one particularly large stall with metal support bars bolted to each wall. Handicap accessible. Things you don't think about. That not all members of the prison population are big, tough guys. Some are injured or aging or otherwise impaired.

I wouldn't want to be them in here. I couldn't even stand it being me.

Of course, none of the stalls offered frosted glass doors or even cheap vinyl shower curtains. Just wide-open exposure. Apparently, showering in prison was a full-monty affair.

I still eyed the stalls with longing. My hair hung down in lank clumps. I'd sweated through my orange jumpsuit, could feel the salt riming my skin. I tried to figure out if I could partially disrobe, try to use the slow dribble of sink water to at least rinse off my torso.

But I couldn't bring myself to do it. I remained too afraid of alien beetles, who might burst through the cell door at any time. Not to mention the look that would come into Mick's crazy blue eyes if he could catch me partially unclothed.

Prison had eyes, Justin had said.

Even now, they were watching us. Watching me.

I sipped more water, turned away from the cell door and discovered Justin, now awake on the lower bunk, staring at me.

"Ashlyn," he croaked.

"Asleep." I brought over the jug of water. Helped hold up his head while he took the first few sips. He winced the moment I touched him, but didn't comment.

"They didn't . . . come back?"

I didn't know what he meant, eyeing him in confusion.

"After they got me. They didn't . . . come for you?"

"No," I assured him.

"I hoped . . . not. As long as they were beating me . . . I knew they couldn't be . . . hurting you. But then, Z. He disappeared. I didn't know . . . what that meant."

"We didn't see him."

"Okay."

"Justin . . . why? If this is about money . . ." I gestured to his horribly swollen and distorted features. "Why?"

"I don't . . . know. They kept telling me . . . to stop. Stop what?" Justin grimaced, sipped more water. "Then they'd say they were the ones asking the questions, and hit me again."

I frowned, considering the matter. "Have you . . . have you been doing something you shouldn't?"

My husband smiled, but it was a sad expression on his battered face. "You mean other than cheating on my wife?"

I flushed, looked away.

"I ended the relationship, Libby . . . as you requested . . . six months ago. I never should've started it in the first place."

"Maybe, something else? Maybe related to work?"

But Justin wouldn't be put off. "I'm sorry. You know that, right?"

I didn't answer, just looked away.

"But you're still not happy," he said, and again, the expression on his face . . .

"I'm trying," I said at last.

"I looked forward to our date night."

"Me, too." But I still wouldn't meet his gaze, couldn't meet his gaze. I wasn't prepared for this conversation. It was easier for me to view my husband as the bad guy. He had lied, he had cheated. If I kept that perspective, then the total collapse of my life didn't have to be my fault.

I didn't have to consider my own secrets, my own betrayals, my own dishonesty. If I didn't forgive, then I didn't have to repent.

"Is there something else I can do?" Justin asked now.

I smiled faintly. "Break us out of prison?"

He seemed to take my request seriously. "Libby, honey, I built this place. Take it from me, there's no breaking out. That was part of my job, my crew's job. The walls are tunnel proof, the floors are dig proof, the windows shatterproof. Not to mention the seven electronically controlled locks between us and freedom. Even the medical ward, the kitchen, the common areas, they're constructed to the same standards, just stocked with different equipment. As long as one of our kidnappers stays in the control room, which seems to be their standard operating procedure, that team member has eyes on us at all times, and could shut down our escape efforts at a moment's notice."

"What if we could overpower them?"

"Who? How? You already took on Mick, but to what end? I got Tased, Ashlyn got Tased and you ended up with a concussion. Even if we took out both of our escorts, got really lucky and somehow subdued Mick and Z, Radar could still simply tap the control system's touch screen, and instantaneously lock down the entire facility. We'd be trapped in whichever room, corridor or prison cell we'd started in, waiting for Z or Mick to regain consciousness."

"And exact revenge," I added softly.

"Exactly."

"What if we could lure Radar out of the control room?" I suggested. "Or, better yet, if this control room is so powerful, instead of trying to get *out* of the prison, let's try to get *into* the control room. Then we could use the control panel to trap Z and his crew in a dayroom, or a sally port, whatever. Give them a taste of their own medicine.

"Then, we could trip the alarm system," I added with growing excitement. "Local law enforcement would have to investigate sirens, right? Mothballed prison or not. They'll arrive, save us, arrest our kidnappers. Done!"

Justin didn't immediately dismiss my idea. "Don't break out, break in," he mused. He nodded shortly, then winced at the pain. "Possible. The control room is operated via a touch screen. If you can figure out an iPad, you should be able to run the system. Also, the control room was built to serve as a mini 'safe room' within the prison. A place the correction officers could use to make a last stand. The ballistic-rated glass installed there is four times stronger than the glass used in the cells, meaning it would take a full hour for Z or his crew to break their way through. That should buy us enough time to sound the alarm, and wait for the cavalry."

"So now we just have to figure out how to get their designated person out of the control room," I said. I had moved closer to my husband on the bunk bed. Both of our voices had picked up. This was prob-ably the longest we'd spoken to each other in months. It brought back memories of other times, when our marriage was still young, and we'd spent hours discussing everything from the best preschool for Ashlyn to a particular issue Justin was hav-ing with a bid, or who to invite to our up-coming dinner party. We'd been a good team back then. At least, I'd thought of us that way.

"We should threaten Z or Mick," I de-cided. "Not just overpower them, but look like we're ready to deliver a mortal strike. Radar will have to leave the control room in order to assist."

Justin didn't look convinced. "Threaten them with what?"

"A shiv?" Only thing I could think of, as we were in prison.

"Made from . . . ? We don't have a plastic comb, toothbrush or ballpoint pen. Furthermore, Z and Mick are following prison protocol—not carrying any lethal weapons that could be captured and used against them."

"Z has stuff in his belt. All those compartments? There are things there."

"Not big enough to be a knife or gun."

"Something!"

Justin smiled. "Fair enough. But even considering their Tasers, how do we make our play? Manage to disarm and somehow overpower both Z and Mick? I haven't looked in a mirror just yet, but somehow, I don't think I'm as fit-looking today as I was yesterday."

Which combined with my own physical limitations . . .

"Fire," I tried next. "We start a fire. In the kitchen, I guess. Oil on the stove, maybe something that appears accidental, except we panic and instead of dousing it in flour, fan it with a towel. They'd all have to work together to put out a fire."

"The entire facility is equipped with a fire suppression system," Justin said. "Single tap on the control room systems menu, and good-bye, fire. Hello, wet us."

"Then what?" I asked in frustration. "There has to be a way out. There's always a way."

"Ransom," my daughter said. Justin and I both startled, glancing up. We hadn't realized Ashlyn was awake. Now, almost as a reflex, we blushed guiltily.

I waited for my husband to soothe. He surprised me, then, by stating calmly, "I don't think that's what they want, honey. They seem to be after something else. I'm not sure what."

"I know," Ashlyn said bluntly. "I heard that much. But did you tell them about the insurance?" My daughter had a look on her face that gave me a sense of déjà vu. Then I got it. She looked like Justin. She looked exactly like my husband when he was working through a major build crisis, determined to make this latest two-hundred-million-dollar facility submit to his will.

"Yes. But the policy is only four million. Our hosts . . ."—he used the term dryly—"are a team of three. I don't think a little over one million apiece is adequate incentive for them."

"We can pay more." I spoke up quickly. "From our funds."

"Honey . . ." Justin paused. The silence dragged out. "We don't . . . We don't currently have those kinds of financial resources."

"Excuse me?"

"I haven't been taking a salary, Libby. For the past sixteen months. There's been a couple of major bids we haven't gotten, cash flow's tight . . . I've been leaving the money in the company, so we can make payroll."

I didn't speak right away. Not that Justin's words scared me. We'd done this before. Justin considered his employees family, too, and he often put their payroll requirements above his own.

No, what silenced me was that he hadn't said anything before now. Sixteen months.

A year and a third. I guess that's how long we'd really been drifting apart.

"We have resources," I said at last. "Antiques, jewelry, cars, two homes. We could liquidate . . ."

"I believe ransom is a cash biz."

"Maybe the company could pay out from the cash reserves. It'd be a hit, sure, but so would your death, right? I mean . . ."

Justin gave me a look. Then, in the next instant, his expression changed. "My death," he murmured.

Ashlyn and I studied him uncertainly. "What?"

"Libby, you're right. My death. That would do it."

"Justin," I ventured, "we're not going to kill you for ransom funds. No killing, no dying. Ashlyn and I, we forbid it."

"You don't have to. You don't have to do anything at all. It's kind of funny, really." Justin's swollen lip twisted. "Z, Mick, they've already done the hard part. Fuck 'em. We're going to ransom our own damn selves. And I know exactly how we can do it."

Chapter 25

CHRIS LOPEZ LIVED IN SOUTH BOSTON. And not the recently gentrified, up-and-coming part of Southie, but the hard-core, dilapidated triple-deckers with rotting-out front porches and cheap vinyl siding. Walking distance to several neighborhood pubs, of course, but still . . .

Tessa drove over with Wyatt in her car. The other New Hampshire cop, Kevin, had stayed behind to contact various emergency rooms and methadone clinics in northern New Hampshire for possible Libby Denbe sightings.

Tessa found it unnerving to drive with a guy in the passenger's seat. Wasn't sure why. A Lexus SUV had plenty of interior space. And true to her initial assessment, Wyatt wasn't exactly prone to blather. He sat reasonably relaxed, resting against the passenger-side door, leaving the middle console as neutral territory.

She had to make a couple of quick driving moves. Merging here, tucking in there. He whistled once in appreciation as she veered deftly around a particularly aggressive driver. But Wyatt didn't comment, or appear unduly tense.

"God bless the mountains," he muttered once, which she took to explain his feelings on Boston drivers.

She'd selected for her vehicle's GPS the British butler's voice. Jeeves, she called him. She'd picked the accent to amuse Sophie, who would then attempt to mimic it, but also because it seemed less grating to be told to make the next available legal U-turn in the Queen's English. Wyatt had broken into a grin at the first voice command, so apparently he was a man with a sense of humor. She could appreciate that.

He was also freshly showered and in a clean uniform. A man who planned ahead.

She liked that, too.

Okay, so, Chris Lopez.

They parked in front of a local bar, then walked to the corner and inspected the crumbling white triple-decker that served as Chris Lopez's legal address.

"Fixer-upper," Wyatt stated, not a question. "Bet he picks on it, when he's around. Man's got skills and connections. Might even funnel some 'extra' supplies from job sites. Build a little personal equity from corporate overages."

Tessa nodded. Not a bad bet. Place looked quiet at the moment. Lights off. They'd kept the Denbe crew up late last night, answering questions at headquarters. Even then, she wouldn't be surprised if the build team had grabbed a few beers afterward, sharing suspicions, fears, guilt over the fate of their missing boss.

Would it be work as usual on Monday, she wondered, flying out to whatever job site? Or would the guys hang closer to home, desperate for word? The FBI hadn't issued any travel restrictions with regard to Denbe's core management team.

Maybe, after talking to Lopez, that would change.

Wyatt approached first, testing out the sagging front steps with his heavier weight, gesturing at several spots to avoid. They weren't approaching with strict caution, and yet Tessa was aware that both of them had fallen silent, Wyatt in the forward position, herself, automatically a couple of steps back, where she could help cover him, even as his larger mass shielded her approach.

Sophie had climbed into her bed at four this morning. Not said a word. Just snuggled up close. Then, when Tessa's alarm had gone off at six:

"Mrs. Ennis says you're helping a family."

Tessa, halfway across the room, focused on getting ready: "Yes."

"What's wrong with them?"

"They . . . got a little lost."

Her daughter, sitting up in bed: "Someone took them."

"We don't know for sure."

Sophie, repeating firmly: "Someone took them. Do they have a little girl?"

"They have a big girl. Teenager."

"Does she know how to fight?"

"I'm told the whole family knows how to fight."

"Good. They'll be someplace dark. That's what kidnappers do. They take you, and lock you up someplace all alone and very dark. You should search those places first."

Tessa, turning away from her dresser to meet her eight-year-old daughter's gaze as somberly as her daughter met hers. The therapist had advised a straightforward approach to dealing with Sophie's trauma: Acknowledge the incident, encourage communication and promote empowerment. No dismissing of fears or placating of nerves.

Sophie had learned the hard way that adults couldn't always protect her. There was nothing Tessa could do or say about that now.

"What else would you recommend?" Tessa asked her daughter.

"You should check the windows for a sign. Maybe the word *help*. You can write on dirty windows, you know. Just lick your finger and use your spit to draw each letter. Except you have to keep licking your finger, and after a while, your finger doesn't taste so good."

"Got it."

"They might need food. You should bring snacks. Kidnappers don't like to feed kids. Especially bad kids, and when you're scared, it's hard to be good."

A small ache tearing into Tessa's heart. Trying hard not to think too much about what her daughter must have endured two years ago. Keeping her own voice steady and resolute: "What kind of snacks should I bring?"

"Chocolate chip cookies."

"Okay. I'll stock my car with blankets and chocolate chip cookies. Maybe a thermos of hot chocolate?"

"Yes."

"Thank you, Sophie. That's very helpful."

"Are you going to shoot someone, Mommy?"

"I'm not planning on it."

"But you're going to bring your gun?"

"Yes."

"Good, Mommy. I think you should."

Now, Tessa couldn't help but think that Chris Lopez's triple-decker appeared cold and dark. And the lower windows were very dirty, the kind that would make a finger taste particularly awful when smearing out a message for help.

Tessa placed her right hand inside her open coat, on the butt of her gun. She turned her body slightly sideways, to make it less of a target.

Then, she nodded once to Wyatt, who raised his left hand and knocked.

A BLACK LAB OPENED THE DOOR. Older dog, with a graying muzzle that stood out in sharp contrast to his sleek black coat. He released the rope that had been tied around the door handle, then sat, staring patiently at Tessa and Wyatt while thumping his tail in welcome.

"Hello?" Tessa called out.

"Say, good dog," a man's voice called from upstairs. Chris Lopez.

"Good dog," Tessa muttered. The black Lab thumped his tail a couple more beats.

"Good dog, Zeus," the voice called from upstairs.

Tessa still had her hand on the butt of her gun, slowly scanning the shadowed interior for signs of other life. "Good dog, Zeus," she repeated.

The dog yawned. Apparently, her voice wasn't too convincing.

"Chris Lopez?" she called out. "It's Tessa Leoni, Northledge Investigations. Got a couple of questions for you."

A few seconds later, the staircase creaked, then shuddered as Lopez went rat-a-tat down the upper half. When he rounded the lower landing and spotted Wyatt as well, his steps slowed. He was holding a rag, wiping what appeared to be white clay from his fingers and forearms. Now, he gripped the rag tightly, coming to a halt two steps from the bottom.

"Do you have . . . news?" He spoke the words tightly, as if already anticipating that any word that took two investigators to deliver wouldn't be good.

"No. Just more questions. May we come in?"

"Yeah. I guess. I mean, sure. Couldn't sleep, so just, um . . . been grouting the upstairs bath. Give me a sec. I'll wash up in the kitchen."

He gestured toward the back of the

house, and Tessa and Wyatt followed him through the entry, past the staircase to the rear-facing kitchen. Zeus, the elderly guard dog, plodded along beside them, apparently content to join the party.

The kitchen turned out to be gutted. Stripped down to the subfloor, with a lone refrigerator, jury-rigged sink and several sawhorses topped with plywood serving as counters. In the corner sat an old blue card table big enough for four. Chris nodded toward it, so Tessa and Wyatt each grabbed a metal folding chair and took a seat.

"Sorry for the mess," Lopez said as he banged on the faucets, started scrubbing the grout from his hands. "I bought the place two years ago. Figured I'd have it fully functional in eight months. You'd think, as a construction professional, I'd know better."

"Doing the work yourself?" Wyatt spoke up.

"Exactly."

"Licensed?"

"'Course not. But I got buddies who are. They already helped update plumbing and electrical. Now, I'm mostly down to finish work. In theory, I can manage that."

"You like carpentry?"

"Most days, more than it likes me."

Zeus circled the table. Handsome dog, with broad head, silky ears. He stopped in front of Tessa, cocking an eyebrow in clear expectation. Tessa's husband, Brian, had had a beloved German shepherd. Her own experience with dogs was limited, making her uncertain. "What does he want?"

"What does any man want? Your undying devotion and a decent back scratch."

Tessa held out a hand. The dog moved until his head was underneath. She took that as a hint, and rubbed between his ears. The old dog closed his eyes and sighed contentedly.

"You can have a dog even with your travel schedule?" she asked Lopez. He'd stopped scrubbing and moved on to rinsing.

"For starters, Zeus is hardly a dog. He considers himself human, plain and simple. Two, he lives with my neighbors. But they work most weekends, so if I'm around, Zeus hangs with me. We hammer things, sand floors, belch. You know, guy time."

"And he can open doors?" Wyatt, with a touch of awe.

"When he's not fetching beer. Hey, these are valuable life skills." Lopez banged off the faucet, grabbed a roll of paper towels to dry his hands and crossed back to them.

Zeus opened one eye at his approach, then resumed sighing blissfully beneath Tessa's touch.

"Yeah, yeah, yeah," Lopez muttered. "So much for the code of brotherhood. Keep that up, and I'll have no choice but to rat you out, buddy. Mention to the pretty girl that, sure, you can open doors, but walk over a metal sidewalk grate? Cross a suspension bridge? Turns out, Mr. Handsome is afraid of heights, which I learned the hard way, having to carry him down the Lion's Head trail on Mount Washington as he trembled like a baby. Hiking up, all good. But then, turning, looking down . . . Black Labs can turn green. Don't let anyone tell you differently."

Zeus didn't seem to care that his deepest darkest secret had just been revealed. He placed his head on Tessa's lap and sighed again.

"You're a hiker?" Wyatt again.

"When I can. Gotta say, this project's keeping me busy."

"White Mountains?"

"Yep."

"Favorite trails?"

Lopez rattled off several. By the sound of it, he knew his way around the Presidential Range. Interesting, given the location of Justin Denbe's jacket in northern New Hampshire.

But if Chris Lopez was damning himself, he didn't seem aware of it.

"So," Lopez said shortly, "I'm kind of thinking you didn't come all the way here to ask me about hiking."

"Nope," Wyatt agreed.

"What can I do for you?"

Tessa decided they might as well get straight to it: "Tell us about Kathryn Chapman."

The effect was immediate: "Ah, shit. Do you mean my stupid niece? Or my boss's even stupider ex-girlfriend?"

CHRIS'S SISTER HAD ASKED HIM FOR A FAVOR: Could he find a job for her daughter, Kate, at Denbe Construction? Unfortunately, given that business was slow, there was a temporary hiring freeze. But then Chris heard that the building's travel agency had an opening for a receptionist. Perfect. He got his niece an interview and a couple of weeks later, Kate was employed and Chris's sister was happy.

"All I wanted," Lopez emphasized slowly, his dark eyes still snapping, "was to get my niece a job. So I got her a job. Not in my company, but in my building. End of story."

Except, of course, it wasn't.

Chris became suspicious in January. Over the holidays, it became clear that Kate had a new boyfriend. She kept sneaking off to check her phone, blushed when anyone asked about her job, hell, was so obvious about trying not to be obvious that even Chris had teased her a couple of times.

Then, just two weeks later, Lopez had walked into the travel agency to arrange for a couple of plane tickets and saw them: his boss, Justin Denbe, leaning over Kate's desk, and Justin had this smile and Kate had this look on her face, half dazed, half dazzled, and just like that, Chris knew.

"Not the first time," he said bitterly. "Justin? Shit. You gave me a hard time"—he shot Tessa a look—"but I just talk a good game. Hell, I travel three hundred and forty days a year and spend the majority of my waking hours with a bunch of hairy-backed guys who are barely evolved enough to walk upright. I only wish I could find a good woman who'd want me. But Justin . . . What can I tell you? That apple didn't fall far from his old man's tree. Justin liked women. Women liked him. But my niece? I mean . . . My twenty-year-old *niece*?"

Lopez sounded extremely offended.

No, he had not confronted Justin. What could he say? Instead, he'd cornered Kate, trying to get her to listen to reason. Justin was married. Justin was never leaving his wife. This whole thing would only end in heartbreak.

Kate hadn't cared. She was special. She was the one. She just knew it.

Which, slowly but surely, started to piss Lopez off.

"You gotta understand," he said, "my niece . . . she may not have a brain in her head, but she's sweet. She's trusting. She's not looking at Justin the same way he's looking at her. He's twice her age and twenty times more experienced. For him, having his cake and eating it, too, is more than a lifestyle choice, it's gene pool. Like a fucking family legacy."

This caught Tessa's attention. "You mean, Justin cheated on his wife the way Justin's father used to cheat on his mother?"

"Yeah, and being the other woman was no great shakes in Dale's world, either. Just ask Anita Bennett."

"What?"

Tessa stared at Chris Lopez. She noticed that beside her, Wyatt appeared faintly smug.

"Anita's youngest kid," Lopez extrapolated. "You know, the son who doesn't look anything like Anita's husband but could be Justin's younger brother? The boy who five years back was the recipient of Denbe's first and *only* full-ride college scholarship? Come on, you haven't figured that out yet? I thought everyone in the company knew."

Tessa composed herself quickly. Of course. Anita Bennett and Justin's father. Just as Wyatt had predicted. He kicked her lightly under the table. She kicked him back.

"But the thing is," Lopez was saying, "Justin's mother was known for being a drunk. Maybe she drove the old man to it;

not my place to judge. But Libby? She's beautiful. She's talented. She's gracious. You know how many nights I've been to their house? I don't know. Because it's been that many. The entire team can be fresh off planes, still coated in mud and reeking of five days on a job site, and Libby will welcome us through her doors. How are you, nice to see you, how's the build, how's the family, how's the kids. Hey, who needs a beer, or boys, are we drinking wine tonight?

"That's Libby. He doesn't fucking deserve her."

Tessa had stopped petting the dog. She was too busy staring at Lopez, who was obviously madly in love with his boss's wife.

Well, well, well.

"Is that why you decided to text her?" she asked quietly. "You thought she deserved to know the truth?"

"Yeah. I just . . . couldn't take it anymore. It was only a matter of time before Justin broke Kate's heart. Figured it was only fair to mess with him first."

"Did it work?"

"Libby booted his sorry ass," Lopez said, but he didn't sound convinced. His gaze dropped. He scuffed his foot against the subflooring.

"Justin never found out I dropped the dime," he said. "Best I can tell, he thought Libby had finally gotten suspicious, checked his cell. He and Kate had been texting. Stupid thing to do, and he knew it. There was a big scene. Yelling, screaming, drama. He got to move to the basement."

"He told you that," Wyatt pressed quietly, "or Libby told you that?"

"He did. Libby didn't know I was even part of this. I bought a TracFone to text her. Hell, just because I was ruining their marriage didn't mean I wanted to be part of it." His lips twisted dryly.

"But Justin talked to you about the home situation?" Wyatt said.

"Yeah. To the whole team. It was clear something had happened. Justin showed up the Monday afterward, totally off his game. I mean, it's funny. When it comes to women, he's always been so . . . slick. I guess I didn't even take his marriage that seriously. But when the shit hit the fan . . . The dude actually appeared remorseful. Claimed he'd been a total idiot, no better than his old man, but now he'd seen the light and would do anything to get his wife back."

"Did he?" Tessa asked.

"He dumped my niece," Lopez said flatly. "Like a hot potato. And trust me, that I got to hear about. She called me five, six, seven times a day, crying hysterically, demanding to know what she should do, how to win him back. Christ. I had to start turning off my cell just to go to work. I'm lucky she didn't rat me out."

"How do you know she didn't?" Wyatt again.

"Justin would've confronted me. He's not a beat-around-the-bush sort of guy. He's got a problem with you, you know it. No stabbing in the back. Just a direct hit, full-on to the jugular."

"Did Kate get him back, or did the relationship truly end?" Tessa asked, because based on her conversation with Kathryn Chapman, she wasn't convinced the girl was totally forthcoming. Some things, at least, had remained unsaid.

"Best I know, over and done with."

"Bet she must've had some opinions about the wife," Wyatt commented. "Not easy to lose your first big love like that."

"Oh, leave Katie out of this. She's just a stupid kid. Trust me, she wised up soon enough. Probably tried a couple of foolish stunts to get Justin's attention, and when he knocked her back down, took the hint. It was June when this whole thing blew up. And trust me, my sister can tell you, Katie spent most of the month sobbing in her room. But by July, not so much so. And August . . . She'll have a new boyfriend, soon enough. She's a pretty girl, and getting smarter all the time."

"You think she ever went after Libby?" Tessa asked.

"Not that I ever heard."

"And Libby, did she track down Kate?"

"Not that I ever heard."

"What about a divorce lawyer?" Wyatt spoke up. "Did things get that far, for either him, or her?"

Chris Lopez looked up at them. He suddenly smirked. "You don't know, do you?"

They didn't answer.

He leaned forward, crossed his arms on the table. "I can't tell you if Libby actually called a lawyer, but I can tell you what would happen if she did."

"Enlighten us," Tessa said.

"Prenup. Justin's bragged about it several times. A simple one-page document that Libby readily signed. In it, she renounced all claim to any share of Denbe Construction, in return for being entitled to fifty percent of any and all personal assets accrued during her marriage. Sounds reasonable enough, right? Company was Justin's to begin with, inherited straight from his father. Except, then you get to the fine print, which is . . ."

He paused a beat, eyed them expectantly.

Tessa got it first. It gave her claim to the crime scene after all. "There are no personal assets," she murmured. "He runs everything through the company."

"Ding, ding, ding, give the woman a prize. The Boston town house, the cottage on the Cape, the cars, the furniture, all held by Denbe Construction. Even Justin's year-end bonus, he graciously declines, leaving it in the corporation as cash reserves. If Libby left Justin, she would be entitled to half of exactly zero. I'm telling you, this is Justin's thing, Mr. Benevolent Dictator. Promises his wife he'll always love her—here's a five-million-dollar town house. Promises his employees he'll always take care of us—I'm not even gonna take my bonus, but leave it in the company. But really, he's only looking out for himself. As both my niece and Libby got to find out the hard way."

TESSA AND WYATT DANCED AROUND WITH LOPEZ for another thirty minutes. What had he been doing on Friday night?

"Local bar. Circulate my photo; at least half a dozen regulars will confirm I was there."

Last time he saw Libby and/or Ashlyn Denbe?

"I'm telling you, you're barking up the wrong tree. Just because I got a beef with how my boss handles women doesn't mean I'd harm a hair on his head."

But he had access to the security code for the Denbes' residence.

"Sure. All of us on the build team know it. Justin isn't the most organized guy in the world, and sometimes he'd have us pick up a few last-minute things. If Libby was around, she'd feed you a cookie. I'm telling you, Justin deserves to be knocked down a peg or two. But not his family."

And Ashlyn?

Lopez's face had turned red. "I'm not talking about her! I can't even think about her. Assaulted in her own home . . . You want to save the legal system some dough? When you find out who did this, just say the word and me and the guys will take care of the rest."

Using the skills he'd learned as an army ranger? Probably had some contacts, too, the kinds of guys who'd know how to quietly break into a house and quickly subdue a grown man and his wife and daughter?

"I'm fifteen years out. The guys I know are either picking sand from their teeth, having been called up from the reserves, or are finally being cut loose because they now dive for cover every time a car backfires. The first group of guys is deployed too far away. The second group is too drunk. You want to make some headway, go hound Anita Bennett. Now, there's a woman who has reason to eliminate the entire family. Starting with the fact that it would make her own child the sole surviving Denbe male. Don't royals do that sort of thing all the time? Why not big business? Hell, we're talking a hundred-million-dollar corporation. Some imperial inheritances have gotta be smaller than that."

"We'll take that under advisement," Tessa assured him. She glanced over at Wyatt, who'd returned to perusing the evidence log. When he didn't offer up any more questions, she pushed back her chair. They'd learned as much as they were going to learn, she judged. At least until they had time to research the pieces of Lopez's latest story and push back harder. For now, however, probably best to hit the road.

The old black Lab had curled up at her feet. Now he stood to his feet with a giant yawn. She gave him a final pat on the head, feeling an unexpected pang. She liked his company. Thought Sophie would like his company. Something to consider, getting a dog. Then maybe, both she and her daughter would finally sleep through the night.

Lopez escorted her and Wyatt back to the front door. The conversation had clearly agitated him. Tessa just couldn't decide whether he was frustrated they didn't magically accept his claims of innocence, or nervous that they were still poking around.

Wyatt had been right about two things: Anita Bennett had been involved with Justin's father. And, yes, the whole crew seemed to be a bunch of liars.

Wyatt waited until they were around the corner to start speaking. Tessa had assumed his first words would be *I told you so*, so he startled her by declaring:

"I think you're on to something."

"Me? You're the one who caught Anita's personal relationship with Denbe, senior."

"Which is interesting if the rumors about her youngest son are true. But you got me thinking about Justin's affair. After all, the Anita Bennett, Dale Denbe thing is at least twenty years old. Whereas the biggest recent stressor for Justin and Libby has been his involvement with Kathryn Chapman."

"Which Libby found out about six months ago," Tessa countered.

"Because one of Justin's own guys decided to rat him out," Wyatt filled in.

"Except it doesn't sound like the marriage is necessarily over. We're hearing more stories of date night than divorce lawyers."

"Maybe Libby isn't as naive as Lopez thinks. Maybe she looked up the prenup, did a little digging and realized just how financially devastating divorce would be."

"So she arranged for them all to be kidnapped?" Tessa wasn't following.

"I'm not saying the affair led directly to the kidnapping. I'm wondering if the *fallout* from the affair didn't put things in play for Friday night."

"Such as?" They'd arrived at her car.

"Well, we got Lopez, Justin's second in command, looking at his boss with fresh, angry eyes. Combine that with maybe disgruntlement over the direction things are going at the company level and . . ."

"Then there's Anita Bennett," Tessa picked up. "She was once the other woman, even, possibly had a son. Got her nowhere. Now Justin is engaging in similar behavior, perhaps aggravating old wounds, new prejudices."

"Then we got Libby, doping herself up with Vicodin to cover her pain. And maybe engaging in other new behaviors as well." Wyatt slid into the passenger seat, holding up the evidence log. "While you and Lopez wrapped up your tango, I finished reviewing the inventory list for the trash recovered from the Denbes' brownstone. Garage bin. Item thirty-six down. Best guess, based on trash pickup, is that the contents are no more than two days old."

Wyatt pointed. Tessa peeked.

"A *pregnancy* test? A positive home pregnancy test?"

"Yep. Question is, does Justin Denbe know he's a father again? Or . . . is he?"

Chapter 26

Is my husband a chauvinistic pig? I suppose, if you look at our marriage, he appears sexist. And yet, he is the father of an amazing fifteen-year-old girl. Who he personally taught to cluster six shots to center mass time and time again. Let alone, from the day of her birth, he's actively spoken of Ashlyn's future as head of the family firm. No need to try for a son. For Justin, from the moment he held his daughter in his arms, she was absolutely, positively perfect.

I always preferred to think of us as co-workers whose areas of expertise happened to fall along traditional lines. My husband works. He loves his job; he's at his best when wrestling with a multimillion-dollar-contract issue. And I love my job, which includes creating our house, raising our child and crafting a lifestyle that reflects who we are as a family.

I've never thought of my role as lesser. I've never thought of Justin as the "one in command." At least, not until six months ago. But even then, I didn't view myself as the weak half of the marriage. I simply viewed myself as a failure. Because if part of my job was to meet the needs of the family, how well could I be doing, considering my husband had taken up with another woman?

Of course, I understand deep down inside that from the beginning, one of the things Justin had most loved about me was my independence. And eighteen years later, there wasn't much of that left.

There is a breed of men out there, you know, who are attracted to strong women. They just don't know what to do once they win us over.

So that's how I view my husband, the strong man, driven to pursue a strong woman, then mostly at a loss forever after. If that's patronizing, well then, maybe that makes me the chauvinistic one. Because given the family history, I can't say I was totally surprised that my husband cheated on me. I was mostly ashamed for not figuring it out sooner. And hurt, because I had wanted us to be different. I had imagined myself to be special enough, attractive enough, smart enough, to forever hold Justin's interest.

Love is risk.

I took it, and I got burned.

But someday, my daughter will take the same risk. And I don't have the heart to tell her to take the easy road. Because there is a breed of women out there who are attracted to alpha males. We just don't always know what to do with them once we have them.

JUSTIN WAS CONVINCED he knew how to handle Z. Let him do the talking, and we'd be ransomed out of our prison cell by the end of the day. Which meant the first thing Ashlyn and I had to do was talk him down. We'd tried fighting fire with fire. We'd made a stand, we'd even attempted rebellion. To date, it had gotten us Tased and battered.

If Z and his crew were former military, then warfare was their specialty.

We needed a different approach. One outside the alpha dog's normal realm of experience. I had a few ideas on the subject, which Ashlyn seconded. Given Justin's current condition, we slowly but surely wore him down. One of us, he might have dismissed. Two of us, he eventually gave way. My idea, our plan. We would execute as a team, our first family project in six months. And we would win. I was convinced of it. There was finally enough at stake.

The hardest part was waiting.

We sat, Ashlyn on the top bunk, Justin and I below. First rule of psychological warfare: He or she who initiates the discussion has by definition given up ground. We couldn't afford to give up ground.

So we practiced patience.

My tremors were returning. My headache, the deep, dragging exhaustion, punctuated by moments of excruciatingly painful cramping. The pills, whatever Radar had given me in the middle of the night, seemed to be waning, placing me once more on the withdrawal express.

I could confess to Justin. Tell him once and for all what I'd spent the past few months doing. Just how great a spouse and parent I'd turned out to be.

But again, she who initiates the discussion has by definition given up ground.

So I held my tongue.

We had no sense of time anymore. Daylight outside. Constant fluorescent lighting inside. Morning, mid-morning?

Eventually, we heard footsteps. Steady, not rushing, but I found myself holding my breath, hands already forming into fists. On the top bunk, I saw Ashlyn ease into the farthest corner of the bunk, assuming the crouch position . . .

The steel door swung open. Z stood there, Radar beside him.

"Breakfast," Z stated crisply.

And in that one word, I knew we could win.

PER PROTOCOL, JUSTIN LEFT THE CELL FIRST, hands secured at his waist. Z stood with him, while Radar came in to fetch me. Radar kept his back to the door, blocking the window and, I realized, the security camera, as he slid two round white pills into the palm of my hand.

No words were exchanged. I had a brief image of the flat white tablets, numbers stamped in the back, then I dry swallowed both pills without question. A millisecond in time, then he had the restraints secured around my wrists and I joined my husband in the dayroom. Radar followed with Ashlyn and we fell in line, Z leading Justin by the arm, Radar escorting me and Ashlyn half a dozen paces behind.

We offered no resistance, behaving as three dutiful hostages who'd just spent a long night learning their lesson.

Our captors were freshly showered. Their hair still damp, Z in a crisp new outfit of 100 percent commando black, Radar in a fresh pair of baggy jeans and a new dark blue flannel shirt. I tried not to hate them, but given my own rank smell, it was difficult.

In the kitchen, our wrist restraints were removed and we were once more tasked with cooking. I conducted a quick inspection of the pantry and walk-in refrigerator. No additional supplies. Then again, when would they have had the time to restock? The lack of refurbishment reassured me, however, spoke of a set timeline. Z and his crew didn't plan to spend eternity here, just long enough.

I pulled butter, bacon and eggs from the cavernous refrigerator, then an assortment of dry goods from the walk-in pantry. I'd have to do the recipe off the top of my head, but after all these years, that wasn't a problem.

I put Justin in charge of crisping bacon and scrambling eggs. Ashlyn already knew her assignment: She was to set a table. Use whatever she could find, but somehow create the impression of a real, honest-to-goodness kitchen table.

While I made homemade cinnamon rolls.

Z disappeared, leaving Radar alone. Our youngest captor took a seat by one of the stainless steel counters, paying more attention to Justin, who stood, with half his face battered and one eye swollen shut, over a sizzling frying pan. I prepared the dough, then sprinkled flour onto the stainless steel prep surface and started rolling out. Once I'd created a large, thin rectangle, I spread butter across the entire surface, followed by liberal handfuls of white sugar, brown sugar and cinnamon. I rolled it up into one long cinnamon-dusted snake, then sliced it into inch-thick sections.

The ends appeared ragged and ugly. Without saying a word, I trimmed off both, handing one doughy piece to Ashlyn, her favorite part of the cinnamon-roll-making process. The second, I handed to Radar.

He didn't even acknowledge me. But he picked up the bite of dough and popped it in his mouth. Just like that.

Some negotiations are not a matter of heavy battery, but slow advancement. Gains made so subtly, your opponent doesn't realize you've even moved until they're forced to watch the victory dance.

I made two dozen rolls, given that men of Z and Mick's size ate at a certain volume, let alone if one homemade cinnamon bun was a treat, then three to four was an act of gluttony destined to be followed by a state of satiated lethargy, if not an outright sugar coma.

This kind of yeastless roll, thin and flaky versus thick and doughy, was Ashlyn's favorite. I'd evolved the recipe twelve years ago, when my three-year-old hadn't the patience to wait hours for homemade baked goods. Turned out, basically using pie dough halved the prep time while still yielding plenty of cinnamony delight. Our family recipe, now being shared with our family kidnappers.

While the commercial kitchen filled with the warm scent of baking cinnamon and caramelizing sugar, I inspected Ashlyn's table. My daughter has always been creative, and her latest efforts didn't disappoint.

She'd taken over one of the rolling stainless steel prep tables. Given that the overall color scheme in prison had a tendency to be stark white, she'd placed six red cafeteria trays to serve as institutional placemats. Each red tray was topped with a plain white plastic dinner plate. Then, she'd taken smaller salad plates, centered each on a dinner plate and written, in brightly colored condiments, the individual's name.

Z's single initial was particularly impressive, standing out in bright red ketchup script. For Radar, she'd used yellow mustard. Mick got green pickle relish, and for a moment, my child and I shared a smile;

Ashlyn loathed relish. Always had, always would.

In the middle of the table, Ashlyn had filled a glass bowl with multicolored layers of dried lentils, topped with an artful arrangement of three eggs, a wire whisk and a single piece of cooked bacon, stolen from her father's pan. Add in the collection of plastic cups, silverware and rolled-up paper napkins, and the overall effect was rustic and charming. A piece of home.

The oven timer chimed. The cinnamon rolls were ready. Justin plated the eggs and bacon. We positioned the platters on the table, and just like that, showtime.

Z appeared five minutes later.

His own power play, I would guess, as he entered the kitchen in slow, measured strides, his face perfectly expressionless even as the wafting scents of fresh-baked buns and crisp-cooked bacon must've hit him like a wall.

Radar was already at the table, perched on the edge of a metal stool. He had a slightly glazed-over look on his face and was staring at the cinnamon rolls as if they were the last drop of water in a desert. But he remained still, hands at his side.

Z took in the table, still advancing steadily. Now his gaze flickered to me, where I stood next to my waiting stool, as did Justin and Ashlyn.

He smiled and I could tell he saw right through me, understood completely every step I'd just taken and why.

Z dished up first. Two rolls, half a plate of eggs, half a dozen pieces of bacon. He passed each platter to Radar, who filled his plate, then dished up a plate for Mick, presumably working the control room, before returning the remaining food to the middle of the table. I hadn't been around last night, but Justin and Ashlyn seemed to be waiting for something.

"Eat," Z ordered at last, and they each took a seat.

A reminder of who was in charge. I wasn't concerned. Second bite of the cinnamon roll, Z's eyes fluttered down, the quick rush of buttery pastry and gooey cinnamon sugar hitting his bloodstream, intoxicating his senses.

I wondered what he was remembering right now. A mother, a grandmother, even just a moment in time when Z had felt warm, safe and loved. The true power of comfort food. It didn't just fill one's belly, it evoked a mood. And now, my food was triggering Z's memory, forming an association between my handmade rolls and his own sense of well-being that would be difficult to break. Hence the past eighteen years I'd spent making homemade treats for Justin and his build crew. Because nothing earned undying devotion faster than freshly baked chocolate chip cookies. Then, even the toughest of the tough turned instantaneously into a little boy, savoring a childhood treat while gazing upon the provider of that treat with fresh adoration.

I could use some adoration right about now.

My family was already eating. I picked at my own food, avoiding the greasy bacon, nibbling on a single roll. I should eat to build my strength, but I didn't completely trust my stomach yet. Not to mention Z and his crew had commandeered the majority of the food. I didn't want to take even more away from my daughter and husband.

"You're going to ask for something," Z said after the second cinnamon bun, while reaching for a third. "You anticipate my mind will be so muddled by your homemade rolls, my senses so overwhelmed by this lovely display of domesticity that I will say yes."

"We're not going to ask for something, we're going to give you something."

"You have nothing to give. And you're wrong about the rolls. Cooking as good as this . . . now I have even less incentive to let you go." His gaze flickered to my husband and there was a look on his face I didn't understand.

"You've invested a lot of time in this operation," I stated evenly. "Time, money, resources. I'm sure you and your team don't want to walk away empty-handed."

"Not about money. Didn't I already say that?" Z glanced at Justin, my husband's battered face, swollen eye.

"Mom." Ashlyn nudged me, voice low. For the moment, I ignored her.

Z pulled his attention away from Justin long enough to eye me skeptically. "Besides, hasn't your husband told you everything yet? That business isn't going so well? That he no longer takes a salary? That, in fact, you don't have money to offer?"

My face didn't change expression. I had just learned these things, of course, but it surprised me that Z knew such details as well.

"Did he tell you about all the pressure he's under?" Z continued in a bored voice. "Use that as his excuse for all of his *extra-curriculars*. Poor Justin, just trying to feel like a big man."

Justin flinched. I could feel his leg tensing up next to mine, preparing to stand. And do what? Pound the table? Take on the bigger guy with the cobra tattoo?

"Mom." Ashlyn again, voice still low. She'd pushed away her red tray, her shoulders hunched as if with trepidation.

"Nine million dollars," I said, ignoring both my family members.

For the first time, I could tell that I'd caught Z off guard. His face froze, the green cobra tattoo staring at me with twin beady eyes. Radar was less circumspect. He did a short double take, jaw hanging open, before quickly composing himself.

"We start today," I continued calmly, "and it can be wired to the account of your choice by three P.M. tomorrow. We do the work. You get the money. But the demand has to be delivered today, and you have to let us go. Price of ransom. The victims must be recovered safe and sound."

Z frowned at me, which, in fact, made the cobra's fanged mouth move in unsettling ways around his left eye.

"Nine million dollars," I repeated. "Guaranteed payday. You'll leave this prison rich men. Not bad for a few days' work."

Z didn't immediately say no. Almost absently, he pulled apart his third roll, biting into one half, flaky pastry catching around the corner of his hard-set mouth.

"How?" he asked.

"Insurance policy. On Justin, but also Ashlyn and me."

"Company policy?"

"Yes. Perk of being an owner. Justin might not currently draw a salary, but he still gets great benefits."

"They'll pay?"

"That's why you carry insurance."

Another bite. Z chewed. Z swallowed. "Cash?" he asked abruptly.

"Wired to the fund of your choice."

"I will not go on camera."

"We have it all worked out."

"One wrong word . . ."

"It's in our best interests to have this all go as planned."

"Nine million dollars," he repeated, a concession of sorts.

"Three apiece. Or, more likely, five for you, two for each of your men."

Radar didn't look concerned by this split. Z actually smiled. And once again, the cobra tattoo seemed to twist and shudder around his perfectly shaved head.

"The background report," he declared dryly, "had not indicated that you would be a problem."

"Would you like another cinnamon bun?"

Z smiled again. Then his gaze switched to my husband, and the sudden coldness in his eyes made me start. He despised my husband. I could see it clearly, in the directness of his gaze. Hatred at a level that was beyond professional, had to be personal.

And for just one second, I hesitated. Maybe ransom was a bad idea. The exchange of money for hostages was inherently complicated. So many things could go wrong. A simple misstep could lead quickly and catastrophically to further violence, even death.

Especially when dealing with a man who'd covered his head in a giant fanged viper.

"Radar." Ashlyn's voice from beside me. My daughter no longer reaching toward me, but across the table toward the youngest commando.

Radar? Why would my daughter ask for . . .

I turned quickly, grabbing for Ashlyn's arm but missing, as without another word, she slid off the back of her stool and dropped limply to the floor. Blood, so much blood, pooling on the lower half of her orange jumpsuit.

"Ashlyn!" Justin, already on his feet, then immediately drawing up short. "What the . . ."

Ashlyn's staring up at me. Eyes, so much like my own, now filled with regret. "I'm sorry, Mom."

And in that moment, I understood.

The men were scurrying around. Radar pushing back his stool, Z announcing in an authoritative voice for Justin to come with him, for Radar to tend to us.

I ignored them all. I focused on my daughter, who'd tried to warn me yesterday that we didn't talk to her anymore. Not just moments in a marriage, I realized now, but moments in an entire family, when you stopped seeing one another. When you shared space, but no longer yourselves with one another.

I did my best to see her now. To gaze into her eyes. To comfort her with my own presence. As I knelt on the floor and held my daughter's hand while she miscarried.

Chapter 27

WYATT GOT THE CALL just as he and Tessa were leaving Chris Lopez's neighborhood. Nicole, or should he say, Special Agent Adams, sounding crisp and cool as always, reporting that contact had been made. Justin Denbe himself, shortly after ten this morning, had appeared in a video presenting the ransom demands.

Tessa knew how to drive. Her years as a state trooper? Or just a lifetime living in Boston? Wyatt couldn't begin to hazard which, but half a dozen white-knuckle moments later, they were careening down the alley that ran behind the Denbes' town house, where sure enough, the FBI's huge mobile command center squatted like a fat linebacker in the middle of an old lady's tea parlor.

Inside, they found Nicole's partner, Special Agent Hawkes, manning a laptop at a small table, flat-screen monitor mounted above. Nicole paced in the limited space behind him, obviously agitated. As Tessa and Wyatt walked in, she gestured to the oversize monitor with a jerk of her chin. Nicole had her arms crossed over her chest, one finger tapping her elbow restlessly.

She wasn't just agitated, Wyatt realized. The FBI agent was upset.

He and Tessa exchanged a glance. He gestured for her to take the remaining seat across from Hawkes, while he stood next to Nicole. With all of them in viewing position, Hawkes hit the play button on his keyboard, and the rest of the story emerged.

The ransom demand had been delivered via a video message. It featured a single close-up shot of Justin Denbe, his face a black-and-blue battered mess, staring into the video camera with one good eye as he slowly listed the kidnappers' demands. Nine million dollars, to be wired directly into a single account by 3:00 P.M. EST on Monday, at which time the entire Denbe family would be safely released. Failure to meet the demands would result in further harm to the Denbe family. More details to follow.

At the end of the twenty-second clip, Justin held up the front page of the morning paper. A brief close-up of the Sunday edition's date, then the screen went blank.

"*Union Leader.*" Wyatt identified the Manchester-based newspaper. "Means they're still in New Hampshire."

"But no word on the rest of the family?" Tessa asked. She was leaning toward the computer screen, as if that might help.

"Justin Denbe contacted his insurance company via telephone at ten twenty-three this morning," Nicole provided, fingers still tapping. "He demanded to speak to a manager, saying that he and his family had been abducted. He was afraid for his life and evoking the special circumstances clause in the kidnapping policy: Essentially, in the event that the policyholder faces credible risk of imminent death, the company will pay out half of the value of the life insurance policy as additional ransom. Given that a dead Justin Denbe would cost the company ten million in life insurance, it's in the company's own best interest to pay up more now, in order to save later."

Wyatt turned that around in his head: "So, instead of paying out just the four million in ransom insurance, the company will pay that, plus an extra five from the life insurance policy?"

"Precisely."

"Nine million in ransom versus ten million in death benefits," Tessa murmured. "Once again, the captors seem to know a great deal about the Denbes' personal affairs, including just how high they can go with their ransom demand before capping out."

"Our theory has always been that the kidnappers are professionals." Hawkes spoke up, recuing the video. "Given that, it makes sense they'd do their homework before embarking on this enterprise."

Enterprise. It sounded so clinical, even businesslike, Wyatt thought. Until you looked at Justin's battered face. The man had been worked over good. A ring of crusty blood still plastered to the hairline at his left temple. His lower lip cut and puffy, his right eye entirely swollen shut. Not to mention a massive bruise on his other cheek, plus half a dozen larger and smaller lacerations combining to form one grotesquely misshapen mess.

Yet, the man had stared into the camera directly and spoken in a firm voice. Still holding up, then. Maybe because the kidnappers were picking on him, and not his wife and daughter? Meaning Justin's own demeanor was a sort of proof of life for the rest of his family?

"We think she's pregnant." He hadn't meant to blurt it out like that, but it happened. Staring at Justin's battered face, wondering if the guy even knew what all was going on within his own family.

"What?" Nicole, clearly surprised.

"The evidence log. Last page, contents from the garbage in the garage trash bin—"

"When did you get a copy of the evidence log?"

Wyatt shrugged, looked her in the eye. "When didn't you read it?"

Nicole scowled, clearly taking his point. In her defense, it was a thirty-page document, and given everything she had to review as the lead agent. But still . . .

"One of those stick things from a home pregnancy test," he continued now, aware of Tessa and Special Agent Hawkes watching him. "Marked positive."

"You think Libby's pregnant? But if it came from the trash, it could have been anyone's."

Wyatt arched a brow. "You mean like the sixty-year-old housekeeper's?"

The FBI agent kept her chin up. "Or the daughter's. She's fifteen. That's old enough."

"True. Any talk of a boyfriend, or sleeping around?"

"Not yet, but that's not going to be the first piece of knowledge shared by her closest friends. Frankly, interviewing teenage girls is tougher than approaching Mafia henchmen. They'll either close ranks, or feed you so much gossip you don't know what to believe. It's going to take us at least a couple more agents, not to mention several more days to sort all those stories out."

"In the meantime," Wyatt stated evenly, "what was good for the gander may have proved good for the goose. Justin cheated on his wife. She cheated back."

"Ending up pregnant?" She still sounded dubious.

"As well as addicted to Vicodin. Don't pity those kidnappers."

Nicole sighed, abruptly rubbed her forehead. "Meaning we possibly have four hostages. God, what a mess. Well then, all the more reason to make this ransom exchange happen. Shall we?" And she gestured once more to the monitor.

"JUSTIN'S INITIAL PHONE CALL WAS SHORT," Nicole explained now. "Unfortunately, as we hadn't anticipated a call directly to the insurance company, we didn't have a phone tap in place. As a matter of protocol, however, the call was recorded. Our audio experts are working on it now, hoping to enhance the background noises in order to assist our efforts. Moving forward, of course, we'll establish a designated line at the insurance company, as well as get one of our agents in place. Next time around, a professional negotiator should be able to drag out the conversation, allowing us the opportunity to trace it."

"Why did he call first?" Tessa asked. "Why call, then send a video?"

"Proof of life," Hawkes provided. "He needed to determine the insurance company's requirement for 'credible risk' of imminent death. You know, what kind of evidence would he need to deliver to support a nine-million-dollar ransom demand?"

Tessa shuddered slightly.

Wyatt agreed: "How does a question like that *not* lead to chopped-off body parts?" he murmured to no one in particular.

Nicole nodded shortly. "The customer service manager was obviously shaken by the call, but she held up well. She said they would need visual confirmation that Justin and his family were alive. Justin asked if e-mailing a video would suffice. She agreed, but said they'd need evidence the video was real-time, not something that had been previously recorded. They agreed that Denbe would hold up today's newspaper, SOP for these kinds of situations. Also, the manager gave Justin a code word to use at the beginning and end of the video—Jazz, which apparently is the name of her cockatoo—that way she'd know the footage had been filmed after he'd spoken to her.

"At the end of the call, you can hear Justin mutter that his face should take care of the rest. We presume that means he felt the image of his bruises, lacerations, et cetera, should suffice for evidence of credible risk."

"Where's the call center?" Wyatt asked.

"Chicago."

"And he e-mailed the video there?"

"Directly to the manager's corporate addy, which she provided."

"How long did it take," Tessa asked, "between the initial phone call and arrival of the video?"

"Approximately forty minutes," Hawkes supplied. He tapped the keyboard, and an e-mail appeared on the monitor before them. He scrolled to the end, where a long string of technical fine print appeared. "See this? This is the kind of data that's present on all e-mails, including time and date sent. More relevantly, it also includes the various servers used to route the e-mail from origin computer A to destination computer Z."

"You mean you can trace the e-mail?" Wyatt asked with fresh interest. He wasn't a computer guy. Liked numbers fine, a good white-collar crime always being a fun puzzle to solve. But technology, computers . . . definitely more Kevin's domain.

Hawkes's turn to grimace. "In this case, probably not. Look, this line here is the X-Originating-IP: in other words, the IP address of the computer that sent the e-mail. We'd love a name, of course, Evil Kidnappers' Computer from Boston. What we got, however, is a string of numbers that will only become relevant later, should we recover a computer to match up. Now, if you move to the next line, the Received lines, you'll see each server that the e-mail passed through on its journey from the kidnappers' computer to the life insurance company's desktop. Sometimes, these servers are identified by a name, indicating the e-mail passed through a major corporate server on its way around the world, say Hotmail, or Verizon. In this case, however, you'll see the Receiving-IPs have domain names such as FakeItMake-It, HotEx, PrescriptMeds, interspersed with lines of complete gobbledygook."

Hawkes paused, looked up at them. "My best guess? The sender turned this e-mail into spam. Some of these funny-sounding domain names, that's what they are; massive servers that sit around the globe and spit out e-mails for Viagra, Canadian drugs, et cetera. These servers survive by being hard to trace. Our sender took advantage of that. Meaning at least one of our UNSUBS has significant computer expertise. Maybe even runs spam as a side business, that sort of thing.

"Now, we got people," Hawkes provided with a shrug. "They'll analyze, dissect, attempt to unravel. But . . ." He shrugged again, and Wyatt got the message. Tracing the e-mail would be a long shot.

"The video itself looks homemade," Tessa observed, moving along. "Single focus, up close and personal."

"We're thinking a cell phone," Nicole stated. "Something with average resolution but not a quality video camera. As for the narrow focus, two considerations: One, Justin was counting on his injuries to motivate the insurance company to pay out an additional five million, meaning he needs the primary shot to center on that damage. Second, the narrow frame also obscures the background, limiting the amount of information we can glean on their current location."

"Professionals," Wyatt sighed.

"We do have one hint." Hawkes tapped the arrow on the screen, and they watched the video play yet again, everyone staring intently at the battered face of Justin Denbe as he stared back at them.

The shot was neck to forehead. No excess space below, above or around. Just a gray-toned wash of Denbe's battered features that darkened slightly at the edges.

"No flash," Hawkes said. "In a focus this tight, flash would wash out the subject's face, render most of his nose, cheeks stark white. However, no halos around his head, either, meaning the light didn't come from behind him. Best guess, the room was sufficiently lit by overhead lights, allowing for even illumination of Denbe's features."

"Rules out some of the northern campgrounds," Wyatt mused, mental gears churning. "A lot of them cut the power for the winter, meaning if the kidnappers were staying there, they'd have to rely on flashlights, candlelight, whatever. Not to mention, those old cabins . . . not many windows for natural lighting."

"I'm thinking the place has modern lighting," Hawkes said. "And if not a landline, would have to have reliable access to a cell signal given the length of the first call. Rules out some of your mountain parks as well."

"Good point."

"I want to see the wife and daughter," Tessa murmured. "I don't like that we're not seeing Libby and Ashlyn."

"Don't think they want all three members of the family together," Wyatt said. "Three together is harder to control. Not to mention filming gets more complicated. But I think Libby and Ashlyn are doing okay. That's why Justin sounds better than he looks. He might've gotten the shit beat out of him, but his family is untouched. Otherwise, he'd sound more stressed, rattled."

Wyatt turned to Nicole. "Is the insurance company going to pay?"

"Going through the chain of command now. But either way, they've promised to cooperate with us. We got people traveling to the offices as we speak. Give us another twenty minutes, we'll have a tapped line, not to mention several agents in place. Justin has to make contact again—not enough information has been provided to complete the transaction. So there'll be another call. And this time, we'll be ready."

Chapter 28

WE MADE IT DOWN TO MEDICAL, Radar's boyish face set in an impassive expression as he helped get Ashlyn situated on the steel bolted bed.

Not much to do, according to him. Miscarriage was a natural event, the body's way of coping. Best he could offer was Tylenol for the pain and water to counter the blood loss. Later, I should watch Ashlyn for signs of fever, which could indicate an infection. In which case, she would require immediate medical attention.

Radar didn't expand upon that statement. Such as, would Z permit one of his nine-million-dollar hostages to visit an ER? I had a feeling our ransom demand was about to come back to bite us. Especially the way Z had looked at Justin . . . Had we really managed to negotiate a deal with Mr. Big Bad Commando? Or had we somehow just played right into his hands?

Radar left, and I went to work removing Ashlyn's blood-soaked jumpsuit, carefully covering her with a towel as I went. A camera was mounted in the corner of the room, and I couldn't bear the thought of Mick, sitting in the control center, getting off on my daughter's pain. I wondered if I could reach up, smear water, or maybe Vaseline across the tiny electronic eye. But I figured Z would never tolerate such a blatant act of insubordination. He'd materialize, there would be consequences, and looking at my daughter, myself, Justin . . . How much more abuse could we take?

I washed Ashlyn's underwear the best I could in the sink, noticing some tissue, trying not to think about it.

Our captors had not considered new undergarments, so I redressed Ashlyn in her still-damp panties, now lined with feminine hygiene pads set out by Radar. He'd muttered under his breath that they made handy field dressings, hence his stash. Clean towels above. Blood-soaked towels below. Again, best not to think of it.

I forced myself to sit, stroking Ashlyn's arm. Her eyelids had stopped fluttering. She appeared to be drifting into sleep. The body doing its best to heal, as Radar had predicted.

Radar finally returned. In hindsight, I realized he'd probably been gone a good thirty to forty minutes. Ironically, the longest time Ashlyn or I had been left unsupervised, let alone unshackled. Just hours ago, we would've run for it. But now . . .

Z seemed to know so much about us. Including how completely we would implode. Had he counted on it to make us easy marks? Known that eventually we would hinder ourselves? Ashlyn and I didn't even require management anymore. We'd hamstrung ourselves with our own secrets. How accommodating of us.

"Methadone," Radar murmured. One word. He spoke with his back to the camera. I thought about it, and then I understood. I bent over my daughter, my lank hair obscuring my own lips, so I appeared to be comforting Ashlyn. They could see us but not hear us meaning that appearances were everything.

"Those are the pills you gave me? I've heard of it."

"It's a synthetic opioid. Helps with withdrawal from other narcotics, such as Vicodin." He turned toward a metal supply case, opening drawers as if searching for something. "But it's also addictive. Eventually, you'll have to wean off it."

He was trying to advise me. For life after this. Assuming the ransom was a success. "How many pills should I take?"

"I've been giving you ten-milligram Diskets. First dose was four tablets. You seemed to struggle again this morning, so I gave you two more. It's not an exact science. A real clinic would spend the first few days of detox figuring out the appropriate dosage for your situation. I'm just winging it."

"I don't feel . . . they're not the same as Vicodin."

"No high," he said bluntly, still rearranging drawers. "Methadone manages the worst of the withdrawal symptoms, as you're still on a narcotic. And the pills last longer. You should be able to take one dose a day in order to mitigate the depression, nausea, headaches. But like I said, you're swapping one problem for another. Good-bye, Vicodin addiction; hello, methadone addiction. You'll need to see a real doctor in order to manage the rest of your withdrawal. Assuming you want to."

"You seem to know a lot about painkiller addiction," I said at last.

He shrugged. "Drug abuse du jour."

"You're a good doctor, Radar. I appreciate your help. For me, and my daughter."

He didn't say anything, appeared uncomfortable.

I couldn't help myself: "Why do you do this? Work with Z and Mick? You seem to have real skills, real talent. You could get a job, in a hospital—"

"Don't."

Single word, filled with more menace than I had anticipated. I drew up short, hesitant, then resumed holding my daughter's hand.

The atmosphere in the tiny room now felt tense. Strange, really. Radar was a captor and we were captives. How else should it feel?

Except, of the three commandos, I trusted Radar the most. He was the caretaker, smuggling me methadone that clearly Z knew nothing about. And he was good with Ashlyn. Competent, even compassionate in his administrations.

Then again, what had Z said about him? Radar would sell out his own mother if the price was right.

Yet this young man, kid really, knew things about Ashlyn and me that Justin didn't even know. And not only had Radar kept my secret, he seemed to be trying to help me. To prepare me for life beyond these prison walls.

I tried to picture my old life, or maybe the new life that would begin sometime after 3:00 P.M. tomorrow. Wearing my own clothes. Sleeping in a room with the lights off. Returning to my family and friends, one of whom had most likely set us up, meaning none of whom I'd be able to trust.

And suddenly, unexpectedly, my eyes filled with tears. I ducked my head, not wanting Radar, let alone Mick in the control room, to see me cry. Oh my God, where were we going from here? We didn't need Z and his prison cells and orange jumpsuits to break us. We'd done it to ourselves, ensconced in our luxurious Boston town house, going through the everyday motions of our extremely privileged lives. Once a real family, now three mere clichés. The pill-popping wife, the unfaithful husband, the pregnant teenage daughter.

Justin seemed fixated on our rescue as some sort of magical switch. Our kidnappers would deliver us in return for the insurance money, and that would be that. We'd click our heels three times, whisper there's no place like home and instantly wake up in our own beds. Justin would go back to work. Ashlyn would go back to school, and I'd . . .

I'd visit a methadone clinic and get my addiction under control? Or say fuck it, and rush back to my lovely orange bottle of pills first chance I got?

I didn't know. I honestly didn't know, and for a moment, the thought of going home, of returning to our real lives with all the unsolved problems . . . it terrified me.

At least in here, we knew who the enemy was. Whereas, once we were home . . .

Beside me, Ashlyn suddenly jerked

awake. Her hazel eyes flew open, panic written all over her face. "Mom!"

"It's okay. I'm here. Shhh . . ."

"Oh, Mom . . ." I could tell the second she finished coming round, as her hands dropped down automatically, cupping her tender stomach. She gazed at me a long time, her expression still young, but already older than I wanted it to be.

"I know, honey," I murmured. "I know."

"Don't tell Dad," she whispered, the words nearly automatic.

I had to smile, but it was a sad expression on my lips. "He'll always love you, sweetie."

"No, he won't. He has standards," she said, and her tone was clearly bitter.

I didn't know what to say about that, so I resumed my bedside vigil. A daughter who had kept her mother's secret. And now a mother charged with keeping her daughter's secret.

"I'll . . . um . . . grab a new jumpsuit," Radar muttered, clearly uncomfortable. He exited, leaving us once more unsupervised and unshackled.

Merely trapped in our own self-induced misery.

I brushed the tears from my daughter's cheek and we waited, together, for the worst of our pain to ease.

WE COULDN'T HIDE IN MEDICAL FOREVER. Z must have demanded an update. Upon hearing that Ashlyn was stable enough, it was back to the family cell for us. Radar walked on one side of Ashlyn, I took the other. She moved gingerly but didn't require much support. To be fifteen again, so young and fixable.

Her footsteps slowed as we entered the cavernous dayroom.

I didn't blame her. Justin had never been one to run from a fight. Sure enough, the cell door barely clanking shut behind us:

"I want to know his name." Justin rose to standing in the middle of the tiny space, arms crossed over his chest, voice stern and cold. Not asking, but demanding.

Ashlyn pulling her arm away from me, bringing up her chin. "Maybe his last name is Chapman. As in your girlfriend's younger brother. He'd be about my age, right?"

My eyes widening, just as my husband paled.

Justin whirled on me. "How dare you tell her—"

"I didn't."

"I did!" Ashlyn, in full glory now, arms flung out, thin body nearly levitating with hostility. "I checked your phone, Dad. I read your e-mails. Quite a little exchange you had with a girl young enough to be my sister. Wonder what her father would think. Maybe she's not supposed to sleep around, either. Maybe, she was also supposed to wait for a boy who would *honor* her and *love* her and *respect* her. You know, all that crap you used to feed me, before running out the door to cheat on your family. Hypocrite! Fucking liar!"

"Ashlyn!" Myself, stepping quickly between my daughter and my husband, as if that might keep Ashlyn safe.

Justin's face, already terribly misshapen, had taken on the color of eggplant. Steam should have been pouring out of his ears. Certainly, every blood vessel in his body appeared ready to burst.

"Don't you *ever* speak to me like that, young lady!"

"Or what?"

"Stop." My voice came out too shaky. I cleared my throat, forced myself to sound more forceful. "Both of you. Take a second."

Ashlyn, turning on me now. "Why? You afraid I'm going to tell him about your drug problem."

"What?"

I wanted to laugh. I understood it would be wildly inappropriate. But the sheer rage on my daughter's face, followed by the sheer bewilderment on Justin's. I wanted to giggle. Except I was pretty sure the first hiccuping laugh would lead straight to tears.

Ashlyn, still on a rampage: "Jesus Christ, Dad. She's been stoned out of her mind for months now. The glazed-over eyes? The way you ask her a question and it takes a full minute before she answers? I mean, come on, Dad. It took me two weeks to figure out she was abusing prescription painkillers. I'm a kid. What the hell is your excuse?"

Justin, officially too stupefied to speak. Me, a hand now clasped over my mouth because, heaven help me, any second now, I was going to burst into hysterics.

"I mean, really. You're out all the time with your new girl. Mom's doped out of her skull. Of course I decided to have a little fun. Even took a tumble in your bed. Not like you two are using it."

Justin lunged. I got my arms around his waist, not that it really mattered. He weighed twice as much as me and, even bruised and battered, moved like a freight train. He roared something. Maybe that he would kill him, the mythical boy. And Ashlyn screamed something. Maybe that she hated him, her own father.

He was swatting at her. Trying to get at our child. Our own baby, who just hours before had been pregnant with a baby of her own, and I felt this incredible pressure build behind my eyeballs. A pain beyond any pill's ability to deaden. A hopelessness beyond any wonder drug's ability to lift.

Then, I was in the fray. Digging in my heels, shoving back at my husband, heaving, heaving, heaving as I screamed at the top of my lungs:

"You stupid idiot! I didn't want your money. I didn't want your house. I didn't want your precious business. I just wanted you to love me. You stupid, stupid asshole. Why . . . couldn't you . . . just love me?"

Our legs tangled up. Justin went down hard, hands over his swollen face. I fell to my knees beside him. Pounding his shoulder, sobbing hysterically, while Ashlyn wept next to the bunk beds.

"And it wasn't just her, was it? There were other women, too. Lots of others. Jesus Christ, you are just like your father. And now I'm just like my mother except popping pills instead of cigarettes, and we were both supposed to be better than this. What happened? God, Justin, what happened to us? How did we become exactly the people we never wanted to be?"

I couldn't stop hitting him. My rage was a feral beast, finally off its leash. I hated my husband. I hated my life. But mostly, I hated us, the ways we'd both failed, proving ourselves human, when so long ago, we'd been sure we'd rise above all that. Mortals were fallible. We'd been in love.

At the last second, I saw my husband's shoulders shake. I saw the tears on his cheeks, the defeated bow of his head . . .

I couldn't take it anymore. I threw my arms around him. I held him close, promising forgiveness I wasn't sure I had in my heart to give, but for now, this moment . . . If he would just be all right. If we could just pretend to be a family . . .

Ashlyn joined us on the floor, her arms around both of us, damp cheek pressed against my neck. "I'm sorry, Mommy, I'm sorry, Mommy, I'm sorry, sorry, sorry."

Justin moaned. We cried harder.

"Oh, for the love of God."

Z stood in the open doorway, staring at us as if arriving at the scene of a car accident.

"You people . . ." He couldn't complete the sentence.

And I agreed with him. We defied description. What kind of family behaved like this? What kind of people loved one another, and hurt each other anyway?

"Three P.M. tomorrow. Not soon enough." Z stopped shaking his head, stabbing a finger at me instead. "You. Off him." Another finger, pointed at my daughter. "You, too. Stand and present."

Ashlyn and I climbed shakily to our feet. Z stared at us harder. We threw our shoulders back, assuming the posture of good soldiers. He grunted his approval. Then, his gaze went to Justin, now uncurling on the floor.

"Whatever happened, I'm sure you deserved it. Ladies. With me."

We started walking forward just as Justin rose unsteadily to his feet.

"Wait."

Ashlyn continued marching, but I stopped. I couldn't help myself. I'd loved this man so much of my life. The afternoons at the firing range, our first home, the birth of our daughter, the way I used to wake up and find him watching me so intently.

All those moments when I know I had really, truly seen him. All those moments when I know he must've really, truly seen me.

"I didn't realize," Justin murmured. "What was going on with Ashlyn, with you . . . I didn't realize. And Ashlyn's right. I should've. A good man, an attentive father . . . I fucked up, Libby. That's on me. When we get home, if you want a divorce, I'll do whatever you want. I'll even rip up the prenup. House, company, whatever you'd like, I won't fight you. In fact, you can have it all. It's the least you deserve and shame on me for not realizing that sooner. But I wish . . . I would miss our family, Libby. I would miss us."

I waited for him to say more. But he swallowed instead, choked up.

I thought of all the things I could offer in reply. Forgiveness. Acknowledgment of my own crimes. Or more importantly, that I missed us, too. Had for months, and no pill in the world had been able to fill that void. All the nights I had wandered down to the darkened basement, my hand pressed against that closed bedroom door, willing my husband to feel my presence, to open his door to me.

I said: "How many other women, Justin?"

"You're the only one I've ever loved," he said.

Which told me enough.

I turned away from my husband and walked toward my captor instead.

Chapter 29

Wʜɪʟᴇ ᴛʜᴇ Bᴏsᴛᴏɴ ᴄᴏᴘs ᴀɴᴅ FBI went to work on strategizing possible ransom scenarios, Tessa and Wyatt decided to follow up with Anita Bennett. In her house, surrounded by pictures of her family, hopefully, including her youngest son, who might or might not be Justin Denbe's half brother.

Being the local, Tessa drove. Wyatt resumed his easy sprawl in the passenger's seat, except this time, he was scowling.

"You don't look happy," Tessa ventured

at last, threading her way from Storrow Drive to Route 2 toward Lexington, Massachusetts.

"I'm disgruntled."

"Personally or professionally?"

"Professionally. I don't have a personal life to get disgruntled about."

"Really?"

"I like carpentry, making things with my hands. Other than that, I work a lot. No wife, no kids, no girlfriend."

"Okay."

He turned, regarding her steadily. "You? How does the life of a corporate investigator compare with your days as a state trooper?"

"Better hours, better pay," she said.

"But do you love it?"

It took her a bit to answer. "I like it," she said at last. "For my daughter's sake, that's enough."

She could feel him watching her from the passenger's seat. Not speaking. Not scrutinizing. Just . . . being.

She found herself saying: "You haven't asked me about my husband."

"Your business, not mine."

"Two years ago," she heard herself continue, "Brian was shot dead, and my daughter went missing. I confessed to shooting him, but was also charged with killing my own kid."

"Your daughter's alive. You said so."

"I found her. Some of my methods didn't necessarily . . . color inside the legal lines. I won't ever be welcomed in law enforcement again. But I have my daughter back and that's what matters most."

"You know," he drawled slowly, "now that you mention it, that case rings a bell."

She stiffened, steeling herself for the inevitable comments on her shooting skills, or even a crack on how her husband must've deserved it.

Instead, he asked: "How's your daughter holding up?"

"She told me to look for the Denbe family in cold, dark places. Also, to bring cookies and carry my gun."

"Smart kid."

She found herself nodding. And thinking that she liked Wyatt Foster. Liked him a lot.

"You ever been married?" she asked.

"Yep. Total train wreck. But I've got nothing against domestic life. And between you, me and the lamppost, I like kids. It's one of those things guys can't really say, though. Comes out sounding creepy. Which, given how much I respect your skills, is not the impression I'm trying to make."

"I don't date much." This must be what happened when you went too long without adult company, she decided. First attentive listener and it was like she had diarrhea of the mouth. She continued: "My focus is my daughter, creating a safe, stable home environment for her. She deserves that much."

"Ah, hence the scraped-back hair—"

"That's the second comment I've received in two days! What is it about my hair?"

"You're too young to look that old," Wyatt said matter-of-factly. "Besides, it doesn't work for me. I see something pulled back that tight, mostly, I get curious how it might look down. You know, preferably after a nice dinner, followed by a couple glasses of wine, that sort of thing."

Tessa was no longer watching the road. She was staring at the man sitting in her passenger's seat, and she was pretty sure she was blushing. *Blushing*, for heaven's sake.

"But I imagine you don't date on the job," he continued now, voice still perfectly even.

"Exactly," she managed, and returned her eyes to the road.

They fell back into silence.

"So," she drawled after another few minutes. "You're disgruntled."

"Yes. The kidnappers are exposing themselves. They're making phone calls, buying local newspapers and most likely getting supplies to treat a woman in the midst of pretty serious withdrawal. And yet, we still can't get a bead on them. It's pissing me off."

"We don't have a description," Tessa pointed out. "It's hard to make headway without a tangible description of the suspects to circulate. I mean, what can local law enforcement do right now? Ask local gas stations if any strangers bought a newspaper today? At this rate, we should feel disgruntled. We're still skirting the perimeters of the crime. We haven't reached the heart of the matter."

"I called my office," Wyatt said. "Got them working with the local wireless providers to identify chunks of real estate that don't receive adequate cell coverage. Sounds like that will eliminate a great deal of the White Mountain National Forest. 'Course, most of the real estate in question is high altitude or deep country . . . not exactly accessible for hiding hostages anyway."

"Process of elimination is still something; a no that helps lead to yes."

"Forest rangers have been making progress, too, visiting campgrounds and trailheads. At this rate, we may work ourselves down to a mere fifth of the state left to search by tomorrow."

"See, smaller haystack. Well done."

Wyatt stopped scowling, grinned instead. "I like you," he said. "Hairdo aside, I'm going to ask you out one day. But not today. Today, we're going to focus on the Denbe family."

"Not much time left," she murmured, taking the exit for Lexington as she followed her GPS's directions for Anita Bennett's house.

"Exactly," he agreed, fingers drumming against the middle console. "Exactly."

*   *   *

ANITA BENNETT OPENED HER FRONT DOOR after the first ring. She took in Tessa, wearing black Ann Taylor slacks topped with a
fitted white shirt, and frowned slightly. Then
she spotted Wyatt, standing in full view of
her neighbors in his brown sheriff's uniform, and positively scowled.

"Come in!" she said, less of an invitation, more of a demand. They did.

Anita wore a long dark skirt with slim
black boots, topped with a heather-colored
cable-knit sweater. She matched the
white-painted, black-shuttered house,
Tessa thought, a perfect advertisement
for refined New England living. Currently,
the woman was fidgeting with her long
string of pearls, and looking at Tessa and
Wyatt as if she didn't know what to do
with them.

"We have some more questions," Tessa
said by way of explanation.

"I would've met you at the office. As it is,
we've just returned from church."

"It will only take a minute."

A last scowl, then Anita seemed to give
up. Her shoulders came down slightly; she
gestured for them to follow her.

"Honey, who's here?" A man's voice from the end of the hallway.

Anita didn't immediately answer, but kept walking, leading them past a massive kitchen with black granite countertops and cherrywood cabinets, then the formal dining room, until they finally arrived in a smaller sitting room, boasting a fireplace, a pair of silk-covered wingback chairs and a vintage 1920s love seat.

Tessa found this interesting. She would've described the COO's office as modern, while her home was clearly New England traditional. She wondered what other differences distinguished work Anita from home Anita.

An older man in black slacks and a cranberry-colored sweater had been sitting in front of the lit fire. Now he rose, moving gingerly, and offered a hand. He had a full head of striking gray hair, topping a broad, friendly face with wire-rimmed glasses.

"Daniel Coakley," he said, by way of introduction. "Anita's husband. And you are?"

"These are two of the investigators looking for Justin and his family," Anita said crisply. But Tessa noticed the woman's gaze softened when she looked at her husband. She moved closer, placing a hand on his arm in an almost protective gesture. "It's okay, Dan. They just need to ask me a few more questions. Do you mind?"

Dan seemed to take that as his cue to depart. He nodded at both of them, then worked his way slowly down the hallway in the direction they had come.

"Heart attack," Anita said, in answer to their unspoken question. "Last year. He died twice on the way to the ER. You have no idea how much that puts your life in perspective."

She gestured to the forest-green wing-back chairs. Tessa took one, Wyatt the other. Anita perched on the edge of the gold-and-green-covered sofa. Putting plenty of distance between her and the investigators, Tessa noticed, while sitting ramrod straight, hands clasped on her knees, body language radiating wariness.

Given the woman's discomfort, Tessa took her time, letting the silence drag out while she took inventory of the room, seeking out family photos. She spotted two larger framed prints. One close-up shot of three school-age boys, piled up on a hillside, bright faces beaming. Then, the classic family shot, a younger Anita seated in one of the wingback chairs, three now teenage boys kneeling around her while a noticeably larger, healthier Daniel Coakley stood behind them all, hand on her shoulder.

In this photo, Tessa could see that Anita's husband had had blond hair, which complemented his fair complexion. Before going silver gray, Anita appeared to have been a strawberry blonde with equally pale skin. Which left their youngest son with noticeably darker features than the rest of the family.

She and Wyatt exchanged a look. He was seated comfortably in the other wingback chair, one leg crossed casually on the other, elbows resting at his side. He was going with his quietly accessible demeanor. Not pressuring their interview subject, but letting her come to him.

Effective approach given how much Tessa herself had volunteered in just one car ride.

"We have received a ransom demand," Tessa said.

Clearly, this was not what Anita had

been expecting. Immediately, the COO was on her feet, fingers once again working her pearls. "How, when? What do they want? Are Justin and his family okay?"

"Demand is nine million dollars. Justin evoked some special clause that allows an additional life insurance payment in situations of extreme danger."

"Oh my God." Anita's hand, covering her mouth. "Is he . . . all right? Ashlyn? Libby?"

"Justin states they are currently safe, but we haven't received visual confirmation yet."

"Will the insurance company pay?"

"Being worked out as we speak."

"Of course they'll pay," Anita said, no longer looking at them, but seeming to speak to herself. "That's why one carries such policies. So that when the worst happens, the company will pay, and Justin and his family will be returned safe. When?"

"Soon. We hope."

Anita sat back down. Her earlier wariness was gone. She appeared intent now. "So what do you need from me? How can I help?"

Tessa and Wyatt exchanged another glance. If Anita had a vested interest in the

Denbe family's disappearance, she was doing a good job of hiding it. Or maybe, none of this was news to her. The ransom had been part of the plan, and all was proceeding on schedule.

Tessa decided to cut to the chase. "Tell us about your youngest son."

The COO froze. For one moment, Tessa thought the older woman might fight it, but then she conceded their point with a single, stiff nod. "I see the rumor mill's been busy as usual."

Tessa and Wyatt just waited.

"You want to know why I didn't just tell you everything yesterday," Anita continued unprompted. "First second you arrived in my office, I should've aired my dirty laundry, dragged all the skeletons out of the closet. Because of course, Justin's disappearance must have something to do with my son. Families are like that."

Again, Tessa and Wyatt said nothing.

"He doesn't even know," Anita said abruptly. "Timothy, I mean. Daniel does. And, yes, it was a very difficult time in our marriage. But we survived it. And Daniel loves Timmy. Views him as just as much his son as our other two children. In the end, we decided to let it be. Daniel is happy, Timmy is happy, why rip apart our family for no good reason?"

"Does Justin know?" Wyatt spoke up.

Anita shrugged. "People in the company have whispered about it for years, of course. But I've never directly stated that Timmy is Dale Denbe's son. Frankly, the first ten years I wasn't even sure myself. Of course, as Timmy's grown up, the family resemblance . . ."

"Does Justin know?" Wyatt pressed again.

Anita seemed to be struggling. "I'm sure he must suspect it," she finally allowed. "But again, for Timmy's sake as much as anyone's, I've never gone there, and I never will."

"For Timmy's sake?" Tessa repeated, allowing disbelief to color her voice. "Because being in line for a hundred-million-dollar family business can't possibly be in his best interest?"

Anita smiled faintly. "Do you know what Tim is studying at college?"

They shook their heads.

"Animal husbandry. He wants to move to Vermont and start his own free-range all-organic all—environmentally correct dairy farm. Timmy isn't interested in building two-hundred-million-dollar prisons or hospitals or colleges. He wants to be one with the earth."

"So he sells his share of the business and uses it to start his farm."

"What share?" Anita said calmly. "Dale didn't leave the firm to his surviving heirs. He left it to Justin, specifically, by name. Even if I wanted to subject my family to the strain of declaring Timmy's parentage, it wouldn't change anything. Besides, given the shape the firm's in, I'm not sure it could survive the drama. And again, for what? Justin is the right member of the Denbe family to be heading the company. He loves it. My son has his own dreams. Nothing is broken. Nothing needs to be fixed."

Tessa wasn't buying it. "You're denying your son part of his family, let alone the choice of getting involved with the business—"

"Excuse me. I *am* the business and Timmy's spent as much of his childhood at the Denbe Construction offices as my two other boys. At any point, if he was interested in construction, I could've gotten him involved with the firm given my own position, let alone his possible gene pool. He's *never* been interested."

"And Justin's really okay with this?" Wyatt again, sounding just as skeptical as Tessa.

"We've never spoken of it. Ever. Timmy was just a baby when Dale died. Then, by the time he hit ten, and started looking more and more like Justin, and less and less like Daniel, what was the point? People suspected. Rumors swirled. But Justin has never asked me and I've never volunteered."

"But Timothy got a college scholarship. First one Denbe ever paid."

Anita hesitated. Her gaze slid away. "Justin offered," she murmured. "Company had had a good year. Who was I to argue?"

"So he knows," Wyatt pressed.

"We've never spoken of it," Anita repeated stubbornly. Apparently, in her world, denial made it so.

Daniel was back, standing in the doorway.

"Justin knows," he said. The words came out hoarsely. The man cleared his throat, as if to speak again, but Anita was already moving to his side.

"Honey, it's okay, they're just leaving."

Daniel stood his ground. "Justin knows," he said again, the words firmer this time. "Those bonuses he gives to you. They're profit sharing, for Timmy, too. Like the checks he sends to his mother."

Anita flushed, didn't say anything

Tessa and Wyatt regarded Daniel with fresh interest.

"Why do you say that?" Tessa asked.

"Dale, whatever else you wanted to say about him, always met his obligations. Justin's like that, too. Takes care of his mother, given her a share of the proceeds of the company, even though she hasn't spoken to him in years. He takes care of his half brother likewise, even if Timothy has never been acknowledged."

"You don't know—" Anita started.

"You set the money aside," Dan interjected loudly. "You dole out part of your year-end bonus to Timmy, but not to Jimmy and Richard. You think I don't know why? You think some year Tim won't ask?"

Anita flushed, didn't say anything.

"Justin knows," Daniel repeated. "But he doesn't pry. After all these years, it's just one of those things. The arrangement works, as long as no one questions it."

"And Tim has never questioned it?" Tessa asked.

"No, ma'am."

"And Justin's never questioned it?" Wyatt pressed.

"Not that I know of."

"We're going to pull your financials," Tessa warned, glaring hard at Anita. "Anything else you'd like to tell us now, before we read about it later?"

Anita flushed again. "I have nothing to hide. Whatever happened to Justin . . . whoever is holding him for ransom, it has nothing to do with me or my family."

"Any fresh ideas who might be behind it?" Wyatt again.

Anita regarded him curiously. "It doesn't have to be any of us, does it? I mean, if it's a ransom case, and he's been taken by professionals . . . Well, I mean, anyone can tell Justin is a wealthy man. His homes, his cars, the company. Maybe he was targeted because of who *he* is, not who he works with."

"They knew the security code to his town house," Tessa rattled off. "They knew the family's schedule, the home's layout and exactly when and where to strike. This was an inside job, and you'd better believe

Justin is as aware of that as we are. Meaning the second he and his family are safe at home . . . You really think Justin's going to just let this whole incident slide?"

Anita had paled. She shook her head.

"It's going to be warfare," Tessa continued. "Justin himself is going to go after each and every one of you, even if it means dismantling his own company brick by brick. The more you know him, the bigger your exposure is going to be. So speak now, Anita. We're willing to listen. Justin, on the other hand, after having watched his wife and daughter suffer . . ."

"I don't know anything," Anita insisted. "I wouldn't harm Justin, let alone his family. And I can't think of anyone else in the firm that might."

"Not even someone who was unhappy with the direction things were moving?" Wyatt pressed. "Might think he or she could do better, if they were in charge?"

A slight hesitation. "You should talk to Ruth Chan."

"The CFO?" Tessa asked. "The one on vacation?"

"We finally spoke this morning. She was going to head straight for the airport, try to get on the first available flight out. But in the beginning, when I told her what had happened to Justin . . . She got real quiet. It's not that she said anything, or confessed anything. Just . . ."

Tessa and Wyatt waited.

Anita finally looked up. "She didn't seem shocked. I told her Justin and his family had gone missing, and it didn't seem to surprise her at all."

Chapter 30

Z LED ASHLYN AND ME through a maze of broad corridors. At first I thought we must be heading to the kitchen for lunch duty, but after we bypassed those doors, I gave up guessing our destination and simply followed in his wake.

He hadn't bothered to shackle our wrists. Nor did he walk between us. Instead, he strode forward several paces, shoulders loose, body language relaxed, a man who might as well be on a Sunday stroll.

Now that the ransom wheels were set in motion, did he figure he had little to fear regarding an attempted escape? Or, when it came to him versus us, did he just figure he had little to fear?

Ashlyn was moving slowly. She should be resting in bed, not roaming a vast, hard-floored building. When we got home, I'd take her directly to the doctor. As well as have a long-overdue heart-to-heart chat.

Z finally arrived at a heavy steel door. He opened it and we entered a modest room, with floor-to-ceiling wood paneling against one wall and a raised dais. A gold cross was mounted on the wood paneling. Chapel, I realized. We had reached the prison's sanctuary.

Radar was already there. He had every light on and was walking around the space with his iPhone, either filming or snapping photos. He looked up when we entered, but his face was as expressionless as always.

"We'll start them here," he said to Z, pointing to a spot on the dais. "Should give us enough light, with a neutral-enough backdrop. I gotta go with a wider frame to include two people, so the viewers are going to see more. But wood paneling's pretty nondescript."

"Their jumpsuits?" Z asked.

Radar held up his phone, aimed it at Ashlyn and me. "Not gonna happen. Orange collar clearly visible."

Z nodded, apparently having expected this answer. He gestured toward the corner, where I saw a pile of clothing on the floor. Our clothing. From the first day. Was that yesterday, or the day before? Time grew murky when you spent 24/7 under the glow of fluorescent lighting. I didn't know how lifers learned to stand it.

"Tops only," Z instructed us. "Just throw them on over your jumpsuits, then we'll figure out the collars."

I finally understood what they were trying to do. Disguise us and our location. Of course, the ransom demand had to be beamed to the authorities, who would scrutinize the video footage for any clues as to our whereabouts. For example, cinderblock walls, orange prison jumpsuits, anything else they could see in the frame. So we'd film against the one noninstitutional wall in the entire facility, while wearing our last known garments.

As usual, Z had thought of everything.

I handed Ashlyn her baby blue waffle-knit shirt. Raising her arms over her head clearly pained her, so I helped drag the form-fitting sleep top over her oversize jumpsuit. The jumpsuit top bulged awkwardly, while the bright orange collar poked through the waffle shirt's crewneck like an out-of-place bird of paradise flower.

Z took one look and shook his head. "Top of the jumpsuit, off."

Ashlyn and I looked around. The room was one open space. No alcove to tuck inside, or half wall to duck behind.

"We need privacy," I stated primly.

Z stared at us, cobra tattoo nearly hissing. "Why? Radar's already seen it all, and I could care less. Get it done."

We remained standing there, staring at him. Myself, I could do it. But strip my daughter, bare her to these two men who'd already taken so much from us? Ashlyn's shoulders had hunched, her body unconsciously rounding as if to make herself small. I couldn't take it. I positioned myself in front of her, crossed my arms over my chest, and faced off against Z.

"We need privacy," I repeated.

Z sighed. He spoke as if addressing two small children. "Let me explain how this is going to work: You will do exactly what I tell you to do. You will say exactly what I tell you to say. Or, if you misbehave"—he leveled his gaze at me—"I'll let Mick beat the shit out of your daughter. Or, if you misbehave"—his gaze switched to Ashlyn—"I'll let Mick beat the shit out of your mom. Now, fix the wardrobe."

"It's okay, Mom," Ashlyn whispered behind me. "Remember, when I was little, at the beach? We can figure it out."

When Ashlyn was little, it was often just her and me at the beach, given Justin's work schedule. Ashlyn hadn't the patience for the overcrowded changing room, let alone the long line. So I would hold a towel around her as a makeshift curtain, while she wiggled her suit on or off. Later, I got to the point where I could lie in the sand with a towel draped over the top of my body, and make my own wardrobe adjustments while my four-year-old giggled uncontrollably.

If I thought about it, it had been her and me against the world for a long time. And my daughter was right: having come this far, no reason we couldn't figure things out.

She reached her hands under her waffle shirt and worked the snaps. She got one arm out, then the other. With the waffle shirt hanging loose around her shoulders, she divested the short sleeves of the jumpsuit top, then got her arms back in the waffle top. We left the top of the jumpsuit hanging down at her waist, where it would be out of the video frame.

Next, my turn. I'd been wearing a champagne-colored wrap top. Also form-fitting, and never going to work layered on top of a baggy jumpsuit. I gave Z and Radar my back, and got to it. Undressing wasn't so bad. Snap, snap and the top of the jumpsuit dangled down while I kept my arms crossed protectively over my chest. Ashlyn handed me my top.

For a moment, I smelled oranges and my eyes welled with longing before I realized it was simply the citrus notes of my perfume, embedded in the silky fabric. Postcards from another life, one that I knew hadn't been that long ago—one day, two days?—and yet already was completely alien to me.

It felt wrong to pull such a delicate fabric over my sweat-encrusted skin. To surround myself in silken finery after days of wearing a stiff, oversize man's jumpsuit.

My hair was too rank, my nails too dirty. A jail cell made the filth easier to take. But this, a visit to the past, a note of refinement amid the abyss . . .

"Mom? Let me."

I'd been trying to fasten the complicated tie system at the waist of the wrap shirt, but my fingers were shaking too badly. Now Ashlyn brushed my hands away and took over working the knots.

I admired her dexterity as much as I admired her bravery. We had screwed up, obviously. A family of three absolute fuckups. And yet, each of us, in our own way, was holding up. My fifteen-year-old, highly privileged, officially sexually active daughter had not collapsed. She was not sobbing hysterically or shutting down or whining constantly. She was functioning. We were all functioning.

We would get through this, I told myself. We'd survive, we'd return home and we would . . .

We would forge on. We'd forgive, we'd forget. That's what families did, right? Muddled through in full, imperfect glory.

Ashlyn and I finished our preparations. Her top in place, my top in place. We moved to the spot Radar indicated on the dais, then Z handed me a newspaper, the Sunday edition. I tucked it beneath my arm as he gave each of us a one-page script. He had the piece of paper flipped over, blank side up.

Now he said, "On the count of three, Radar will start filming. You will each start reading, alternating line by line, Ashlyn going first. Remember, no adlibbing, no straying from the script, or the other one pays the price."

My first tingle of apprehension.

"One."

Why wouldn't he let us preview the script?

"Two."

Why the need to threaten us with Mick?

"Three."

Radar nodded his head. We flipped over our pages and once again, my heart sank in my chest.

"MY NAME IS ASHLYN DENBE," my daughter whispered. In the background, Z scowled at her, cupping his hand around her ear.

"My name is Libby Denbe," I filled in, my voice louder, as he'd indicated.

Ashlyn cleared her throat. "Today is Sunday."

I provided the date, then, following the note from the script, hastily unfolded the newspaper and flashed the front page.

"We are here with my father, Justin Denbe," my daughter intoned.

"To secure our freedom," I read, "you must wire nine million dollars to the following account." I read off a long list of numbers. The script instructed me to repeat. I licked my lips, and repeated.

"Tomorrow, three P.M., eastern standard time, we will call you," my daughter recited.

"On Justin Denbe's iPhone," I read. "The call will be in FaceTime. You'll be able to see us. We'll be able to see you."

"You will verify that we are alive," Ashlyn said. Her eyes flew up; she glanced at me almost eagerly.

"You will then have ten minutes to wire the money."

"Once the full payment is received," Ashlyn read, "we will provide the address of the location where we can be retrieved unharmed."

"By three eleven P.M.," I said, "if the full nine million dollars has not been successfully wired to the account provided . . ."

"The first member of our family . . ." Ashlyn paused, glanced up. Z stared at her hard, both willing the words from her mouth and reminding her sternly of the consequences if she failed to utter them. "The first member of our family will be killed," Ashlyn whispered.

"To be selected at random," I intoned, my voice equally quiet.

"There will be no negotiation."

"No additional contact."

"The money will be received," Ashlyn murmured.

"Or one by one, we will die," I finished.

"Pay the money," Ashlyn read flatly.

"Keep us alive." Did my voice sound pleading?

"Jazz," Ashlyn said.

I frowned, spotted the word on my own script. "Jazz," I repeated.

Then, just like that, Radar lowered his phone and the show was over.

Ashlyn and I didn't talk again. We retreated to the corner of the room, peeling off the clothes that were once ours and now felt as if they belonged to other people from another life.

Radar had exited immediately. Probably to deliver the short video. E-mail it? I wasn't a techie, but he seemed to know what he was doing.

Z waited for us beside the door, hands in the front pockets of his black cargo pants. He didn't attempt to sneak glances as we changed, seeming immune to our presence. Of our captors, he was the one I could least figure out. Clearly, he was the leader of this operation. The brains who was equally respected for his brawn.

Former military. Current private mercenary? The kind of man who would do whatever, hurt whomever, as long as the money was good? Kidnap a family, beat a husband, terrify a wife and teenage daughter?

As of this moment, was he double-dipping? Receiving payment from whomever had wanted us taken, while also attempting to earn an additional nine million in ransom funds?

Or, would that be unethical? A break in some mercenary code?

There was a thought there. A kernel of an idea I struggled to hold. Given what we knew thus far—the locked front door, the insider knowledge of our routine—we'd assumed someone we knew must've hired Z and his team to take us. Except, we'd never figured out who or why. Which brought up the logical question, would this same person who was willing to pay for us to disappear really want us returned home again, safe and sound? The ransom exchange made sense for Z, Radar and Mick, each of whom stood to receive millions of dollars. But what about the mystery mastermind? What did he get out of all of this?

Surely it had to be in his best interest for us to never be found alive. Which might explain the current take-it-or-leave-it approach to the ransom demands. Certainly, the script that Ashlyn and I had just read hadn't allowed any room for negotiation, good faith exchanges or counteroffers. Just pay nine million dollars by 3:00 P.M. tomorrow, or members of the Denbe family will start turning up dead.

It was as if Z was waiting for an excuse to kill us.

Maybe because that was still his overarching charge, the terms of the first contract. And as strange as it sounded, Z struck me as the ethical type. A man as good as his word. The kind of guy who made a promise, then kept it.

I shivered, and once I started, it was hard to stop.

Twenty-four hours, I thought.

Twenty-four hours and then either a miracle would occur, and we'd find ourselves safely back in our own home.

Or, we were as good as dead.

Chapter 31

WYATT WAS NOT HAPPY. His fellow investigators were not happy. He and Tessa had returned to the Denbes' Boston town house upon receiving word of fresh contact. A short video of Libby and Ashlyn Denbe had been e-mailed to the life insurance company approximately thirty minutes ago. Now they were all once more huddled in the back of the FBI's mobile command center staring at the computer screen. The video had just ended. Special Agent Hawkes hit replay. Again, then again. None of the subsequent viewings improved any of their moods.

No contact information for follow-up questions. No room for renegotiating the ransom terms or demanding a good-faith gesture, such as the release of the youngest family member. Just a flat-out exchange. Pay the money or pick up the bodies.

"How do we know they won't kill the Denbes the second after we wire the money?" Nicole scowled. She was twirling a loose strand of blond hair around her finger, a nervous habit Wyatt knew she hated, but couldn't break.

"We don't," her fellow FBI agent, Hawkes, countered. "Sounds like the whole exchange happens long distance. We pay, the Denbes provide an address, then we get to rescue them."

"Talk about a KISS approach to kidnapping," Wyatt drawled. "Keep it Simple, Stupid. Which is exactly what they're doing."

"Insurance company won't go for it," Nicole warned.

"Denbe Construction will threaten to sue if they don't," Tessa countered. She was standing next to Wyatt. Her hair smelled like strawberries, and he really did want to remove that plain black hair elastic, just to see how it fell around her shoulders. Now was not the time or place to notice such things, of course, and yet he did. "After all, the policy contains a risk-of-imminent-death clause, and here's a video of the insurants stating they'll be killed if monies aren't delivered. Seems pretty slam dunk to me."

"We need more information," Nicole continued primly. "That's the whole point of the negotiations. We should be demanding concessions, such as the release of the girl. Instead, we're being squeezed just as tightly as the insurance company. Told nothing. Ordered to deliver everything. We take all the risk, they gain all the reward."

Wyatt held up his hand. "Let's talk about that. Before we get too far into what this video doesn't tell us, let's discuss what it does." He ticked off one finger: "Experienced captors."

"Professionals! We already knew that!" Nicole, still twirling her hair.

"We thought in terms of hired muscle, most likely former military. But what about prior kidnapping-for-ransom experience?

You guys have databases. Got any lists of professionals, known offenders who've done this kind of thing before? That might tell us something."

Nicole frowned, but nodded. She gestured to Hawkes, who started typing.

"They're using an iPhone." Tessa continued brainstorming. "Given that tomorrow's phone call will be in FaceTime. They'll dial Justin's number in the FaceTime mode and once we pick up, it'll be like a video conference. We can see and hear them, and they can see and hear us."

"Given the quality of the video," Hawkes said, "an iPhone would work. Now, FaceTime requires a Wi-Fi connection, but that's not really an issue in this day and age. Could be they have Wi-Fi available at their location, or they brought a Mi-Fi, creating their own hotspot."

"Can we trace it?" Wyatt, the nontechie, asked.

"The Wi-Fi signal? If the signal were unsecured and we were within distance to receive it, yes, there are some tools that could lead us to the source. But that means being able to pick up the Wi-Fi signal, identifying it's the one being used by the UNSUBs and already being within a few hundred yards—or less—of the broadcast location."

Wyatt took that to mean no. "What about the iPhone?"

"Don't have a phone number to trace; the call number was blocked when Justin dialed customer service. Best guess, given these guys are pros, is that the iPhone is either stolen or a knockoff. Big black market for consumer electronics, making it easy enough to pick up a couple of disposable phones for a job like this. At least"—Hawkes shrugged—"that's what I would do."

"The girl was surprised," Tessa said quietly. "Justin appeared to be talking off the cuff, but this video, the way they intoned the words. It's almost like Ashlyn and Libby were following a prewritten script. The threat of death . . . You could tell that caught Ashlyn off guard."

"She didn't freak out," Wyatt murmured, though the look on her face, the moment after reading that line, would haunt him.

"They're unharmed," Nicole said. "Not beaten, like Justin. Also, holding up well given the situation. Seems to indicate that thus far, they've been treated better than he has."

"They're not worth more if beaten to a pulp," Wyatt said bluntly. "Justin is. But I agree. Whatever threats the kidnappers are using, it's enough to gain cooperation without rendering them hysterical."

"Professionals," Tessa murmured, the obvious distinction.

Wyatt bent over, scrutinizing the video. "Background looks like wood paneling," he said.

"Agreed," Hawkes seconded.

"Consistent with many hiking lodges." He turned this around in his mind, trying to think through the logistics. "The Denbes will provide the address of their location once the money is transferred," he muttered out loud. "Meaning the kidnappers have to wait around to ensure their demands have been met, most likely somewhere close enough that the family continues to play by the rules, even when on the phone with us. Then, the moment the payment has been wired to the designated account, two things will happen at once: Law enforcement will descend upon the provided address, and the newly wealthy kidnappers will flee the premises. If you ask me, proves once and for all they're definitely in northern New Hampshire."

Three pairs of eyes greeted him with open skepticism.

"City cops," Wyatt informed them dryly. "You're accustomed to dozens of uniformed officers who can be anywhere and everywhere in five minutes or less. Now, in my neck of the woods, closest backup is an easy twenty, if not forty, minutes away. Plenty of time for experienced kidnappers to make their exit, before we can make our entrance.

"So"—he straightened, warming to the subject—"we should check out roads. The kidnappers would look for multiple byways. Otherwise, they risk driving directly past arriving officers. Their target hideout would include rural lodges, campsites that lie near multiple points of access . . . I need a map. And not one of your digital screens. But a real, impossible-to-fold-up paper map that we can mark up with highlighters and abuse with drippings from our lunch."

"Got it," Nicole said, and headed for the rear of the mobile command center, where apparently even the FBI kept things as antiquated as real maps.

While Nicole dug through a pile, Wyatt used the opportunity to ask, "Any luck interviewing Ashlyn Denbe's friends?"

Hawkes took the liberty of answering. "Yes and no. According to Ashlyn's BFF, Lindsay Edmiston, Ashlyn didn't have a boyfriend and wasn't the type to sleep around. However . . ."

Wyatt and Tessa eyed him expectantly.

"Even Lindsay thought Ashlyn was keeping a secret. Friday night, when the parents were supposedly on their date night, Lindsay had invited Ashlyn over to her house, but Ashlyn had refused. According to Lindsay, that was unusual, Ashlyn not being the type who preferred staying home alone. Lindsay had begun to suspect there was a boy in the picture. In fact, Lindsay wondered if on Friday night when the parents were out, Ashlyn had really been all alone in her bedroom."

"She had the boyfriend over?" Tessa asked sharply.

Hawkes glanced up at them. "Maybe. But Lindsay already swears not anyone from the local high school."

*   *   *

NICOLE AND HAWKES HAD MORE INTERVIEWS to conduct. They departed, leaving Tessa and Wyatt to work the map. Wyatt fixated on roads, towns and wilderness areas in northern New Hampshire. He couldn't get Ashlyn Denbe out of his head. The way she'd perked up, looking briefly excited at the promise of her and her family's safe return. Only for her face to freeze over again, as she and her mother continued to read down the script, getting to the part detailing what would happen if the kidnappers' demands were not met. The killing of the first member of the Denbe family.

Wyatt got on the phone with his deputy, Gina, who'd apparently been working with the cellular providers to block out sections of the mountains that lacked cell service. Then, he contacted Fish and Game, as well as the wildlife agency, updating their own tireless searches of dozens and dozens of campgrounds and trailheads with more Xs, more Os.

In the end, he marked up the map with multiple games of tic-tac-toe, while identifying a mere quarter of a million more acres to search. Taking into consideration major thoroughfares, he homed in on his three "most likely" northern cities: Littleton, which had a major interstate, 93, running right through it, ready to bring the captors down to Boston or up into Vermont. Second choice, Colebrook, on the New Hampshire/ Vermont border, with Route 3, as well as 26 and 145, all converging in one extremely isolated town. Finally, Berlin, on the eastern side of New Hampshire's narrow tip, bisected by Route 16, but also very close to Route 2 into Maine. Bigger than the first two options, and a rougher town given the boarded-up mills, but then again, probably a comfortable enough place for hired muscle.

Wyatt drew three big Os, based solely on assumptions and guesses and gut feel. A lot of maybes, given an entire family was on the line. Ashlyn. Libby. Justin Denbe.

Wyatt set down his pen.

He sighed heavily.

Tessa, standing across from him, seconded the motion.

"Tomorrow, three o'clock. It's not going to happen," she stated simply.

"No," he agreed. "Even if the insurance company pays . . . No good reason for a bunch of professionals to let that family walk away."

"We have to find them."

"Yep." He glanced at his watch. "Twenty-six hours and counting."

"I want to know the identity of Ashlyn's mysterious boyfriend," Tessa muttered. "Innocent bystander, or one more person with access to the security code for the house?"

"Good point."

"Is it just me, or does every member of this family have a secret?"

Wyatt shrugged. "Find me a family that doesn't."

"Good point." But her tone said she wasn't happy about it. For that matter, neither was he.

Wyatt looked around. FBI's command center had emptied out, everyone pursuing various leads, their own insider information. Dividing and conquering, the best way to cover the most investigative ground in the shortest amount of time. Frustrating, though, when others were covering the questions you wanted answered most.

"FBI is covering Ashlyn," he stated now, refocusing. "That puts us on Denbe Construction. You know, interviewing all the various liars on the management team."

Tessa brightened. "I wonder if Ruth Chan's plane has landed."

"Excellent idea."

They left the mobile command unit, and went to find the CFO instead.

Chapter 32

MICK ESCORTED US TO DINNER. The moment he appeared at the cell door, Justin was tense. By unspoken agreement, Justin took up position on one side of Ashlyn, while I stood on the other.

In contrast, Mick seemed relaxed, positively grinning as he gestured for all three of us to exit the cell, no hand restraints, no person-by-person procession. Like Z, he took the lead, allowing the three of us to walk unhindered behind him. He kept his right hand lightly caressing the Taser holstered at his waist. Otherwise, Mick strolled along as if he hadn't a care in the world.

The promise of nine million dollars making him giddy? Or simply the joy of the final countdown? In twenty-four hours or less, this would all be over. We'd be gone, one way or another. Picked up by the police, or . . . killed by our captors? Maybe Mick wasn't as excited about the possible payout as he was the opportunity to finally exact his revenge. I couldn't picture Radar shooting us down in cold blood. But Mick, he would do it with gusto.

While Z would keep it quiet and quick. Nothing personal. All business.

I missed Radar. For one thing, my nausea was returning, not to mention a general sense of gloom and doom. Withdrawal symptoms, creeping up on me as insidiously as any black-clad commando. I needed a pill. Wanted a pill?

My beautiful orange prescription bottle. Two, three, four hydrocodone tablets. That lovely feeling of melting. The world slipping sideways, till no hard edges existed anymore. Don't worry. Don't overthink. Just go with the flow.

Fuck the methadone. I wanted real drugs.

We arrived at the commercial-grade kitchen. Mick spread his arm expansively.

"Liked the cinnamon buns," he said. "Now go work some magic."

I walked through the refrigeration unit and dry storage, trying to muster some enthusiasm, but mostly thinking I'd like to poison the whole lot of them. Undercooked hamburger? Improperly handled chicken? People got sick off meals all the time. Surely I could think of something.

Of course, we ate the same food. Meaning what would I gain in the end? Six people down with a GI bug? If our captors were incapacitated at all, most likely they'd leave us in our cell to rot. Maybe even postpone the ransom exchange. Earn us another night in this hellhole while they recovered.

No. No food poisoning. Comfort food. An iron-rich, carbo-loading, strength-building meal to fortify my own family, so that tomorrow, come game time, we'd be as ready as we could be.

I wanted hamburger, but couldn't find it in the refrigerator. Funny, because I could've sworn I'd seen some this morning, when I'd grabbed the bacon for breakfast. Of course, they must've fed themselves lunch. Maybe they grilled up burgers?

I settled for cans of stew meat from the dry storage, then returned for a block of cheese, only to discover it was also gone. Sliced up to toss on their burgers?

My head ached. The stark overhead lights, bouncing off all the stainless steel, hurt my eyes. But I forced myself to contemplate both the walk-in pantry and the massive refrigeration unit. Both were definitely sparser. In fact, if I conjured up that very first meal of pasta and sauce, what I'd inventoried then versus now . . . Z and his team were either eating up a storm or . . . cleaning out.

Our captors were covering their tracks. Preparing for the end.

"Hello?" Mick called out, voice already threatening. I forced myself to return to work.

I set up Ashlyn with two cans of spinach. She promptly wrinkled her nose. I added canned corn, a jar of onions and canned carrots.

Mick gazed at me doubtfully. "That ain't cinnamon rolls."

"Quiche?" I asked him.

"Gesundheit," he said.

"Shepherd's pie it is."

I put Justin in charge of making mashed potatoes from a box mix, while I dumped the stew meat into a skillet with olive oil and the drained pearl onions. It looked like dog food and smelled about as good. I reminded myself of the cold Hormel raviolis my mother and I used to eat from cans all those years ago. Of our elderly neighbor who did eat canned cat food because it was cheaper than tuna and she had to save as much money as she could in order to buy more vodka.

After Ashlyn had drained the vegetables, I had her add them to the stew meat. In the pantry, I found garlic powder and Worcestershire sauce. I added both liberally, while Ashlyn and Mick continued to wrinkle their noses.

Next I found a lasagna pan. Vegetables and stew meat on the bottom. Instant mashed potatoes, dotted with butter, spread on top. The pan went into the oven and I set about making rolls while Justin did the dishes and Ashlyn set the table.

"Seriously?" Mick asked me.

"Seriously what?"

"That . . . food."

I shrugged. "Fresh hamburger and

potatoes would be better, but you work with what you got."

"That's disgusting."

"Don't eat it."

"Hey, I've lived on MREs. I can eat that slop."

"Then don't complain."

"What is this, housewife warfare?"

"Sure. Now, be nice, or next time, I'll dust you."

Mick laughed. Which might have made me feel better, except his eyes were too bright and the laugh too long and in the end, Ashlyn moved closer to her father while I switched to the other side of the prep table to roll out the dough.

Compared with the morning's cinnamon roll fest, my makeshift shepherd's pie was greeted with considerably less enthusiasm. But as Mick had said, soldiers were used to low standards.

Mick filled half his plate with a look that said he'd eat it all just to spite me. Z inspected the layers with a scientist's cool-eyed study, then shrugged and dug in. A plate was set aside for Radar, then my family had their turn. Justin took easily as much as Mick. Ashlyn sighed heavily and delicately scooped out just enough to feed a bird.

"Spinach." She shuddered.

"Iron," I corrected my daughter, who'd started her day with massive blood loss.

"Spinach," she insisted.

I ignored her, tended to myself for a change. It really wasn't too bad. Four hundred times our recommended daily allowance of sodium, not to mention the vegetables were mushy and tasteless, while the meat was stringy and gray, but other than that . . .

I really could've used a pill. A glass of wine. Something.

"You entertain much?" Z asked abruptly. He was staring at Justin. Z had taken seconds. Mick as well.

"What?"

"In that town house of yours. You own a business that depends on landing big contracts. Probably doesn't hurt to have the right people over, wine and dine."

"On occasion," Justin allowed. My husband was sitting tightly, his beaten face wary.

"She cook?" Z stabbed a fork in my direction.

"My wife is an excellent cook. You've had enough opportunities to evaluate that for yourself."

"What's her favorite food?"

"Excuse me?"

"What's her favorite food? Bet she knows yours." Z turned, stared at me.

"Beef Wellington," I provided quietly.

Z turned back to Justin. "So?"

My husband kept his gaze on Z. "Fresh oranges," he said slowly. "We had them on our honeymoon. Picked them ourselves straight off the tree. You can't get anything like that from the grocery store."

He was right. I had loved them then. Memories of a past life. The current taste of my pain.

I found myself looking down at my plate, wishing both men would stop talking about me.

"You plant an orange tree for her?" Z asked Justin.

"In Boston?"

"Build her a greenhouse. Or don't you know how?"

Justin's jaw tightened. Clearly he was being baited, but even I didn't know why.

Z suddenly swung toward me. "Gonna leave him?"

I glanced up. All eyes were on me, including Ashlyn's.

"When you return. Tomorrow night," Z prodded. "Decision time."

I forced my chin up. "None of your business," I said clearly.

"Leopard never changes its spots."

"Don't you have someone else to go kidnap?"

He smiled, but it wasn't warm. I swear the cobra tattoo was coiling and uncoiling restlessly around his head. "Don't know. You're going to be a tough family to top. Most people just cry a lot. You guys are much more . . . eventful."

He contemplated Ashlyn next: "Boyfriend, or are you just a slut?"

She went with my approach. "None of your business."

Which was a shame, because Justin and I had really wanted to know her answer. Probably, she had felt the same about us.

"Pretty girl like you should have higher standards."

My daughter gave Z her best flat-eyed stare. "Really? What's this, advice from a professional fuckup? I mean, first you kidnap us, now you're a life coach?"

Z smiled. If Mick's laugh scared me, Z's smile terrified me. He leaned back, placed his fork across his plate.

"Family," he said at last, "is a terrible thing to waste."

Then, he looked at me, and in his eyes, I saw it all. Resolution and regret.

We were dead.

Tomorrow, 3:00 P.M., they would receive the payoff, and then, they would kill us. Business. Plain and simple. Especially when dealing with a man with a fanged cobra tattooed around his head.

No one spoke again.

Z left. We cleaned up the kitchen. Radar arrived for his dinner, slipping two pills under his napkin, which I whisked away when bringing him fresh rolls. I returned the leftover shepherd's pie to the walk-in fridge, dry swallowing the tablets the second I was out of sight and wishing bitterly they were hydrocodone instead.

Finally, Mick escorted us back to our cells, still no hand restraints, still the illusion of freedom.

Dead family walking.

When the cell door finally clanked shut behind us, I turned to find him grinning broadly. He winked, waggled his tongue and mouthed, *Soon.*

Last glance at the ever-present camera, then he disappeared.

ASHLYN WAS ASLEEP inside a matter of minutes. She climbed up to the top bunk and collapsed. She needed the rest. Justin and I needed to talk.

"They're not going to let us go," I said without preamble, perching restlessly on the lower bunk. "Tomorrow, three P.M., they're going to take the money, then kill us."

"Nonsense." Justin was lying on his back across from me, hands tucked behind his head, staring up. "They're professionals. No way they're going to mess up a chance at nine mil."

"None of this makes any sense. This huge sum of money is wired to their account, then they magically leave us alone? I mean, the second they have the money, what's to stop them from harming us? We're still in a prison. We're still at their mercy."

"We'll be in the control room, safe from them. That's what I set up with Z: Tomorrow, come deadline, we'll use Radar's phone to call my cell. Some federal agent in Boston will most likely answer. We'll see him, he'll see us. Visual confirmation. Then you, me and Ashlyn will move into the control room, locking it down and ensuring our own safety while the funds are being wired. The minute ransom has been received, Z and his team will exit stage right. While we await local law enforcement, who will return us to Boston and allow us to get on with our normal lives."

"What if the authorities won't pay the ransom? There's no way to renegotiate or confirm . . ."

"Z's terms. He wanted to keep things simple. And actually, I agreed. Better to make it all or none. Puts more pressure on the insurance company."

"But if the company won't pay—"

"The company will pay, Libby. They have to. We delivered the proof they requested, the policy is up to date and frankly, the feds will probably make them. It's in everyone's best interest for tomorrow to go as planned. Trust me, in another twenty-four hours, we'll be able to put all of this behind us."

I studied my husband, still not convinced. My hands were shaking. I'd taken the methadone, which was supposed to reduce my withdrawal symptoms, but my sense of doom and gloom still wouldn't go away.

"We don't even know why they kidnapped us," I muttered next.

"Does it matter?"

"They beat you!"

"I'm doing okay."

"They terrorized Ashlyn."

"She's a strong girl."

"How can you be so calm—"

Justin sat up so abruptly, he nearly hit his head on the upper bunk as he swung around to glare at me. "Still don't trust me, Libby?"

I opened my mouth, but no words came out.

"We're going home. That's what matters here. One way or another, tomorrow, three P.M., you and Ashlyn will be on your way to Boston. My family will be safe."

Then I got it, the source of my unease.

There was a set to my husband's shoulders I recognized. An edge to his voice. He'd made a decision, one that clearly put the safety of Ashlyn and me above his own.

"You're not going to do anything stupid," I heard myself say. "We all need to go home, Justin. We're a family."

He smiled, but it wasn't a nice twist of his lips. "Family? I cheated on my wife. Hell, I never even suspected what was going on with my teenage daughter. You tell me, Libby. How terrible would it be if I never made it back?"

"Don't even talk like that. Your daughter needs you!"

"And you, Libby? What do you need?"

I wanted to tell him I needed us. I wanted to tell him if we could just get home, everything would be all right. But mostly, heaven help me, I saw in my future a lovely orange prescription bottle filled to the top with fresh white pills . . .

Z had been right. Family was a terrible thing to waste and that's exactly what we'd done. We'd battled one another, we'd betrayed one another, and in the end, for what?

We'd return home, except instead of finding solace, we'd have to confront the wreckage of our lives.

And still my eyes welled up. I gazed at my husband. A man who'd hurt me. A man I'd lied to in return. And I found myself crying. For the home we used to have. For the marriage I'd thought we'd built together. For the future I'd always hoped to give my daughter.

Justin got off his bunk. He put his arms around me, and though I was stinky and smelly and awful, he tucked me against his chest.

"Shhh," he murmured. "I'm going to fix this, Libby. Trust me, just trust me. Tomorrow I'll make everything all right."

I let my husband hold me. I focused on the reassuring strength of his arms, the sound of his heartbeat. Then I pressed my head into the curve of his shoulder because, once upon a time, I had loved this man so much and I knew, one way or another, I'd never get to feel that way again.

Three P.M. Monday.

Dead family walking.

Chapter 33

TESSA AND WYATT FOUND RUTH CHAN in the baggage claim of Terminal E. The petite CFO sported large sunglasses, a dark tan and a bad case of nerves. When she spotted Wyatt, approaching in his sheriff's uniform, she visibly flinched.

Then, she squared her shoulders, adjusted her grip on her lone suitcase and marched toward them.

"Any word on Justin or his family?" she asked.

Tessa pegged the woman at late forties, early fifties. Obviously Asian in descent, but something else as well. An exotic woman, beautiful even in simple black yoga pants and a cream-colored wrap top. Though oversize sunglasses covered half her face, it was obvious she'd been crying. Tear tracks stained her cheeks, while a hoarse rasp thickened her voice.

"We have some questions," Tessa began.

"I don't want to go to the office," the CFO stated immediately. "Someplace neutral, that would be best."

Ruth had yet to eat. They settled on Legal Sea Foods, even though it meant switching terminals, as the restaurant had booths suitable for a private place to talk. Wyatt offered to carry the woman's suitcase, but Ruth declined, marching resiliently forward, as if keeping moving was the secret to keeping composed.

Fifteen minutes later, they were ensconced in a back booth of the dimly lit restaurant. Ruth had parked her suitcase after removing a slender laptop, which she was now firing to life.

She had yet to speak to them, appearing to be on a mission. For now, Tessa and Wyatt were content to wait. They ordered clam chowder. Ruth ordered grilled salmon and a glass of white wine.

Then, the CFO took a deep breath and finally faced them. She had removed her sunglasses. Up close, she was a wreck. Wan skin, bruised eyes, haggard expression. A woman who'd either had the world's worst vacation, or was taking the news of her boss's disappearance very hard.

Ruth spoke first: "Anita said they were taken Friday night."

"Justin Denbe and his family have been missing since Friday night," Tessa supplied.

"Any word? Contact? Leads?"

"We have received a ransom demand. Nine million dollars, due tomorrow, three P.M."

Ruth flinched. "Denbe Construction doesn't have that kind of money."

"Justin contacted the life insurance company. He's invoking the risk-of-imminent-death clause."

"Of course," Ruth murmured. "Half the life insurance, plus the kidnapping insurance . . . that makes sense. Will the company pay it?"

"Not our call."

"They'll pay it," Ruth said, almost as if speaking to herself. "They have to pay it. If something happened to Justin . . . the public fallout, let alone potential legal liability . . . They'll pay it."

Tessa and Wyatt didn't say anything, just continued to study her.

"So." The CFO released a pent-up breath, her shoulders coming down. "This is really a kidnapping-for-ransom case. Justin is an obviously wealthy man. Unfortunately, that made him and his family a target."

Again, Tessa and Wyatt didn't say anything, just continued to study her.

"It's just . . . When I first heard the news, when Anita called . . . I thought for sure . . . I mean." Ruth took another deep breath, then, when that wasn't enough, a fortifying sip of wine. "I was so scared something worse had happened. That Justin . . . that maybe, someone had felt a need to hurt him. And I worried . . . I worried it was my fault."

The food arrived. A cup of chowder for Tessa, a bowl of chowder for Wyatt, the salmon for Ruth.

Wyatt dug into his chowder. Ruth attempted her own meal, but when she picked up her knife and fork, her hands were shaking too badly. She returned to her glass of wine.

"Why don't you start at the beginning," Tessa suggested. "Tell us everything. If you want to help Justin, that would be best."

"I wasn't in the Bahamas on vacation," Ruth stated. "I was there on business. Justin sent me. Someone has been embezzling money from Denbe Construction. I've been following the money trail."

Tessa got out her phone, set up the record app and they got down to business.

In August, Ruth had noticed a minor billing mistake. Numbers on an invoice had been inverted, and instead of paying the vendor twenty-one thousand dollars, accounts payable had cut a check for twelve. Obviously Denbe Construction owed an additional nine thousand dollars; unfortunately, by the time the mistake was discovered, there wasn't time to release the additional funds before payment deadline.

Ruth had decided to call, personally apologize for the error and assure the vendor that the appropriate check would be placed immediately in the mail. Except when she called the number, it was disconnected. She had then Googled the company's name for additional information, only to discover that no such company seemed to exist.

To be sure, she'd followed up on the physical address of the listed company, a street address in New Jersey. Further investigation revealed the street address belonged to a UPS store, while the suite number corresponded to a PO box.

Which had told her enough. The address was fake. The phone number fake. The vendor fake. Denbe Construction was being scammed.

Immediately, Ruth had dug deeper. She'd determined that the vendor, DDA, LLC, had sent a total of sixteen bills over the past three years for a total of nearly four hundred thousand dollars. The contractor was attached to a major senior care facility with a total build cost of seventy-five million. Four hundred thousand dollars, spread out over sixteen payments, was relatively small potatoes. The invoices listed miscellaneous finish materials plus installation costs, nothing out of the ordinary for such a project.

Meaning, at first glance, the invoices were logical enough, and the amounts due small enough, not to attract notice or arouse suspicion. But where had DDA, LLC, come from?

Given the number of ongoing construction projects, not to mention the widespread use of subcontractors, new vendors were regularly added into Denbe's system. Authorized bills arrived with a code in the memo section that attached them to the appropriate build project; generally Chris Lopez, as head of the build team, or even Justin himself, provided the vendor with the code, a stamp of approval. DDA, LLC's invoices all had the appropriate bill code in the memo section, meaning there was no reason for Ruth or her staff to question the bills.

Now, once a month, Ruth issued a report to both Chris and Justin itemizing all income and expenses associated with the various projects for their review. On the one hand, this should have been an opportunity for one of them to spot the name DDA, LLC, and question it. Then again, the monthly reports often ran half an inch thick, an endless blur of vendor names and subcontractor expenses, starting with checks in the tens of millions of dollars and ending with personal reimbursement requests in the tens of dollars.

Ruth could see where a relatively small check to a relatively minor vendor might get lost in the shuffle. In fact, she was guessing that was the theory behind the crime—rather than defraud a hundred-million-dollar company out of four hundred thousand dollars at once, go after it in drips and drops. Twenty thousand here, fifteen there. While it might sound like a lot of money to some people, for a company of Denbe's size, those amounts weren't even rounding errors on most of their projects.

A solid little scam that had slowly but surely been adding up.

Ruth had checked with Denbe Construction's bank to see if they could tell her anything more about the cleared checks. They could; based on the information stamped on the back, each check had been deposited into an offshore bank account. In the Bahamas.

So the fake vendor billed to a post office

box in New Jersey, then deposited Denbe's checks into an account in the Bahamas. And had been for three years without anyone suspecting a thing.

Four weeks ago, Ruth had waited for Justin to stay late at work. Then, when no one else was around, she'd entered his office and made her case. As she'd expected, he'd been furious, then just plain insulted that someone had dared to steal from him.

Ruth had proposed taking the case straight to the FBI. Offshore accounts were involved, and they would need major investigative guns to demand information from a bank in the Bahamas. Even then, she wasn't sure what level of cooperation they'd get. Banks were notoriously prickly about releasing a customer's private information, though rules were finally loosening, thanks to the war on terrorism.

Justin, however, hadn't wanted to involve the police just yet. Instead, he wanted to bait the perpetrator.

"He asked me to go to the Bahamas. I have the bank account information for DDA, LLC; I got it from our bank. So Friday, I was supposed to walk into the Bahamas bank and close DDA's account. Take the money and run, I suppose, except it is our money."

Ruth gazed at them expectantly.

"How can you close out an account that's not yours?" Tessa asked. "Don't you have to have signing authority or something?"

"I was going to wing it. Our assumption is that whoever is behind the fraud doesn't visit in person, right? So just do it. I'm a CFO, I can talk the talk. And Justin wanted the money transferred back to Denbe, which I'm fully authorized to do."

"He wanted the person who stole from you to know you'd stolen back from them," Tessa filled in. "Hence the transfer to Denbe."

"Exactly."

"Did it work?" Wyatt asked with a frown.

Ruth shook her head. "I was one day too late. The person, the *thief*, had transferred out all the funds on Thursday. But this is the crazy part: When I told the clerk that the transfer had been a mistake and I wanted to know who'd authorized the transaction, the clerk became very nervous and asked if that meant there was an issue with the other accounts as well. Turns out, whoever set up DDA didn't have just one account. He or she had *fifteen* accounts at the bank. For a total of eleven-point-two million dollars."

"That's a little bit more than four hundred thousand," Tessa said blankly.

Ruth had given up on dinner completely. She sat, twisting the stem of her wineglass.

"I called Justin Friday afternoon. I told him the account was closed, that I'd been too late. But I didn't tell him about the other accounts, the other money. I wasn't trying to lie or mislead him. It's just . . . I already had a suspicion, and in these kinds of situations, you can't afford to be wrong. I told Justin I needed a couple more days. I'd call him again on Monday."

"How'd he take it?" Wyatt asked.

Ruth shrugged. "He was frustrated that we'd missed out on reclaiming the money. But . . . we'd known it was a long shot. And while Justin wasn't happy that someone had possibly stolen four hundred thousand dollars from his company, that kind of loss, over three years, we could live with it."

"Except you're saying the perpetrator had actually accrued eleven-point-two million," Tessa pressed.

Ruth sighed, dark eyes miserable. "I stayed up all Friday night, all last night. I've been poring over contractor lists, project P and Ls, picking out small, random vendors, then Googling them. I've found six more that don't exist. It will take a full forensic audit, easily a good six months of work, but I'm guessing, in the end, all eleven-point-two million came from Denbe Construction. Was stolen from right underneath our noses."

Tessa's eyes widened. She could tell Wyatt was equally startled. "Someone scammed eleven million dollars in the past three years? And you're just now noticing?"

"That's the thing. The invoices, the fake vendors. The amounts are all so small. In some cases, literally a couple thousand dollars. The kind of payments designed to slip between the cracks."

"But you said eleven million—"

"Exactly!"

Then, Tessa got it. "You're not talking about the past three years."

"No!"

"You're talking . . . ten, fifteen?"

"Maybe longer."

"Twenty?" Now Tessa was definitely caught off guard.

"Predates me," Ruth said, "so it's hard to be sure. But some of those years were the company's biggest. Justin had just taken over, landing three two-hundred-million-dollar builds at once. The amount of billing and invoicing going on, with employees who were overstretched and a computer system that was relatively antiquated. To end up with over eleven million dollars, the embezzler must've had at least a couple of big years, and those were the years when you could've gotten away with faking very large invoices and no one would be the wiser."

"Fifteen to twenty years," Tessa murmured.

"Predates Chris Lopez," Wyatt said.

"Predates most of us," Ruth commented. "Except . . ." She wouldn't meet their eyes anymore. She picked up her glass, swallowed the last of her wine. Her hand was still trembling, the misery once more etched into her face.

A longtime employee. One who'd have access and authority. Also, by virtue of being one of the only females in a predominantly male business, possibly even a close personal friend of the CFO.

Anita Bennett. Denbe Construction's current COO and Dale Denbe's former mistress.

Chapter 34

I DOZED OFF, dreaming of a long hot shower. I stood in my own bathroom, custom glass doors steaming up as I let the hot spray cascade down my naked body. Then, lathering up with my favorite shampoo. Watching thick white suds slide down my arm, chasing away the salt-encrusted itch of my own sweat and grime.

In my dream, I could feel my skin sloughing away, like an exoskeleton to be shed. Prison bars, cinder-block walls, hard concrete floors. I watched their remnants dissolve into a faint gray crumble, then wash down the drain.

If I stopped, looked down the drain, I knew I would see Mick's face. Radar. Z. They were gone, melted like Dorothy's Wicked Witch and now spiraling down the bowels of Boston's sewer system where they belonged.

But I didn't stop. Didn't want to look. To seek them out would be to resurrect evil. And this was my dream, my shower. Where the soap smelled liked fresh-picked oranges, and I was no longer in my Back Bay town house, but on a beach in Key West, where I would emerge from the bathroom to find my husband waiting in bed, wearing nothing but cool white sheets tangled around his long, lean body.

Oranges. He would feed me oranges. The promise of pleasure.

The taste of my pain.

My shower changed. The water disappeared. Pills sprayed out instead. Hundreds, thousands of long, oblong tablets. Hydrocodone. My precious painkillers, returning to me. Complete with orange-colored bottles, of course.

The promise of pleasure.

The taste of my pain.

I fell to my knees on the hard tile, and let the pills bury me.

*   *   *

I JERKED AWAKE, my eyes momentarily blinded by the overhead lights. I blinked, feeling my heart race in my chest. Justin was standing in front of the cell door. I must have made a noise for he was staring at me.

"You okay?" he asked.

Funny question coming from a man whose face looked like a badly beaten side of beef with one eye still completely swollen shut.

"Ashlyn?" I asked.

"Asleep, top bunk."

I gave him a look, and Justin double-checked. He nodded, confirming Ashlyn was definitely sleeping. Seemed like lately our daughter had become very good at faking it.

I got up, crossed to the stainless steel sink and attempted to get a sip of water.

"Why is the water pressure so lousy?" I asked, if only to break the silence.

"Big building, demanding many miles of pipes to bring the water from there to here. Installing a more efficient system would cost more money, except, for what?" Justin shrugged. "Inmates got nothing better to do than wait."

He crossed to me, rubbing the back of my neck, like he used to do once upon a time.

"I dreamed of a shower," I murmured. "A long hot shower with unlimited soap."

He smiled. "I smell that bad?"

"No worse than me."

"It'll be over soon, Libby. This time, to-morrow, you can be showering all you like."

I wanted to believe him. Could use the reassurance. And yet . . .

"Shouldn't you be sleeping?" I asked. "You know, conserving your strength?"

"Tried. Can't get used to the narrow bunk. Or maybe it's the tight walls."

"You're not cut out for hard time?"

"Nope. I just build 'em. Me, I'm all about wide-open spaces."

He was. Cold, rainy, snowy, miserable, it never mattered to Justin. He was always happiest outdoors.

"Has Ashlyn been sleeping?" I asked.

"Like a baby," he said, then, a second later, the irony of the comment hit him, and he grimaced, stepping back.

I looked away. If it was hard for a mother to realize that her teenage daughter was sexually active, it had to be excruciating for a father. Especially for Justin, who'd placed her in an ivory tower from her first moment of birth. Daddy's little princess. His perfect girl.

I wondered which was worse, his horror or his hurt.

"Did you know?" he asked now, voice hushed. "I mean, even suspect?"

I shook my head.

"She hasn't mentioned a boy's name? Been spending more time out, buying new clothes . . . I don't know, doing what teenage girls do when being stupid about a boy?"

"What are you going to do, Justin? Load a shotgun?"

"Maybe!"

"I didn't know."

"But—"

"Did you?" I kept my voice even. "You're her father. Did you suspect anything?"

He scowled, shifted uncomfortably. "Of course not. But I'm the dad. Fathers . . . We don't get these things. We can't look at our daughters that way."

"What's the name of her best friend?"

"Linda."

"Lindsay."

"Lindsay! I was close."

"Are you?" I shrugged. "Ashlyn's fifteen years old. According to her, she's spent the past six months spying on us, given that we've spent the past six months no longer speaking to her. She's lonely, she's vulnerable and we . . . we checked out on her. And by we, I mean *we*, Justin. You're her parent, too."

He didn't like that assessment, his displeasure showing in the tightening of his jaw. But he didn't immediately refute the argument. Instead, being Justin, he went on the offensive.

"When did you start popping pills?"

I kept my gaze as level as his own. "When did you first cheat on me?"

"It's not the same. You're the primary caretaker and you know it. Meaning you've spent the past six months impaired on the job."

"Versus spending your lunch breaks on booty calls? Do you really want to have a competition about which of us sinned worse?"

"You confronted me, Libby. You demanded an explanation—"

"I caught you once. Clearly there've been others—"

"I feel I have the right to know. Do you have a dealer? Are you inviting criminals into our home? Maybe one of them took an interest in Ashlyn. Maybe, one of them knows Mick or Z or Radar."

My mouth hung open. I could feel my temper rise. My first instinct was to scream no, how ridiculous of him. I got my drugs the honorable way—by lying to any medical professional who carried a prescription pad. Instead, I heard myself say, "AIDS, herpes, syphilis, gonorrhea. Did you invite them into our home? Blackmail, drama, extortion. Maybe, one of your lovers knows Mick or Z or Radar."

"Libby—"

"Justin! It's not right. You betrayed my trust. And not once. But multiple times. And somehow, that's okay? You said you were sorry, so now I'm supposed to just move on? I don't know how. I *loved* you, Justin. You weren't only my husband, you were my whole family. Except, my father couldn't wear a helmet and my mother couldn't stop smoking and you, you can't keep it in your pants. They failed, then you failed and I don't know how to rebuild this time. So, yes, I started taking pills. Because while you might be sorry, I still . . . *hurt*."

Justin's battered face, set in stone: "So it's my fault? You're an addict, and it's *my* fault."

"I didn't say that."

"Do you think it's your fault I slept with that girl?"

I couldn't take it. My gaze slid down. I wanted out. Out of this conversation, out of this damn cell. Out of this life, really, which explained the gratuitous use of painkillers.

"Do you think it's your fault I cheated?" Justin continued relentlessly. "That if you just looked different or behaved different, or maybe were more adventurous in bed, I never would've strayed?"

I covered my ears with my hands. "Please stop."

"I love you, Libby. I never loved her."

"But you gave yourself to her. You took a piece of yourself away from me, and gave it to her instead."

"Do you want to know why?"

"No." *Yes.*

"Because she looked at me the way you used to. I went down to make a damn plane reservation and she . . . The way she looked at me . . . I felt important. I felt the way I used to feel when we first met and all I had to do was show up on your doorstep and you would . . . you would light up. It's been a long time since I've seen you smile like that. It's been a long time since I've felt . . . like you saw me that way."

"So it is my fault you cheated."

"No more than it's my fault that you abuse painkillers."

"I don't even understand this anymore!"

Justin shrugged. He no longer appeared implacable, just tired. "Of course not. We're married, Libby. We've spent eighteen years with our lives all tangled together. To say I don't affect you, or your actions don't affect me . . . How can *that* make any sense? A marriage is greater than the sum of its parts. At a certain point, that's what we forgot; we stopped doing the math, tending the whole. We became selfish. A pretty girl smiled and I behaved selfishly. And you were hurt, in need of a quick pick-me-up, so you behaved selfishly, too. We forgot each other. Which is what selfish people tend to do."

"You'll cheat again," I whispered. "It's what cheaters do."

"And you'll find a new source of painkillers," he said, just as quietly. "That's what drug addicts do."

I hung my head, feeling the shame that was six months overdue. I had been right before; it was easier to hate my husband. To avoid the obvious, such as that eighteen years did take its toll and both of us had stopped making the time for our marriage. Until one day . . .

"Why did you keep her texts on your phone?" I asked suddenly. "You must've known I might see them."

My husband's turn to look away.

"You wanted to get caught," I murmured, understanding finally dawning. "You wanted me to find out what you'd been doing."

"Haven't there been moments in the past few months when you swore to yourself you'd stop? Not take another pill? Clean up your act, live the straight and narrow?"

Slowly, I nodded.

Justin raised his head, met my eyes.

"Me, too. I hated being a liar, Libby. I hated knowing I was hurting you. I don't know . . . I can't explain all of it. Maybe we all turn into our parents in the end. Or maybe, I'm just weak. But I'd meet a girl . . . and one thing would lead to another . . . And immediately afterward, I'd feel terrible. A liar, a cheat, a failure. I reached a point . . . I didn't want to feel that way again. So, yes, I think some part of me wanted you to catch me. I hoped it would force me to get myself under control. I would take responsibility, you would finally forgive me and then I wouldn't have to feel so lousy anymore."

Justin, still gazing at me. "Do you know what my mother did when my father died?"

I shook my head.

"She took a fifth of vodka and poured it on his grave. She hated him, Libby. Absolutely, positively hated him. I don't want you to hate me. I don't want to be the kind of guy who's not even missed by his own wife. I never wanted to be that man."

Justin sighed heavily. He placed his hands on my shoulders and gazed at me so seriously. So somberly. Had I ever seen him look like this? Eighteen years of memories, and yet . . .

"I love you, Libby. I was stupid. I screwed up. And I failed. But I love you. Whatever happens next, I want you to know that."

My first ping of alarm. "Don't talk like that—"

"Shhh. I need you to tell me you're going to quit the pills. You must be already detoxing, yes?"

"Yes—"

"Then promise me when you get home, you'll continue. You'll take care of yourself. You'll be there for Ashlyn. You're right. Our daughter needs us."

My second ping of alarm. He sounded like a man who'd already made a decision. A man who was now simply preparing himself for the consequences. "*Us,* Justin," I countered sharply. "As in, we're *all* going home tomorrow. No doing anything rash. We need you, Justin. We need you."

My husband, still eyeing me intently. "Are you going to quit?"

Myself, still thinking of oranges, the taste of my pain. "Yes."

He pulled me into his arms. "Good girl," he whispered against the top of my hair.

"Don't worry about the rest. No matter what, tomorrow, you and Ashlyn will be safe. I promise you, Libby. I swear it on my life."

Chapter 35

THEY BROUGHT ANITA BENNETT in for questioning at 10:15 P.M. They did it properly, two dark-clad FBI agents appearing on her doorstep and requesting her presence at the FBI field office. It was difficult to say no to FBI agents and finally, shaking and uncertain, Anita had acquiesced, kissing her husband lightly on the cheek, telling him it was nothing, she'd be home shortly.

The investigative team was already waiting in the Boston field office. Special Agent Adams, Special Agent Hawkes, then Tessa and Wyatt. They were seated in the viewing room, another trick of the trade—forcing the suspect to confront a new set of interrogators, which would add to her confusion.

The FBI had a dedicated fraud squad, a whole team of financial wizards who lived and breathed corporate embezzlement, money laundering, white-collar crime. It had been Special Agent Adams's idea to let them take the lead—they could ask more specific questions concerning Denbe Construction's P and L. Also, if they could keep Anita on the defensive, switching up focus while retelling parts of her story to a fresh set of investigators, they increased the odds of her tripping up, muddling a minor detail that might open major floodgates to what really happened to Justin and his family.

One thing they all agreed on: Time was ticking.

Ransom exchange was now a mere seventeen hours away. The life insurance company had agreed to play ball, but the overall mood remained skeptical. The terms of the exchange were too broad, with not enough safeguards for the Denbe family in place.

And now, given this whole embezzlement angle . . . Wyatt had already expressed what most of them feared: The kidnapping was not a kidnapping case at all. Ransom was merely a smokescreen to cover the real motive: Anita Bennett had been stealing from Denbe Construction for the past two decades. Justin had finally caught wind of the scam, perhaps even confided in his wife, Libby. Meaning he and his family now had to disappear. Their untimely demise might invite undue attention from the police. Hence a kidnapping for ransom. How many times had Anita herself tried to say Justin's disappearance might have nothing to do with the firm, that he was a target simply because he was wealthy?

And of course, in kidnapping-for-ransom cases, exchanges didn't always go as planned. Sometimes, wealthy victims even wound up dead. Say, Justin, Libby and Ashlyn Denbe. Tragically killed, 3:00 P.M. tomorrow, during a botched rescue attempt.

The firm would soldier valiantly on, Anita Bennett now securely ensconced as CEO, where her first major decision would be to fire Ruth Chan. Then, the firm would be all hers, as well as her eleven-million-dollar secret.

A lot of motive for murder. Certainly, entire families had been killed for less.

Anita Bennett was escorted to the interview room. The two agents, Bill Bixby and Mark Levesco, produced paperwork. Anita agreed to be interviewed on camera. She'd been informed of her rights, understood anything she said could and would be used against her in a court of law. She could end the interview anytime and maintained the right to call an attorney. Anita signed the form. They were off and running.

Bill was an older agent, Mark his younger counterpart in a pink-and-gray Brooks Brothers tie. Bill took the lead, striking a collegial tone. Sorry to interrupt Anita's evening. Thanks so much for her cooperation. Surely she understood time was of the essence and they were all working diligently toward the safe return of Justin, Libby and Ashlyn Denbe.

Anita nodded. She'd changed out of her church clothes from the morning for a somber pair of gray knit slacks and a blush-colored turtleneck. She looked older to Tessa, as if the day had already worn her down. She also appeared wary, her face clearly guarded as she accepted Bill's statements but didn't immediately gush information.

The FBI had had only six hours to prepare for this moment, but they'd done their homework well. The second Tessa and Wyatt had called Nicole Adams with news from their interview with Ruth Chan, the CFO had been whisked off to the Boston field office, where she'd spent the next few hours ensconced with the financial agents, going over the books and explaining what she'd found. Additional agents had immediately pulled Anita Bennett's records, compiling lists of bank assets, major purchases and, of course, trips to the Bahamas. They were still only at the tip of the iceberg, according to Special Agent Adams, but given the time pressure, they decided it was better to ambush the COO sooner versus later.

They weren't as interested in a confession of corporate embezzlement as they were an admission of a physical address for the safe return of the Denbe family.

And they still had a few tricks up their sleeves.

Anita's initial responses were pretty much as Tessa had anticipated. Collegial cop, Bill, wrapped up his spiel, and young guy, Mark, started to smack down financial reports. What did Anita know of this transaction? Was she aware of this vendor? Had she heard of this company? Where was she on June 12, 2009? What about this project, what about this new automobile, what about this transaction, had she really visited the Bahamas twice in 2012, on and on.

Anita started with denial, transitioned to confusion, then appeared simply shell-shocked as Levesco rained down piece after piece of the embezzlement puzzle. Sixteen years of phony invoices from non-existent vendors.

"What? I would never."

Over eleven million dollars defrauded from Denbe Construction, then funneled through offshore bank accounts.

"I don't even know how to do something like that. I'm in operations, not finances. I don't even know our billing systems anymore."

During which time, Anita purchased several cars and one house as cash transactions.

"My husband and I are debt averse. If you look at my bonuses for each of those years, you'll see we paid for those items with legitimate income."

Three kids paid through college.

"I make a good living. Again, look at my tax returns. Six hundred thousand in salary covers three kids in college."

The scholarship for her youngest?

She flushed. "I've already spoken to two detectives about that. Justin offered the scholarship to my youngest son. His decision, not mine."

Interesting, since Justin wasn't around to comment.

"Ask Ruth Chan! She issued the checks. Signed by Justin. She'll vouch for the arrangement. It was hardly a secret. Everyone in the company knew."

And eight vacations in the Bahamas in the past six years?

"We like the warm weather. Besides, it was nice of Justin to offer his time-share."

A small hiccup. The Denbes had a time-share in the Bahamas? News, but given all the ground they'd been racing to cover in just forty-eight hours, hardly surprising that they'd missed it.

Last visit by Anita Bennett was for fourteen days.

"My husband was still recuperating from open-heart surgery. The time away was good for him."

Paid off one hundred thousand in hospital bills.

"And if you'll look at my savings account, you'll see the hit!"

Which was true. While it would've been nice to magically discover Anita had eleven million dollars sitting in the bank, her finances were currently depleted. Then again, according to Ruth Chan, the embezzlement money had been sitting in a bunch of fake corporate accounts in the Bahamas until just five days ago. A defrauder who'd been smart and disciplined enough to keep the illicit gains at arm's length was hardly going to dump them into personal savings now. Most likely, the funds had been moved to a single new account under an alias, probably at another offshore bank. The FBI would work on tracking that next, but such things took time, not to mention a bit of luck.

Poker or blackjack?

"What?"

Receipts. Ten years of receipts for the Mohegan Sun Resort and Casino?

"I was entertaining clients! I don't gamble. I work in construction. That's risky enough!"

Brand-new 2008 black-on-black Lexus. Cash.

"My oldest son. His college graduation present."

New 2011 Cadillac Escalade.

"For Dan. His other vehicle was seven years old!"

Which brought them to a Florida condo in 2010, a Mazda Miata just four months ago. On and on Levesco went. Fake billings here. New purchases for Anita there. Tessa had thought the COO would grow more defensive. Clam up. But instead, Anita picked up her own tempo, until she was matching the younger FBI agent beat for beat. Which was impressive, really. Not just the amount of money that Denbe Construction had paid out to fake vendors each year, but how unapologetically Anita spent her own income. She made a good living, as she informed her interrogators again and again. Salary, bonuses, lawfully declared on her taxes year after year. And, yes, she spent her money on her family.

Houses, cars, vacations. She worked hard, they lived well. She had nothing to be ashamed of.

Around and around they went. Consistent denials of embezzlement, full admissions of major purchases. Finally, Tessa glanced over at Special Agent Adams and nodded once. Nicole had been expecting the signal. She picked up the phone and buzzed the room next door.

Two agents appeared in the hallway. They had Daniel Coakley, picked up fifteen minutes after his wife, between them. Now they led him past the interview room, just as the older FBI agent, Bill, opened the door, ostensibly to get something to drink.

Anita looked up. Spotted her frail husband walking past, and froze.

"What . . . what is he doing here? You didn't tell me!"

"Eleven million dollars stolen," Mark stated crisply. "A family of three, vanished. Do you really think we're going to leave any stone unturned?"

"But Dan's health! You can't interview him. His heart. He gets tired, he needs to rest."

"And we need answers, Anita. By three P.M. tomorrow. We're going to keep going till we get them."

In that instant, watching through the two-way glass, Tessa felt bad for Anita Bennett. She even felt guilty, as bringing in Dan had been her idea. But if she'd expected the older woman to cave, to magically confess all, she was mistaken.

Instead, Anita Bennett simply shook her head. "But I can't give you answers. I didn't steal from the company. I didn't even know funds were missing. And I don't know what happened to Justin. I didn't do this. Justin is like family to me. And I take care of my family. Just look at my financial record. That is what I do. Work hard and tend to the ones I love. You can't squeeze blood from a stone, Agent. You can't squeeze blood from a stone."

She stared up at both FBI agents beseechingly.

And in that moment, Tessa, who never trusted anyone, believed her.

"Damn," she murmured.

Wyatt, who was seated beside her, seconded the motion.

*　　*　　*

THEY KEPT ANITA BENNETT TILL MIDNIGHT. Then, when her story and her husband's story never wavered, Nicole Adams personally escorted both back to their home. The task force remained at the conference room table, but no one had anything to say.

"We'll keep digging," Nicole's partner, Special Agent Hawkes, offered at last. "Get an agent down to the Bahamas, see if we can get a description of the person who closed out all the shell accounts. It's a new lead; we just need more time to chase it.

No one stated the obvious: They didn't have more time.

"Let's talk three P.M. phone call," Wyatt suggested.

Hawkes obliged: "I'm thinking the call to Justin Denbe's cell will come from a restricted number, probably from another iPhone, given the FaceTime feature. We have Justin's cellular company on standby to assist us with tracing the source of the call through triangulation of cell towers. That takes time, however, so we'll want to keep the caller on the phone as long as possible. Ask questions, maybe get confused about the wire transfer numbers, require clarification."

"We have ten minutes max," Tessa pointed out. "Remember the instructions: By three eleven the ransom funds must be transferred, or the first member of the Denbe family . . ."

"You're thinking of taking the call in the Denbes' town house?" Wyatt asked Hawkes.

"That's our current plan."

Wyatt was quiet for a moment. "Why?"

Hawkes frowned. "Why not?"

"I'm thinking the action is up north. The jacket tossed in central New Hampshire. The requirements of the hideout location, given the logistics of housing that many people while remaining out of sight of cops, locals, et cetera. You take the call here, and odds are, you're at least three hours away from the party. Or, say, you bring Justin Denbe's iPhone to my offices. Still take the call, no problem, but now be closer to the heart of the matter."

Tessa perked up. She hadn't thought about that, but she liked it. "Their instructions don't cover where we or the phone have to be," she pointed out. "Nothing stopping us from heading north."

Nicole Adams had returned, was standing in the doorway. "I wouldn't want to spook them," she said cautiously. "This is the one contact we get. If we do something unexpected, even if not explicitly against their instructions . . ." She let the rest of the warning go unsaid.

"Nine million dollars is a lot of reason not to spook too easily," Wyatt commented.

"Or we do what they've been doing," Tessa interjected with growing excitement. "They're sending us video with tight focus, little background, right? We can do the same. We'll grab artwork from the Denbes' town house, say . . . the big print of the red flower that hangs in the family room. Stick it on a wall in your office"— she glanced at Wyatt—"and take the call there. Just enough background to be familiar. Might be interesting, actually, to have the kidnappers think the task force is safely tucked in Boston, when really, we're three hours north."

"Steal a page from their book," Wyatt murmured. "I like it."

"Unless their demands involve activity down here in Boston," Hawkes warned.

Wyatt shrugged. "You have a whole field

office of agents five minutes from the Denbes' town house. What can't they handle?"

"Well, when you put it that way . . ."

They all looked at one another.

"Makes me feel like we're finally doing something other than play catch up," Wyatt said at last. "All along, the kidnappers have been calling the shots. They say jump, we say how high. Now, I don't know how much this will help us in the end, but . . . it's something. I'd like to feel as though we're doing something."

They agreed.

Tomorrow, 8:00 A.M., they'd reconvene at the Denbes' town house. Take the phones, borrow a painting and stage their own video conference call at the North Country sheriff's department.

Tessa liked it. Less than fifteen hours now. Then the task force would take on the kidnappers. At stake, an entire family. Including fifteen-year-old Ashlyn Denbe, reading her own ransom instructions, the look on her face when she reached the death clause . . .

They would do this. Wire the money, receive the Denbes' location, then rescue the family safe and sound.

Unless of course, this whole thing was really about the embezzled 11.2 million dollars.

In which case, they would never see the Denbes alive again.

Chapter 36

THEY DIDN'T COME FOR US first thing in the morning. The sky lightened through our narrow outer window. I woke up, tossed and turned. Dozed back off, only to dream of striking cobras and orange pill bottles. The second time I awoke, I forced myself to sit up, confront the cinder-block reality of my jail cell. I could hear Ashlyn above me, also thrashing in her sleep, murmuring something low and agitated under her breath.

Justin wasn't in his bunk, but sat on the floor, his back against the steel door as if keeping guard. I wondered if he'd passed the whole night there. He was awake now, head up, arms resting on his hiked-up knees, but he appeared lost in thought, one finger tapping absently against his other hand, as if working out a problem.

I played my morning game of guessing the hour. The day seemed fully under way. Eight A.M., nine A.M., ten A.M.? Maybe if we survived this afternoon, I'd sign up for a survival course. Become the world's oldest Girl Scout, learning how to pinpoint compass directions based on the moss growing on trees, or the hour of the day based upon the shadow that same tree cast upon the ground. I could learn some new skills. Certainly, my old ones weren't doing a whole lot for me.

I crossed to the toilet. Justin gave me his back, the closest we could get to privacy.

Afterward, when he remained preoccupied and Ashlyn continued to thrash on the top bunk, I scrubbed my face, using only my hands because we didn't have any soap or towels. Then, acting on impulse, I picked up our empty plastic jug and worked on filling it with water from the sink. I leaned my head over the tiny sink, pouring half the water jug over my hair, then worked at my scalp furiously with my fingertips. I could feel myself spraying water everywhere, but I didn't care. I just couldn't take one more second of the rank smell of my own hair, the constant itch of dirt and grime on my skin.

I scrubbed and scrubbed and scrubbed. Maybe I was trying to slough off my own skin, shed my miserable existence. Or maybe, a year from now, this would become the DNA evidence that would be used to convict Z and his team on all charges. The castoff cells of my dead skin, sprayed over this tiny sink in this tiny cell in this much too big prison.

I missed soap, the soft feel of lather, the reassuring scent of cleanliness. But I continued scrubbing, pouring the second half of the jug slowly over my head, down the fine strands of my shoulder-length hair. Finally, I splashed more water onto my neck, then shoved up the jumpsuit sleeves and scoured at my arms. By the time I finished, I was soaked, my jumpsuit was soaked and the cinder-block wall was thoroughly sprayed with water. And I felt better. Prepared for the day. As ready as I was going to get.

"Can I have a turn?" Ashlyn, now awake and watching me from the top bunk.

Wordlessly, I began to refill the jug.

"Beautifying yourselves for your rescuers?" Justin drawled from the floor.

"We are women." I handed my daughter the water jug. "Now hear us roar."

THE MORNING WORE ON, slowly and surely eroding our nerves. My hair dried as I took up pacing between the bunk beds. My jumpsuit, too. I still wouldn't call myself clean. Just . . . less dirty.

Justin gave his swollen face and short hair a quick douse. Then, when the vast common room remained quiet, just the never-ending hum of fluorescent lights, he started a light regimen of push-ups, followed by sit-ups, then finally pull-ups using the top bunk.

Ashlyn watched us both as if we were insane. She had assumed the fetal position, curled up in the corner of the top bunk where she could see everything while remaining carefully tucked away. She reminded me of a feline. Not at all relaxed. Just waiting for the first excuse to spook or pounce.

I forced her to drink water, given that she was still recovering from yesterday's miscarriage. I wished I had food for her as well. I finally had my own appetite back, my stomach actually growling as I prowled around the narrow cell. It seemed fitting that I would finally be ready to eat the day our kidnappers stopped feeding us.

Did they want us weak, fatigued, uncertain? All part of Z's campaign of psychological warfare. By the time 3:00 P.M. rolled around, we'd do whatever he wanted just as long as he tossed us a bread crumb.

Or had something else happened? Our kidnappers had become sick, or were otherwise impaired? They wouldn't just leave us, would they? Drive off, disappear? No one knew we were here. We would rot, literally die like forgotten animals trapped in a cage. Sure, the water would keep us going for the first week. But after fourteen, fifteen days of no food . . .

A new sound. A snap, then a flicker of the lights as the hum died out, taking the overhead lights with it. Our cell went from overbright white to shades of gray, illuminated only by a sliver of window, while the common area went to immediate shadow, a stage suddenly devoid of spotlights.

"Powering down," Justin murmured.

And I got it. What our captors were doing. Preparing to leave the prison. Preparing to end the game, make their getaway.

What was the time? I couldn't figure it out based on the angle of the sun.

But it was coming. Three P.M.

The hour of reckoning.

I stopped pacing, climbed up to the top bunk and held my daughter's hand.

After another moment, Justin joined us. We sat together, arm in arm, and waited for whatever was going to happen next.

TESSA WOKE UP AT FIVE THIRTY. Her room was still dark. She'd been asleep three, four hours tops and couldn't figure out what had woken her. Then, she watched her door soundlessly open, Sophie's pale form appearing.

Her daughter drifted into the room, moving so quietly Tessa wasn't even sure she was awake. Sometimes Sophie sleepwalked. Sometimes, she also talked in her sleep. Or, more like sleep-screamed.

Now Sophie materialized at the edge of Tessa's bed, her eyes round and alert in her face.

"Mommy?"

"Yes."

"Did you find the family?"

"Not yet." Tessa drew back her covers. Sophie climbed aboard.

"You checked the cold, dark places?"

"Some of them."

"What about the mountains? Did you try all the cabins in the mountains?"

"Tomorrow . . . today, actually . . . I'm going to head north. We'll check more."

"Bring cookies."

"Absolutely."

Sophie tucking against her. "That girl needs you."

Tessa, hesitating. Her daughter was identifying with the victim, and given how things might turn out . . . She should hedge her bets, better manage her daughter's expectations. And yet, in a case like this, was such a thing even possible? She found herself saying: "Losing you was the worst thing that ever happened to me, Sophie. Returning home, discovering that you weren't there. It hurt. Like someone had punched me in the stomach."

"I didn't want to go. They made me."

"Of course. I knew you never would

have willingly left me. I hope you know, I never would've willingly let you go."

"I knew, Mommy. Just like I knew you were coming. And I knew you'd make them pay."

Tessa, wrapping her arms around her daughter's bony shoulders. "We were lucky, Sophie. It sounds funny, but we got each other back. That makes us lucky."

"And Mrs. Ennis."

"And Mrs. Ennis."

"And Gertrude."

Sophie's doll. With the eye they had carefully sewn back on. "I want this family to be lucky, too, Sophie. I'm going to try very hard to help them. There's a whole bunch of detectives, in fact, who are working hard to help them. But sometimes, it also takes a bit of luck."

"Cold, dark places."

"Got it."

"Bring cookies."

"Yep."

"Carry your gun."

"Yes."

"Then, please come home. I miss you, Mommy. I miss you."

*   *   *

WYATT DIDN'T SLEEP. He worked his phone, clearing messages, catching up with the rest of his department. His deputies had some news: a break-in at a methadone clinic in Littleton, sometime Saturday night. Could be related to their case, or then again, maybe not. Gas station attendant had called in about filling up a white van on Saturday morning. Driven by two tough guys. Made him nervous, he said. Figured they were running drugs, given the plain white van, the dead man stares. They'd headed north on 93, all he could offer. One had three tears tattooed under his left eye. Definitely, the dude had served time.

Fish and Game had found another van parked off road by Crawford Notch. Older model, painted dark blue. Abandoned when they found it, the back littered with empty beer cans and smelling strongly of marijuana. Sounded like it belonged to some people up to no good, but probably not trained professionals up to no good.

And so it went. A string of a dozen or so possible sightings or maybe leads, if only they knew what they were sighting or leading.

At 2:00 A.M., Wyatt gave up on calls,

stared at their map instead. He fell asleep with his head upon it, dreaming of Xs and Os and Ashlyn Denbe telling him to hurry up, there wasn't much time left.

Six A.M., he was up, showered and back in yesterday's uniform. He met Kevin down-stairs, both of them checking out, grabbing coffee, then heading for the Denbes' town house. They arrived thirty minutes early and were still the last ones to arrive.

Special Agent Hawkes already had the Denbe family cell phone. Nicole already had the picture.

Nothing new to report. Agents were still working the financials, while a pair of uniformed officers now sat outside Anita Bennett's house. Feds were in place at the insurance company headquarters in Chicago. Cellular company still awaiting final go-ahead for the 3:00 P.M. EST call.

They knew what they knew. They had what they had. It was what it was.

They headed north, reaching the county sheriff's department by 11:00 A.M. By noon, the Denbes' picture was on the wall, and they'd run through half a dozen ransom scripts. Nicole would handle the call, with the rest of them providing backup.

Twelve thirty, they ordered lunch.

One o'clock, Wyatt finished debriefing local PDs as well as the state police. They'd set up a designated channel through dispatch, ready to broadcast information the second they had any.

He once again reviewed the map.

One thirty, two o'clock. Two fifteen. Two thirty.

What'd they miss, what'd they miss? Always something. You planned, you prepared and yet, in the end, it was always something.

Wyatt, back to staring at his map.

Two forty. Two forty-eight. Two fifty-two. Two fifty-five.

What if the suspects never called? What if this was how the case ended, not with a blaze of glory but in total radio silence? The family was already dead, an embezzler covering his or her tracks. There wouldn't be any rescue. Just a sad, drawn-out search that would consume days, weeks, months, maybe even years.

Three P.M.

Three oh one.

Three oh two.

Justin Denbe's phone rang to life.

Chapter 37

Z MATERIALIZED OUTSIDE OUR CELL DOOR. For the first time since this ordeal started, he appeared tense, and his wired alertness immediately put our own nerves on edge. He was bearing a black plastic garbage bag that turned out to be filled with our original clothing. Now he fed each item through the wrist slot in the door with terse orders for us to change.

Our first step back into the real world, I wondered, our Boston garb? But I already doubted it. Ashlyn and I had also been commanded to change for our segment of the ransom demands; not because Z had wanted us to look our best on video, but because he hadn't wanted to give away any information on our whereabouts, such as prison jumpsuits. I had a feeling the same logic applied here.

If the ransom demand was met, the police would learn of our location soon enough. But it wasn't Z's style to give away any advantage before he had to.

Once we were changed, it was time to exit the cell.

"Denbe first." A barking command.

Z indicated to the slot in the door. Justin presented his wrists, which were immediately bound with zip ties. I went next. Then Ashlyn. When we were all secured, Z made a motion with his hand, and with a buzzing snap, our steel door swung open.

Z kept his gaze on Justin, who walked out with his shoulders back and chin up, his bruised face clearly defiant.

Immediately the tension ratcheted up another notch.

Don't do anything stupid, I found myself thinking. Please don't do anything stupid.

Except I wasn't sure what that was anymore. Here we were, once again bound and helpless. Stupid only applied if our captors really were going to let us go. They had other options, of course. For example, placing a bullet through each of our heads the second the ransom funds appeared in their account. Not like we could stop them. Not like the police were standing by to help us the moment the money was delivered.

One way or another, we were still on our own, and I could feel the tight restrictions of the plastic zip tie digging into my wrists.

Z took Justin by the elbow. He indicated for the ladies to walk first. Once Ashlyn and I ventured uncertainly forward into the shadowed dayroom, he and Justin fell in step behind us. Clearly, Z had pegged Justin as the primary threat, to be monitored at all times. I wish I could disagree, chortle gleefully to myself that if only he knew. Instead, I felt a rising sense of hysteria and had to suppress the ridiculous urge to tug on my freshly washed hair.

At the sally port, we had to pause. I wondered who was in the control room. Mick or Radar? Z gestured to the security camera and the first set of doors rolled open. We stepped inside. Another pause. The clang of steel slamming shut behind us, plunging us into a deep dark, broken up only by the dim glow of green emergency lights, illuminating faint puddles of floor. I could feel Ashlyn shudder beside me, and move closer.

Then, more slowly than I would've liked, the next set of heavy steel doors slowly opened. A broad hallway loomed before us. Also lit by emergency lights. We must've come this way before, but everything looked different without the bright wash of overhead lights. The prison had taken on the spooky feel of a haunted house, and while I knew it was daylight outside, already I felt isolated, my shoulders hunching, my chin tucking down as if the ceiling were lower, the walls closing in.

"Walk," Z ordered, and very tentatively, Ashlyn and I shuffled forward.

We followed the puddles of green glow to another set of doors. Turned out to be a second sally port. More clanging as steel doors slammed shut behind us. A sound that got under the skin. A sound I never wanted to hear again.

The closing doors once more plunged us into darkness. We waited, Ashlyn bouncing on her toes beside me, until the forward set of doors slowly rolled open. Was it just me, or had this set of doors taken much longer? Had to be Mick in the control room. Having a little fun at our expense.

I willed my face to be impassive. I would not give him the satisfaction of showing my fear.

Z urged us forward. We walked, losing our sense of direction in the shadowy green maze of prison corridors. Suddenly, the hallway lightened. We came to a stretch with large exterior windows awash with daylight. Then, across from that, an enclosed chamber lined with windows that had been heavily fortified with horizontal bars.

The control room. Had to be. I could see monitors and panels and all sorts of crazy computer equipment that meant nothing to me but probably everything to my husband.

They were going to do it. Exchange us for ransom. We would go home; they would get nine million dollars.

We would go home.

I stared at the now empty room, door open, our ticket to safety.

I took one more step, then from behind, Z grabbed my arm and drew me up short.

He said, "Not so fast."

And I shuddered, feeling my heart stop in my chest.

"HERE'S THE DEAL," Z continued shortly. "It's two fifty-five P.M. I'm going to let you into the control room. I'm going to hand you a phone. I'm going to remove your wrist constraints."

Z stopped looking at Ashlyn and me, staring at Justin instead. "At which point, you have the power to lock down this prison. You could even attempt to trap me inside. But you should know, Radar and Mick are already out. They're armed with a full arsenal of weapons, which they are exceptionally well trained at using. I'm guessing that between them, they could pick off at least thirty-six to forty-eight first responders without even breaking into a sweat. I know you might not care about that"—his gaze went hard, his fanged cobra tattoo moving restlessly as he frowned—"but I'm counting on the ladies to be your conscience." His gaze flickered to us. "Play it smart, everyone goes home safe and sound. Try something stupid and there'll be a lot of funerals on Friday. In-

cluding your own. I'm not a man who for-
gives, Denbe. And I know where you live."

Justin said nothing.

I stepped forward, inserting myself into
the space between them. "Tell us what
you want us to do."

Z switched his attention to me. "The rest
is easy. Call your husband's cell phone
using FaceTime. Wave to the nice FBI
agent who plans on building her career
around your safe return. Reiterate the wire
transfer instructions. Radar is monitoring
the account. The second we have confirmation the funds have been received,
we're gone. By three eleven, on the other
hand, if no money has been received, we
start with plan B."

Z's gaze back on Justin. "Want to know
Radar's real expertise? He's a demolitions
expert. Sure, your control room has
ballistic-rated glass. But trust me, Radar
can take out an armored tank. Your reinforced fish tank, not a problem. Better hope
the FBI has their act together. Better hope
they're also going for smart today, and not
planning anything stupid."

I hadn't even thought of that, and now I
felt my nervousness ramp up double-time.

"Wait a minute, wait a minute. But we don't control them, we have no way of knowing . . . What if they don't wire the money? It's not our fault!"

Z merely shrugged his massive shoulders as he dragged us toward the open control room. I wanted to dig in my heels. All of a sudden, this didn't seem like such a great idea. I'd been worried about my husband's rash actions. Now I had to worry about an entire law enforcement team as well?

"By three eleven, if we don't have the money, you'll get to hear a very large boom. You might want to duck for cover. You know, just to give yourselves a sporting chance."

Then, we were in the control room and Z was wielding a knife. No time to panic. No time to scream.

Slash, slash, slash.

Our wrists were free.

A phone was shoved into Justin's hands.

Then Z was gone, the heavy control room door booming shut in his wake.

We were alone, unshackled, and for the first time ever, in charge of our prison.

I stood stock-still, my first taste of quasi-freedom leaving me completely immobilized.

Not my husband.

"All right," Justin declared briskly. "This is what we're going to do."

THE IPHONE CONTINUED TO CHIME. After a split second, Nicole kicked into gear. She waved a hand, indicating for everyone to take position.

Then she stood in front of the Denbes' family-room painting, now hanging in a sheriff's office three hours north, and answered the phone, activating FaceTime.

Hawkes had wired the phone to a larger TV screen so the rest of them could watch the show.

Justin Denbe's face appeared, his swollen eye and misshapen nose a pulpy mess. But there was no mistaking the determination on his face.

"This is Justin Denbe. I'm here with my wife, Libby, and daughter, Ashlyn." A quick sweep of the phone screen. Libby Denbe appeared briefly, seemingly frozen in place, nearly petrified with fear. Their fifteen-year-old daughter, Ashlyn, however, was literally bouncing up and down in agitation. "We are safe and secure. Please wire the money by three eleven, or they will blow us up."

Hawkes made a rolling motion with his finger to drag out the call. Nicole tapped her foot once to indicate she got it.

"This is Nicole Adams, special agent, FBI. We are happy to be in contact with you, Justin, and to receive confirmation that you and your family are alive and well."

"You have eight minutes," Justin replied crisply.

"We understand. And the account number for the wire instructions is . . ." Nicole rattled off the long string, repeating it twice. At the computer, Hawkes continued to tap the keyboard frantically, exchanging messages with Denbe's cellular provider, who would now be working to trace the incoming call. Tessa stood at Hawkes's shoulder, Wyatt beside her. She found herself holding her breath.

"The insurance company has instructed us to wire one million dollars as a good faith deposit," Nicole continued. "They won't release the remaining eight million without further assurances of your safety."

"In six minutes," Justin replied tersely,

"that account either receives nine million dollars or they blow us up."

"Are they there, Justin?" Nicole continued evenly. "Can I speak to the person in charge?"

"No."

"No, I can't speak . . . ?"

"No, they aren't here. We're alone in the control room. We can keep them locked out, meaning we are safe from immediate physical assault. Explosives, on the other hand . . ." Justin's tone was droll. He didn't seem nervous to Tessa. Just . . . grim. A man who knew the score.

Beside her, Wyatt mouthed the words *control room*. Wyatt studied her. Tessa shrugged.

"Libby and Ashlyn are with you, but not your captors? You are alone?" Nicole continued. While her face remained impassive, one leg trembled beneath her. High-stakes poker, with other people's lives at stake.

"Five minutes," Justin said. Then, for the first time, his tone broke. "Look, I know you're trying to trace this call. They know you're trying to trace this call. I'm telling you, you don't have time. For the next five minutes, my family and I are safe.

That's as good as it's going to get. Now you get that fucking money in that fucking account, or your next visual will be myself, my wife and my daughter being blown to shit!"

"I understand. Your safety is our number one concern. Of course, we have to work with the insurance company—"

"Listen to me. This is not a negotiation. I am not in touch with our captors, they are not on this line. They are standing very far away, holding a detonator. They are monitoring the account. Either the money appears by three eleven, or they flip the kill switch. Those are the options."

"Control room," Wyatt muttered again beside Tessa. He was nudging her with his arm, as if that term should mean something to her. "The pile of personal possessions on the kitchen counter—wallet, jewelry . . ."

"Justin," Nicole was saying, "I understand your concerns. Trust me, we're on your side. But if they have wired your room with explosives, how do we know they won't activate them either way?"

"Because rich men have incentive to get away. Poor men don't."

Then, Tessa got it. She turned toward

Wyatt, keeping her voice low even as her eyes widened. "Prison. Prisons have control rooms. But, how could you smuggle a family into a prison unless . . ."

Wyatt was already one step ahead: "The new state facility," he supplied grimly. "Completed last year, never been open. Locals still furious over the lost job opportunities, the waste of taxpayer funds. How much you want to bet—"

"It was built by Denbe Construction."

"Meaning Justin knows exactly where he is. And if he's still not providing his location . . ."

"He's scared."

"Suspects must really have access to explosives." Wyatt grabbed a yellow legal pad. Wrote in giant black marker: *WIRE $$ NOW*. And held it up for Nicole.

The special agent never blinked, simply stated into the phone: "Good news, Justin. The insurance company has approved the full nine million. The money is being transferred as we speak. Couple of minutes more, Justin. Then you and your family will be safe."

Tessa and Wyatt didn't wait for the rest. They were already bolting from the room,

Wyatt on the radio, sending out the request for backup over the preset emergency channel. Then, they were in the parking lot, piling into his cruiser.

"Thirty miles north," Wyatt declared. "We should be there in twenty."

He hit the sirens and roared onto the road.

Chapter 38

Justin was on the phone. Talking, talking, talking.

Beside him, Ashlyn was bobbing up and down, looking more like herself, in her old pajamas, and yet not at all like herself, with her tightly drawn features and the anxiety radiating from every taut line of her body.

And myself . . . Facing the possible final ten minutes of my own life, I didn't know what to do. I wandered around the room, which was bigger than I would've thought, with a broad, horseshoe-shaped control desk plopped in the middle of a larger area lined by charging walkie-talkies and several doors I assumed led to supply closets. I found the infamous key drop, an open metal tube into which, in case of emergency, a corrections officer would drop all keys, rendering them inaccessible to attacking inmates, and thus keeping all ammunition and firearms closets secured.

I turned my attention to the massive control desk, gliding my hands over the plain white Formica desktop, the various flat-screen monitors inlaid at an angled rise, then the half a dozen microphones that sprouted up like weeds. The corrections officers were locked in here, I thought, isolated by their very powerfulness. A mini set of wizards of Oz, seeing all, commanding all, but forever trapped behind the barred curtain.

Above me, mounted from the ceiling, hung a line of four flat-screen TVs. They were off now, but I bet this was how our captors had monitored us, reviewing various images from the dozens if not hundreds of security cameras. They had watched us cry. Watched us fight. Watched us slowly but surely break down into lesser beings, the total deconstruction of a family.

It made me suddenly furious. That they'd violated our privacy like that. Sat here in this locked room, maybe even took bets on our misery. Ten bucks says the woman cries first, five bucks says the girl can't pee with an audience.

I hated them. Intensely. Virulently. Which, perversely, made me want to see them. Turnabout is fair play. If they'd once been able to study us like animals in a zoo, well, we had the control now. And there was nothing in Z's terms that said we couldn't monitor them.

I bent over, and while my husband cursed out some FBI agent for not having magically done exactly what he'd told her to do exactly when he'd demanded that she do it, I started powering up control screens and exploring the surveillance options.

"Mom?" Ashlyn appeared beside me.

"Just kicking the tires, honey. Now, if we wanted to see the view from the cameras outside the prison, which buttons would you hit?"

Ashlyn leaned around me, tapped the control screen where a white button indicated security and we both studied the menu that came up next.

The screen had a clock in the lower right-hand corner. It read 3:09. Two minutes till our captors gave up and launched a counterattack. Possibly even blew us up, as Justin was alleging.

I didn't think Z would take out the room. He struck me as the kind of man who'd neatly eliminate the door. That way he could march through the smoking rubble, pull out a Glock 10 and tend to the rest of his business up close and personal. Waste less ammo.

On the monitor, a white van suddenly came into view. Growing larger and larger until it nearly filled the screen. I found myself staring at Radar, sitting behind the wheel. He was not looking up at the camera, no doubt mounted above the prison's intake door, but was looking toward the passenger's side, as if expecting someone.

Picking up. He was picking up Z and Mick, his cocaptors.

But he was supposed to be on the roof. Armed to the teeth and ready to fire upon first responders.

Unless the money had been paid. Wired straight into the account. Justin had been right: Rich men had nine million more reasons to make a quick getaway than poor men.

The clock on the bottom of the screen hit 3:10.

Radar, holding up his phone, saying something I couldn't hear to a person I couldn't see.

My gaze, flying up to find Justin. "Did they pay? Is it okay, did the insurance company pay?"

Justin, into the phone: "Have the funds been received? It's three eleven, tell me the funds have been received?"

The FBI agent, her voice as crisp and authoritative as ever: "Justin, I have word that the money is being transferred right now."

Radar, still studying his phone, hitting some buttons. Talking to the person I couldn't see.

"Justin, the funds have been delivered. Can you please advise us as to your location? We have officers standing by for the safe recovery of your family."

"Mom!" Ashlyn cried, clutching my arm, bouncing even higher at the news. We were safe, funds received, we were safe, the police would be on their way.

Justin, sounding abruptly tired, as if the good news had taken more out of him than our impending deaths: "We are currently at the new state prison. Located—"

Boom!

I turned toward the control room door, breath already catching. Expecting to spot Z, striding through the smoke and rubble like the Terminator, ready to mow down all the officers in the police station, or, in our case, a helpless family stuck in a control room.

The locked door was intact, the bank of barred windows intact. No Z. No smoking rubble.

"Mom!" My daughter, yanking on my arm as she screamed hysterically.

I turned back just in time to see Mick come barreling out of the door I'd assumed was a supply closet. He was grinning madly and, true to Z's words, was armed to the teeth.

"Miss me?" he called out.

Then he leveled his semiauto, and while we stood there, the proverbial fish in a barrel, he opened fire.

While Wyatt drove, Tessa worked the phone. She got Chris Lopez on the line, demanding to know anything and everything he could tell them about the state prison Denbe Construction had built in the wilds of New Hampshire.

Surrounded by six hundred acres of mountains, marshes and deep wilderness. Closest town twenty miles away. Nearest PD even slightly beyond that. A facility so remote it was set up to house its own security team, except given that the prison was never funded, those barracks remained empty.

Help wasn't anywhere close. Looking at fifteen to twenty minutes ETA for first responders.

While the police radio crackled to life with fresh reports. Sound of shots fired coming over Justin Denbe's cell phone. Sound of female screaming. Call now dropped, unable to reconnect with the Denbe family.

"Drive faster," Tessa ordered Wyatt.

"Now see, this is why you should hang out with sheriffs. We not only know how to drive faster, but we can also drive smarter."

Abruptly, Wyatt swung the vehicle left. They careened onto a dirt path Tessa would've sworn was a deer trail. She grabbed the oh shit handle just as he hit the gas.

The cruiser launched, then settled into a bone-crunching gallop.

"In the state of New Hampshire, the shortest distance between two points is rarely paved. But if you know where to look, you can almost find a dirt road. Ten minutes," he announced. "Ten more minutes, then we'll have the prison in our sight."

"THE DOOR," Justin was yelling. "The door, the door, the door!"

At first, I didn't understand what he meant. Justin had gone down, the first shot from Mick's gun dropping him like a rock, red blooming across his shoulder. Ashlyn had screamed, then instinctively dove behind me, leaving me standing alone, on one side of the vast control desk, Mick, still grinning madly, on the other.

He turned his gun toward me. I ducked, then heard a grunt and watched him rock to the side; Justin, down but not out, had kicked him in the side of the kneecap.

"Door!" my husband yelled again.

Then I got it. We were trapped. In a space this small, Mick would mow us down in a matter of seconds. Escape back into the prison, where we could get out or at least spread out, was our only chance at survival.

I bobbed up, ducking my head as I frantically stabbed at the touch screen, willing myself to stumble upon the door controls. We'd been in the security menu. I'd seen a door lock override. Where, where, where . . .

Another shot. Two, three, four. My shoulders hunched reflexively and I practically felt the whistle of the last bullet as it whizzed by my ear.

Then my daughter was suddenly standing, her eyes wild, her long hair a tangled mass as she heaved up a rolling desk chair and threw it at Mick with all her strength.

"I hate you!" she screamed. "I hate you I hate you I hate you I hate you I fucking hate you."

A second desk chair went flying and now Mick was ducking for cover, swearing as he tangled briefly in one set of rolling chair legs, went down, tried to recover, got nailed by Justin again in the kneecaps and landed hard.

There! Override. I jabbed at the bright red button. "Are you sure?" a dialogue box squawked at me. Override releases all inner and outer doors . . .

Override, override, override! Yes, yes, yes, yes, yes!

Ashlyn had found the walkie-talkies. A dozen had sat in a neat row of charging stations around the outer perimeter. Now she turned them into missiles, humming them one after another at the top of Mick's head. He cursed again, pinned behind the control desk by her relentless assault.

The control room door swung open just as Ashlyn hurled the last walkie-talkie. I couldn't see Justin, but I heard his voice, commanding clearly:

"Run, goddammit. Get her out of here!"

I didn't need to be told twice. We had our deal, parent to parent. Either one of us was expendable. It was Ashlyn who mattered.

I grabbed my daughter's hand and pulled her from the control room.

While behind us, Mick once again opened fire.

WYATT HIT THE CREST OF THE HILL HARD. Briefly, the cruiser was airborne, and in that moment, Tessa spotted it. A vast compound at least ten miles away, perched up on a knoll, dominated by a large, obviously institutional building, and surrounded by miles and miles of razor-wire fencing.

The cruiser landed. They both grunted on impact. Then Wyatt was fishtailing back down the dirt road, hurtling them out of the woods, onto pavement. A hard right, and they were headed north, flying up a newly paved road as trees blurred into a long green tunnel around them.

"That's huge!" Tessa exclaimed. "How will we find them?"

"Follow the sound of gunshots. You wearing a vest?"

"Yes."

The whole team had donned them at two thirty. Expecting that the call might lead to action, and while you hoped for the best, a good cop always planned for the worst.

Tessa couldn't help but think of Sophie, her daughter, who'd already lost a parent. And then, her daughter's own prophecy, *Look for them in a cold, dark place.* What could be colder and darker than a mothballed prison?

As Sophie had said, Ashlyn needed her. The whole family needed her.

"I want the shotgun," Tessa said.

Wyatt flattened the accelerator to the floor, and once again, they shot forward.

WE CLEARED THE CONTROL ROOM into the main corridor.

"Dad," Ashlyn gasped, her hand still clasped in mine.

"Out, out, we need out."

"Dad!" My daughter actually dug in her heels, tried to halt our progress.

I whirled on her, my expression so fierce, or maybe just so insane, my daughter gasped. "You forget him, Ashlyn Denbe. You forget me, too, if it comes to that. You get out of here. This is your last order, the one instruction I want you to remember. You survive. Your parents demand it of you."

"Mom—"

"Shut up, child. He's coming. Now *run*!"

She did, straight down the hall toward the outer doors. I'd like to say Ashlyn was motivated by my speech, but far more likely, she was spooked by Mick's inhuman roar as he finally cleared the control room, staggered into the hallway and turned toward us.

I had a brief image. A huge pumped-up bear of a man with blood streaming down one half of his face where some of Ashlyn's missiles had found their mark. He was clad all in black, covered in some kind of vest that virtually sprouted guns and ammo. And a knife. Strapped to his outer thigh. A huge, gleaming hunting knife that I could already tell he'd love nothing better than to use to gut me.

He leveled the gun first. Aimed it straight at me while I stood, still rooted in place. He pulled the trigger. Forty feet back, an easy distance for a man of his training and marksmanship. The gun clicked empty.

I couldn't help myself. I smiled at the irony.

Then, Mick threw the gun to the side and charged.

I ran, following my daughter's lead to the front doors. If we could just get outside, so many places for cover. And the police had to know. They'd been on the phone, they had to have seen something, heard everything. They'd be coming.

If we could just get outside.

Ashlyn hit the double-glass doors first. She was running so hard, the doors parted like water before a diver. I spotted a thin seam of brighter daylight, then she was through.

Mick's heavy-booted footsteps, growing louder and louder behind me.

I tried to pour on the speed, a forty-five-year-old woman, suffering from withdrawal, nearly completely broken down, trying to reclaim some of her lost youth.

I wasn't going to make it. Mick was fit and well trained. And I was just me, a middle-aged woman whose heart was already pounding too hard in her chest. I felt simultaneously light-headed and nauseated, trying to find that inner gear, realizing there was nothing left. This is your body on drugs, I thought inanely. Apparently, a four-month diet of prescription painkillers did not do a body good.

The glass doors, so close, if I could just get through . . .

Then, daylight magically appeared before me. The door opening all on its own.

Z stood directly in front of me, face impassive as I raced straight for him. He had Ashlyn's arm in a tight grip, twisting it behind her back as she grimaced in pain.

Beyond him, Radar waited in the idling van, side door open.

Of course, I'd seen them pull up. How stupid of me. We'd run right toward them, straight into the waiting arms of our captors.

I couldn't help myself. I screamed. In rage, frustration and sheer exhaustion.

Then, because I had nothing left to lose, I hurled myself at Z, the man who held my daughter, and went for his eyeballs.

"WHERE IS IT, where is it?" Tessa demanded to know. They had hit the first sign advising motorists not to stop for hitchhikers. Then, a sign notifying them they were on state property. Next should come the perimeter fencing, topped with rolls of razor wire, to be followed finally by a guardhouse marking the turn into the six-hundred-acre compound.

But so far, nothing.

Sky remained quiet overhead. No sign of the FBI chopper, which had probably launched from Concord. No roar of other sirens, though the local PD had to also be en route, not to mention the activation of the state's SWAT team.

Then, up ahead, the first glimmer of the sixteen-foot-tall, razor-wire-topped, fully electrified double-lined fence.

"Rifle," Wyatt ordered.

She went to work removing it from its rack, as he shot past the fence, made a squealing right-hand turn and finally entered the prison grounds.

Z WENT DOWN. I'm not sure what he'd expected. That I'd surrender, give up, fall apart. But certainly, not that I'd attack.

Ashlyn stumbled to the side, then I was on him, raking my ragged nails across his face, trying to dig my thumbs into his eye sockets. The fanged cobra around his left eye hissed at me, but I ignored it, intent on my mission. Maim. Hurt. Make him bleed.

Then I was unceremoniously plucked from Z's body. Mick had me in his massive arms, lifting me up. I heard the fragile fabric of my fine wrap top tear; so much for Boston clothes. Then, Mick tossed me through the air. I landed hard on the asphalt drive, gasping as the breath was knocked from my body.

Z leapt to his feet, clutching his left eye with one hand, while Mick yanked his knife from his leg holster and squared off against me and my daughter.

I'd been right earlier. The blade was huge and serrated. And Mick was looking forward to using it. Very much. He wiped the last of the blood from the gash on his forehead, and grinned at us.

My daughter was still on the ground beside me. She hiccupped slightly and I could see the fear on her face as she scrambled to her feet.

Mick tossed his knife from his right hand to his left, then back again. Putting on a little show.

Z, on the other hand, walked slowly backward to the waiting van, hand still covering his eye. Clearly, he thought Mick could handle us.

"When I tell you to go," I murmured to my daughter, "I want you to head back into the prison. Disappear. Hide anywhere you can. The police are coming, you just need to buy time."

Ashlyn didn't speak. I could tell she understood the decision I'd made. And maybe she would've protested or hedged, but that knife, that giant, stainless steel blade, flashing from hand to hand . . .

I wish Mick hadn't run out of ammo. I would've much rather faced a bullet. But a knife attack was up close and personal. He was going to have to approach, then assault, and the ensuing struggle would buy the time for Ashlyn to escape. Justin had done his part in the control room. Now I would do mine.

But I wondered, just for a second, if Mick had any other guns tucked into that vest. If I could just put my hands on a trigger. A single, up-close shot . . .

I'd just started to take inventory when Mick charged.

No roar this time.

Just a swift, silent lunge that caught me flat-footed and completely unprepared. I saw the knife arc out, heard Ashlyn's startled scream, then suddenly my vision was filled with two hundred pounds of snarling menace.

Was my daughter running? I hoped she was running.

I did the only thing I thought I might get away with, a brief memory of some article I'd read on a website, or maybe a story once relayed at Justin's gun club, but when facing a larger opponent in hand-to-hand combat, close the gap between you. Actually move inside the kill zone, where your opponent can no longer hit you with the full force of his windup.

In this case, I stumbled toward Mick. He was forced to stop short, his forward momentum and wildly swinging arc twisting him off balance. In that split second, I was beneath his arm, knocking against his chest. It must've looked like I was locking him in a lover's embrace, but really I was frantically running my hands down his weapons vest, searching out anything that might help me.

I was an experienced shooter. If I could just get my hands on a firearm, anything at this point-blank range . . .

Mick grabbed my shoulders and savagely ripped me away from him. I stumbled, tried to counter with my own body weight, but at a mere hundred and ten pounds . . .

He threw me across the covered causeway and I felt the instant burn of a hundred tiny rocks ripping the skin from the palms of my hands. I was still trying to climb to my feet when Mick once more assumed the position, legs crouched, blade flashing brightly as he tossed it expertly to his right hand.

I didn't have any more tricks up my sleeve. I simply raised my head and watched death come for me.

The glass doors of the prison burst open.

Justin lurched into the open space, bright red blood drenching his favorite blue dress shirt, his lips peeled back into an inhuman grimace. Twisting right, spotting me. Twisting left, spotting Mick.

Then lunging head-on at the knife-wielding brute who'd attacked his family.

"Noooo!"

Justin's scream. My own. Eighteen years of our lives so entangled, including this one final moment.

Mick brought up his blade, half surprise, half defense.

Justin continued charging. And Mick stabbed my husband straight into his chest.

A gasp. A fresh scream. Ashlyn's this time, from the doorway of the prison, where she'd reappeared, a fifteen-year-old girl still certain her father could slay monsters.

Then, a new sound, faint, but closing the gap.

Sirens. The cavalry, arriving at last.

Too late for Justin.

But maybe . . .

I glanced up sharply. Saw it clearly in Z's eyes from where he was crouched in the waiting van. Regret. Not for killing my husband, I was certain. But because they had run out of time to kill us, too.

Justin had collapsed on top of Mick, one arm entangled in the other man's vest, his body large enough to pin both of them in place. Now Z leapt out of the van. Given the approaching sirens, he seemed to reach some sort of internal decision. Rather than take the time to untangle Justin from Mick's vest, he helped Mick heave Justin's flopping corpse into the vehicle, Mick rolling in after him. Then, Z resumed his position.

The van door slid shut.

Radar gunned the engine.

And they roared away. Just like that. Nine million dollars richer. Cold-blooded murderers of my husband. Making their getaway.

My daughter wasn't screaming anymore. Or crying.

She just stood there, completely shell-shocked.

After another moment, I crossed to her and put my arms around her trembling shoulders. We stood together, listening to the sirens come closer, and wondering if we'd ever again feel safe.

Chapter 39

TESSA SPOTTED LIBBY AND ASHLYN DENBE
FIRST. They stood under a covered carport
outside the main prison entrance. Libby's
clothing appeared torn to shreds and
streaked with blood. In comparison, Ashlyn appeared in relatively better shape, but
with a blank expression on her face.
Shock, trauma, stress.

Wyatt braked hard twenty feet back, and
they threw open the doors, hands on their
weapons.

"Libby and Ashlyn?" Wyatt called out,
still tucked behind the protective cover
formed by his open door.

The woman answered first. Her voice hoarse but surprisingly steady. "Yes."

"How many remaining on the property?"

"They're gone. It's just us. The commandos . . . all gone. My husband. *Gone* . . ." Libby's voice broke. She folded her arms around her daughter's still-frozen form, but whether she was seeking comfort or giving comfort remained unclear.

Wyatt and Tessa exchanged glances. In a crisis situation, first order of business was to secure the scene, next tend to the victims, then give pursuit.

They got to work.

In Tessa's days as a state trooper, she'd carried enough supplies to outfit a small village. Wyatt clearly thought the same. From his trunk, he produced blankets, water and energy bars. Without a word, Tessa went straight to the women, while Wyatt, weapon drawn, conducted a rapid inventory of the building.

"My name is Tessa Leoni," she introduced herself as she approached, voice calm, movements brisk. "I was hired by Denbe Construction to assist with finding you."

Libby and Ashlyn both stared at her. Up

close, Tessa could see that the girl was unnaturally pale. She was also starting to shake. Small shivers now, but her condition would grow to full-on tremors if not dealt with quickly. Tessa threw two dark wool blankets around the girl's shoulders, handed her a bottle of water and instructed her to drink.

Libby Denbe was already rubbing her daughter's shoulders. Her hands appeared lacerated and there were already bruises forming around her face and neck. And yet she still seemed in better shape than her daughter.

"Ashlyn?" Tessa prodded more gently. "Ashlyn, honey, I need you to look at me. You're going into shock. If we don't do something about that, you're going to feel a lot worse in a very short amount of time. I need you to drink some water, maybe have a bite to eat . . ."

The girl simply stared at her, Libby rubbing, rubbing, rubbing her daughter's bundled-up form.

Tessa made a second attempt: "Ashlyn. Can you tell me how old you are?"

The girl slowly blinked. Bit by bit, her too-large hazel eyes came into narrow focus, a small frown forming on her brow.

"Fifteen?" she whispered at last, more of a question than an answer.

"I'm with law enforcement, Ashlyn. See that uniformed officer over there? He's with the county sheriff's department. Soon you're going to hear even more sirens. We're all here for you, Ashlyn. You and your family. We're here to make you safe."

"My father . . . ," Ashlyn whispered.

She glanced abruptly at her mother, and Tessa could see tears now sliding down Libby's face.

"He saved us," Libby provided hoarsely. "Mick was hidden inside the control room. He had a gun, knives, so many weapons. He shot Justin, we just got out . . . Then he was chasing us, with this huge blade. And he was so much bigger than me. So much stronger. I told Ashlyn to run and hide. I didn't want her to see . . . but she found Justin in the hallway. Even shot in the shoulder . . . He'd sworn to me he'd keep us safe. No matter what. No matter how. He wouldn't let us down."

"Mick stabbed him," Ashlyn erupted suddenly. "He took his knife, and he, and he . . . I hate him! I hate him I hate him I hate him. We Tased him. We hit him, we fought him. Why can't a man like him just die!"

The dam broke. Ashlyn burst into tears, falling into her mother's embrace. Libby grabbed her daughter tightly, and they clung to each other, a family of three now forever a family of two.

Tessa didn't say a word. That snowy night years ago, she and Sophie had done the same. In fact, they still did. Because some kinds of pain didn't magically fade away. While knowing they at least had each other helped make the bad days easier to take.

Wyatt returned, murmuring low in her ear. "Tire tracks, headed down the hill. Must be on open road by now."

Tessa got the message. "Libby, Ashlyn? I know you are hurt. I promise, we're here to help. But first, we need your assistance. The men who did this. They're getting away. Wouldn't you like to do something about that?"

Her words got their attention. In a matter of minutes, she had them ensconced in Wyatt's cruiser, more blankets, more water, Ashlyn now tearing into one of the energy bars while Libby did most of the talking.

Plain white van. Neither of the women remembered any identifying marks, had not really seen it much from the outside anyway. Their captors, on the other hand, they could describe in great detail. Three men, a huge guy with a cobra tattoo, a second big guy with crazy blue eyes and checkerboard hair, then finally, the smaller born-again nerd.

Libby and Ashlyn talked, Wyatt worked the radio, getting the description circulating immediately to all available law enforcement officers.

More vehicles arrived, state police cruisers, unmarked detective's vehicles, not to mention the feds, tearing up the long, snaking drive.

Not much longer now, Tessa knew. The feds would take over and with at least two members of the Denbe family safe, her assignment would wrap up, with even Wyatt finding himself relegated to cleanup. Except the kidnappers were still out there. Men so brutal that even after being paid nine million dollars, they'd been willing to slaughter an entire family.

The feds' black sedan making the final climbing turn.

Tessa studied Libby Denbe and she made her decision.

Tessa squatted down, taking Libby's hands in her own. "You are strong. Your daughter is strong. Trust me when I say you are both doing remarkably well. Now, I just need a couple more things from you. You understand, right, that whoever did this knew you, knew your family?"

Libby got it immediately. "Inside job," she murmured. "They overrode our security, knew everything about us, even mentioned having done research."

"Do you think they were professionals?"

"Yes, former military. Justin thought the same."

"Did you know them?"

"No. I think they were mercenaries. Hired to do the job."

Tessa nodded, not surprised, but troubled. Because if someone had hired professionals to take the Denbes away, would that person really be happy to have them reappear in Boston?

"I know," Libby said quietly, as if Tessa had spoken out loud. "I think that's why

Mick tried to kill us. Because while they didn't want to say no to all that money in ransom, the fact remained, their assignment was to kill us."

Sitting beside Libby, Ashlyn didn't even flinch. Which said something about her past three days.

Behind Tessa, the sedan had come to a stop. The sound of car doors opening . . .

No more time to beat around the bush. "What about your drug problem?"

Libby flushed, replied steadily: "The younger one, Radar, had experience as a medic. He took care of me, including providing methadone."

Tessa frowned, something about that niggling in the back of her mind.

Car doors, slamming shut.

Her voice lower, more urgent: "Did you cheat on your husband? I need a name—"

"No! Why would you even? We were working on our marriage—"

"Then who's pregnant?"

Libby's eyes widened. She glanced almost involuntarily at her daughter.

Tessa's turn to be surprised. Not the mother, but the daughter, the teenage daughter. Meaning . . .

"Ashlyn—"

"Libby Denbe, Ashlyn Denbe? I'm Special Agent Nicole Adams. This is Special Agent Ed Hawkes, with the FBI." Nicole had appeared, standing stiffly at Tessa's side, voice impressively commanding.

Tessa took that as her cue to leave. She rose, giving Libby and Ashlyn one last reassuring smile. Then, with Nicole Adams pointedly stepping forward, asking about immediate medical needs . . .

Tessa checked in with Wyatt, who was still working the radio.

"Any luck?" she asked, meaning with capture of the kidnappers.

"Negative. But good news is, there's only one access road coming in and out of this prison. Given that we got cops pouring in from all directions, as well as choppers en route, one white cargo van shouldn't be so hard to find."

Tessa nodded, waited a beat. "You sure about that?"

"No," he declared flatly.

They watched more cop cars pour into the property and start climbing the knoll, vehicles that, by definition, should've already come across any and all white cargo vans traveling a lone access road.

"They knew this place," Tessa murmured. "According to Libby, the kidnappers were professionals. Not only knew all about the family, but mentioned doing research. Meaning, they probably picked this location deliberately, having run across it while researching Justin Denbe—"

"Or being informed of its availability from someone else inside Denbe Construction," Wyatt filled in. "Someone who could provide them with access, show them how to run the place, probably even identify an old back road, maybe used during construction, for getting heavy machinery on site."

Tessa sighed heavily. They didn't have to say the words out loud to know the truth; the plain white van wouldn't be discovered anytime soon. Once again, the kidnappers were one step ahead.

"Justin Denbe is dead?" Wyatt asked, having only gotten to hear bits and pieces of her conversation with Libby and Ashlyn.

"Died protecting his family from one of the guys . . . Mick?"

"His body?"

"Took it with them. Covering their tracks, maybe? I don't know all the details yet. I ran out of time to ask questions."

Wyatt smiled faintly, understanding her dilemma perfectly. Then, his expression grew more serious. "The family was attacked even after the ransom was paid."

"Libby believes the kidnappers' primary assignment was to kill them. The ransom money was just a nice perk."

"Kill *them*," Wyatt pressed, "or kill Justin? Assuming it's Anita Bennett, wanting to take over the company, Justin's death alone would be enough."

"Or," Tessa followed his train of thought, "ditto with a mystery embezzler who feared Justin's tracking efforts were growing too close." The thought that had bothered her earlier clicked into place. "One of the kidnappers has medical training. He assisted Libby with detox, even provided methadone. Now, if the mercenaries were just going to kill her in a matter of days, would they really go to that much trouble?"

"Meaning Justin was probably the intended target," Wyatt supplied. "The kidnapping was a nice way of framing the incident so it wouldn't be immediately traced back to, say, the company. Justin died in a ransom exchange gone bad, not an 'accident' that might lead to undue police questioning."

Tessa frowned, still not liking it. "All very elaborate."

"No more so than embezzling eleven million over nearly two decades."

"True. So, we're looking for someone patient. Who has inside knowledge of the Denbe family, the firm's finances and the prison project. Who would also have the connections to hire some ex-military mercenaries. Who would instruct those mercenaries that it was okay to kill Justin, but supply Libby with medical attention should she need it." Tessa stopped. "Is it just me, or is it too obvious?"

Wyatt looked equally disturbed. "He wasn't even around when the embezzling began," he warned.

"And yet?"

"Chris Lopez." Wyatt sighed.

"Chris Lopez," she agreed.

MONDAY AFTERNOON, 3:22, plain white cargo van heading west. Not toward the main entrance of the prison compound, but toward the side of the property, where the hard-packed ground showed traces of the access route once used by scores of construction vehicles during the first phase of the building project.

Earlier in the day, after shutting off the power, Mick had spent quality time clipping away at the perimeter fencing, until he could roll aside a section just large enough to form a van-size hole. Now, Radar drove slowly through the opening, braking long enough for Mick to jump out and unroll the fencing back into approximate position. Nothing that would hold upon closer inspection, of course, but they didn't care about eventualities. They cared about the next thirty minutes. All they needed more or less. Thirty minutes for law enforcement to interrogate the woman and the girl, compare notes, activate additional resources and churn, churn, churn.

At which time, the chase would begin in earnest.

Not that it would matter, as the men would already be gone.

White cargo van, through the perimeter fencing, heading due west deeper into the woods. Earthmovers had once traveled this way. Excavators ripping off the top of the knoll, to make it flatter and more suitable for a massive building. Then, dirt haulers bringing in new, better dirt for fill, topsoil, whatever the plans required.

The access road was broad, the kind of hard-packed earth that couldn't yield any tire tracks, as it had nothing left to give. The sparse vegetation that had managed to grow in during the ensuing two years bowed under the weight of the relatively light van, before springing back again.

Their base camp was six miles in, at the base of a hill that Radar had studied for weeks before finally deciding it would do. A rocky hill. Not huge, but comprised mostly of boulders, New Hampshire being the Granite State and all.

He pulled forward, then carefully backed his way in between two rocky outcroppings, the mountain version of parallel parking. Satisfied he was as close as possible to the target, ensconced on three sides with stone, he killed the engine and they began the next phase of operations.

All necessary supplies were in the van. Z had a bag of tricks. Mick had a bag of tricks. Radar had a small bundle, being the most nondescript of them to begin with.

Z started with his "tattoo." Solvent to sponge, sponge to shaved skull, and inch by inch, the green cobra disappeared, scrubbed away as if it had never existed. Next, he exchanged his black commando gear for a pair of broken-in men's jeans, comfortable T-shirt, oversize gray hoodie bearing the Red Sox logo and even larger L.L. Bean barn coat. Since a tinge of green remained on his skin, he donned a Red Sox cap. Add a pair of scuffed-up hiking boots, and he could be any white guy who lived in New England. Just a dude, hanging out in the mountains until the right plane could take him to a better location . . . say, a beach in Brazil.

For Mick, the transformation was even easier. Pop, pop and two bright blue contact lenses were out, leaving behind warm brown eyes framed by surprisingly thick lashes. Quick buzz of the electric razor and the checkerboard hair was gone, leaving a smooth, round skull. If Z was a mountain dude, then Mick went for Euro chic. Straight-legged black jeans, a fine-knit cranberry-colored sweater covered by a slightly rumpled dark sports jacket. A tourist, probably visiting from Canada, which, as a native French speaker, worked for him. Over his shoulder, he slung a black leather attaché case, carrying fresh ID, not to mention paperwork on his new bank account, now flush with $1.5 million dollars. His cut; Radar had received the same, while Z, being the brains of the operation, had pocketed $2 mil. As for the remaining $4 million . . . there were brains and there were masterminds. Masterminds, it turned out, were very expensive.

Not that Mick was complaining. Any operation was only as good as the planning behind it, and given how smoothly this operation had gone, it would be the easiest 1.5 million Mick had ever made.

Last person to swap out his disguise: Radar. He changed clothes. That was it. From jeans, flannel and baseball cap to Dockers, white button-up dress shirt and designer wire-rim glasses. He looked like any young professional in Boston. Maybe a recent MIT grad, now killing it at a software firm. A job he probably could've excelled at, had he been inclined to do things such as real work.

Now Radar placed his old gear in the van. So did the others. A pile of incriminating evidence, not to mention the bloody knife as well as additional gore. They stepped away, putting some distance between themselves and the vehicle.

Z hadn't been lying. Radar's true expertise was demolition.

And given that forensic techs were so good that even blowing up a van couldn't completely destroy all the evidence, they were going for one step better. Disappearing. Burying the van in a small avalanche of boulders, the kind that occurred naturally all the time in the Granite State, just ask the Old Man of the Mountain. With any luck, the van, the remnants of their operation and all traces of evidence would never be seen again.

They donned protective eye gear, as taking a rock fragment to the cornea at this stage of operations would be just plain stupid.

Z gave the signal. Radar pushed the button. A small rumble. Not terribly loud. Explosives are as much about placement as power, and Radar had worked hard to identify the hillside's natural weaknesses.

Then with almost a groan, the top half of the rocky terrain gave way, and the ensuing slide whomped down upon the white van. The shatter of glass, the squeal of crumpling metal, then, the van was gone. Random boulders continued to rain down for a few minutes afterward.

The men waited patiently; for, again, to rush at this stage of the operation would be stupid.

When the dust settled, they made their final inspection. The van, every square inch of it, was gone, a fresh pile of rocks forming the perfect tomb.

Z made the call.

"Men," he declared. "*Vamos.*"

Mission complete, each helped himself to one of the waiting four-wheelers. They would not race through the woods together, but set out alone, each heading to his own vehicle, waiting for him at a spot he'd chosen ten days prior and discussed with no one. Life would be resumed under a new name, known by no one and probably never shared. These men could work together. But they survived alone.

Radar was still considering tropical

beaches and large-breasted women. As for the others, he could care less.

He pulled away first. One by one, so did the others.

Monday afternoon, 4:05, the whine of four-wheelers scattering north and north-west. Staying off major roads and away from clearings where one might be spotted by, say, a police chopper flying overhead.

North, northwest, as if approaching Vermont, or even Canada.

Except for one driver. Who, thirty minutes later, arrived at his vehicle and promptly headed due south.

Back to Boston, and some unfinished business there.

Chapter 40

THE FBI AGENTS TOOK ASHLYN from me. I wanted to protest. Wanted to grab her hand and hold my daughter close. But the EMTs needed to check her out, they said, and as I'd been the one requesting a doctor, I had to let her go. Not to mention, the last of the adrenaline was leaving my bloodstream and I could feel myself crashing.

Each word became harder and harder to find. Each question took longer and longer to answer. A tunnel formed in my vision, with the light very far away.

The EMTs came for me, too. They sat me in the back of an ambulance, taking my vitals, fussing over my low blood pressure, the abrasions on the palms of my hands. But I wasn't seriously hurt. That was the irony. I was detoxing and shocky and traumatized, but strictly speaking, I didn't suffer from a single incapacitating injury.

The last look on my husband's face. The grim determination bracketing his mouth as Justin went at Mick head-on. The blade, that huge, serrated blade, sinking into my husband's chest. He'd said he would keep Ashlyn and me safe, and in so many ways, Justin had always been a man of his word.

My modern-day caveman. Incapable of being faithful to me. But willing to die for me instead.

The EMTs cut me loose with instructions to follow up with my doctor for a full detox regimen. One of the medics already appeared skeptical, as if he'd met too many others like me, and already doubted my success.

I missed Radar. I didn't have to explain myself to him. He knew all my deepest, darkest secrets and none of them had shocked him.

Ashlyn finally emerged from the back of the ambulance. A medic was offering his hand, but she climbed down on her own. I watched my daughter cross the parking lot toward me, fifteen years old, chin up, shoulders back. She hurt. I could feel her pain radiating from her. But she walked, step by resolute step, her father's daughter, and that made me ache all over again.

She arrived and the feds pounced. We were ushered into the back of a black sedan, and with an impressive line of law enforcement vehicles in tow, we sped away.

OUR DESTINATION WAS the county sheriff's department conference room, where we met a whole group of county, state and federal officers who needed to ask us some questions. Because our kidnappers were still out there, a blond FBI agent explained, and time was of the essence, and surely we wanted to help catch these terrible men, let alone recover our loved one's body.

Justin's body. I wondered if even now Z and Mick were tossing him into a ditch.

The sheriff's detective was there, the one who'd first arrived at the prison and brought us blankets. I focused on him, because even though the crisp-talking blond FBI agent—Adams?—was the one who seemed to be running the show, Officer Wyatt had a steady demeanor I needed right now.

I noticed the investigator, Tessa Leoni, was beside him, both of their expressions carefully neutral. I thought she stood closer to him than strictly necessary. And I thought they both held themselves slightly apart from the rest of the room, as if they wanted it understood up front that they were only part of the circus, not the ones running the show.

Ashlyn wanted food. A deputy disappeared, returning shortly with a stack of take-out menus. She shook her head, asked if they had a vending machine. Two Snickers bars, two bags of potato chips and one can of Diet Coke later, my teenager was happy.

I went with coffee. And water. And a trip to the bathroom, where I washed my hands and rinsed my face over and over again.

When I stood up and confronted the face in the mirror, I had to pause, touch my own reflection with a trembling hand, because truly a woman who appeared that gaunt, that exhausted, that *old* couldn't be me. The hollows beneath my cheeks. The bruises beneath my eyes. The sheer fatigue etched into each line of my face.

I had failed that woman. I had not taken care of her. And here I was, maybe exactly where I deserved to be.

When I opened the bathroom door, Tessa was standing in the hall, obviously waiting for me. She smiled faintly, as if she knew exactly what I'd just done, the thoughts that had gone through my head.

"It gets better," she murmured. "Even if it doesn't feel that way right now, eventually you will feel like something more than a shadow of your former self."

"How do you know?"

"My husband was killed two years ago. I almost lost my daughter as well. Her name is Sophie, and she's been very worried about your family. She told me to look for you in cold, dark places, and bring you hot chocolate and chocolate chip cookies."

I smiled faintly. "I could use some hot chocolate."

"Does Ashlyn have a boyfriend?"

I shook my head, no longer surprised by any question. "Not that Justin and I knew."

"The pregnancy was a surprise?"

"We only figured it out when she miscarried in prison. My family . . . we haven't been doing so well, even before this happened."

She seemed to accept that. "The medic person helped her?"

"Yes."

"You like him. You speak of him with respect."

I shrugged, feeling, ironically, as if I was betraying Radar's trust. "He took care of us when we needed him. I respect that."

"Did you like the other two as well?"

Immediately I shuddered. Not when I thought of Z. Even with the cobra tattoo, there was something commanding about him, an admirable quality of extreme self-control. On the other hand: "Mick, the one with the checkerboard hair, I don't think he's sane. He promised to hurt me, but only after hurting Ashlyn first."

"So if he was in the military," Tessa said out loud, "maybe not honorably discharged?"

I nodded, understanding now where she was going with this.

"And Chris Lopez?" she asked abruptly.

Now I was surprised. "What about him?"

"He likes you."

I shook my head, already dismissive. "He works for my husband. He's one of the guys. I don't . . . They're like a gaggle of boys. I don't even look at them individually. They're just . . . Justin's sidekicks. Very talented, each and every one of them, but not entirely sane."

"Did you know Lopez is Kathryn Chapman's uncle?"

"What?"

"And he's the one who sent you those texts six months ago?"

I gaped at her, couldn't help myself. In turn, the investigator nodded slightly, as if that had been half the point: to see my reaction and gauge it for herself.

Down the hall, the conference room door opened, a reminder of the rest of the task force, still awaiting our return.

Tessa produced a card. She handed it to me. "If you think of anything, of course, please call. But also . . . if you ever need to talk. Just talk. I can't promise to understand everything, but I think given my own experience, my own family . . . I will understand enough."

She offered me one last bolstering smile, then led me back to the conference room. I took a seat, and the blond FBI agent announced that, per protocol, they would be separating Ashlyn and me. Of course, if I wanted to call a lawyer, a family member for support . . . but again, time was of the essence and they really needed to get started.

I gazed at my daughter. She had chocolate smudging the corner of her mouth, and absurdly, that reminded me of when she was four years old and had smeared brownie batter all over her face, even on the tip of her nose, which she then tried to reach with her tongue again and again. I'd laughed till I cried, while Justin had grabbed the camera and we'd been happy then. I swear, we had been so, so happy . . .

I must've made a sound. Maybe distress. Because my daughter reached across the table and squeezed my hand.

"It's okay, Mom. We've made it this far, right? I can do this."

She got up and followed two agents out the door, while I fisted my hands on my lap in order to let my baby go.

The second the door closed behind her, Special Agent Adams got down to business.

She started with the basics. How we'd been taken, where we'd been taken. How much did our captors know about us, what had we managed to learn about them?

I relayed Radar's medical expertise, several of his comments that led me to believe he was former military. Justin's initial belief that they didn't mean us harm, as they carried Tasers, not guns. Also when Mick attacked me, Z had Tased his own man to get him to back down.

Except then they'd pulled Justin from the cell and beaten him to a pulp without any explanation.

The investigators exchanged several glances at this.

"You mean," the blonde, Special Agent Adams, reiterated, "the kidnappers did not start by talking of ransom?"

"No. That was our idea. After the beating, it occurred to Justin that he could evoke the imminent-death clause of his life insurance policy, making us worth nine million dollars. And that kind of money might be what it would take for them to let us live."

"In the days leading up to the kidnapping, did you feel any threat? Such as someone watching you? Notice people loitering around your neighborhood, perhaps contractors across the street? Feel any sense of danger?"

I shook my head.

"Did they know about Justin's affair?"

I recoiled, wondering how this would be relevant, but then again . . . "Actually, Z seemed to know about Justin's . . . extracurriculars." I wanted to keep the bitterness out of my voice. I didn't.

"How would you describe the state of your marriage?"

I shrugged tiredly. "Strained. Awkward. But we were trying. Date night. This whole thing . . . Date night." The taste of oranges mixing with champagne upon my lips.

"Did you ever contact a divorce lawyer after discovering that Justin was cheating on you?"

I shook my head.

"Why not?"

The question confused me. "We have a daughter. We have a life. Maybe some people throw that away after . . . one mistake, but I wasn't going to."

"Are you aware of the terms of your prenup?" the second FBI agent asked me. Special Agent Hawkes.

I nodded uncomfortably, still not understanding this line of questioning. "Yes. I renounced all claim to Justin's company, in return for fifty percent of our personal assets. The company was from Justin's father and predated me. The concession seemed fair enough."

The blond agent studied me. "Are you aware that you have no personal assets? That, in fact, Justin ran your entire life, your homes, your cars, your furniture, everything, through the company?"

I shook my head, feeling dazed. The interview wasn't going the way I'd thought it would. I'd hoped it would be about the men who'd just murdered my husband and assaulted my family. Not about . . . me. "Justin paid the bills. I never thought to question . . . But it wouldn't have mattered. I hadn't asked for a divorce. Not to mention, in prison, Justin offered to rip up the prenup, give me anything I asked for. He was sorry."

"So you were going to divorce him." The second FBI agent again.

"I didn't say that. Justin also said he'd miss me. He'd miss our family."

"Well, it's all a moot point now." Special

Agent Adams, not sounding harsh, just matter-of-fact.

"He swore he would keep us safe," I whispered. "Justin knew he wasn't the perfect husband, the perfect father. He worked too much, was absent too often, let alone the whole matter of faithfulness. But he swore he would keep us safe. We were his family and he would not fail us. And he didn't."

I stared them in the eye. Dared these investigators to besmirch my dead husband. Dared them to question a marriage and life that had already cost me so much.

They didn't.

Instead, another investigator, with wire-rim glasses, spoke up for the first time. "So, what can you tell us about the missing eleven million dollars?"

I stared at him blankly, and felt the ground open up beneath my feet yet again.

By the time Ashlyn returned to the room, I was done. I couldn't answer one more question, I couldn't absorb one more "truth" about me, my husband or the family business. Someone had embezzled money from the firm. A lot of it. For a long time. And apparently, in the past few weeks Justin had stumbled across the theft and taken some countermeasures.

Except he'd never related anything to me. Maybe because for the past few weeks, he'd still been sleeping downstairs in the basement, a husband kicked out of his own marital bed.

The firm's financial future was rocky. Not insurmountable, I was told, but rocky. Which, given that the firm owned my homes, my car and my furniture, was probably something I should care about, if not for my own sake, then at least for Ashlyn's. Except I wasn't sure I could absorb one more shock.

My husband was dead. Someone close to us had been stealing from us for over a decade. And most likely, that same person had hired Z and his team, probably not because of ransom at all, but to remove Justin from the picture before he uncovered the full extent of the embezzlement scheme.

Which must have had Z and his team laughing on the inside. Here they were, already paid to kidnap and torment us, probably with instructions to buy time, maybe even to kill Justin but have it look like part of a separate crime. Then we'd gone and offered them an additional nine million. Win Z over? Manipulate him into doing our bidding? Please. Talk about double-dipping. First, he got paid by some shadowy client, then, got even more money from his own victims.

The man was an evil genius, and I almost wished I could return to our incarceration just so I could poison him this time. While starting a kitchen fire and burning the whole damn place down around their ears.

I hated him. Every time he'd looked at me with respect. The background report hadn't indicated you'd be a problem . . .

He'd lied to me.

My husband had lied to me.

Except my husband had also died for me.

My thoughts were such a tumultuous mess. My head hurt and I was tired. So unbelievably tired.

The feds wanted to put us in a hotel, safe house, something of that nature. Our kidnappers were still on the loose. No sign of the white cargo van, just a hole in the perimeter fencing where they'd made their getaway. Until they had more information, Special Agent Adams felt it was best to keep us safe.

But I saw the expression on my daughter's face. Felt its match on my own.

After all we'd been through, the days, the nights. The look on Justin's face, the knife, the knife, the knife, the knife, sinking into his chest . . .

We wanted to go home. Safe or sorry, we *needed* to be home again.

More consultation. A phone call with the Boston PD, further discussions.

Finally, it was agreed. The agents would graciously permit us to return to our own residence. But given that Z and his team also knew where we lived and might have incentive to finish what they'd started, basic precautions needed to be taken. I would immediately change our security passwords the second I stepped foot into my house. In addition, the Boston PD would assign a uniformed officer to keep watch from the street, as well as beef up patrols in the area.

Special Agent Adams also suggested that I not immediately invite over any family or friends. In fact, if there were people we wanted to see, she recommended that we meet them in full daylight, at public places.

You know, because someone we trusted had clearly betrayed us. And that person hadn't escaped with eleven million dollars just yet.

It was okay, I said. We didn't just want to go home; we wanted to be alone. No more eyes watching. No more audience judging.

It was time to just be. Once a family of three, now a family of two, battered, shaky, grief-stricken, but still hanging in there.

Shortly after ten, the cops finally let us go. The feds provided the escort, a black sedan heading three hours south to Boston. Ashlyn fell asleep in the back. I think I dozed off a time or two.

Then, we were there. Our home, which would never completely feel like our home again. The crime-scene tape, subtle but present on the doorway. Evidence placards, still marking random places in the foyer.

My wedding ring, buried in a pile on the kitchen island. I took it out. I slipped it on, and felt the first wave of grief hit me like a wall.

But I would not succumb. Not yet, not now.

Off to the security system's control panel. Running through the instructions Justin had given me time and time again. I needed a code, a string of numbers no one would know but I could easily remember. I went with a date: the day I'd moved out of the tenement housing. The first step toward building a better life. If only I'd known then what I knew now . . .

I told the agents we were all set. I let them graciously out the front door, then promptly activated our security system, listening to various dead bolts fire home.

Ashlyn was still standing in the foyer, looking at the spot where I had vomited. Just three days, but already a lifetime ago.

"Can I sleep in your room?" my fifteen-year-old daughter asked.

"Yes."

"I want a gun."

"Me, too."

"I want it loaded, underneath my pillow."

"Everything we learned not to do in firearms safety," I observed.

"Exactly."

"Loaded clip next to the unloaded firearm, in the top drawer of the bedside table," I countered.

"Okay."

"Ashlyn . . . I'm proud of you."

My daughter didn't look at me, but stared at the vomit stain. She said, "I've been sleeping with Chris Lopez. He likes you, he's always liked you. But he can't have you, so he settled for me instead. And I knew it was wrong, but I didn't care. You and Dad . . . you just seemed so far away, and I wanted someone to make me feel special again."

I opened my mouth. I closed my mouth. "Oh, honey."

"I just want it to go away now, okay? Don't tell anyone. Don't do anything. Just . . . make it all go away."

"Did you tell the police?"

"Of course not! I just want it to be over. Please, can't it all be over? I can't stop seeing his face, Mom. Dad and the blood, and that knife! He died for us. He died because of me!"

Ashlyn collapsed. Hunched over on the bottom step, her arms over her head, as if that would block the terrible images. And I understood what she meant, because I had the same visions stuck in my own head. As well as way too many unwanted revelations. Chris Lopez, Justin's most trusted second in command, sleeping with our teenage daughter. Is this why Tessa Leoni had asked about him specifically? Because she already suspected him in my family's kidnapping? After all, he'd meddled in my marriage, then seduced my fifteen-year-old daughter.

Why, if Justin were still alive . . .

Then, all of a sudden, so many things finally made sense. Including why my husband, my modern-day caveman, had to die.

I went to my daughter. "It's okay, Ashlyn. We've come this far. We're going to get through this." I was unconsciously repeating her words from the sheriff's office. I gave her a bolstering hug. Then, I got on the phone and dialed Tessa Leoni.

Chapter 41

CHRIS LOPEZ WOKE UP to the barrel of a gun, dug into his right temple.

"If I were you, I wouldn't move," Tessa said. She sat beside him, on the edge of his mattress. She hadn't bothered with any lights, using the glow of a penlight to jimmy his rear window, then creep through his house, up the main stairs. She'd found the elderly Lab, Zeus, sleeping in the hallway. He'd lifted his head once, seen it was her, then gone back to sleep with a sigh.

All in all, she was feeling very comfortable with her nighttime adventure. Which was good, as she was extremely pissed off.

Now she offered up conversationally: "When did Ashlyn first tell you she was pregnant?"

"What?"

Lopez tried to sit up. She used her left fist to whomp him hard in the middle of his sternum.

Lopez collapsed back down against the mattress, gasping for air.

"Fifteen-year-old girl? The daughter of your boss? A child you swore you thought of like your own daughter? You fucking pervert!"

Lopez, moaning now. "I know, I know. I'm a total douche bag. Just pull the god-damn trigger. I deserve it."

His self-pity made her angrier. She hit him again. "Hey, I'll do the threatening around here!"

"I don't know . . . I never should've . . . I *am* a pervert. What the hell was I think-ing!" Lopez sounded as if he was crying. Jesus Christ. Tessa reached over and snapped on the bedside lamp.

Yep, Lopez had worked himself into quite a state.

"Start at the beginning," she instructed

sternly. "Tell me everything. Maybe I won't shoot you."

"There was no beginning. I mean, it's not like I planned it." Lopez seemed to pull himself together. He dragged himself up to sitting; this time, she didn't try to stop him. At least he was partially clothed in a threadbare white T-shirt and gray boxers.

The ruckus had awoken the dog again. Zeus padded in, then went to Tessa's side and whined softly. She patted his head and he settled, curling up at her feet.

"Look, Ashlyn found out about Justin's affair. I'm not sure how. Probably eavesdropped on her parents' fighting, hell if I know. But she also figured out the other woman was my niece, Kate. I heard a story she even confronted Kate in the lobby, and Anita had to run her off. All I know is my niece called me one night to say the crazy girl was back, standing outside her house, and wouldn't go away. What was I supposed to do? I headed on over to handle things best I could."

"Best you could?" Tessa's tone was dry.

Lopez flushed. "I took Ashlyn to a nearby coffee shop and tried to talk some sense into her. I gave her my whole spiel—Katie was just a stupid girl, I knew for a fact Justin had ended things, and her parents really were trying to work things out. She needed to just give everyone some space and time. Ashlyn seemed to finally calm down. I drove her home. Figured that would be that."

"But?"

He shrugged, appearing once again self-conscious. "She started calling me. Said she needed someone to talk to. Her parents were both shut down, it's not like her friends understood and given that I already knew everything that had happened. I don't know. She'd talk. I'd listen. She was just so . . . angry. I mean, she'd really idolized her parents. Both of them. To have them do something so . . . human. It messed with her. It's like if they weren't perfect, then the whole world must not be perfect. She was kind of freaking out."

Tessa simply stared at him.

He flushed again. "So, uh . . . yeah. She came over one day, after school. Bad day, had gotten in a fight with her best friend. Started to cry. So of course, I put my arms around her. Next thing I knew, she was kissing me. I don't . . ."

He stopped talking, dropping his gaze to the bedcovers. "I didn't seduce her, if that's what you're thinking. I don't expect you to believe me. But as strange as it sounds, she was the one using me. She was really pissed at Justin, remember? And what better way to get back at her father who'd slept with a younger woman than to be the daughter sleeping with an older man?"

"This is what you tell yourself?" Tessa stated flatly. "This is how you sleep through the night?"

Lopez's head shot up. "I've been regrouting the bath, remember? Who the fuck says I've been sleeping?"

"So when did she tell you she was pregnant?"

"What pregnancy? I'm not kidding, I have no fucking clue what you're talking about!"

"She miscarried, you know. While your goons had her locked up in prison. Interesting, too, because I would've thought a *gentleman* such as yourself would've requested no harm come to ladies. Justin, on the other hand . . ."

"Not my goons! Not my instructions! And what do you mean she miscarried while in prison? What the hell is going on?"

Tessa paused. She eyed him thoughtfully. Wyatt had been right in the beginning; the Denbe Construction management team was full of liars. Anita Bennett. Chris Lopez. And yet, they were both incredible actors as well, or they truly didn't know everything.

"Ransom," she stated.

"I heard there'd been contact. No one has told us anything else."

"The insurance company paid the money." She continued to watch him.

He sat up straighter. "So they've been released? Are they home? Christ." Lopez ran a hand through his hair, appearing to be simultaneously agitated and relieved. "How is Libby?"

"Seriously? You're sleeping with the daughter but you're still in love with the mom?"

"Told you I was a douche bag."

Tessa played one last card. "Well, you'd better be a douche bag with a valid passport, because Justin knows you're the one who got his baby girl pregnant. She might have miscarried, but that doesn't mean he won't be gunning for your head."

Lopez paled. Abruptly, his shoulders

came down, his chin up. "I'll see him myself. First thing in the morning. Head right over. My fault. I did the crime. I'll serve the time."

"Goddammit!"

Tessa shot off the bed. She twirled violently, disrupting the sleeping dog and causing Lopez to gape at her. She jammed her pistol back into her shoulder holster. If she'd been extremely angry before, she was extraordinarily frustrated and furious now.

"Justin Denbe's dead."

"What?"

"Kidnappers planned a double-cross after the ransom had been paid. He died, saving Libby and Ashlyn."

Lopez, completely slack-jawed now. "But you said . . ."

"I lied. Mostly to test if you were a liar. But you honestly have no idea what happened shortly after three P.M. yesterday, do you?"

"Lady, I'm so confused right now, the only thing I have is a headache. Are Libby and Ashlyn all right?"

"Relative scale, yes. But Ashlyn did miscarry, and Libby knows you were the father."

If the threat of Justin's rage scared him, then to judge by Lopez's face, the thought of Libby's hurt shamed him.

"Oh," Lopez said, then seemed to lose all further words.

Tessa perched in a nearby chair. The old Lab whined nervously again. She stroked one of his ears in comfort as her mind whirled around and around.

"I don't get it," she said at last.

Lopez still wasn't talking.

"Whoever did this knew Justin, Libby and Ashlyn. He or she also had the kind of contacts necessary to hire three mercenaries. Most likely, the same person has been embezzling funds from Denbe Construction for the past fifteen to twenty years—"

"I haven't even worked there that long," Lopez interjected with a frown.

"Which is why we started by suspecting Anita Bennett."

"She wouldn't steal from the company. It's her one true love. Besides, she wouldn't hurt Justin like that. He's nearly a fourth son to her. The fact that her youngest may or may not be his half brother seems to actually make her feel closer to the family.

I'm not saying that's logical, but that's the way things are."

"Then who? We're talking an employee who's been around for nearly two decades, knows the Denbes' home inside and out, is familiar with the company's financials as well as understands the inner workings of a recently built New Hampshire prison. Who would know, have that kind of access . . ."

Tessa's voice trailed off. And just like that she knew. A suspect so obvious, they'd never ever considered him. And yet . . .

Lopez was still regarding her blankly.

She sprang to her feet, stopping just long enough to give Zeus a quick kiss on top of the head. Definitely, she and Sophie should get a dog. But for now:

"Entry code for the Denbe Construction offices. I need it. *Now.*"

WYATT WANTED TO GO HOME. He understood Libby Denbe's instinct perfectly. Hell, he'd only been working the past forty-eight hours, not held captive against his will, and already, he wanted nothing more than to return to the sanctuary of his personal space for a hot shower, a home-cooked meal (fine, a microwaved freezer meal) and a good night's sleep.

But here was the part of policing no one told you about until it was too late: The doing was the smallest piece of the job. Writing up reports detailing what you'd just done, on the other hand . . .

He was filling out paperwork. Lots of it. So was Kevin, but Kevin actually liked paperwork. He was annoying that way.

Two A.M., his cell phone rang. Nicole Adams. Didn't surprise him, and not just because Nicole was an upwardly mobile FBI agent, but because she genuinely cared about her work. If a case didn't have a resolution—and this one certainly lacked many key answers—she'd stay nose to the grindstone till it did.

Out of professional respect, not to mention for old times' sake, he took the call.

"Found the white van?" she asked immediately. His department was handling the APB on the white cargo van, not to mention Justin Denbe's corpse.

"No van, no band of merry men and no dead body."

"Seriously? With all the officers in the area?"

"I'm getting the impression the hired muscle involved a brain or two."

Deep sigh. "The body bothers me," Nicole muttered. "They're not going to keep something that incriminating, let alone smelly, in the back of their vehicle."

"Oh, I doubt they're driving the van anymore. Best guess, given their complete disappearance off the radar screen, is that they had another vehicle waiting. Tomorrow morning, we'll start sending divers into nearby lakes and ponds. Most likely, we'll find the van completely submerged with Denbe's body in the back. That would explain the whole now-you-see-'em, now-you-don't act." His turn to ask a question: "Any trace of the missing funds?"

"No, and I'm told the financial gurus have turned Anita Bennett's personal finances inside and out. It's possible she has the monies stashed under an alias in yet another offshore account, of course. But as of this moment, we're mostly chasing our tails."

Wyatt grunted, Nicole's frustration on the subject mirroring his own.

"Libby and Ashlyn?" he asked.

"Returned to their townhome." Where

they could magically pick up the pieces of their lives. Nicole didn't say the words out loud, but they were implied.

"Are you going to see her?" Nicole asked abruptly.

"Who?"

"Tessa Leoni. She stands next to you, you know. With everyone else, she maintains a good three- to five-foot barrier. But not you."

Wyatt thought he might be blushing. He covered his face with his hand, while hedging carefully. "Why are you asking?"

"It's late. I'm tired. I'm curious."

"Tessa is an interesting woman."

"You're going to ask her out." Nicole supplied the words not as a question but as a statement. She didn't sound angry about it, though. More like satisfied.

"What's his name?" Wyatt asked.

Nicole's turn to blush, at least that's what he told himself.

"Well, now that you mention it . . ."

Turned out she'd met a financial planner six months ago. They were very happy together. Which made Wyatt feel surprisingly better about things. Not that they owed each other anything, but still . . . Always nice to know the other person was happy, and all's well that ends well.

"You'll call me when you find the van?" Nicole requested now. "Or better yet, when you've located our three suspects."

"Sure. Likewise?"

"Likewise."

"Now go get some sleep. One of us has to."

Wyatt hung up the phone. Then he laced his fingers behind his head, leaned back in his chair and frowned. Personal life aside, Nicole's update on the missing funds bothered him. A van with three commandos and a body vanishing into thin air made some sense. The right pond, forest gully, overgrown pile of bramble. Plenty of places in the wilds of New Hampshire convenient for disappearing a vehicle. But the embezzled funds? Eleven million dollars that had been sitting around in a variety of fake bank accounts for the past fifteen or so years suddenly gone without a trace?

"Kevin," he called out. Across the task-force room, where they'd spread out to do their paperwork, Kevin's head popped up.

"What?"

"You're a smart man. If you had eleven million dollars, what would you do with it?"

"Stuff my mattress," the resident brainiac replied promptly. "Bedding doesn't require any paperwork. Better yet, it can't testify against you in a court of law."

"But the funds were in the Bahamas just a week ago," Wyatt countered. "In real bank accounts. That's what Ruth Chan said. She went to steal the money back, so to speak, only to discover there were even more accounts than she'd suspected." Which sparked another thought. "What's harder to believe, Kevin? Getting away with embezzling from a major corporation for sixteen years? Or stealing the money, but not touching a penny of it during all that time?"

Kevin was intrigued. He pulled himself away from his own pile of paperwork and walked on over. "Implies the person didn't need the money yet. Not a drug addict or a gambler skimming money to feed a habit. More like, a disgruntled employee building a rainy-day fund."

Kevin raised an interesting point. Most embezzlement cases still went back to motive—addiction issues, pressing medical bills, perhaps alimony and/or child support that was squeezing the person's bank account. But embezzlement was generally carried out by an employee with a high degree of financial knowledge and authority in the company. Meaning these were people who were intelligent, respected and trusted. Most didn't go to the dark side without some kind of underlying justification.

"So we're talking a patient person. No immediate pressing financial issues. He or she created the first fake company approximately sixteen years ago," Wyatt reviewed out loud. "Then, maybe when that didn't trigger any consequences, simply kept going along. One year into two, then five, then ten, fifteen . . . skimming money, always small amounts, nothing that would make the radar screen. So disciplined. Almost gamesmanship."

Wyatt tried the word on for size, liked it. "We're talking someone who most likely, at a certain point, embezzled for the sake of embezzling. A personal little secret that enabled her or him to giggle on the inside during all management meetings, whatever. The classic if-only-you-knew . . .

"Of course, all good things must come to an end. Which in this case is August, when purely by accident, Ruth Chan discovered the first fake vendor. She does a little more digging, gets her ducks in a row, then discloses the fraud to Justin four weeks ago."

Kevin frowned at him. "Justin knew about the missing money for a whole four weeks."

"Yes and no," Wyatt found himself correcting. "At the time, Chan thought the total amount skimmed was only four hundred thousand, an amount more annoying than horrifying for a hundred-million-dollar company. In fact, Justin decided the amount was so low that, instead of involving the police, he devised a strategy for stealing his own money back. He sent Ruth Chan to the Bahamas to close out the fake account, except the money was literally transferred out the day before."

"So when does Justin know the full extent of the damage?" Kevin asked.

"He . . . didn't," Wyatt murmured, thoughts hitting overdrive.

"Huh?"

"He didn't. Chan called him Friday afternoon. Told him the one account had been closed already but didn't mention anything else. She asked for more time to investigate instead. Then . . . just hours later, Justin and his family were abducted from their own home."

Kevin was staring at him. "To cover up the embezzlement," the brainiac stated, as if this should be obvious. "So Justin would never know about the full eleven million that had been stolen from his family firm."

"Maybe." When he walked through the timeline out loud, what Kevin said made sense. Ruth Chan discovered the embezzlement was actually twenty times worse than they'd suspected, and within hours, Justin had been kidnapped. No such thing as coincidence in policing. Meaning the two events had to be connected. And yet. And yet . . .

"Ruth Chan!" Kevin declared abruptly. "She was the embezzler, and she arranged Justin's kidnapping to cover up her own crime. Better yet, she's not even in the country, meaning she has the perfect alibi."

Wyatt frowned at him. "Without Ruth Chan, we wouldn't even know there had been sixteen years of fake billing. Since when does the thief report the theft?"

"To evade suspicion?" Kevin suggested.

Wyatt rolled his eyes, shook his head. "Who knew?" he asked abruptly. "That's the question we need to answer. Who knew Ruth Chan had discovered the fake vendors? Who knew Ruth Chan would be in the Bahamas Friday morning to close out the first account? Who had enough inside information to transfer out all the money one day prior, to get his or her ducks in a row . . ."

Wyatt's eyes, suddenly widening.

"Ruth Chan told someone," Kevin was saying. "Or Justin did. Someone they trusted, but shouldn't have, obviously."

"Or, she didn't tell anyone at all. She didn't even want to talk to Justin about it, right? Not until she'd done all her homework first. That's the kind of person Ruth Chan is, meticulous, discreet. We didn't understand that. We didn't pay enough attention to that. If anyone talked, it wasn't Ruth Chan, it was Justin. Shit, I gotta make a phone call!"

Chapter 42

ASHLYN NEVER MADE IT TO THE BEDROOM. After the past few days spent desperately
anticipating sleeping in her own bed, she
barely made it out of the shower before
crashing with wet hair and a T-shirt on the
family-room sofa.

I'd been on the phone while she showered. Talking to Tessa Leoni, who was
kinder and gentler than I would've expected.
She assured me she would personally handle the situation with Chris. With discretion,
of course. As well as the appropriate use of
force. Her tone told me enough and only
made me like her more.

I wanted to feel satisfied. Vindicated as an appalled mother, a betrayed friend. All those times I'd had him over to my house. And, yes, somewhere along the way, it had become clear he harbored a schoolboy's crush on me. Certainly, right after I learned of Justin's affair, Chris starting hanging around the house more, clearly willing to be a shoulder to cry on.

But I hadn't leaned on him. I'd turned to painkillers instead.

I showered my way through my outrage. Washing my hair again and again and again. Lathering up, rinsing down, repeat, repeat, repeat. It was late, after 2:00 A.M. I should finish up, go to bed. I applied deep conditioner, then scoured my skin with the same ruthless diligence I'd just spent on my hair.

I wanted to think the worst of our experience was behind us, but I already understood from this evening's ordeal that the grillings from various law enforcement agencies had only just begun. In the morning, they'd be back. More questions, maybe even a request for a formal statement regarding Ashlyn's relationship with Chris. Maybe they'd require a medical exam. Maybe I should think about hiring a lawyer.

What were your rights when you were a victim of a kidnapping and other violent crimes? What kind of counsel was involved in prosecuting a grown man for sleeping with your teenage daughter? What if Ashlyn wouldn't press charges, or answer questions? Should I demand it of her, or would it only traumatize her further?

Then, in the middle of the shower, rinsing the conditioner from my hair, it hit me:

My husband was dead. I was alone. For now, for always, there would be no partner to ask these kinds of questions. Ashlyn's best interests sat solely on my shoulders.

My husband was dead.

I was now a single parent.

Justin . . . the knife protruding from his bloody chest.

I went down. Dropped to my hands and knees on the tiled floor, the water beating at my back while I panted, gasping for breath.

Moments in a marriage. All those times when I know I saw my husband. All those times I wanted to believe he saw me. The first time we made love. The priest, declaring us man and wife. Him, holding a squalling newborn in his arms. And Justin, dying before my eyes.

He'd looked at me. He'd known, maybe even felt the serrated blade already sliding between his ribs. He'd known he was dying. And he had not looked at me with anger and blame, only regret.

I would miss us, he'd said. He would grant me a divorce if I wanted it, but he would miss our family.

Was I crying? It was hard to be sure, with the shower spray pouring down my neck, around my face.

I would have to plan a funeral, I thought, but how did you plan a funeral with no body? Wait for the police to find it, I guess. Wait for that sheriff's detective and his deputies to return my husband to me. And Ashlyn. She would want to say good-bye to her father. She would need closure, just as I had needed it thirty years ago.

And that thought stung me all over again. That for all my planning and sacrifice, in the end I hadn't spared my child my deepest pain. She'd lost her father, just as I'd lost mine. Now I would play the role of my mother, trying to hold it all together.

Meaning wading through finances that sounded like they were already strained.

What if we lost the house, what if we moved into tenement housing, what if Ashlyn never got to go to college, but became collateral damage of her father's poor planning, just like I had been?

I couldn't breathe. I was gasping, and yet no air would come into my lungs. I had survived three days in an abandoned prison, only to succumb in my own shower.

Then, in the back of my mind . . . hydrocodone. My orange-bottled pills. Maybe still downstairs in my purse in the center island. But if not, I had other stashes, a woman who knew how to keep her secrets. Half a dozen pills tucked in the back of the silverware drawer, ten more in my jewelry travel bag, four or five in the bottom of a crystal vase in the china closet. Close to two dozen emergency pills.

I stood up. I tasted oranges and I didn't care. I was going to get out of this shower. I was going to head downstairs, raid the first hidden supply. Just this once, of course. After the past few days, I'd earned this.

I rinsed my hair.

I shouldn't do it. I'd promised Justin I'd

be strong for our daughter. He'd pressed me in the cell, probably already suspecting something would go wrong with the ransom exchange, needing the reassurance that I could raise our child without him.

Just two pills, I thought. Enough to take the edge off. My whole body ached and I needed the rest. I would be a better parent if I got some rest.

I wondered if this was how my mother had felt, the look on her face every time she'd gazed at a pack of cigarettes. Knowing she shouldn't. But feeling the weight of the world upon her shoulders, the burden of single parenthood. She worked so hard. She deserved at least a little treat.

Justin had died for me.

Shouldn't I be able to give up Vicodin for him?

I turned off the water.

One pill. Just . . . one. To help manage my own withdrawal. The sensible thing to do.

I should.

I shouldn't.

I would.

I wouldn't.

I opened the shower door, reaching for a towel.

And found a man standing in my bathroom instead.

IT TOOK ME A MOMENT. Maybe a full minute, while I stood in the glass enclosure, water dripping from my naked body. Then he leered at me, and that did it. The eyes were the wrong color—deep brown instead of crazy blue. And the checkerboard hair had been shaved, replaced by a smooth skull. Finally, his clothes, from commando black to European upscale.

But his face, his mean, merciless face hadn't changed one bit, not to mention the fresh bruise over his left eye where my daughter had nailed him with a walkie-talkie only hours earlier.

I grabbed the towel, held it in front of me. Not nearly a good enough defense as I stood, trapped in my own bathroom by the man who'd murdered my husband.

"Miss me?" Mick drawled. He leaned against the doorjamb, his massive shoulders effectively blocking my exit. He knew there was no place I could go, nothing I could do. He seemed content to savor the moment.

"How . . . ?" I had to lick my lips to get the words out. My throat was dry, my thoughts racing. Ashlyn, asleep downstairs on the sofa. Please let her still be asleep.

Then: She'd asked for a gun. Why hadn't I made it to the basement gun safe yet? Why hadn't I retrieved firearms first, then climbed into the shower?

"But I changed the security codes . . ."

"We got our own override code. You'd have to know about it to deprogram it, and you didn't know about it. My intel is better than your intel." He smirked at some joke only he understood. "It's called irony, babe."

"The police are watching the house," I tried.

"Yep. Two patrols, one front, one back. Alternating intervals. And not a problem, since I only required sixty seconds to punch in my access code, open your rear garage door, then close it again. Police return to a secure-looking residence, and everybody is happy."

"You're wrong. Two detectives are coming over any moment. There's already been a new development in the case. That's why I was showering, so I'd be ready to answer their questions."

He stilled, cocking his head to one side while studying me. One second passed, then another.

"You're bluffing," he declared. "Nice try, though. I like to think I'm worth the effort."

He lunged. So quick I didn't even have time to gasp. I wanted to leap back, into the glass-enclosed shower, but that would only trap me and I didn't think for a second hard shower tiles would keep him from doing what he planned on doing next.

I snapped out with my towel. Was rewarded by his sharp cry as I caught him in the side of the face, hopefully on his bruise. I whipped the towel again, except this time, he grabbed the end, yanking me toward him.

I let go, and the sudden loss of counterweight made him stagger back. I bolted, heading for the door, jabbing out with my elbows, trying to catch him in the head again as I passed.

He grabbed at my waist, but my damp skin slipped through his fingers. Then I was free, flying through the master bedroom, hurling things behind me.

I didn't know where to go, what to do. Instinct propelled me down the stairs toward the lower foyer. The police were outside. I didn't care that I was buck naked. If I could just reach the front door, bolt out into the street . . .

Ashlyn, asleep in the family room. I couldn't leave her behind.

I heard the thunder of pounding footsteps. My own muffled sob as I tried to pick up steam, faster, faster, faster. Hadn't I already run this race today? Hadn't I already lost it?

I rounded the corner onto the bottom landing. Looked up. Caught a brief glimpse of Justin's face. Set. Grim. Determined. Wait, not Justin, Ashlyn. My daughter, Ashlyn . . .

"Duck," she said firmly.

I did, as she swung her father's golf club with both arms straight at Mick's descending form.

He roared, twisting at the last second, taking the hit in his shoulder. Then he was bellowing with pain as he wrenched the club from my daughter's trembling hands and heaved it over his own head.

I threw myself back at him, catching him around the knees as he stood on the second step.

Off balance, he stumbled, releasing the golf club to grab at the railing instead.

Ashlyn and I were off again. Front door wasn't going to work. Too many locks, not enough time. We headed for the kitchen, driven by some primitive instinct toward the room best stocked with makeshift weapons.

I'd read somewhere that women should never grab knives. We were too easily overpowered, then the knife was used against us. Better, the proverbial cast-iron frying pan, which required little skill to bash over your opponent's skull.

I had my mother's frying pan. I was already flinging open the lower cabinet, scrabbling for it, when Ashlyn yelped.

She'd halted by the center island, grabbing my purse and throwing it back. But Mick had dodged effortlessly and now had the hem of her oversize T-shirt fisted in his hand. My daughter wasn't going down without a fight. She was throwing back her elbows, stomping down with her bare feet, screaming at the top of her lungs.

And I could tell, from eight feet away, that Mick was enjoying every second of it.

Inside the cabinet, my groping hand found its target. I closed my fingers around the handle of the heavy pan and withdrew it, straightening slowly and confronting a man I loathed.

In return, he let his gaze wander up and down my still-naked form.

Then, like a man tossing garbage, he threw my daughter against the center island and advanced.

"How'd you know?" he drawled. "I've always liked it rough."

Ashlyn hit the island hard, her head colliding with the granite. Now, out of the corner of my eye, I watched as her body slid bonelessly to the floor.

Don't look. Don't be distracted. One opponent. One chance to get this right.

Mick charged.

Too soon, too fast, I thought, and instead of swinging my pan, I dashed right just in time for Mick to feint left. I darted out of the kitchen, moving away from my unconscious daughter, toward the living room. If I could topple a lamp, make a disturbance visible through the front windows, maybe the passing patrol car would see it. The uniformed officer would stop to check it out.

Mick was moving. Sidestepping right, then left, then ducking, then lunging. The sliding, shifting rush confused me. Up, down, right, left. I had my frying pan up, trying to be prepared for anything, for everything, as he suddenly dove low, caught me around the waist and crashed us both to the floor.

I went down hard, fingers still locked around the handle of my pan. I brought it down onto his head, hammering, hammering, hammering. Except Mick had used my own trick against me. He was in too close, I couldn't get enough momentum in the swing to really hurt him. His face was buried between my naked breasts and now, as I beat against him ineffectually, I could hear him laughing into my chest.

"That's right, fight, fight, *fight!*"

I wasn't going to win. He was too strong, too big, too well-trained. My best efforts, he found funny.

He suddenly reached up, caught my right wrist in a bone-crushing grip. I cried out. My cast-iron skillet fell to the floor.

And that was that.

He rose to his feet, grabbing my shoulders and dragging me to standing. This close, I could see that his brown eyes were just as crazy as his blue eyes had been. He was enjoying this. Relishing every second as his face lit up with the possibilities.

Behind him, the door to the basement stairs suddenly opened, a shadowy maw that revealed a second impressively large male, stepping soundlessly into my kitchen, while pressing a single finger to his lips. Z. Sans the green cobra tattoo and black commando gear.

I didn't move. I didn't make a sound. I stood there, totally bewildered, my wrist aching, my shoulders bruising, as Z walked smoothly forward, leveled a .22 caliber pistol and shot Mick at point-blank range through the side of the head.

Mick collapsed sideways.

Z stood over his man and fired twice more.

Then, at long last, my house fell quiet.

*　　*　　*

Z HANDED ME THE GUN, wrapping my right hand around the grip.

"Neighbors will call in gunfire," he announced crisply. "Police will arrive momentarily."

He reached behind me, dragging a throw off the sofa and draping it around my bare shoulders.

"I was never here. You fought him off. Well done."

"You killed him."

"He accepted the terms of the assignment: You and Ashlyn were off-limits. He broke the rules twice. In our line of work, failure has consequences."

"You . . . you knew he'd come back?"

"I suspected."

"I don't understand. It was okay to kill Justin, but not Ashlyn and me?"

"The terms of the assignment," Z repeated. He had a crumpled piece of paper. Now he pressed it into my hand. "Radar asked me to give you this. You won't want to share it with anyone. And it's probably only good for the next twelve hours."

He turned, heading for the basement door.

"Wait."

He didn't break stride.

"I want to know the override code," I blurted out. "The code you're all using to get into my house!"

He didn't break stride.

He was leaving. Just like that. Arrive, survey, conquer. My frustration bubbled up. As well as my loathing at always feeling so powerless. At the last second, it occurred to me that I wasn't in the prison anymore, and that I was hardly helpless.

I raised the .22, the pistol Z himself had handed to me, and leveled it at the back of his head. "Wait. I said wait!"

Z finally paused, turning slightly. "Your daughter probably requires medical attention," he commented.

"I'm tired of being a pawn!"

His voice, as calm as ever. "Then pull the trigger."

My arms were shaking. My whole body, now that I noticed. And all of a sudden, I wasn't exhausted anymore. I was enraged. At this man, for violating my home, my family. At myself, because heaven help me, I was already going to pop that first pill. But also, mostly, perversely, at Justin, because he'd gone and gotten himself killed and I still loved him and I still hated him and what in the world was I going to do with all those conflicting emotions? How would I ever get closure?

Z staring at me patiently, his expression almost testing. I wasn't the one who would give him any trouble. His research said so.

I pulled the trigger.

And the chamber clicked hollowly. Of course, Z, the omnipotent, always one step ahead. He'd loaded his pistol with exactly three bullets, discharged all three rounds into Mick's head, then handed me a useless weapon. I expected him to smile mockingly.

Instead, he said simply, "Good for you. Welcome to the first step of taking your life back."

Then he was gone.

I checked my daughter first, who was slowly regaining consciousness. Next I found the phone, calling 911 and requesting the police as well as an ambulance. Finally, I went upstairs and retrieved a bathrobe, still gripping the gun with my right hand as I slipped the piece of paper from Radar beneath my pillow and prepared for whatever was going to happen next.

Chapter 43

IT TOOK WYATT THREE TRIES to reach Tessa Leoni. By then, it was 4:00 A.M., but it hardly mattered. Buzzed on adrenaline and the knowledge of who, what, when, where, why and how, he was already in his cruiser, over state lines, heading for Boston.

"Chris Lopez didn't do it," he stated without preamble, when Tessa finally answered her cell.

"No shit. I put a gun to the man's head— hang on, you never heard that from me— and he still pled innocent."

"I never heard anything, and he didn't do it."

"He was sleeping with Ashlyn," Tessa supplied. "Though he wants the record to show *she* was using him—"

"Is this the part where you don't tell me that you shot him?"

"Please, bullets are much too expensive to waste on the likes of him."

"Good point."

"However, we had an interesting conversation on who would have enough *access* to Justin Denbe, to plot against him and his family."

"Funny, Kevin and I just had the same conversation."

"For the record, while you and Kevin and me and Lopez were all conversing, someone else was doing. One of the kidnappers returned, broke into the Denbes' home and attacked Libby and Ashlyn, apparently intent on finishing some unfinished business."

Wyatt was just taking the exit onto 93 southbound. He pulled his steering wheel sharply right. "What?"

"Exactly. Libby identified him as Mick; the Boston PD are running his prints now to get his real identity. Apparently, he'd taken a special interest in her during incarceration, but had been held off by the ringleader, Z. Well, assignment over, Z gone, Mick decided to make good on some earlier promises. He used a special override code to access the home—having timed the Boston patrol cars, FYI—then surprised Libby in the master bath. She took evasive maneuvers, Ashlyn entered the fray and the two women managed to lead him on a pretty good chase through the home until Libby finally grabbed a loaded twenty-two she'd left next to the sofa—"

"She had a loaded gun in her family room?" Wyatt wasn't sure whether to be surprised or impressed. He remembered the accounts of the Denbes' shooting prowess. Still, to leave a loaded gun lying around a family home was a fairly aggressive act.

"Considering what they had been through," Tessa supplied, "not to mention Special Agent Adams' multiple lectures on how the three men were still out there . . ."

"Fair enough."

"Libby shot Mick dead. Three times, left temple, up close and personal. Professional-grade work."

The way Tessa said it struck Wyatt as odd.

"Meaning?"

"Meaning her fingerprints are all over the gun, but interestingly enough, no GSR is on her fingers."

"She fired a gun three times without getting any gunshot residue on her hands?"

"She claims she washed her hands before calling the police."

"You can't remove *all* traces that easily."

"You're singing to the choir. But she's not budging from her story."

"Did they check Ashlyn's hands? Maybe she's covering for her daughter."

"Her daughter was slammed into a granite countertop and is still recovering from a concussion. But, yes, Boston PD swabbed Ashlyn's hands. Nada."

"There were just the two women in the house?" Wyatt asked.

"Exactly."

The tone of Tessa's voice said it all. Odds were, Libby had not shot commando Mick. But she felt a need to cover for whoever did. Which, if it wasn't her daughter . . .

Wyatt took a deep breath and declared, "I think Justin Denbe might have been embezzling from his own company. An In Case of Divorce fund. Except sixteen years later, he also started talking about it. I think he told his lover, Kathryn Chapman, who saw Ruth Chan's travel itinerary. She took the steps to wire out the funds before Chan ever landed in the Bahamas. Then ordered Justin and his family kidnapped, in order to keep the eleven million for herself."

"I think you're part right," Tessa Leoni said. "I think Justin Denbe definitely embezzled from his own firm. I think he's also very much alive."

"WHO ELSE HAD ENOUGH ACCESS?" Tessa quizzed shortly. "We're looking for someone who worked for Denbe Construction for at least sixteen years, who knew intimate details of the Denbes' home life, including security code, interior layout, family schedule. A person who might know former special forces, current guns for hire—which we've established are part and parcel of the construction trades. Not to mention someone brilliant enough to devise such a scheme, and ballsy enough to pull it off. I say, Justin Denbe, Justin Denbe, Justin Denbe."

Wyatt wasn't arguing with her. Hearing the words out loud only fit the lightbulb already going off in his head. "The kidnappers weren't supposed to harm Libby and Ashlyn," he muttered by phone. "Hence Mick was Tased for attacking Libby. Most likely, instructions from Justin himself. He had nothing against traumatizing his wife and daughter. He just didn't want them hurt."

"But he *needed* them," Tessa countered. "If he just faked his own kidnapping, his own death, it would be suspicious. Hence, for his Embark on a New Life plan, he needed them all abducted from their home and held against their will. Libby and Ashlyn became his witnesses, two people who could swear under oath they saw him die before their very eyes."

"Knife to the chest. Not so hard to fake with a blood packet. And we still haven't found the body."

"Exactly."

"I think he cheated on her," Wyatt said abruptly. "Pure conjecture, but the money skimming started sixteen years ago. I think it was triggered by the first time Justin was unfaithful to Libby. She would've been pregnant with Ashlyn right about then.

A stressful time in any marriage. He fell off the wagon, followed in his father's foot-steps, whatever. But at that moment, Justin realized he was his father's son—fidelity challenged. And he started to worry, because Libby wasn't necessarily his mother, the kind of woman who would turn a blind eye. If she left him, divorced him . . ."

"Fifty percent of all personal assets," Tessa supplied.

"So he stopped taking money out of the business, bought the town house in the company's name. Except that meant he didn't really have cash. So he created an offshore slush fund. Why not? From his perspective, it was his money, after all. But as any corporation is subject to audit, of course he couldn't just have the accountant write him a check. He had to create a fake vendor, bill his own firm, then pocket the cash. Amounts small enough not to be noticed, large enough to give him peace of mind. Ingenious, really."

"Except Libby didn't find out," Tessa picked up. "He got away with that affair, she gave birth. Maybe they were going to live happily ever after, except then he met another girl—"

"Leading to another fake billing cycle . . ."

"And continued with a crazy dual life as a loving husband/cheating husband, great boss/embezzling boss."

"It happens," Wyatt said.

Which was true. When it came to crime, innocent people hemmed and hawed all the time, how could he, how could she, why I never suspected a thing. That was because innocent people had consciences. And guilty people, such as Justin Denbe, didn't.

"Sixteen years," Tessa murmured. "Then, finally, the shit hit the fan. Libby found out about the latest woman, and Justin started devising an exit plan. Ironic, really, given that Libby still wasn't planning on leaving him."

"I don't think that mattered," Wyatt said curtly. "Where are you?"

"Denbe Construction offices, looking for Justin."

"He's not there."

"Given that I'm here, walking the offices, I already know that. So here's a question: How do you, by phone, also know that?"

"Because Libby wasn't leaving Justin. You heard her—they were working on their marriage. Meaning . . ." He paused a beat. Tessa finally got the rest of the story.

"He was leaving her."

"And why does any husband leave his family of eighteen years?" Wyatt asked.

"Fuck. He thinks he's in love with Kathryn Chapman."

"Meaning . . ."

"He's hiding at Kathryn Chapman's house. Most likely getting everything in order before they hop a flight to some exotic locale first thing in the morning."

Wyatt said, "Last one there buys dinner."

"Please. I'm already in the city."

"Yep, but at this point, so am I."

KATHRYN CHAPMAN LIVED IN MATTAPAN. Her mother's house, a white-painted triple-decker. Tessa had the address, because she'd gotten it off Chris Lopez. Wyatt, on the other hand, had police dispatch, an in-vehicle computer system, not to mention GPS, which explained how he managed to pull up just seconds before her. She literally veered around him as he parallel parked four blocks over, where his sheriff's cruiser wouldn't spook Kathryn Chapman or Justin Denbe.

He gave her a cheery wave. Tessa rolled her eyes and drove around yet another city block in search of parking. Always fun in Boston.

She found parking two blocks over and trotted back to Wyatt's vehicle, where he was leaning against his cruiser, waiting for her. She thought he looked particularly good in his brown sheriff's uniform, which was just as well.

"Dinner," he declared. "Your treat."

"Do I get to pick the restaurant?"

"Fair is fair."

"I want to wear heels. Maybe a skirt."

"Hell, I'll pay for that."

"No, my dinner. But I expect a jacket from you. Maybe even a tie."

"And you're in heels?" he pressed.

"Yes."

"Done."

They turned their attention to Kathryn's darkened duplex, a couple of blocks down. Five A.M. Sun would be rising soon. Already, lights were appearing in homes with early morning commuters. Not the best time of day for stealth.

"How do you want to play it?" she asked.

"We don't have a warrant."

Tessa shrugged. "More your problem than mine. And you don't even have jurisdiction in Massachusetts."

"You're right, we should call for backup." She gave him a look.

"Or," he countered, "I could close my eyes, and if the front door happened to open, giving me cause to worry about the safety of the individuals inside the residence . . ."

"Then as a conscientious representative of law enforcement, naturally you'd have to check it out."

"Naturally."

"Three minutes," Tessa said, and walked away.

She could feel his eyes on her back as she departed. And it wasn't a bad thing. More like a warm, giddy feeling that promised good times to come.

Tessa reconned the house. Front door had a bolt lock and a chain. Too time-consuming. She turned her attention to a back garden door. Older, only the key-in, key-out lock, which five minutes later finally gave way to her steadily improving lock-picking skills.

She took her first step into the rear-facing kitchen, already breathing hard.

Sky was lightening. Shadows disappearing. Full daylight dangerously close.

She got halfway across the peeling vinyl floor.

Then heard a floorboard creak above her head.

If that was Kate Chapman's bedroom, she definitely wasn't asleep anymore. Most likely, neither was Justin. A man experienced with firearms, and with at least eleven million dollars on the line . . .

Moving carefully now, feeling out each old, creaky floorboard . . .

She made it to the front door, located at the base of the main staircase. Above her, a toilet flushing. Footsteps, padding along the hall.

Don't come down, don't come down, don't come down . . .

Easing out the chain lock. Carefully twisting the bolt lock. Then, the final twist of the knob . . .

The front door groaned open. Noticeably, audibly. Then, above her, silence. Total silence. And not the good kind of silence. The *aware* kind of silence. Justin, Kathryn, or all of the above, knew someone had arrived.

Wyatt appeared in the open doorway.

He was moving cautiously, his body turned sideways, approaching from an angle to be less of a target. Tessa held up a single finger to her lips, then pointed to the ceiling. He seemed to take the hint, easing silently through the door, to join her at the base of the staircase.

"I think they know," she murmured low. "Other egresses?"

"Fire escape," Wyatt whispered back. "First and second floor. I might have greased the rungs. But you didn't hear that from me."

Tessa was impressed. Good trick for future reference.

"We gotta move fast," she murmured.

"Isn't Chris Lopez alive because of your previous restraint?"

She nodded.

"Then I say, he owes you one. Kathryn is his niece, after all."

Tessa got the message. Lopez did owe her one. She made the call, then, sixty seconds later, was holding out her cell at the base of the stairs, while Lopez boomed through speakerphone:

"Kate. I know you're awake. Now stop

fucking around and get your ass down here. I just heard what happened to Justin. Cops are gonna be here any second and we gotta get our stories in order. Come on, I've already been waiting . . ."

Total silence.

"Kate! I'm not joking around. You either talk to me, or that's it. I'm washing my hands of this. Police come around, I'm gonna tell them all about it. Yep, my niece was sleeping with my boss. Yep, she wanted his family to go away. In fact, I actually heard her say on several occasions, if only they'd drop dead . . ."

A woman's voice suddenly, from the top of the staircase. "Uncle Chris?"

"Duh!"

"You sound funny."

"I'm screaming up a goddamn staircase. Throw on some clothes and get down here."

Tessa could hear floorboards now, as well as low, indistinct murmuring. She was holding her breath. Slowly, she forced herself to release it, keep a light grip on her firearm.

Then, the first floorboard creaking.

"Uncle Chris?"

Tessa moved her phone slightly, cued Lopez.

"In the kitchen," he called over speaker-phone.

Another stair groaning. Tessa and Wyatt easing back into the shadows of the landing.

Kathryn Chapman appeared moments later. She wasn't in pajamas, but already clad in jeans and a tailored navy blue top. The kind of clothes, Tessa thought, you might wear to board a plane.

The girl turned toward the kitchen, and just like that, Wyatt stepped forward, slapped his palm around her mouth and dragged her back.

Kathryn's face paled, her blue eyes widening into saucers. She spotted Tessa and, far from being reassured, struggled even more. Which told Tessa a couple of things, such as Kathryn clearly viewed her as the opposition, and as such, during their first conversation, had most likely lied through her teeth.

"He's up there, isn't he?" Tessa murmured now.

Kathryn attempted to shake her head, though Wyatt's thick arm held her in place.

"He's told you he's taking you away. Got some money set aside."

Kathryn didn't try to respond, just flushed.

"Forget for an instant that the man has betrayed his own wife. He's also betrayed his only child. This is the guy you want to run away with?"

Kathryn's gaze turned mutinous, which Tessa took to mean yes.

Clearly, no help from this woman. So Tessa went with plan B. She opened her mouth and screamed at the top of her lungs.

"No, Mick. Don't hurt me. I don't know where he is. Mick! No, no, no! Mick!"

Footsteps, hard and fast. Justin Denbe responding to the evil mercenary's name and springing into action. Hammering down the stairs. Careening into the foyer, pistol at his side, already in a crouched position in the open doorway.

Tessa watched his gaze ping-pong from the open door, to Kathryn's restrained form, to herself, who already had her firearm leveled at his head.

"Justin Denbe," she declared. "Drop your weapon. You are under arrest."

*   *   *

JUSTIN DIDN'T IMMEDIATELY DROP HIS GUN. Figured, a man like him. He remained crouched, appraising the situation, gaze darting to the open door.

"We know what you did," Tessa said, aim perfectly level. This close, she had all the time in the world. She continued conversationally. "And I wasn't making that up. Mick did return last night. He attacked your wife and daughter."

Justin straightened, finally giving her his full attention.

"What? Is Ashlyn okay? Is Libby okay? I told them, the terms of the agreement . . ."

"No hurting your wife and child," Tessa filled in. Beside her, Wyatt was on the move, cuffing Kathryn's arms behind her back. "That was the deal, right? You hired the men with the explicit instructions not to hurt your wife and child. But they could hurt you. Had to for the nine million dollars in ransom. That's how you paid them, right? They received at least part of the ransom funds, as promised. That way, you still didn't have to share your eleven million."

Justin Denbe, clad in dress jeans, button-up shirt, leather shoes, more clothes suitable for a plane: "Are Ashlyn and Libby all right?"

"Other than terrified? Traumatized? I mean, seriously, who the hell are you to be so concerned about them now? After all you put them through?"

"They were not to be harmed," he reiterated stubbornly.

Wyatt shoved Kathryn's cuffed form to the side. "Sixteen years," he stated. "You embezzled from your own company for sixteen years."

"Don't be ridiculous." But he wasn't looking at them anymore, his gaze once more darting to the open doorway. "Can't steal from yourself."

"Oh, you can," Tessa corrected, grip tightening on her gun. "Because anything you put in your personal accounts you risked owing to your wife, who was bound to figure out about your affairs and demand a divorce. Or you could siphon money into slush funds no one ever knew about. Until sixteen years had passed, and you found yourself with eleven million dollars, a dying business and a jilted wife. Must not have been too hard to make your decision after that. Time to get out, while the getting was good."

Justin still didn't say anything. He wasn't even making eye contact with Kathryn Chapman. Instead, skittishly, he continued to lean toward the open door.

"What time's your flight?" Tessa asked.

He flinched.

"We got your girlfriend. Gonna travel without her?"

Belatedly, he glanced at Kathryn. Wyatt no longer had his hand over her mouth. She gave an involuntary moan.

"Yep, this is your boyfriend," Tessa told her. "A man who hired his own kidnappers, faked his own death and abandoned his own family. But, hey, he's all yours."

Beside her, Wyatt said, "Mick's dead. Your wife shot him."

Justin's eyes widened. He appeared startled.

"But your daughter has a serious concussion," Tessa pressed. "She needs you. In fact, your miraculous return from beyond the grave might be exactly the kind of thing that would enable her speedy recovery."

It was interesting, really, to watch the agonized look that overcame Justin Denbe's face. The clear internal struggle. Be there for the daughter he adored, but also return to the life of responsibility. Or go. Just go. No commitments, no obligations, a free man with eleven million dollars in his pocket.

He looked at Tessa.

He looked at Kathryn, not even speaking, just making pleading sounds in the base of her throat.

And then . . .

He ran for the doorway. Leapt through it. Got as far as the deck. Tessa yelled his name, gun coming up, but holding fire as she couldn't very well shoot a man in the back. Wyatt thrust Kathryn aside, preparing to give chase.

As somewhere in the distance, a rifle cracked. Tessa registered the sound, then dropped instinctively to the floor, Wyatt joining her, as together they watched Justin Denbe's head explode on the front porch.

Now you see him, now you don't.

Justin's body collapsed.

Kathryn started to scream.

There wasn't a second shot. Or a third. The first round had gotten it done.

After an eternity had passed, Tessa climbed shakily to her feet. Wyatt rose to stand beside her. They took in Justin's lifeless form.

Wyatt said: "Told you the hired muscle involved a brain or two."

THEY PHONED SPECIAL AGENT ADAMS. Let the federal agent flex her muscle as neither one of them had legal standing. Plus, it meant she'd inherit the paperwork. Kathryn was led away, still screaming. Most likely would be taken to a local emergency room and treated for shock.

In the meantime, uniformed officers patrolled the neighborhood. Rooftop deck, two houses down and across the street, they recovered a rifle and a single brass cartridge. Serial number filed off the rifle. Fingerprints wiped off the cartridge.

"Professional-grade work," Nicole said, stating the obvious.

"Dead men tell no tales," Wyatt intoned.

"One of the kidnappers?"

"You take Justin into custody, he's bound to talk," Tessa supplied with a shrug. "Most professional arrangements involve signed confidentiality agreements. Let's just say, Justin appeared at risk for violating his."

"You see anything?" she asked.

"No," they replied honestly.

Nicole sighed, returned to her vehicle to update the APB. Not needed for anything else, Wyatt and Tessa finally departed, Wyatt walking her to her car.

"Think Libby and Ashlyn are now safe?"

"Well, think about it. If Justin was here when Mick attacked his family . . ."

Wyatt nodded. "Kind of thinking the same thing. One of the hired guns, maybe the leader, took out his own guy."

"Interesting profession. Very strict rules of employment. But said guy also left Libby and Ashlyn alone afterward. So, yeah, hopefully dust will now settle and they can start rebuilding their lives."

"Is that what you're doing?" he asked.

She answered him as honestly as she could: "Some days better than others."

They'd arrived at her Lexus.

"So," he said.

"So," she answered.

"This is the awkward part. 'Cause technically you're buying dinner, and yet I'm dying to ask you out."

"Can't meet my daughter," she warned seriously. "Not for a bit."

"Wouldn't expect it."

"I got space issues."

"Noticed that. I got a thing for wood. Sometimes, I have to build things. Just do."

She nodded. "I look really good in heels," she said at last.

"Really? Because I'm told I'm damn hot in a jacket and tie."

"No tie. Just the jacket."

His gaze warmed. "Still the heels?"

"Still the heels."

"Friday night?"

"Next Friday. I need to spend some time with Sophie."

"Fair enough."

Wyatt leaned forward. Caught her off guard with a low whisper to her ear. "And wear your hair down."

Then he turned, already sauntering down the street. Tessa remained standing there a moment longer, a slow smile spreading across her face. She thought of families, old and new, and survivors, then and now.

Then, she got into her Lexus and drove home to her daughter.

Chapter 44

THIS IS WHAT I KNOW:

My husband started siphoning funds from his own company sixteen years ago. Not just a slush fund, but an Exit in Case of Emergency fund. The federal financial wizards believe he accrued a little over thirteen million dollars by setting up dozens of fake vendors in his own company books, then vouching for their authenticity.

According to e-mails recovered from his computer, he began to make his exit plans back in June, approximately five days after I discovered his affair. By the time Ruth Chan caught wind of the embezzlement in

August, it hardly mattered. Justin's escape strategy was well under way. No doubt he sent her to the Bahamas simply to get her out of town for the big event. Certainly, he'd already purchased a forged passport, later found on his body, for the name Tristan Johnson. He'd also used that name to purchase a plane ticket for the Dominican Republic, as well as open a new bank account, where he most likely planned on transferring the bulk of his illicit gains.

Those funds have yet to be tracked down, maybe still sitting in another bank under a different alias; the forensic accountants are working on it.

Finally, the Great Escape: My husband hired three professionals to kidnap his own family. He gave them a security code to enter our home (the date I'd discovered Kathryn Chapman's texts on Justin's cell phone; Paulie, Justin's top security guru, discovered it when auditing the system). Justin then prepped the men with all the information they would need to successfully ambush us in our own home, while also providing a secure location for our incarceration.

He gave them guidelines: They could

not harm his wife or his daughter. And apparently, he granted them permission to Tase and beat the shit out of him. After all, the kidnapping needed to appear genuine in order for his death to appear genuine, not to mention he needed the insurance company to cough up nine million dollars in ransom. It's not like Denbe Construction had that kind of money, and heaven forbid Justin should dip into his own cash reserves.

Z and his team performed their job admirably. But I think, in hindsight, Z became increasingly disgruntled about working for a man whose master plan involved, at the very least, terrorizing his unsuspecting wife and daughter. Hence the expressions of frank hatred I caught so many times on his face.

Was that why Z and/or Radar assassinated my husband? I doubt it. I think if Z had truly wanted Justin dead, he would've taken care of it up close and personal during those final moments at the prison. Plus, Z always struck me as a professional; the kind of guy to get the job done whether he approved of his client or not. I think Radar was probably assigned the job of tailing Justin, to make sure he got safely out of town, just as Z took on the job of tracking Mick. Tying up loose ends, so to speak. When Mick attacked me, Z took the necessary steps to eliminate an untrustworthy associate. And when Justin was collared by the police, Radar took the necessary steps to eliminate an untrustworthy client. As Justin had said, they had nine million reasons to make a clean getaway, which they did.

Mick's fingerprints ID'd him as Michael Beardsley, a former marine, dishonorably discharged five years ago, and with a reputation for working the "private sector." For a while, the FBI visited Ashlyn and me nearly daily with photos of Mick's known associates, hoping we could pick out Z or Radar from the photo array. So far, we haven't recognized any of the men in the pictures. And so far, the police haven't been able to find any trace of e-mails or other means of contact between Justin and Z.

No doubt, Z took many precautions on that front. Given that, in the end, he saved my life, I haven't gone out of my way to provide information that could aid with his capture. Ashlyn knows what happened that night, and shares my opinion. So we do our thing, and let the cops do theirs. I doubt they'll ever catch Z or Radar. But I also doubt they'll ever bother us again. Job over, they've moved on. Maybe, someday, we will, too.

I miss my husband. Maybe that's perverse of me. But you don't love a man for nearly twenty years and not feel his absence. Yes, I had signed a prenup forfeiting all claims to Denbe Construction, in return for half of all our personal assets. And, yes, Justin ran all our personal possessions through the business, so that had I decided to divorce him, I would've been entitled to nothing at all.

He cheated on me. Physically, emotionally, even financially. And in that regard, I still can't feel special because it turned out he cheated on everyone. Stole from his own company, denied assets to his own employees. In his own way, he tried to compensate by giving out generous bonuses during the boom years, but still . . . He drained thirteen million dollars from the company coffers, denied even his closest and most loyal employees the chance to buy into the firm, all while presenting himself as a great guy and considerate boss.

In the end, I think there were two Justins. The one I cherished as my husband. The one Ashlyn loved as her father. The one his guys respected as their leader.

Then, there was the one who stole from all of us, while constructing an elaborate ruse in order to leave us forever. Because thirteen million dollars apparently mattered more to him than the love of his family and the admiration of his firm.

I don't understand that Justin. I can't picture what would make someone already so successful value money over his family and friends. All I can guess is that he really wanted his freedom. No more responsibility, no more decisions, no more obligations. Though ironically enough, we would've helped him with that, too. He could've sold the firm to his management team. He could have run away to Bora-Bora with Ashlyn and me. We would've gone. We loved him that much. Or thought we did.

This is the part both Ashlyn and I struggle with. The Justin we knew had strong values, rigidly upheld expectations of himself and others. Whereas the kind of man who betrays his whole family, going to the extreme length of kidnapping and terrorizing his own wife and daughter just so he can make a clever getaway . . .

Would he have ever looked back? Missed us? Mourned us at all?

Because we mourn him. We can't help ourselves. We mourn the man we thought we knew, the father who taught Ashlyn how to use a cordless drill, the man who used to hold me at night. The man we thought we watched die for us.

Because we'd believed in that man. And we miss him still.

The DA brought charges against Chris Lopez. He pleaded guilty to all counts, sparing my daughter the trauma of a trial. I wonder if that makes him feel noble. He seduced a vulnerable fifteen-year-old girl, but this one act somehow makes it right.

I haven't spoken to him. Frankly, I have nothing to say.

I am working on myself these days. Whether my husband was a liar or not, I'm trying to make good on the promise I made: to quit prescription painkillers and be there for my daughter. I am working with a detox specialist now, having gone from hydrocodone to methadone and now weaning off the methadone. I made Ashlyn go with me through the entire house. I showed her all my little hidey-holes, and one by one, we emptied out the pills, then handed them over to my doctor.

I can't say it's been easy. I dream of oranges all the time. I wake up tasting birthday cake and I feel an overwhelming sense of guilt. I had wanted to save my family. Even after discovering Justin's affair, even after popping that first pill, I still thought we'd somehow make it. We'd get our acts together, forgive, forget, carry on. Justin, Ashlyn and me against the world.

I work with an excellent therapist now, who likes to ask me questions. Such as, Why? Why should our family have survived intact? Because we were so happy? So loving? So nurturing of one another?

Justin wasn't the only one with problems. I'd become an addict and my fifteen-year-old daughter was sleeping with a forty-year-old man. Maybe, just maybe, the three of us together wasn't working out so well.

And maybe now, the two of us surviving can do better.

Ashlyn and I are talking again, sharing our pain, but also our fledgling hopes and dreams. My daughter is officially a wealthy young woman. In keeping with the tradition of his father, Justin left the entire company to her, by name. Meaning she now owns one of the largest construction firms in the country, not to mention two homes and a nice collection of cars.

She doesn't want them. We are working with Anita Bennett and Ruth Chan to put together a deal for the employees of Denbe Construction to purchase 51 percent of the firm. As for our Boston brownstone, Ashlyn would like to part with that as well.

We both agree it's too big and filled with too much regret.

We like the idea of leaving Boston, maybe heading west, to Seattle or Portland. We'll buy a charming Craftsman-style bungalow, maybe something with a detached garage we can turn into an art studio. I can work on my jewelry. Ashlyn would like to take up pottery.

We can nest for a bit. Have less. Do less.

Find more.

I like the idea and, being a wealthy older woman, can afford for the first time in my life to do as I please. That piece of paper Z delivered on Radar's behalf? It bore the number of an offshore bank account held in Justin's name. Justin had three go-to passwords. In this case, it took me only two tries to guess the right one. At which point, I electronically transferred all 12.8 million dollars to a new fund under a corporate name I invented on the spot. A few more transfers here and there, and Justin's Exit in Case of Emergency fund became my Sole Surviving Spouse fund.

Imagine, after all the lengths Justin went to in order to make sure I would never be entitled to a single penny of his money, I got it all.

I wonder if he's rolling over in his grave.

And I confess, some days that thought makes me smile.

This is what I know:

Pain has a flavor.

But hope does, too.

Author's Note and Acknowledgments

I've always wanted to kidnap a family. It's one of those ideas that has spent years churning around in the back of my head. Then one day, I had the opportunity to tour a recently constructed prison, and my writer's brain immediately fell in love.

Endless coils of razor wire. Solid bars of saw-proof steel. Narrow slivers of ballistic-rated glass. All combining to help form one vast, soulless structure where footsteps echoed for miles and the clang of heavy doors slamming shut sent shivers up my spine.

Yep, it was love at first sight.

Meaning first and foremost, I owe a huge debt of gratitude to Michael Duffy for providing a tour of the facility his company helped build. He also educated me on the number of unopened and mothballed penitentiaries nationwide, as ongoing budget crises have frozen the funds needed to open and/or operate the facilities.

In this particular case, the prison has since opened. Also, the building I describe in this novel is a work of fiction. Having toured one prison and read about many others, I amused myself by cherry-picking the particular details I liked best. It's good to be an author, where I can construct anything I want out of pure words.

Along those same lines, any mistakes are mine and mine alone.

For the making of this novel, I also decided it was time to create a new character, an honest-to-goodness New Hampshire cop. I didn't fully appreciate just how unique the county sheriff's departments are in New Hampshire, until I tied up hours of Lieutenant Mike Santuccio's well-intentioned time. His insightfulness, not to mention patience with my endless questions, definitely saved me on several occasions. Thank you, Lieutenant, for a fascinating look at rural policing, not to mention fresh respect for the men and women who must police these crazy mountains I love so much. Once again, any mistakes are mine, and mine alone.

Sarah Luke helped with much of the addiction information. While fellow suspense novelist and one of my favorite authors, Joseph Finder, set me straight on the inner workings of Back Bay Boston. Thanks, Joe!

Congratulations to Michael Beardsley, nominated for death by his loving wife, Catherine, who won the annual Kill a Friend, Maim a Buddy Sweepstakes at LisaGard ner.com. Also to Stuart Blair, winner of the international Kill a Friend, Maim a Mate, who nominated his new bride Lindsay Edmiston for a star-making turn in the novel. Since no females die in the making of this novel (a first for me!), Lindsay graciously agreed to the role of Ashlyn's BFF. Don't worry, you can still visit the website, where the next contest for literary immortality is already up and running. Maybe 2014 can be your year to fictionally maim that special person in your life.

Speaking of love, Kim Beals was the

winning bidder at the annual Rozzie May Animal Alliance auction. Her generous donation to Rozzie May, which assists with low-cost spaying and neutering of dogs and cats, was in honor of her stepdad, Daniel J. Coakley. Her one request, he be a decent guy in the novel, as he is a great guy in real life. Hope you both enjoy!

Being an animal lover, I also donate one opportunity for pet immortality to be auctioned off by my local no-kill animal shelter, the Animal Rescue League of New Hampshire–North. This year's winners, Michael Kline and Sal Martignetti, asked me to commemorate their beloved black Lab, Zeus, who passed away during the writing of this book. Zeus was one of those amazing dogs who seemed more human than canine. As his owners put it, while most Labs could be cadaver dogs, Zeus could've been a detective.

Finally, my deepest, most heartfelt appreciation to my editors, Ben Sevier from Dutton and Vicki Mellor from Headline. In the way the writing process sometimes goes, I grew a little frustrated with this book. As in burning it or shredding it, or shredding, then burning it started to sound like great ideas. But my editors insisted on offering insightful comments that dramatically improved the novel instead. Fine. Just remember, what happens in the first draft, stays in the first draft . . .

Clearly, writing a novel is a lonely, if not always sane, pastime. I am so fortunate to have a truly amazing and supportive family who puts up with me even when my dinner conversation consists of muttering under my breath followed by staring off into space. Then there's the best friends a girl could ask for, Genn, Sarah, Michelle and Kerry, who know when to make me laugh and when to simply pour another glass of wine.

Finally, my heartfelt adoration to my enormously talented, incredibly gracious, favorite-person-in-the-whole-world agent, Meg Ruley. Yes, she's that good and I'm happy to have her on my side.

Oh yeah, and just in case you thought I hadn't noticed, thank you to my amazing readers, who make all this pain worthwhile.

About the Author

LISA GARDNER is the *New York Times* bestselling author of fifteen novels. Her Detective D. D. Warren novels include *Catch Me, Love You More, Live to Tell, The Neighbor, Hide*, and *Alone*. Her FBI profiler novels include *Say Goodbye, Gone, The Killing Hour, The Next Accident*, and *The Third Victim*. She lives with her family in New England, where she is at work on her next novel.